Praise for
SPIN

"The tag line is: 'How far would you go to get what you always wanted?' and Kate Sandford, protagonist of Catherine McKenzie's first novel, *Spin*, goes so far she makes you cringe.... Full of pop-culture allusions, some really funny ones.... *Spin* is a compelling, fast-paced read."

—*Globe and Mail* (Toronto)

"McKenzie successfully portrays a group of young friends as they struggle to figure out who they are and what they want . . . [and] steers the novel to a satisfying conclusion."

—*The Gazette* (Montreal)

"Imagine if Bridget Jones fell into a million little pieces, flew over the cuckoo's nest, and befriended Lindsay Lohan along the way, and you are beginning to grasp the literary roller-coaster ride that is Catherine McKenzie's *Spin*. Filled with brutal honesty and wry humour, *Spin* is a story for anyone who has ever woken up hungover and thought, 'Do I have a problem? Yes—I need to find a greasy breakfast.' And by that I mean everyone I know."

—Leah McLaren, *Globe and Mail* columnist,
author of *The Continuity Girl*

"With McKenzie's engaging debut, you'll be up late rooting for the lovable and broken Kate Sandford as she stumbles her way towards sobriety by way of a bit of tabloid journalism. *Spin* is honest, funny, and fresh."

—Julie Buxbaum, author of *The Opposite of Love*
and *After You*

"In Kate Sandford, Catherine McKenzie has created a twenty-first-century Bridget Jones—dark and delicate, broken yet strong. *Spin* is all at once comic, heartbreaking, and life-affirming."

—Tish Cohen, author of *Town House* and
The Truth About Delilah Blue

"Kate Sandford is someone you know: she's snarky and a little bit fragile, and when she has the chance to make up for blowing the opportunity of a lifetime, you can't help but root for her even when she's not rooting for herself. Catherine McKenzie has written a winning first novel—*Spin* is funny, touching, and impossible to put down."

—Shawn Klomparens, author of *Jessica Z.* and *Two Years, No Rain*

"With *Spin*, Catherine McKenzie taps into both the ridiculous and sublime elements of the world her characters inhabit, and, more important, points out how those are often exactly the same. A thoroughly engaging debut."

—David Sprague, music journalist and contributor to *Variety*, *Village Voice*, and *Rolling Stone*

SPIN

SPIN

CATHERINE McKENZIE

WILLIAM MORROW

An Imprint of HarperCollins*Publishers*

First published in slightly different form in Canada in 2009 by HarperCollins Canada.

Excerpt from *Arranged* copyright © 2012 by Catherine McKenzie.

HarperCollins books may be purchased for educational, business, or sales promotional use. For information please write: Special Markets Department, HarperCollins Publishers, 10 East 53rd Street, New York, NY 10022.

FIRST U.S. EDITION

Library of Congress Cataloging-in-Publication Data is available upon request.

ISBN 978-0-06-211535-5

12 13 14 15 16   BVG   10 9 8 7 6 5 4 3 2 1

For my grandparents,
Roy and Dorothy McKenzie

and

For my friends—
Best. Friends. Ever.

Chapter 1
Must Love Music

This is how I lose my dream job.

It's the day before my thirtieth birthday when I get the call from *The Line,* only *the* most prestigious music magazine in the world, maybe the universe. OK, maybe *Rolling Stone* is number one, but *The Line* is definitely second.

I've wanted to write for *The Line* for as long as I can remember. It still blows me away that people get paid to work there since I'd pay good money just to be allowed to sit in on a story meeting. Hell, I'd sit in on a recycling committee meeting if it'd get me in the front door.

So, it's no surprise that I almost fall off my chair when I see their ad in the Help Wanted section one lazy Sunday morning. I sprint to my computer and wait impatiently for my dial-up to connect. (Yes, I still have dial-up. It's all this struggling writer can afford.) When the scratchy whine silences, I call up their webpage and click on the "Work for Us!" tab, as I have too many unsuccessful times before, and there it is. A job, a real job!

The Line *seeks self-motivated writer for staff position. Must love music more than money because this job pays jack, brother!*

Send your CV and music lover credentials to kevin@theline.com.

I spend the next twenty-four hours agonizing over the "music lover credentials" portion of my application. How am I supposed to narrow down my musical influences to the three lines provided? Then again, how am I going to get a job writing about music if I can't even list my favorite bands?

In the end I let iTunes pick for me. If I've listened to a song 946 times (which, incidentally, is the number of times I've apparently played KT Tunstall's "Black Horse and the Cherry Tree"), I must really like it, right? Not a perfect system, but better than the over-thought-out lists sitting balled up in my wastepaper basket.

And it works. A few days later I receive an email with a written interview attached. I have forty-eight hours to complete the questionnaire and submit it. If I pass, I'll get a real, in-person interview on *The Line*'s premises! Just the thought of it has me doing a happy dance all over my living room.

Thankfully, the questionnaire is a breeze. *Pick five Dylan songs and explain why they're great. Pick five Oasis songs and explain why they suck. What do you think the defining sounds of this decade will be? Go see a band you've never seen before and write five hundred words about it. Buy a CD from the country section and listen to it five times. Write five hundred words on how it made you feel.*

I stay up all night chain-smoking cigarettes and working my way through two of my roommate Joanne's bottles of red wine. She's always buying wine (as an "investment," she says), but she never drinks any of it. What a waste!

When the sun comes up, I read through what I've written, and if I do say so myself, it's a thing of beauty. There isn't a question I stutter over, an opinion I don't have. I've even written it in *The Line*'s signature style.

I've been waiting for this opportunity forever, and I'm not going to fuck it up.

At least, not yet.

The next two weeks are agony. My brain is spinning with negative thoughts. Maybe I don't really know anything about music? Maybe they don't want someone who can merely parrot their signature style? Maybe they're looking for some new style, and I'm not it? Maybe they should call me before I lose my goddamn mind!

When the spinning becomes overwhelming, I try to distract myself. I clean our tiny apartment. I invent three new ramen noodle soup recipes. I see a few bands and write reviews for the local papers I freelance for. I clean out my closet, sort all my mail, and return phone calls I've been putting off for months. I even write a thank-you letter to my ninety-year-old grandmother for the birthday check she sent me on my sister's birthday.

I spend the rest of the time alternating between obsessively reading *The Line*'s website (including six years of back issues I've read countless times before) and watching a young star's life explode all over the tabloids.

Amber Sheppard, better known as "The Girl Next Door" (or "TGND" for short), after the character she played from ages fourteen to eighteen on the situation comedy called—

wait for it—*The Girl Next Door,* is Hollywood's latest It Girl. When her show was canceled, she starred in two successful teen horror flicks, followed by a serious, Oscar-nominated performance for her turn as Catherine Morland in *Northanger Abbey.* She's been working nonstop since, and has four movies scheduled to premier in the next five months.

When she wrapped the fourth film just after her twenty-third birthday, she announced she was taking a well-deserved, undisclosed period of time off to relax and regroup.

And that's when the shit hit the fan.

Anyone really seeking relaxation would rent a cabin in the woods and drop out of sight. But not TGND. She partied all night, slept all day, and dropped twenty pounds from one photograph to the next. There were rumors appearing on such reliable sources as people.com, TMZ, and Perez Hilton that she's into some serious drugs. There were other rumors, of the Enquiring kind, that her family had staged an intervention and packed her off to rehab. It seems like there's a new story, a new outrageous photograph, a new website devoted to her every move every day, and I read them all.

Such is the fuel that keeps my idling brain from going crazy as I wait and wait.

The call from *The Line* finally comes the day before my birthday at 8:55 in the morning.

Mornings are never good for me, and this morning my fatigue is compounded by the combination of another bottle of Joanne's investment wine, and the riveting all-night television generated by TGND's escape from rehab (turns out *The*

Enquirer was right). She lasted two days before peeling off in her white Ford hybrid SUV, and the paparazzi who follow her every move captured it from a hundred angles. It was O.J. all over again (sans, you know, the whole murdering your ex-wife thing), and the footage played in an endless loop on CNN, etc., for hours. I'd finally tired of it around three. The phone shatters my REM sleep what feels like seconds later.

"Mmmph?"

"Is this Kate Sandford?"

"Mmm."

"This is Elizabeth from *The Line* calling? We wanted to set up an interview?" Her voice rises at the end of each sentence, turning it into a question.

I sit bolt upright, my heart in my throat. "You do?"

"Are you available at nine tomorrow?"

Tomorrow. My birthday. Damn straight I'm available.

"Yes. Yes, I'm available."

"Great. So, come to our offices at nine and ask for me? Elizabeth?"

"That's great. Perfect. I'll see you then."

I throw back the covers, spring from bed, and break into my happy dance.

This is the best birthday present ever! I'm going to nail this! After years and years of writing for whoever would have me, I'm going to finally get to write for a real magazine! For *the* magazine. Yes, yes, yes!

"Katie, what the hell are you doing?" Joanne is standing in the doorway looking pissed. Her curly orange hair forms a halo around her pale face. She looks like Little Orphan Annie, all grown up. Her robe is even that red-trimmed-with-white combination that Annie always wears.

"Celebrating?"

"Do you know what time it is?"

I check the clock by my bedside. "Nine?"

"That's right. And what time do I start work today?"

I know this is a trick question.

"You don't?"

"That's right, it's my day off. So why, pray tell, are you dancing around and whooping like you're at a jamboree?"

Despite the inquisition, my heart gives a happy beat. "Because I just got the most fabulous job interview in the world."

Joanne isn't diverted by my obvious happiness. "I think the answer you were looking for is, 'Because I'm an inconsiderate roommate who doesn't care about anyone but herself.'"

"Joanne . . ."

"Just keep it down." She turns on her heel and storms away.

As I watch her leave, I wonder for the hundredth time why I'm still living with her. (I answered her in-search-of-a-roommate ad on craigslist three years ago, and we've had a love-hate relationship ever since.) Of course, she's clean, pays her share of the rent on time, and never wakes me up when I'm trying to sleep in because she's yelping with joy.

Then again, I've never seen Joanne yelp with joy . . .

Ohmygod! I have an interview at *The Line*!

I resume my whooping dance with the sound off.

I spend the rest of the day vacillating between extreme nervousness and supreme confidence. In between emotional fluctuations, I agonize over what I should wear to the interview. I lay the options out on my bed:

1) Black standard business suit that my mother gave me for my university graduation. She thought I'd have all kinds of job interviews to wear it to. Sorry, Mom.

2) Skinny jeans, kick-ass boots, T-shirt from an edgy, obscure nineties band, black corduroy blazer.

3) Black clingy skirt and gray faux-cashmere sweater with funky jewelry.

I settle on option three, hoping it strikes the right balance between professional and what I think the atmosphere at *The Line* will be: hip, serious, but not too serious.

In the late afternoon, I receive a text from my second-best friend, Greer.

U free 2nite?
No. Very important blah, blah am.
Must celebrate bday.
Bday 2morrow.
Aware. Exam in 2 days. Party 2nite.
No.
Insisting.
Must sleep. Need beauty for blah, blah.

Never be pretty enough to rely on looks for blah, blah. Still insisting.

LOL. Need new friend. Still can't.

Expecting u @ F. @ 8. Won't take no for answer.

No.

LOL. 1 drink.

It never ends with 1.

Will 2nite, promise.

Can't.

I'm $$.

Well . . . maybe just 1.

Excellent. CU @ 8.

I throw down the phone with a smile, and try to decide whether any of my outfits will do for a night out with my university-aged friends.

I'm a nearly thirty-year-old with university-aged friends because the only way I've been able to survive since I graduated (and the bank stopped loaning me money) is to keep living like I did when I was a student, right down to scamming as much free food and alcohol as possible on the university wine-and-cheese circuit. I met Greer this way two groups of friends ago. She's the only one who stuck post-graduation. She thinks I'm a fellow graduate student who writes music articles on the side to pay for my education and that tomorrow's my twenty-fifth birthday.

My own-age friends have all moved to nicer parts of the city. They work in law firms and investment banks, have dark circles under their eyes and pale skin. Their annual salaries are twice what it cost me to educate myself, and the only wine and cheeses they go to are the cocktail parties given by their firms to woo new clients.

They mostly don't approve of the way I live—the part they know about anyway—but I mostly don't care. Because I'm doing it. I'm living my childhood dream of being a music writer. It's not a well-paying life, but it's the life I've chosen. On most days, I'm happy.

If I get this job at *The Line*, I'll be over the freaking moon.

Shortly after eight, I meet Greer at our favorite pub in my number two outfit: skinny jeans tucked into burgundy boots, obscure-band T-shirt, and black corduroy blazer to keep the spring night at bay.

The pub has an Irish-bar-out-of-a-box feel to it (hunter green wallpaper, dark oak bar, mirrored Guinness signs behind it, a whiff of stale lager), but we like its laid-back atmosphere, cheap pints, and occasional Irish rugby team.

Greer is sitting on her usual stool flirting with the bartender. The Black Eyed Peas song "I Gotta Feeling" is playing on the sound system. She orders me a beer and a whiskey shot as I sit down next to her.

"Hey, you promised one drink."

"A shot's not a drink. It's just a wee introduction to drinking."

Greer is from Scotland. She has long auburn hair, green eyes, porcelain skin, and an accent that drives men wild. Sometimes I hate her.

Tonight she's wearing a soft sweater the color of new grass that exactly matches her eyes and a broken-in pair of jeans that fits her tall, slim frame perfectly. I'm glad I took the time to blow out my chestnut-colored hair and put on the one shade of mascara that makes my eyes look sky blue. Nobody wants to be outshone at their almost-thirtieth-birthday party.

She clinks her shot against mine. "Happy birthday, lass. Drink up."

I really shouldn't, but . . . what the hell? Tomorrow *is* my birthday.

I drink the shot, and take a few long gulps of my beer to chase it down.

"Thanks, Greer."

"Welcome. So, tell me about this very important interview. Is it for a post-doc position?"

A post-doc position? Oh, right, that bad job you get after your Ph.D. Biggest downside to the fake-student personality? Keeping track of my two lives.

"Nope . . . Actually, I'm thinking of going in another direction. It's a job writing for a music magazine."

"Well, well, the bairn's growing up."

Greer is always tossing out colloquial Scottish expressions like "bairn" (meaning child), "steamin'" (meaning drunk), and her ultimate insult, "don't be a scrounger" (meaning buy me a drink, you miserly bastard). Depending on the number of drinks she's consumed, it's sometimes impossible to understand her without translation.

"Had to happen sometime."

The bartender, Steve, brings us two more shots that Greer pays for with a smile. He only charges her for about a quarter of what she drinks, but since I'm often the beneficiary of his generosity, who's complaining?

She pushes one of the shots toward me.

"No, I can't."

"A wee dram won't hurt you."

"There's no way anyone actually says 'wee dram' anymore. That's just for the tourists, right?"

"I canna' break the code of honor of my country. Now drink up, lass, before I drink it for you."

I upend the shot and nearly choke on it when Scott claps me hard on the back. He's a history major I met about a year ago at, you guessed it, a wine and cheese. We bonded while arguing over who had deeper knowledge of U2 and the Counting Crows (me, and me). His athletic body, sandy hair, and frank face are easy on the eyes, and given our mutual single status, I'm not quite sure why we've never hooked up. Maybe it's the fact that he's twenty-two, which puts him on the outside edge of my half-plus-seven rule. ($30 \div 2 + 7 = 22$. A good rule to live by to avoid age-inappropriate romantic entanglements.)

Scott orders another round. When it comes, he slides shot number three my way. I protest, but he flashes his blue eyes and wide smile, and talks me into it. Into that, and the next one. When Rob and Toni arrive a little while later, they buy the next two. And when those are gone, the room gets fuzzy and I lose count of the drinks that come next.

The rest of the night passes in a flash of images: Rob and

Scott singing lewd rugby songs. Toni telling me she had a pregnancy scare the week before. Me blabbing on about how I'm going to nail my interview tomorrow, just nail it! Greer *Coyote Ugly*-ing it on the bar as Steve plies her with more shots. Someone dropping me off at my door, ringing the doorbell, and running away giggling. Joanne looking disappointed and resigned, then putting a blanket over me.

I lie on our living room couch with the room spinning around me, happy I have so many good friends, and an awesome job waiting for me to take it.

Tomorrow, tomorrow, tomorrow. I bring my watch to my face so I can see the glow-in-the-dark numbers. 3:40 a.m. I guess it's today. Hey, it's my birthday. *Happy birthday to me, happy birthday to me, happy birthday, happy birthday, happy birthday to me.*

"Katie!"

Someone is shaking me violently.

"Katie! Get up!"

The shaking gets more violent.

"Get orf me!"

"Katie, you have to get up. Now!"

Joanne rips the blanket off my face, and my eyes are flooded with light.

"What the hell's wrong with you?"

"Katie, pay attention. You have an interview in fifteen minutes!"

The world sinks slowly into my still drunk brain.

I. Have. An. Interview. In. Fifteen. Minutes.

Oh my God. *The Line.* The perfect job. The interview I have to nail. The interview I have in fifteen minutes.

I bolt out of bed and lurch toward the bathroom. The face that greets me in the mirror is a mess. My hair's sticking out at all angles, and my eyes are ringed with last night's mascara and eye shadow. I'm not completely sure, but I might also be a little green.

I take several deep breaths and command myself to pull it together. Under Joanne's reproachful eye, I fly into a fury of preparation, washing my face vigorously while simultaneously brushing the aftertaste of last night out of my mouth. After a few strokes of my hairbrush, I whip my hair back into a loose twist and pick up the clothes still laid out on my unslept-in bed.

"What happened to you last night?" Joanne asks.

I slip into my skirt and pull the sweater over my head. "Nothing."

"Yeah, that's obvious."

"Thanks for waking me up."

"You know, someday, I'm not going to be around to take care of you."

"Joanne . . ."

"You'd better get out of here."

I take a last look at myself in the mirror (not so bad, considering) and run down to the street, searching desperately for a cab. I'd meant to take the subway to save money, but that plan's clearly out the window.

In a bit of good luck, a cab shudders to a stop the first time I fling my hand in the air. As it jerks and stops its way downtown, I fight a bout of nausea and nervously watch the minutes tick by on the clock.

8:56. 8:57. 8:58. 8:59.

Please, please, please.

9:00.

Shit, shit, shit.

9:01.

Breathe. Nope, can't breathe.

9:02.

Oh, thank God.

I throw money at the cabdriver and sprint across the street through the rush-hour traffic. Cars screech and horns blare, but I somehow make it across alive. In the glass-and-marble lobby, I blank on the floor I'm supposed to go to. I wait through 9:03 and 9:04 at the information counter before I'm at the front of the line. Twenty-ninth floor, thanks! The elevator finally arrives at 9:05; 9:06 and 9:07 are spent stopping at what seems like every single floor between the lobby and the twenty-ninth floor.

I hurry out of the elevator, fling open *The Line*'s glass door, and try to walk calmly to the receptionist's desk. She has spiky purple hair and a ring through her nose. She can't be more than nineteen.

"Are you Kate?"

"Yes."

"Oh good, you're finally here."

It's then that I notice the clock on the wall behind her.

9:15.

I'm so screwed.

"I was stuck in traffic," I say weakly. Even to me it sounds like I said, "The dog ate my homework."

"Yes, traffic *can* be bad at this time of day."

"Yes."

"They're waiting for you in the Nashville Skyline room. It's down that hall."

"Thanks."

I walk down a long hall decorated with framed blow-ups of *The Line*'s past covers, passing a row of conference rooms. Abbey Road. Pet Sounds. Nevermind. Nashville Skyline.

OK. Here we go.

I check my reflection in the glass that frames an iconic shot of Dylan holding his guitar to his chest while he smiles down at the camera. Not quite the impression I wanted to make, but surely I'm not that color.

I knock on the door.

"Come in."

I take a deep breath and walk in. There are six men and women seated around one end of a long oak slab. Another photo of Dylan, singing close-to-the-mike harmony with Joan Baez, dominates the wall behind them.

I smile nervously. "Hi, I'm Kate Sandford. I'm sorry I'm late."

A small woman in her early twenties with short mousy brown hair rises to greet me. She's wearing a tight black sweater dress that emphasizes her ample curves.

"Hi, Kate. I'm Elizabeth. We spoke on the phone? Why don't you have a seat?"

I sit at the end of the table and face the group. I'm having trouble focusing on their faces.

"Thank you so much for seeing me. I'm sorry about being late. Traffic."

"We understand? This is Kevin, Bob, Cora, Elliott, and Laetitia? Got it? Great? Let's begin?"

"Sure."

"Kate, we've been reading your pieces, and we really like them," says a man in his early thirties who I think is named Bob. Or maybe it's Elliott.

"Thank you, Bob."

"It's Kevin."

"Sorry about that."

"No problem. Why do you want to work at *The Line*?"

I clear my throat. "Well, obviously, it's always been a dream of mine. Of course, it would be. Anyway, I love music, and I've read *The Line* forever, and, I don't know, do you believe in soul mates? Well, I've always kind of thought of this magazine as being my journalistic soul mate."

My heart starts to pound. What the hell is wrong with me? Soul mates? I actually used the words "soul mates" in an interview?

I scan their faces nervously. Cora (or is it Laetitia?) looks like she's trying to keep herself from laughing.

"What do you think you could bring to the magazine? What do you have that's different from everyone else out there?" Elizabeth's lilting voice brings back the nausea I suppressed in the cab.

Let's try this again. With feeling.

"Well . . . I have this real pure love of music, you know? Like on my application? I had a lot of trouble narrowing down my musical influences because I really love all kinds of music. Like, I might dig a Britney Spears song, and the next minute be listening to, you know, Korn."

Did I just say I liked Britney Spears's music?

Cora/Laetitia isn't even bothering to cover up her laughter now, and I can't blame her. Elizabeth's way of speaking seems to be catching, and I'm becoming less articulate by the minute. I feel like I'm about to throw up.

"Talk to me about the bands you've been reviewing lately. Who stands out?" asks an older man whose name I can't even begin to guess at.

"Well, I really like this little neighborhood band called . . . um . . . hold on . . . it'll come to me in a minute . . ." The color creeps up my face as I draw a complete blank. "Um . . . I'm sure I'll remember their name in a second . . . Anyway, they're this great mix of . . . you know, that band that's always on the radio now . . ."

Total panic. I've known and remembered more about music than most teenage boys, and I can't remember the name of one of the biggest bands of that very moment. One of their songs was even playing on the radio in the cab on the way here.

I'm completely done for.

"Kate? Are you all right?" Elizabeth asks.

"I feel a little dizzy. Could I excuse myself for a minute to use the bathroom?"

Bob or Kevin, or whoever he is, frowns, but Elizabeth tells me where it is, and says they'll be waiting for me.

I walk quickly past Pet Sounds and Nevermind to the bathroom. The sharp odor of disinfectant catches in my nostrils. I splash water on my face, and grip the side of the sink as the room spins around me.

This cannot be happening! Please, please, please. Not today, not today, not today.

My stomach lurches, and I bolt into one of the stalls and throw up.

And up.

And up.

When I'm done, I slump to the floor and press my aching head against the cold tile wall, wishing I could disappear. The best day of my life has turned into the worst in an instant. I can't believe the interview I've waited half a lifetime for is coming to this.

"Kate? Are you in here?"

Elizabeth. Fantastic. Please, please, let a hole in the ground open up and swallow me. Maybe it can take me right down to hell, where I belong.

"I'll be out in a minute."

I struggle to stand, and the room begins to spin again. I lurch over the bowl and empty the remainder of my stomach's contents.

Elizabeth raps on the door. "Kate. What's going on in there? Kate?"

"I just feel a little sick . . ."

I throw up again, and this time what comes out doesn't resemble anything I've ever had to eat or drink and leaves a rancid, metallic taste in my mouth.

"You're drunk, right?"

"What? No! I just ate something bad. I think it was sushi."

"I can smell it on you? The alcohol?"

As her words sink in, I slide back to the floor in horror, my legs too weak to hold me.

"Maybe this is none of my business? But I've seen this before? There are good places, you know? Like for people with problems with alcohol?"

"I'll be out in a minute, OK?"

"I could give you a name? Like of a group? You know, AA?"

"I just need a minute," I whisper. "Just a minute."

"I don't think there's any point in continuing with the interview? When you're ready you can show yourself out?"

I listen to her leaving the bathroom, immobilized.

I know I have to get out of here, but I don't have the strength.

This is the worst, worst day of my life.

My thirtieth birthday is the worst day of my life.

Chapter 2
Redemption Song

When I finally pick myself up off the floor, I slink out of the building and somehow make it back to my apartment and my bed.

And that's where I stay for the next two days. I don't answer my phone. I ignore all texts. The only email I open is the formal "Thanks, but no thanks" I receive from *The Line*.

When I can't stand to be in bed anymore, I move to the living room couch and watch television twenty out of every twenty-four hours in a depressed wine haze.

There's a lot to watch. After the escape-from-rehab-high-speed-chase fiasco, TGND disappeared. The speculation is that she's holed up somewhere with her on-again, off-again boyfriend, Connor Parks, an actor eight years her senior.

Connor's career exploded when he made the first *Young James Bond* movie four years ago, and he now makes ten million dollars a picture. He's living like it too, having apparently rented (some sources say bought) an island in the South Pacific, and this is where the press speculates endlessly that TGND is hiding.

"How can you watch that shit all day?" Joanne asks in her twenty-seven-going-on-forty voice when she finds me in a nest of blankets on the couch for the fifth morning running.

I kick an empty wine bottle under the couch. "What do you care?"

"I don't. But it might be nice to be able to watch my own TV once in a while."

Ah, crap. Who knew Joanne had feelings?

"I'm sorry, Joanne. I don't mean to be such a bitch."

She gives me a thin smile. "Apology accepted on one condition."

"What?"

"You take a shower, get dressed, and go outside."

"That sounds like a lot of conditions."

"Do we have a deal?"

"Deal."

And because Joanne is right, I take a shower and go outside for the first time in a week. The air is clean and mild in the way it only is in spring. The first buds are on the trees, and everyone on the street is smiling, or at least it seems that way.

For the first time in a week, I'm smiling too. It's hard to wallow in self-pity with warm sunlight on your face and the scent of cherry blossoms in the air.

I walk through my neighborhood, thinking about the state I'm in. Where my life is going. How I've been chasing a dream for eight long years without really getting anywhere. Something has to give, and I have a feeling I know what it is.

So, when I get back to the apartment, I call my best friend, Rory. We come from the same small town a few hours north and have been friends since kindergarten.

I fill her in on why she hasn't heard from me in so long.

"And then she said I should go to rehab, can you believe it?"

"Um, what time did you want to meet?"

Rory's an investment banker on the verge of a major promotion. We meet for lunch in her office building—the only place I know where she won't cancel on me at the last minute. There's this fifties-style diner in a corner of the lobby, and I wait for her nervously at the chrome counter.

"Katie!"

"Rory!"

I give her a quick hug, being careful not to wrinkle her navy banker's suit. Her olive skin rarely needs any makeup, but today she looks pale and drawn. She's even thinner than usual, and her cobalt blue eyes have circles under them that make her look more heroin-chic than city bigwig.

"Don't they ever let you outside?"

She makes a face. "I'll go outside when I make director."

"You could at least go to a tanning booth. Or, they have these moisturizers now that have self-tanner in them. They look pretty realistic."

"You're one to talk. Haven't you just spent the last week holed up in your apartment?"

"True enough."

The waitress takes our orders, and we catch up on the small details of our lives.

"So, why'd you want to meet, anyway?" Rory asks as she picks at the plate of food in front of her.

"I need an excuse to see my best friend?"

"I thought that other girl, Greer, was your best friend."

"Don't be silly. She's just someone to party with."

"If you say so."

"Rory, you know you're irreplaceable, even if you become a big, snooty director-person who never has time for her friends."

Her eyes narrow. "*If* I become?"

"I meant when, of course."

"I hope so. Anyway, don't worry. I'll still have time for you."

"And I promise not to mind if you're too embarrassed to tell people what I do for a living."

"What do you do for a living?"

I start ripping my napkin into tiny little squares. "Yeah, well, that's kind of what I wanted to talk to you about."

"What's up?"

"I was, um, hoping you could get me a job. I'd be willing to do anything, like start in the mailroom or be your secretary. Whatever it takes."

She looks surprised. "You want to work at the bank?"

"Sure, why not?"

"But what about becoming a writer?"

Ouch. I thought I was a writer. Unsuccessful maybe, but still . . .

"I'm sick of eating ramen noodles," I say, trying to laugh it off.

"You can do some awesome things with ramen noodles."

"Yeah, I should write a cookbook or something. So, what do you say?"

She takes a small bite from her sandwich, thinking it over. "You sure you want to do this?"

"Yes."

"OK, let me see what I can do."

"You're the best, Rory."

"Don't you forget it."

"Like you'd ever let me."

Two weeks later, after more interviews than it should take to become president of a bank, I'm officially hired as the second assistant to the head of the Mergers and Acquisitions department. I'm assigned a small interior office next to assistant number one and told I'll be making $50,000 a year.

As I take it all in, I feel both excited at the prospect of solvency and sick to my stomach at the prospect of working ten hours a day in a room with no windows. But beggars can't be choosers, and I'm grateful Rory came through for me.

Besides the money, the most exciting thing about the job is seeing Rory on a semi-regular basis. When my office tour is done, we spread our lunch out on the small worktable in her incredibly cluttered office.

"I know you're going to tell me you have a system, or something, but how the hell do you find anything in here?" I say, crunching on one of the tart pickles Rory discards from her sandwich.

"It's camouflage," she replies, picking up a napkin and tucking it into the collar of her dress shirt.

"Busy office, busy woman?"

"Precisely."

"You're pretty crafty."

Her lips curve into a smile. "Why, thank you."

"And thank you for the job."

"You're welcome."

"We should totally go out tonight and celebrate."

"I can't. I haven't seen Dave in a week. I need to remind him what I look like."

Dave and Rory have been together since our second year of university, and he's the only person I know who works harder than she does. They're scarily alike, and even resemble each other enough to sometimes be mistaken for brother and sister. On paper they make you want to puke, but in person, they're just Rory and Dave: best friends and lovers. We should all be so lucky.

"Oh, I think he'll remember you."

"Well, I'm not taking any chances."

She takes a small bite from the corner of her sandwich. The amount she eats every day wouldn't get me to eleven o'clock in the morning.

"So, I'm on my own?"

She frowns. "Should you even be going out?"

"Yes, Mom."

"It's just . . . sometimes you can't handle your alcohol."

"What?"

She puts down her sandwich. "Look, don't take this the wrong way, but why are you working here in the first place? Because you got drunk when you shouldn't have, right?"

Excuse me?

"It was my birthday."

"It was the day before your birthday."

"Don't wordsmith me, Rory."

"That's not really the point, is it?"

"What *is* your point?"

She hesitates. "That maybe you should cut down. Especially if you want to succeed here."

I ball up my sandwich wrapper and stand up. "I'll see you Monday."

"Katie, I'm only trying to help."

"Well, you're not, OK? I know I fucked up. I made a stupid mistake. But you're talking like I can't have a beer with my friends . . . like I should be in . . . *rehab* or something . . ."

"Isn't that what that woman at *The Line* suggested?"

"She doesn't even know me."

Her mouth forms into a line. "Right . . . all she knows is that you came to an interview at nine in the morning still hammered from the night before. Silly her to think you might need some professional help."

My blood is boiling. "Talk about the pot calling the kettle black."

"What's that supposed to mean?"

"Come on, Ror. What do you weigh now? Ninety pounds? When's the last time you ate even half a meal?"

She stares at me so intensely I think she might hit me. Then she picks up the remainder of her sandwich and shoves the entire thing into her mouth, chewing aggressively.

"That make you happy?" she says through a mouthful of food.

We stare at one another, equally furious.

I'm not sure which of us cracks first, but, suddenly, we're both laughing uncontrollably.

Rory covers her mouth with her hand to keep from spitting out bits of her sandwich. "You know, I think that was our first fight."

"Had to happen sometime."

"Truce?"

"Truce."

Despite, and maybe because of, the fight with Rory, I arrange to meet Greer at the pub. When I get there, she's sitting at her usual stool being plied with free drinks by Steve.

Steve smirks as he hands me a beer. "Hey, birthday girl."

"What was that all about?" I ask Greer when he leaves.

"You don't remember?"

I get a flash of standing on a bar stool yelling, "Who's the birthday girl? That's me! I'm the birthday girl!"

"No . . . wait . . . don't tell me. I don't want to know."

"It's a good story, lass."

"Again with the stereotypical Scottish terms."

"What's wrong with being a stereotype?"

Steve brings me a shot and a beer back, waving me off when I try to pay him.

"You don't have to buy me drinks anymore, Steve. I've got a real job now."

"He's not buying you drinks—he's trying to get in my pants."

Steve colors and pretends he needs to wipe the counter further down the bar.

"You're totally taking advantage of him."

Greer tosses her hair over her shoulder and gives Steve a lascivious look. "Do you really think I could?"

"Please."

"Interesting."

I spin my stool toward Greer. "So, what's new? I feel like I haven't seen you in ages."

"It was your own self-imposed exile, remember?"

"I prefer to think of it as taking a moment. A knee if you will."

"A *knee*?"

"Yeah, you know, in football, when the coach wants to tell the team something, he says, 'Take a knee.' It means, literally, get down on one knee, but also, 'Listen up, I need your attention.'"

She frowns. "Why would you go down on one knee to listen to someone?"

28

"I guess it is kind of strange."

"And football players do this?"

"Yes, and I mean American football, not soccer."

"Yes, yes."

"Anyway, I was taking a time out to process the state of my life."

"And?"

"And, it turns out my life was extremely shitty."

"Was?"

I bring the shot to my nose, breathing in the sweet, hard fumes. "It's on the mend."

She raises her glass. "I'll drink to that."

"Let's."

I pour the shot down my throat and chase it with half my beer. As the alcohol spreads through my bloodstream I feel lighter than I have since my disastrous day at *The Line*.

It's good to be back.

What with one drink and another, I stumble out of bed the next day sometime after noon. I follow a trail of delicious smells to the kitchen, where Joanne is standing at the stove in her weekend uniform of roomy flannel pajamas, making a sauce.

"What is that? It smells great." I pick up a spoon and try to help myself.

She swats my hand away. "It's not for people who don't answer their phones or return messages."

"What's up your butt?"

"I'm not your answering service."

"What are you talking about?"

"Some girl named Elizabeth called for you a million times yesterday."

My heart thuds to a stop. "Elizabeth from *The Line*?"

"Yeah, I think so."

"You must be joking."

But Joanne doesn't joke.

She stirs the sauce vigorously a few times and puts the lid on. "What's wrong with you? Elizabeth called. She wants you to call her back. Urgently."

I still don't completely believe her.

"What does Elizabeth sound like?"

Joanne rolls her eyes. "She sounds like this? Like she's asking questions? All the fucking time?"

Oh. My. God! It *is* Elizabeth! She called. She wants me to call her back. Yes, yes, yes!

I'm so overcome with joy I actually hug Joanne. She stands there like a board while I jump her up and down, but I don't care. Elizabeth from *The Line* called, and all is right in the world.

I spend the rest of the day in a nervous tizzy. Even though it's Saturday, I keep checking my voice mail every fifteen minutes to see if Elizabeth's returned my call. When the sun sets and she still hasn't called, I help myself to several large glasses of Joanne's never-to-be-touched-by-her wine in a futile attempt to sleep. When that doesn't work, I flip on the E! network and watch the latest TGND coverage unfold.

TGND's been busy since I stopped watching TV all day. She broke up with Connor Parks again and went on a woe-is-me bender. Then a video of her sucking on a crack pipe surfaced. A few days ago, her parents took her to a rugged, lockdown rehab facility up north, where she has to stay for a minimum of thirty days. The footage of her entering a succession of clubs, holding a flame to a pipe, and being dropped off at rehab is played and repeated until even the anchors look bored.

I finally drift off around four in the morning, only to be awakened at eight by Joanne looking pissed and holding the phone out to me with a straight arm.

"We have to stop meeting like this," I say groggily.

"It's Elizabeth? From *The Line*?"

I grab the phone. "Hello?"

"Is that Kate?"

"Yes, this is Kate."

"This is Elizabeth from *The Line*? We met a few weeks ago?"

"Yes, hi. I remember you."

"We were wondering if you could come in for a meeting about a position that's come up? Maybe this morning at ten? I know it's Sunday?"

"Of course I can come in for a meeting! Ten is great."

"Perfect. Come to the same place as last time?"

We say goodbye, and I spring toward the bathroom to start getting ready. The sudden movement makes my stomach turn over, but I shake it off and leap into the shower singing, for some reason, "I am, I am Superman!" over and over at the top of my lungs as I lather my hair.

Whoever said there are no second chances in life was a moron.

I arrive at *The Line*'s offices twenty minutes early with my hair brushed, my makeup done, and my clothes pressed. (I pick the suit this time, hoping some of its respectability will rub off on me.) My stomach still feels jumpy, but I chalk that up to nerves. At least I know I don't smell like alcohol, having loofahed every square inch of myself just in case.

At ten on the dot, Elizabeth appears in the Sunday-quiet lobby wearing an extremely short gray skirt and a tight blue sweater.

"Hi, Kate. How are you?"

"I'm great. Thank you so much for giving me another chance."

"Sure. So, you'll be meeting Bob? You remember him from a few weeks ago?"

I think back to the sea of faces sitting around the board-room table. Try as I might, I can't remember Bob.

"Right, of course. Looking forward to it."

"Good. His office is two floors down?"

I take the elevator to a floor where the decor hasn't been updated in at least twenty years. It's *Miami Vice* chic, and there's something kind of seedy about the atmosphere.

Seeing no one, I push the doorbell that's recessed into the

wall next to a solid wood door. A few seconds later, the door buzzes open, revealing a squat, blond man who resembles Philip Seymour Hoffman, which is ironic when you think about it because PSH played a music magazine guy in *Almost Famous* and . . . Focus, Katie, focus!

"Hi, Bob. Thank you so much for asking me back after . . . well, you know. Anyway, I'm really excited to be here."

He gives me a tight smile. "Yes, well, when this assignment came up we thought of you . . . for obvious reasons. Why don't we go to my office?"

OK, so it's an assignment, not a full-time gig, but everyone has to start somewhere, right?

I follow him along a dark hall to another nondescript brown door. He swipes a key card. The room behind the door has a long row of unoccupied fabric-divided cubicles full of abandoned coffee cups.

"Is this some kind of call center?"

"You might say that. This way."

He cuts to the right along a narrow passage through the cubicles. As I turn to follow him, I notice a paper banner hanging on the far wall. It reads: GOSSIP CENTRAL: IF YOU CAN'T FIND ANYTHING MEAN TO SAY, YOU CAN FIND THE DOOR.

What the hell?

I realize Bob's striding away from me, and I hurry to catch up with him. At the end of the passage is another brown door. Bob swipes his key card once again and pushes it open.

"Sorry about all the security. But given the nature of the information we deal with, we have to take every precaution."

Since when did album reviews become top-secret information? "Of course."

Bob points to the chair in front of his cheap-looking desk. "Have a seat."

I sit down gingerly. When is this guy going to put me out of my misery and tell me what my assignment is?

"So . . . I assume Elizabeth filled you in?"

"Actually, not really."

"Well, you'll have to leave immediately because there's no telling how long she's going to be in there. Everything's all arranged, and the staff's expecting you. It'll be a minimum thirty-day assignment if all goes well, but I'm warning you, it might be longer. We'll be covering your expenses and paying the usual per-word rate. We'd like five thousand words, but we'll discuss the final length once we know what you've got."

He picks up a bulky envelope from his desk and hands it to me. "Here's the background information we've been able to put together. It's pretty extensive and will hopefully give you a place to start. Of course, you can't drink or do anything else that'll jeopardize your stay. If you get thrown out, the contract will be forfeit. Do you have any questions?"

What the fuck is this guy talking about?

"I'm sorry, but I really don't understand. What's the assignment? Where am I going?"

Bob gives me another tight smile, but this time there's an undercurrent of glee in it.

"You're going to rehab."

Chapter 3
Houston, We Have a Problem

So, here I am a day after my meeting with Bob, the Philip Seymour Hoffman look-alike, sitting on the smallest airplane I've ever been on. Cocktail service begins in five, and our flying time will be a total of forty-two minutes. We'll be flying at an altitude of twenty-two thousand feet, and yes, the flight will be this bumpy the entire time. Now remember, folks, if the mask falls from the ceiling because of a loss of cabin pressure, place it firmly over your mouth and breathe normally. In case you weren't aware, there's no smoking on this flight.

Now, let's see. Is there anything I've forgotten?

Oh yeah . . . I'm on my way to rehab.

Turns out that besides being one of the editors of *The Line*, Bob is also the editor-in-chief of *Gossip Central*, an up-and-coming gossip magazine in a world of up-and-coming gossip magazines. Its niche is obtaining extremely inside scoop on celebrities. It made a name for itself when one of its reporters posed as a nanny for a movie star who has a penchant for adopting children from Third World countries. Apparently, a lot of people want to know what brand of underwear she wears. By supplying such details, *Gossip Central's* market share grew quickly, and its circulation now surpasses the population of New Zealand. Or, at least, that's what its website says.

Apparently, Bob had been trying to get something on The Girl Next Door for years. The problem is that she doesn't hang out with anyone who isn't quasi-famous, and that includes her hairdresser, makeup artist, and publicist. After several fruitless attempts, the idea was shelved, and *Gossip Central* moved on to other, more accessible, targets.

And then, TGND went to rehab.

No one was quite sure where the idea came from. Someone (Bob told me there were several people taking credit) shouted it out during the weekly editorial meeting, and the idea immediately caught fire. "We should follow her into rehab." "That's perfect!" "Whoever came up with that deserves a promotion!" "It was my idea." "No, it was my idea!"

Once Bob calmed everyone down, they spent a lot of time discussing the thorny issue of who to send. It had to be someone who could convincingly appear to need to be in rehab and also write a kick-ass article. It couldn't be anyone obviously connected with *Gossip Central,* but it had to be someone they trusted. They racked their brains before putting the idea on the back burner when TGND escaped from rehab.

You know the rest of the story. I showed up half-drunk and disheveled for my interview. They loved my work before they met me, but then they met me. TGND's crack video surfaced, and she returned to rehab. Bob had a moment of clarity: what if the writer actually needed to be in rehab herself? Then she'd fit right in, and might even have a chance of striking up a friendship with TGND. Now who did they know who fit that bill?

So that's why they called. *Gossip Central* wanted to hire me to go to rehab to spy on/befriend TGND and write about it. They'd pay the cost of my stay ($1,000 a day) and $2 a word. And if I did a good job (and dried out, he implied), they'd reconsider me for the position at *The Line*, which still hadn't been filled.

When I picked my jaw up off the floor, I agreed to do it.

Embarrassingly quickly.

I wish I could say the decision was a difficult one, that the thought of going to rehab undercover to dig up dirt on a young woman in the middle of self-destructing gave me pause. I wish I could say I was indignant that Bob thought I'd agree to do it, or that I could convince anyone I needed to be in rehab. But that wouldn't be true, and the first step to recovery is admitting that I have a problem, right?

So, OK, I do.

I want to work at *The Line* so badly I'm willing to do whatever it takes to get into Bob's good books. And if spying on TGND in a sober environment for a minimum of thirty days is going to get me there, well . . . *so be it.*

Forty-two minutes and four mini bottles of Jameson and Coke later (hey, I can't drink *at all* for the next thirty days, and I've never been a good flier), the plane lands, and I disembark a little unsteadily onto the sunny tarmac.

I grew up about forty minutes from here in a town nestled at the base of a ski hill that's so small it doesn't even have a real supermarket (just the Little Supermarket, where everything is twice as expensive and has twice the calories). There's no McDonald's, no main street, no town hall, and no courthouse. It does have a liquor store and a Santa's Village, but that's about it. Unemployment's through the roof, the high school's twenty miles away, and most of the residents don't ski, despite the highest elevation in the east sitting at their back door.

My parents are an exception: educated and middle class, they fell in love with the outdoor life and moved to the town in a fit of hippieness in the late seventies to set up a commune with some like-minded friends. Six months, four broken friendships, and two divorces later, only my parents remained in the half-finished house nestled on a back road in a back-road town. The house was finished just before I came along. By the time my sister arrived a few years later, we even had indoor plumbing. Mom teaches English at the high school, and Dad is assistant manager at the ski hill.

I left town the day after high school graduation and never looked back. Fame and fortune hadn't followed, but I was surviving. I was eking out a living in a city that spat out wide-eyed, small-town girls like cherry pits.

I haven't been home in four years.

When I stumble out of the terminal, a pretty woman about my own age is waiting for me. She has caramel-colored hair that falls to her shoulders and round brown eyes. She's wearing khaki pants and a dark blue polo shirt with a white Cloudspin Oasis logo on it.

"Hello, Katie, I'm Carol, the intake administrator for the Oasis." She speaks in the local, drawn-out accent I've worked hard to get rid of.

"Hi, Carol. Thanks for picking me up."

That might've come out, "Sanks for sticking me up," though I'm not exactly sure.

"Have you been drinking, Katie?"

Hello! Of course I've been drinking. I'm supposed to be an *alcoholic*.

"I had a few drinks on the plane to steady my nerves."

Schdeady me nervsss.

"Well, we've got about a half-hour drive to the lodge."

"I know. I grew up around here."

She smiles. "Then you'll feel right at home."

Absofuckinglutely.

We climb into the van, and Carol maneuvers it onto the highway. I fiddle with the radio dial, searching for the station I listened to growing up. It comes in faintly through the crappy radio. The Plain White-T's are singing "Hey There Delilah."

Feeling oddly happy (I've got a good song + drinks buzz going), I roll down the window and breathe in the smell of the mountains. Maybe all woods smell the same, but this combination of loamy earth and tangy pines smells like home to me.

Seven songs later, Carol slows down to make the turn

into the driveway that leads to the Cloudspin Oasis. Three cars are parked across the road. A group of dingy-looking men holding cameras and smoking cigarettes are lounging on the hoods. As we stop at the gate, one of them rises half-heartedly and walks toward the van. I smile at him, but he flaps his hand in disgust when he realizes I'm not worth the effort.

Carol pushes a button on a two-way speaker attached to a metal pole and mumbles something that sounds like "hot soup." The gates creak open and she drives through.

"Why are the paparazzi here?" I ask innocently.

She glances at me. "Sometimes we have famous patients staying here. Just ignore them."

We drive down a long, curving driveway lined with huge pine trees. Carol stops the van in front of the entrance to a large timber-framed building with a long wing on each side. The building looks new, new, new, with green siding and crisp white trim. There's a lake behind it, and the pine-covered mountains rise steeply from its shore.

I get out of the van. The familiar earth and pine smell is more pronounced, making me feel oddly at ease.

What does it say about me that rehab smells like home?

Carol pulls my suitcase out of the back of the van and wheels it toward the entrance.

"Katie, you understand that once you begin the program, there's no leaving for thirty days?"

"So they tell me." I try to sound serious, but I feel like I want to laugh.

I guess the cocktails on the plane haven't quite worn off.

I try again. "I want this. I'm sure."

"Good."

We enter the building through a heavy oak door. The reception looks like the lobby of a hotel, with a round check-in desk in the middle. The decor is a mix of honey-colored wood and robin's egg blue, and the whole space is filled with natural light coming from the huge skylights in the ceiling. I place my hand on the back of one of the upholstered sofas to steady myself. It feels stiff and formal.

"This is Dr. Houston, the head of the medical staff," Carol says, referring to an attractive man in his early forties who's standing behind the counter. He has black hair, hazel eyes, and chiseled features. He's wearing a white coat, and there's a stethoscope poking out of his right pocket. She pronounces the name Houston like the street, "house-ton."

"Welcome to the Cloudspin Oasis," he says.

I shake his proffered hand. It feels cold.

"I'm Katie Sandford."

"Nice to meet you, Katie. Just so you know, we ask that patients not use their last names, to protect their anonymity."

That suits my purposes exactly.

"Sure."

"Good. Carol will help you check in. Once you're done, you'll come to my office for your medical assessment."

"Okey dokey."

He frowns. "Katie, have you been drinking today?"

Come on. Doesn't everyone arrive at rehab drunk, or high,

or both? Aren't they all finishing off their last hurrah in the parking lot? Like what's his name in that movie, the one where the main character hid in rehab because his one-night stand died of a drug overdose. What the hell is that movie called? This is so going to bother me. Ah, got it. *Clean and Sober.* Michael Keaton. Phew.

"Just a little."

Carol pulls a stack of forms from under the counter and hands them to me. "You'll need to fill these out. You can take them to that table over there." She points to a desk tucked into the corner of the lobby. "Let me know when you're finished."

"Right."

I walk/sway to the desk and sit down. It's made of a single piece of cherry wood that's so polished I can see my reflection in it. My hair is windblown, and my eyes aren't completely open.

God, I look like hell! No wonder everyone keeps asking me if I've been drinking. Well, at least I look the part.

I read the first form. It's in legalese, but as far as I can tell, I'm agreeing to give up my right to leave for thirty days. Once I sign it, the only way out is to be thrown out.

I thumb the end of the pen, click, click, click, unwilling to write my name across the bottom of this paper.

What's the hesitation?

It's just . . . thirty goddamn days. That's a long time.

Do you want this job or what?

Of course.

Then sign the form already.

All right, all right.

I take a deep breath and sign on the dotted line. Thirty days in rehab. Done.

I work through the rest of the pages, filling in my personal information and medical history until I come to a page entitled "Are You an Alcoholic?" As I scan the questions, I begin to feel queasy. Drinking in the day (OK, the morning) isn't usually my thing, and it's starting to catch up to me.

I walk the forms back to Carol.

"Are you all done?"

"Do you think I could finish these another time? I'm not feeling too well."

She looks sympathetic. "Of course. Let me take you to Dr. Houston's office."

A wave of nausea passes through my gut, and I grip the side of the counter.

"Do I have to do that now? Can't I just go to my room or something?"

"I'm sorry, Katie, not yet. It's important that we give you a medical exam first."

I breathe in and out deeply, and the nausea retreats. "All right, let's get it over with."

"Of course. Follow me."

She leads me to the wing to the right of the lobby, where I thankfully spy a bathroom. I push open the door and Carol follows me inside. The sight of the toilet bowl speeds up my nausea, and I fall to my knees in front of it, taking long slow breaths. And for a minute I think I might be OK. That I might not throw up in front of this woman I don't even know. But then the nausea returns, and all the drinks and the two packages of nuts I consumed on the plane are leaving my body in a long liquid stream.

That's the last time I drink and fly.

Carol crouches by my side, holding my hair and rubbing my back. If I wasn't feeling like such shit, I might laugh at the fact that this relative stranger is performing boyfriend duty. But instead, I feel like her kind hands are invading my privacy in the worst way.

Now, if cute Dr. Houston were here . . . Oh God. Not again.

When I'm finally done, I rinse the burning, metallic taste from my mouth and dry my face off on a piece of paper towel from the dispenser.

"Are you all right?"

"Just peachy."

When we get to Dr. Houston's office, I change into a thin hospital gown. Carol gathers up my clothes and tells me she'll be back when my exam is done.

Feeling woozy, I lie down on the examining table while I wait. The minutes drift by, and I feel sleepy. I yawn widely. It's cold in here. It'd be nice to have a blanket. So inconsiderate of them not to provide one.

"Carol tells me you were ill." Dr. Houston's pleasant voice startles me from my half-doze.

I open my eyes. He's standing over me with a concerned look on his face.

Mmm. He really is quite cute. Kind of like Jason Patrick's older brother.

"Are you feeling better?"

Better is kind of a relative concept right now.

"I guess."

He pulls up a round, wheeled metal stool and sits down. "Good. I'm going to begin the physical examination, all right?"

"Sure."

"This might feel a little cold."

Dr. Houston loosens my gown and places his *freezing* stethoscope on my chest. I suck in my breath.

"Inhale deeply." He moves the stethoscope around my chest. "OK, you can release it." He takes the stethoscope's earpieces out of his ears. "What are you here for, Katie? Alcohol? Pills? Cocaine?"

He examines my arms one after the other.

Is he looking for track marks?

"Alcohol."

He takes a penlight out of his chest pocket and shines it in my eyes. "Anything else?"

"Nope. I just drink."

"How many drinks do you usually have a day?"

Who keeps count of that?

"It kind of depends."

He slips a blood pressure cuff around my arm and pumps it tight. "Just give me an average."

What does an average alcoholic drink in a day? I so should've done some research before I came here, you know, other than Googling TGND to death.

"I don't know . . . two bottles of wine . . ."

I watch him nervously. Is that enough?

He pushes his hands into my stomach. "Every day?"

Maybe I went too far?

"Yes."

"Sit up, please."

I sit up and he taps his fingers along my back, making a hollow sound.

"How long has that been the case?"

"A year?"

"Is wine your drink of choice?"

I think back to Joanne's dwindling supply of investment wine and my stomach flips over. I eye the sink in the corner, mentally calculating how long it'll take me to get from here to there. I'm pretty sure I'm going to need at least seven seconds.

"Are you all right?"

Breathe in, breathe out. I. Will. Not. Puke. Again.

"I think so."

"You look green."

"Is 'green' a medical term?"

The corner of his mouth twitches. "Your pallor is troubling."

Maybe it's the lingering Jameson and Cokes, but I think he might be flirting with me. I glance at his left hand. No ring. Interesting.

I look into his eyes for some sign of interest. There's nothing there.

Oh my God, will you get over yourself! He's a doctor who works in a rehabilitation center. He's not going to flirt with a patient he's admitting into his facility!

After depressing my tongue and inspecting my throat, Dr. Houston takes a needle and a few color-coded vials out of a drawer. He ties a plastic tourniquet around my forearm and waits for a vein to bulge, then dabs my skin with a swab of alcohol.

"This will pinch a little."

I turn my head away. I've never been able to stand the sight of a needle pushing through flesh.

The needle enters my arm, and I swear I can feel my blood flowing out into the vial. I try to focus on something else. The number of door handles on the cupboards. The spider spinning a web in the corner.

He pulls the needle out and places a piece of gauze firmly on the hole in my arm. He gives me a paternal smile. "We're almost finished."

I can't believe I thought he was flirting with me.

"Good."

"When we're done, Carol will take you to a room in the recovery wing, where you'll begin the detoxification process."

"What is that exactly?"

"Simply put, it's not drinking in a medically supervised environment. It should take two to three days depending on the severity of your withdrawal symptoms."

Sounds lovely.

"What kind of withdrawal symptoms?"

"Have you ever tried to quit drinking before?"

Does not having enough money to buy drinks count?

"Not really, no."

"The symptoms can be both physical and psychological. Common psychological symptoms are depression, anxiety, and cravings. Physically you may experience tremors, headaches, vomiting, loss of appetite, and insomnia. In severe cases, patients can also experience seizures."

Shit, that doesn't sound good. Thank God I'm only pretending to be an alky.

"Seriously? Seizures?"

"I don't think that's likely in your case . . . if you've been honest about the amount of alcohol you generally consume."

I really have to find a way not to flinch when people use the word "honest" while I'm in here.

"Yes."

"Even so, we'll give you some medication for the first couple of days in order to help you through the detoxification and ensure that you don't have a severe reaction."

He wheels his stool over to a metal medicine cabinet in the corner, unlocks a drawer, and tips some pills into a small paper cup. He spins his stool and kicks the ground with his foot, skidding back to me.

He hands me the cup. "Would you like some water?"

I stare at the pills. They look big. "Do I have to take them?"

"I would definitely recommend it, unless you have a specific reason not to."

I don't really, it's just . . . the day before I started high school my father sat me down to have the drug talk. He was supposed to tell me to "just say no," only my still-hippie-in-his-heart dad (who I was pretty sure grew pot in the corner of the garden he was always telling us to stay away from) couldn't quite bring himself to do it. Instead, he gave me a set of guidelines.

"The way I see it, Kid, anything that comes from the ground is OK," my father said. "It's that manufactured shit, pardon my French, that gets people in trouble. If you can consume it in its natural state, and never tell your mother I said this, I don't see why you can't experiment a little."

I stared at him from the middle of my beanbag chair. "What are you talking about, Dad?"

"I'm talking about pot, hash, and 'shrooms. If you stick to those, you should be OK. Not that I'm telling you to take them. But if you decide to do drugs, those are the drugs you should use."

"OK," I said, feeling freaked out. Did my dad just tell me it was OK to use drugs? Rory wasn't going to believe this.

To date, I've followed his advice. I may have done a little pot, hash, or 'shrooms back in the day, but I've never ventured any further down the yellow brick road.

"What's the matter, Katie?" Dr. Houston says.

"I think I want to do this on my own. You know, without chemical help, or whatever. Isn't that the point?"

"It's absolutely the point. But your addiction is more than psychological, it's physical. And if you can't make it through the physical part, you'll never get a chance to work on the rest."

I stare back into the cup, looking at the pills as if they might tell me what to do.

Why are you hesitating now?

It's just . . .

Spit it out!

I didn't think I'd begin my first day in rehab expanding the list of drugs I've taken.

Will you stop being such a priss!

I upend the cup and dry-swallow the pills. They leave a bitter taste in my mouth.

"You can get dressed now, Katie. I'll see you again in a couple of days."

He leaves, and Carol returns with a set of soft cotton pajamas that are a size too big for me. I change into them, and she takes me to my room. As we walk down a long corridor, my slippers make a shuffling sound on the hardwood floor. I realize I haven't seen another patient since I arrived.

"Where is everyone?" I ask.

"There's group therapy every afternoon."

Joy.

"Here we are." She opens a door. The room behind it looks like a dorm room. There's a single bed with a simple blue cover on it underneath a barred window, a fold-out suitcase rack supporting my suitcase at its foot, and a small bedside table. A stainless-steel kidney pan sits on the simple chest of wooden drawers. The air smells clean and slightly institutional.

"The bathroom is two doors down. If you need assistance, you can push the button here." She points to a white button set into the wall above the bedside lamp. "This will be your room until you finish detoxing. Meals will be brought to you three times a day. Do you have any questions?"

I look around the tiny room. "Am I supposed to stay here the whole three days?"

"Most patients generally do, but if you want to go outside, let me know." She takes a folded piece of paper from her pocket. "This is the treatment schedule you'll be following over the next thirty days. Let me know if you have any questions."

I take it from her. "Thanks."

"I suggest you get some rest."

"Right."

"Everything will be all right now, Katie."

Oh God. Is she going to hug me? I'm so not into hugging strangers.

Carol squeezes me tightly to her. She smells faintly of lilac, like my grandmother does, which is pretty odd for someone who seems my age. I know I'm supposed to put my arms around her, but I can't bring myself to do it. Instead, I stand there until she releases me.

After she leaves, I lean over the bed to look through the window at the daffodil-ringed courtyard. The grounds are empty and peaceful.

I sit on the bed and unfold the piece of paper Carol gave me. It's a thirty-day events calendar. I have a larger, erasable version on my own wall at home left over from university. Only, instead of entries like *Kegger @ Delta Phi* or *Matt Nathanson concert*, this says things like *detox* (Days One to Three), *learning the steps* (Day Four), *coping skills* (more days than I can count), *visiting day,* and (oh, please God, no) *family therapy.*

I toss the schedule onto the bedside table. Christ, I'm already bored. How am I going to get through the next three days? Maybe the pills will help pass the time? I wonder when they're going to kick in. I guess I feel a little sleepy. Maybe a nap wouldn't hurt.

I take off my slippers and climb under the covers, closing my eyes to block out the sun seeping through the curtains. In a few minutes, I can feel myself slipping away, the drugs taking effect.

Sorry, Dad.

Chapter 4
Hi, Katie!

I sleep right through the rest of the day and into the next morning. When I finally wake up, there's still light slipping past the curtains, but now it's a pale, morning light.

As I open my eyes, I feel fuzzy from the drugs and hungover from the Jameson and Cokes. I need to drink a huge glass of water, to pee, and to puke my guts out. Maybe not in that order.

I eye the kidney pan on the dresser. Absolutely not. I will *not* puke into something that belongs in a hospital or an old folks' home!

I pull back the covers and stagger down the hall, trying to remember which door Carol said leads to the bathroom. The second handle I try is the right one.

Please let me finish peeing before I puke. Please let me finish peeing before I puke. Please let me . . . not quite the Serenity Prayer, but it works. The clenched feeling in my gut recedes and eventually passes.

I find an empty glass by the sink, still in its hotel-like paper wrapping, and fill it with tap water. The first sip feels like heaven in my cotton-wool mouth, and I drink and drink, refilling the glass again and again. When I'm sure I can safely leave the bathroom, I retrieve my toiletries and fresh clothes from my suitcase. After a shower and a good teeth brushing I feel almost human. Well, OK, a human with a wicked hangover, but this too shall pass.

What I could really use is the hair of the dog, but something tells me they let dogs bite you around here.

When I get back to my room, I realize it's only 6:40, presumably in the morning. I've got a lot of time to kill.

Might as well get to work.

I take the new journal I purchased at the airport out of my bag and start a fake entry that's really notes on what I've seen and heard up to now. All the puking and prodding will make good atmosphere for my article.

When I've captured every sight, sound, and smell I can remember, I pull out a soft case from my bag that contains the iTouch Bob gave me as a way to communicate with him while I'm undercover.

"There aren't any cell phones allowed," he said, handing me a matte black box. "Fill it up with music, make it look like your own."

I felt a moment of panic. A whole month, maybe more, without texting? My friends were going to think I'm dead.

"Is email forbidden too?"

"That's right."

No cell phones, no email. Where are they sending me?

"Sounds strict."

"It's not one of those chi-chi spa places."

Damn. I was already imagining myself immersed in a mud bath.

"So, how am I going to use this?"

"You're going to hack into their Wi-Fi network."

"I wouldn't have the foggiest idea how to do that."

He handed me a slim envelope. "The instructions you'll need are in here. You should memorize them tonight."

I opened it and read them quickly. They looked simple enough for me to follow.

"How did you get the password to their system?"

He looked smug. "We have our ways."

I squash a pillow behind my back and cross my legs into a weak lotus position. I start up the iTouch, hoping the Jameson and Cokes didn't erase the memorized instructions. Thankfully, Apple has made breaking into someone's poorly protected Wi-Fi network a piece of cake, and I'm soon entering the Oasis's password and connecting to the Internet.

I open my email and write a short update to Bob. *Have arrived. In detox. So far, so undercover.* I hit send and scan through my inbox. There are three emails from Greer and two from Rory sent ten minutes apart.

I open Greer's first. It was sent at 6:44 p.m. yesterday.

K, is your phone dead? Let's hook up 2nite. Bring your drinking boots.

The next one comes from someone named Patrick Morrissey, but the subject line says "From Greer," so I know it isn't someone trying to sell me a penis enhancer. It was sent at 8:32 p.m.

Some scrounger banker let me borrow his BB. Where RU?

I smile, thinking of Greer flirting with Steve before shifting her attention to a guy in a suit (she *hates* guys in suits) so she could finagle him into letting her use his BlackBerry. Classic Greer.

At the time of the last email (11:24 p.m.), Greer was clearly drunk.

I'm letting this guy take me home and you can't stop me!

I laugh out loud, then smother my mouth with my hand. I listen carefully, but I don't hear anything other than the birds twittering outside. For all I can tell, some psychotic addict has killed everyone in the place and I'm the last person alive.

Moving my fingers over the touch screen, I write Greer back.

Sorry about last night. It's a long story, but I had to go away suddenly for work. I probably won't be back for at least a month. Don't worry. I'll be in touch. Love, Katie.

I hesitate before opening Rory's emails. The fact that there are two of them isn't a good sign. Rory usually says what she has to say the first time around, and I'm pretty sure the double email has something to do with the breezy message I left her two days ago.

"Rory, Rory, quite contrary, something's come up, and I have to go away on a new assignment! So, I won't be able to take the job after all. I'll let them know. Thanks so much for the help! Love you!"

Maybe I took the coward's way out, but lying to Rory has never been my strong suit. I knew if I told her the truth she'd be horrified and shocked, and would probably persuade me to be horrified and shocked too. And I didn't want anyone talking me out of taking this job.

Joanne was the only one I'd told, because I had to tell someone. She seemed like the safe choice since she has no real connection to my other friends (Rory and Greer both loathe her). Her reaction was typical Joanne—she just shrugged and asked for my share of the rent in advance. The only rehab-related comment she made was that she expected me to pay her back for all the wine I'd drunk when I got out.

I open the email.

You're not answering your phone and you know I can't stand talking to Joanne. I can't believe you abandoned this job. I know it wasn't what you hoped you'd be doing with your life, but it's time to grow up. I thought you'd have a little more respect for me than this.

Jesus. She's madder than I thought. And hurt. I'm an evil, evil person.

The second email picks up where the first one left off. Clearly ten minutes wasn't enough time for her to calm down.

I can't believe you've put me in this position. I really went out of my way to get you this job, you know, even though I knew I'd regret it. Don't expect me to do anything for you ever again.

A tear runs down my cheek as I sit on my bed, in rehab, feeling very alone.

Several hours later, after I've attempted to eat some of the breakfast Carol brings me, stared out the window for an hour, and off into space for another, I get an IM from Greer on the messenger service I downloaded onto the iTouch.

Where the hell RU?
Secret mission.
U've joined the FBI.
No.
CIA?
No.
Cult?
No.
Joanne says UR in rehab.

God fucking shit, Joanne! The last words I'd said to her were "Don't tell anyone where I am."

Joanne's an idiot.
It's OK if UR. I went to rehab 1x.
You did? When?
In 6th form.
How come?
Mam and pap thought I smoked 2 much pot.
Why?
Cuz I smoked 2 much pot.
What was it like?
Like pot.

LOL. I meant rehab.

Talky.

That's it?

Didn't stay long enough to find out.

Why not?

Did you know they don't let you drink there?

There's a knock on my door. I hastily shove the iTouch under the covers.

"Who is it?"

"It's Carol," she says as she opens the door. "How are you feeling today?"

"All right, I guess."

She looks at the tray of mostly uneaten breakfast sitting on the dresser. "How come you're not eating?"

"I don't feel like it."

"It's important that you try to eat, Katie. We can't move you out of the recovery wing until you need less medical supervision."

I sit up straighter. I already want out of the recovery wing very badly.

"I'm sure I'll be ready soon. I just needed to . . . well, sleep it off, really."

"Recovery's not something you can rush through."

"I understand."

"Good. I'll be in to check on you a little later."

She leaves, and I pull the iTouch out. There's another IM from Greer waiting for me.

Where did you go?

Had to talk to the warden.

I knew it!!!

After lunch, I start going stir-crazy. Sure, at home, with the comforts of wine, a couch, and my TMZ, I'm happy to spend days at a time without even thinking about the outside. But put me in a white room and I don't care what I'm supposed to be pretending to be, I need to get out of here.

Right now.

Feeling desperate, I push the emergency button. When Carol arrives a few minutes later, I ask her if I can go outside. She looks at my nearly empty lunch tray and agrees. As she leads me toward the front door, she explains that there are several walking paths through the woods that surround the lodge. She suggests I take the shortest one. I nod my head, barely listening. By the time we reach the front door, I feel almost giddy. She tells me to be back in an hour, and I step outside and raise my face toward the sky. Its weak warmth feels gentle and inviting.

I take the path Carol suggested through the flower gardens, following the meandering stones that mark it. The air is full of the perfume of the daffodils and crocuses that are pushing through the black earth. I round a bend and come across a couple of gardeners digging up one of the flower beds. One of them is about my age and looks incredibly familiar.

I shake my head. It must be the medication, because if I were straight right now I'd swear that was . . . oh no . . . it can't be . . .

I crouch down behind a tied-up rosebush and peer at him through the twine. Right height, right build, right former quarterback good looks. And didn't Mom say something about him starting a gardening service with his brother the last time I talked to her?

He turns his head toward me, and now I'm sure. Zack Smith, my high school boyfriend, is standing a hundred feet away from me shading his eyes from the sun with a weathered hand. In fact, he's looking right at me.

Shit. He's looking right at me. I've got to get the hell out of here. But how am I going to escape without calling attention to myself?

"Katie, is that you?"

Fuck, fuck, fuck. I so did not think coming here through.

I stand up, brushing a stray piece of bush from my jeans. "Hi, Zack."

We walk toward one another and exchange an awkward hug. He smells like earth and sweat.

"What are you doing here?" he asks when we separate.

"Oh, you know, just a little medically supervised detox. You?"

He grins, revealing his still-perfect white teeth. The breeze blows a lock of his chocolate brown hair onto his forehead. "Oh yeah. Same here."

"Are you serious?"

"Nah. You?"

"Unfortunately."

His face grows serious. "Oh. Well, they help a lot of people here . . ."

"Yeah, that's what I heard."

I meet his warm brown eyes and am momentarily transported back to when we were the Perfect Couple and *Mrs. Katie Smith* covered every one of my notebooks.

"So . . . what are you in here for?" he asks.

Christ. I can't believe the guy who taught me how to do a keg stand is looking at me like I'm dying of cancer.

"Oh, the usual, you know. Anyway, you're still living around here, huh?"

"Yeah. Me and the wife and kids."

The wife and kids. Jesus.

"Do I know her?"

"It's Meghan."

Of course it is. My mother mentioned that too. Meghan Stewart. My high school rival. White-blond and bouncy, she couldn't quite manage a full beer bong. Now she's married to my first imaginary husband, and I'm talking to him in a rehab garden. There's a lesson in that somewhere, I know, but I can't quite put my finger on it.

"That's great, Zack."

"Most days. You know, my oldest is in your sister's class."

Shit, that's just what I need, for my sister to know I'm in rehab. I can imagine her reaction—gloating, superior. And, of course, her first instinct will be to tell my parents.

"Huh. That's . . . funny."

"Chrissie didn't tell you?"

"I haven't spoken to her in a while. Look, can you do me a favor and not tell anyone you saw me here? Especially my sister and my parents? They don't know I'm here and . . ."

"You don't need to explain. We have to keep patient information confidential anyway."

"Right. And thanks. Anyway . . . I should get back to my room."

"And I'd better get back to work." He pulls me toward him again, hugging me close. "It's good to see you, Katie."

"Even in rehab?" I ask into the front of his shirt.

"Even in rehab."

When I get back to my room, I spend a long time talking myself out of packing my bags and jumping the fence. I can't believe I thought I could keep coming to rehab a secret, especially so close to home. How stupid can I be?

Do you really want me to answer that?

Shut it.

OK, OK. Calm down. The patients are supposed to be anonymous, right? I mean, the whole world knows TGND is here, but that's because she's an enormous celebrity. Who am I? Nobody. And Zack said he wouldn't tell, or couldn't tell, which is just as good.

Besides, is it really that big a deal if Mom and Dad find out? It's not like they're going to actually think I need to be in rehab. They'll know something's up, and I'll let them in on the secret and it'll be fine.

OK. Sounds like a plan. Though, just to be on the safe side . . .

I take out the iTouch and send my dad an email saying that I'm going on the road with some (made-up) band so my parents don't call the apartment. Then I eat enough dinner to ensure that I don't give anyone the impression that I still need "medical supervision" and try to ignore the strong urge to down several glasses of wine with my Salisbury steak. When I can't, I take the two little pills that came with my dinner, and fall asleep at seven thirty.

In the morning, I feel better than I have in a long time, and I eat every bite of the breakfast Carol brings me. When I'm done, I sit on my knees staring out the window until Carol comes to take me to see Dr. Houston.

"Well, Katie," he says after he's given me another physical exam. "I can see you're doing better. I think we can move you out of detox and into the cognitive therapy wing."

Oh, thank God. *Learning the steps,* here I come.

"That's great."

"However, before we can move you there, we need to perform some diagnostic tests."

I knew it was too good to be true.

"Why? I thought I was OK."

"You are physically, but a lot of addicts have other psychiatric issues."

"I'm not crazy."

I only do crazy things sometimes.

He lifts a pen out of the pocket of his white lab coat and writes something on his clipboard. "It's not a question of being crazy, Katie. We simply need to make sure there aren't any underlying disorders that will impede your recovery."

"What do I have to do?"

He takes some forms from a drawer and hands them to me. "You can begin by completing this diagnostic test. It will give us your basic psychological profile." He unclips a couple of pieces of paper from his clipboard. "You'll also need to fill this out."

I take it. It's the "Are You an Alcoholic?" form from two days ago. Joy.

"As you're filling this out, I'd like you to think about what your answers mean. About the impact alcohol has had in your life."

You mean all the good times? I'm guessing no.

Back in my room, I sit on my bed and work through the tests. The psychological assessment is a series of multiple-choice questions I vaguely remember from an Intro to Psychology class I took years ago. I toy with the idea of answering "C" to every question but discard it as the bad idea it is.

When I'm done, all I have left to do is discover whether I'm an alcoholic. As if they can tell that by answering a few silly questions. Well, here goes nothing.

Do you enjoy social events more when there is alcohol present? Well, obviously. Who doesn't? *Yes.*

Have you ever been unable to remember events from the night before after drinking? Yes, thank God. Who wants to remember everything they've done after a night of drinking? Take that "birthday girl" comment from Steve. I'm pretty sure I have no interest in remembering all the gritty little details of that night.

Has drinking ever caused a problem between you and a friend or relative? Does Joanne count? *No.* Only . . . shit. What about that fight with Rory? She definitely counts. Fine, fine. ~~No.~~ *Yes.*

Do you stop drinking after one or two drinks, or keep drinking until you get drunk? Duh. You've got to keep the drinks rolling once you've started a buzz. Everybody knows that. Coming down from a buzz is, well . . . a buzzkill. And nobody likes a buzzkill. *Yes.*

Have you ever attended an AA meeting or other twelve-step program? No way. Not unless you pay me. Which I guess explains what I'm doing here. *No.*

Have you had unprotected sex because you were drunk? Sigh. *Yes.* Only . . . hold on a sec. It wasn't *because* I was drunk. I was just young and stupid and really, really into Jack from my creative writing class. When we ended up half-naked at his place after many rounds of cheap beer and he said he didn't have a condom, I told myself that he didn't seem gay or have track marks and threw caution to the wind. But I did think about it. I *might* have made the same decision if I was sober. It's possible. ~~Yes.~~ *No.*

Have you missed work or school because of drinking? Well, obviously, who hasn't? If that's a measure of someone having a drinking problem, then every one of my friends, and most of the population, has one too. OK, maybe the kids who go to Mormon college wouldn't qualify, but that's about it. *Yes.*

Can you drink more than most of your friends? Let's see. Greer and Scott can definitely drink more than me. Rob and Toni are kind of lightweights, and so is Rory. Joanne doesn't drink.

Where does that leave me? I read the question again. Mmm . . . "most of your friends." What if it's a tie? Ah, fuck it. *Yes.*

Does it take more alcohol to get drunk now than when you started drinking? Yes. Of course it does. It's called "tolerance," and it takes a while to build one up. And once you have, you have to maintain it. It's a survival tool, really. How else do you make it past midnight at a university party?

Do you get drunk on a regular basis? Well . . . it's not like I drink every day or anything. At least, it's not like I get drunk every day. Not every day. But didn't I tell Dr. Houston that I did? What did I tell him, anyway? The details are a little fuzzy, but I seem to recall something about two bottles of wine a day. Did I really say that? I guess that means . . . *Yes.*

Have you ever tried to cut down on your drinking? Yes. Wait a minute. Maybe that's the wrong answer. Didn't I talk about this with Dr. Houston too? Why the hell is he making me answer all these questions again? How am I supposed to keep all these details straight? I hate this fucking questionnaire. ~~*Yes.*~~ *No.*

Do all of your friends drink alcohol on a regular basis? Finally, an easy question. *Yes.* I bloody well hope so.

Have you ever been arrested for drunk driving? Another easy one. *No.* Hah! See? I obviously don't have a problem. I'm a safe drunk. I take cabs, I walk, sometimes I let other people drive drunk, but I never do. Never. Well, except for that one time when I drove Zack's truck in high school, but that was just in a field, and I'd only had like three wine coolers, maybe four.

Do you have a family history of alcoholism? Mmm . . . didn't Uncle Brad have to go away for a while? Wait. Was that rehab or just a mental institution? How did he end up there again? Oh, right. He found his girlfriend kissing some other guy at a bar and went crazy, smashing up the bar and the guy and maybe even his girlfriend. Then he went on a three-day bender that ended when he wrapped his car around a tree. Or something like that. It was hard to catch all the details my mother was whispering over the phone to her sister. I never saw Uncle Brad drinking any alcohol after that, though. He always asked for seltzer. So, I guess . . . *Yes.*

Last question. *Do you use drugs on a regular basis? No,* I write. *Only since I came to rehab.*

I must've passed the test, because Carol's leading me to my new digs in the women's wing, where I'll spend the rest of my stay. As we walk through the building, she explains that the Oasis presently has twelve patients and that they never have more than twenty at any time.

I guess at $1,000 a day they can afford to keep it exclusive.

"You're going to be rooming with Amy," Carol says as we walk through the large common room that occupies the back of the main building. "We like to pair newcomers with patients who've been working the program well."

"Does that mean she'll be my sponsor?"

"No, you'll get a sponsor when you join an AA or NA group once you go home. Our focus is on cognitive therapy. You'll learn how to develop skills that will help you cope with life without using drugs or alcohol."

Right, I remember. *Coping skills,* Days Five through forever.

"Is that what we do in group?"

"That's right, but also in your individual therapy sessions, which will be more focused on your particular issues. Your first session is tomorrow morning with Dr. Bennett, who also leads group therapy."

"So, that's all we do? Individual therapy in the morning and group in the afternoon?"

"We have guest speakers sometimes as well."

Now that sounds more interesting.

"Like celebrities?"

She frowns. "The speakers are generally former patients who've stayed sober. But since you brought it up . . . As you already know, we sometimes do have celebrity patients, but it's important not to treat them any differently. They're just like you: addicts trying to get help."

"So who's here? Would I know them?"

"Katie . . ."

"OK, OK, I got it. No asking for autographs. Don't worry. I can behave."

She stops in front of a nondescript door. "Good. Well, here we are."

She knocks and opens the door. The room is much like the one I just left (barred window, simple furnishings, blue bedspreads, faint whiff of institution) but big enough for two twin beds with a nightstand in between. There's evidence of my new roommate on the bed nearest the door, but she's nowhere to be seen.

"Group starts in twenty minutes in the common room. I've left a list of the house rules on your bed. Do you need anything else?"

"I'm good, thanks."

She pulls me into another one of her tight hugs. I give her back a few halfhearted pats, hoping she won't notice my lack of response.

"This is where it really starts, Katie. And you only get out what you put in."

Funny, that's the same thing my trainer said when I decided to try getting into shape a few years ago. The gym membership was Rory's Christmas present to me, and I'd been really determined. That was, until I was put through a rigorous series of crunches and lunges by a man who'd just gotten out of the Corps.

"You only get out what you put in, Katie," he said as I was trying to do my first pull-up since the fifth grade. "Are you ready to give it your all?"

"Yes," I managed to squeak.

"What? I can't hear you!"

"Yes," I yelled as I hung inches off the ground, unable to lift myself any further. My body hurt for three days, and I never went back.

"Right, I understand," I say to Carol.

She leaves, and I sit down on my new bed. Lying on the pillow is a single sheet of paper containing a list of rules about mandatory therapy sessions and meals, no fraternizing between patients, and lights out at 10 p.m.

It's funny because, with a few small alterations, this list is identical to the one that adorned the wall at my summer camp. Come to think of it, we weren't allowed to leave there for thirty days, either. Of course, camp was, you know, *fun*. I'm guessing we aren't going to be singing songs around a campfire here.

I fold the list into my journal—more atmosphere for my article—and unpack a few of my things. Then I take out the iTouch and log on. There's no email from Rory, but there is one from Bob.

Kate, please provide a status report on the target. Bob.

What a sinister word, "target." Like I'm an assassin, or at the helm of an X-wing fighter. I'm not here to kill anyone, buddy, just get them to spill their deepest, darkest secrets, or discover them by trickery if that doesn't work.

Bob, they've had me in isolation until now. Expect to see TGND at group in a few minutes. Will send status report when can. Kate ☺.

Is the emoticon too much? Oh, who cares? He can deal with it if it is. I send the email and slip the iTouch back into my bag, hiding it in my dirty underwear.

It's time for group.

Group therapy takes place in the common room, which is in keeping with the hotel-like feel of the lobby. Its main feature is a picture window that frames an amazing view of the lake. Watching the sun play on the water, I feel a momentary urge to get a running start and dive through the window into the black lake. The leap would likely kill me, of course, but if I managed to get away, would they save me or let me take my chances with whatever monsters lurk below?

There are a dozen metal folding chairs arranged in a circle and a pot of strong-smelling coffee brewing on an oak side table that sits next to the window. The chairs hold an assortment of men and women who look in surprisingly good shape for a bunch of drug addicts and alcoholics. Of course, this *is* a class of addicts who can afford to go to the same place as TGND, so maybe they've never looked as depraved as the addicts in the this-is-what-you-look-like-if-you-do-crystal-meth ads. But does crystal meth care whose body it's being snorted or injected into? Or do you smoke crystal meth? I can never remember.

And speaking of TGND, where the hell is she?

A dumpy woman in her mid-fifties with chin-length salt-and-pepper hair comes to greet me. She's a few inches shorter than me and has a round face.

"You must be Katie. Welcome. I'm Dr. Bennett, but please call me Saundra." I shake her soft, small hand. "Please take a seat—we'll be starting in a minute."

I sit down in one of the remaining empty chairs, suddenly nervous about what's to come. Am I expected to talk on the first day? And what the hell am I going to say, anyway? Won't this group of hardened users be able to see right through me?

Saundra calls the meeting to order. "All right, everyone. Settle down. We're going to be talking about coping mechanisms for stressful situations today. But first, we have a new arrival, Katie."

My nerves increase as ten pairs of eyes travel toward me. Shit! I'm definitely going to have to talk today. Couldn't I learn some of those coping mechanisms first?

I raise my hand and give a little wave.

"I'd like to go around the room and have everyone introduce themselves. Katie, you can go last. Ted, would you like to start us off?"

They go one by one. Ted is a banker addicted to cocaine and alcohol. Mary is a novelist addicted to heroin. There's also a pretty famous movie producer, a former child star if you use the term "star" very loosely, a Fortune 500 executive, an up-and-coming director, an investment banker, two lawyers, and a judge. Their addictions range from simple alcoholism to drugs I've never even heard of. Did you know, for example, that if you take fifty cold pills at once you start to hallucinate? Well, that's what the investment banker was doing every day until two weeks ago. Who knew?

As it nears my turn someone climbs into the chair next to me. It's TGND, Amber Sheppard in the flesh.

She's wearing a bright green velour tracksuit that matches her large eyes, and her black hair is in a tight knot on top of her head. She's much smaller than she looks on television (not more than five foot one) and very thin. She's not wearing any makeup, but her skin still glows with youth and pampering. She looks odd, but beautiful.

And, oh yeah, she's behaving rather strangely.

"Amber, what are you doing?" Saundra asks as TGND plants her bare feet in the middle of her chair and crouches on her heels, her arms up in front of her.

"Nothing."

"We've talked about this, Amber."

"My *name* is Polly the Frog."

So that explains the crouching position. And the flitting tongue.

I look around. A few of the patients are laughing, but most of them simply look annoyed.

"This isn't acting class, Amber. Please sit in your chair properly and introduce yourself."

Amber's cheeks flush with anger. "*Fine.*" She untucks her legs and sits in the chair. "My name is *Polly,* and I'm a frog."

"Amber, please."

"OK, OK. My name is Amber."

"And why are you here?"

"Because I was kidnapped by my parents and brought here against my will."

"Amber . . ."

"All right, all right. I'm addicted to alcohol and cocaine."

"Thank you. Katie?"

My heart starts to pound. I've always hated public speaking.

"Hi. My name is Katie. I'm a writer, and um . . . I'm an alcoholic."

"Hi, Katie!" says the group.

"Wrebbit!" says TGND.

Chapter 5
No Rest for the Wicked

After group I speed back to my room so I can get down as much of what I've witnessed as possible. What I wouldn't give for a microcassette recorder, or one of those tiny hidden cameras that fit into your eyeglasses. But Bob thought it would be too risky, so I'm left relying on my memory, never perfect in the best of circumstances.

My roommate nearly gives me a heart attack when she enters the room without knocking. I close the journal quickly, trying to appear nonchalant. It feels like my heart is beating visibly out of my chest like in an old Disney cartoon, but she doesn't seem to notice.

Amy's model-tall and beautiful. Her toffee-colored skin matches her eyes, and her dark hair is tightly curled and chin length. After I introduce myself, she starts to download the details of her life with the ease of someone who's been here for a while. She's a lawyer who works at one of the largest firms in the city. One too many cocaine-fueled deal memos landed her an all-expenses-paid trip to the Cloudspin Oasis. She's been here for twenty-four days, and if all goes well, expects to leave six days from now.

We chat for a while, and then we have dinner together in the cafeteria. It has a bistro-y feel to it, and another bank of windows framing the green lawn that rolls out like a blanket toward the woods. The view is breathtaking, but no one's looking. Instead, everyone's talking, talking, talking about themselves. I look for TGND, but despite the "all patients must attend all meals" rule, she's nowhere to be seen.

The food is good, simple fare (spicy penne arrabbiata, a tart Caesar salad), and after dinner we follow the crowd to the common room to watch a cookie-cutter romantic comedy on the widescreen TV. When the couple that's meant-to-be finally gets together, there doesn't seem to be anything left to do but go to sleep, and so I do.

I'm dreaming a wonderful dream. I'm writing a cover profile about Feist, and I'm meeting her backstage at the Grammys before she performs. A rainbow of musical celebrities surrounds us. Paul McCartney is playing "Blackbird" for Adam Duritz. Madonna is warming up for her duet with Fergie. Kurt Cobain's daughter is about to make her musical debut, singing backup for Lisa Marie Presley. None of it makes any sense, of course, but I feel extremely happy nonetheless.

That is, until I'm awoken by the most ungodly scream.

"AAAHHHHH!"

My eyes fly open, my heart pounding. By the moonlight

seeping through the window, I can see Amy tossing back and forth on her bed, her mouth open.

I jump to the cold floor and put a tentative hand on her shoulder. "Amy."

"AAHH, AAHH!"

"Amy!"

"Get off me!"

I pull my hand away. "You were screaming."

"Who are you?"

"It's me, Katie. Your roommate."

I turn on the light that sits on the night table between our beds.

She blinks slowly. "Sorry. I was disoriented."

"It's OK. I think you were having a nightmare."

"I wish. I was in a K-hole."

"A what?"

"I was dreaming I was using."

Oh. So "K" must be a drug. But what drug? Vitamin K? Special K cereal with cocaine sprinkled on it?

I'm going to be unmasked soon, soon, soon.

"Right, of course . . . I hate those kinds of dreams."

I totally paused for too long between those two phrases.

Amy sits up and runs her hands through her tightly curled hair. Her eyes look unfocused. "That's the understatement of the year."

Phew. She doesn't seem to have noticed.

"Do you want some water? I could get it for you."

"No, thanks. I'm all right." She pounds her fist into the

mattress. "Fuck! I'm so goddamn tired of this. Why doesn't it get any easier?"

"I'm sure it does."

She looks at me bleakly.

"Sorry, what do I know? I just got here."

"Right. I'm the one who's supposed to be teaching you how to cope."

"You don't have to."

"I know. But I should know something by now, especially since I've been here before."

"This isn't your first time in rehab?"

"This is take three. Three strikes and you're out," she mutters.

"How come it didn't work before?"

She shrugs. "Choices I made. People I should've stayed away from. Take your pick."

"Why not try something else?"

"Like what?"

"I don't know. I'm just talking smack."

She almost smiles. "Interesting choice of words."

"Sorry."

"Don't worry about it. Thanks for waking me up."

She reaches out her hand and after a moment's hesitation, I take it. She quietly begins to cry, and the tears well up in my own eyes.

Jesus. Four days in rehab, and I'm already crying with strangers.

The next morning at breakfast I don't have much of an appetite, so I sip my coffee while Amy digs into an omelet.

"Don't worry, your appetite will come back in a couple of days," she says.

"Oh, I never eat much breakfast."

"Have you had any tremors yet? Those are the worst."

I'm not quite sure how to play this. Should I admit to tremors, or counter with something worse, like seeing imaginary bugs?

She's not testing you, idiot, she's just making rehab conversation.

Right. Less paranoia would be good.

"Not yet. Anyway, I should get to my therapy appointment."

"Sure enough. See you later."

I get a to-go cup for my coffee and ask for directions to Saundra's office.

Her office is oddly decorated with all things dog. I mean, *all things dog.* There's a dog calendar, a dog clock, a couple of framed photographs of dogs, and a dog leash sitting on the corner of her desk. The only thing missing is the actual dog itself. Or maybe the leash is for me?

Saundra sits behind her large oak desk. I get comfortable in her matching visitor's chair as she explains that the Oasis's approach is to identify the root, internal causes of my alcoholism and to teach me techniques that will allow me to solve problems without alcohol. If I trust Saundra and work with her, I should acquire the skills I need to stay sober by the end of my thirty-day stay.

I'm guessing the skills I really need to learn by the end of my thirty-day stay aren't what she's talking about.

"Some patients need longer than thirty days, of course, but given that this is your first time in rehab, and the level of your addiction, which is severe but not chronic, it should be sufficient."

"What do you mean by the level of my addiction?"

"You scored a ten out of fifteen on the alcoholism test."

"Is that bad?"

"It's a graduated scale. Answering yes to more than five questions means that drinking is interfering in your life in a substantial way, which is a sign of alcoholism."

"And I got a ten?"

"Yes."

Yowser, that is not good. But wait a second. Not all those answers were really mine, right? At least three were what I told Dr. Houston as my cover story. So my real score is probably like . . . six. That's nothing.

Saundra pulls a pad of yellow legal-sized paper toward her. "Katie, I'd like to begin by trying to discover the origins of your alcoholism. How old were you the first time you got drunk?"

"I was four."

Her eyes widen. "Four years old?"

"I guess that's kind of young, huh?"

"A little. Why don't you tell me about it."

"Well, actually, it's a funny story . . ."

It *was* funny. When my parents finally extricated themselves from their commune-gone-wrong legal problems, they decided to celebrate by holding a party. There was champagne, and my dad poured me a small glass, a splash really, so I could join the toast.

I remember my first taste of that champagne. It was sweet and delicious, like drinkable candy, and the bubbles felt ticklish on my tongue. I loved it and I wanted more. So I asked for some, and my dad, already a bit drunk, gave it to me. That disappeared as fast as I could drink it, and so did the fuller glass I got from him a few minutes later when he wasn't paying attention.

Before I knew it, I was hammered. I felt like my body was floating, and I lay happily in the grass feeling each individual blade with the tips of my fingers. When the party broke up, my parents took us to a restaurant for dinner. My tipsy parents didn't realize there was anything wrong with me until we got there. That's when I thought it'd be a good idea to teach my two-year-old sister, Chrissie, how to pull the tablecloth out from under the dishes. I'd seen a magician do it on TV and he made it look easy. I remember the horrible clatter of dishes, my father's jumble of oaths, and my mother repeating over and over, "Why would you do that, honey? Why would you do that?"

When they finally clued in that I was drunk—Dad confessed to giving me "just a little taste"; Mom's shriek of anger set half the restaurant's eardrums ringing—I was hauled out of the restaurant by my ear and left in the family car to "sober up!"

When my parents calmed down, the whole thing became a family joke. From that point on, whenever I'd act out, my dad would yell, "Sober up!" and we'd laugh and laugh.

"Do you really think that's a funny story, Katie?"

Uh, yeah. I've brought people to tears with that story on more than one occasion, but maybe you need a drink in your hand to really appreciate it. Like therapy.

"Kind of."

"Can you see why not everyone would think so?"

"I guess. They shouldn't have been giving me alcohol at that age, right?"

"Yes, that's one thing. But don't you also think it's problematic that they turned it into a family joke?"

"It's not like I wasn't punished."

"By leaving you alone in the car?"

"I grew up around here. People always left their kids in the car."

Saundra writes a few words on her pad of paper in a cursive script. "Were your parents neglectful in other ways?"

"What? My parents didn't neglect me."

"I'm sorry, Katie, a poor choice of words. What I meant to say was, were there other times you got drunk as a child?"

A flash comes to me of a Thanksgiving dinner when my mother was away visiting her parents. I was thirteen or fourteen, and Chrissie, Dad, and I polished off several bottles of wine. A snowstorm kicked up in the middle of dinner, and my sister and I ran out into the night to make snow angels. We spread our arms wide, the fluffy snow giving way to our sweeping arms. Dad sprang onto the front porch swinging a bottle and yelling, "I've got the last of the wine!" We burst out laughing and couldn't stop for what seemed like hours.

I feel a wave of nostalgia for the fun Chrissie and I used to have together. "Yes, but . . . those events were harmless. They were fun."

"I'm sure it seemed like fun at the time . . . but do you think it's possible that those early experiences laid the foundation for your alcoholism?"

"Are you saying it's my parents' fault that I . . . that I'm here?"

"Of course not. I'm merely exploring to see if we can find the root of what led you here."

There's a knock at the door. Saundra glances at the clock.

"I'm afraid that's all the time we have for today. We'll pick this up tomorrow, all right?"

"Yeah, I guess." I stand up to leave. "I don't think my parents did anything wrong. I mean, they were, are, great parents."

She looks sympathetic. "I understand. I'll see you in group this afternoon."

"Right, sure. See you in group."

So, I have a confession to make. I didn't have only four mini bottles of Jameson and Coke on the plane. There were a few drinks at the airport too.

Now, I don't usually drink in the morning, but there was something about that morning that felt out of the ordinary. It was a combination of things, really. Seeing the tiny plane I was going to have to fly in. Going undercover. Being about to meet a celebrity I'd been watching for weeks on television. Having the opportunity to finally get where I wanted to be as a writer. Going to rehab. It all balled up inside me, and I needed something to calm me down. The chamomile tea I had before I left for the airport wasn't cutting it, so I headed to the always-open airport bar and ordered a gin and tonic.

And it worked. When the drink was gone I felt better. I felt steady. I felt ready.

Then the flight got delayed because of mechanical problems (Mechanical problems? Shouldn't they be canceling the flight or getting a new plane?) and I ordered another drink to soothe my renewed nerves. The plane wasn't ready until I got down to the ice in drink three, and I blame that drink personally for what I did next.

You see, the whole time I was at the bar there was a woman sitting next to me intently reading a book. I kept trying to strike up a conversation, but she wasn't having it. I don't know if she didn't want to talk to me, or she was enjoying her book too much, but I couldn't get two words out of her.

As I sat there drinking, I started to feel pissed off, and the focus of my pissed-offedness was this woman, sitting there all serene and too good to talk to me, reading, reading, reading.

So, *so*, when she got up to go to the bathroom, leaving her book sitting on the bar, I had this uncontrollable urge to take it. I knew it was childish, I knew it was kind of criminal, but I was having a shitty day and I wanted to spread the shit around.

When my flight was called, the book's owner hadn't returned. I gathered my stuff and threw down some money to pay for my drinks. And then, as I walked away, I scooped up the book and shoved it in my bag, being careful not to glance over my shoulder furtively, feeling thrilled that I'd gone through with it.

Take that, too-good-to-talk-to-me lady!

Of course, once the deed was done, I promptly forgot all about it. Until after my therapy session, when a craving for something, *anything*, that might be bad for me sends me rooting through the bag I shoved the book into in a mad search for a (please, God!) forgotten pack of cigarettes. I don't find any, but I do find forty bucks (score!) and the book I swiped.

I pull it out, unsure where it came from until my thievery comes back to me. Oh, right. The airport. The drinks. The woman.

Well, maybe it's a good read?

I turn it over. It's *Hamlet*. *Hamlet*? You've got to be kidding me. That's what airport woman was so engrossed in she wouldn't talk to me? Well, maybe it's one of those modern retellings, like *The Other Boleyn Girl*. I check the author. Nope. William freaking Shakespeare. Just great. It feels thick too, like the movie Kenneth Branagh made. Rory dragged me to it, and it was like four hours long. It even had an intermission.

And I was so hoping it was something delicious and readable. I'm sure we're supposed to spend our free time contemplating how badly we've messed up our lives, but really, how much time can you think about that kind of stuff? And I can spend only so much time writing in my journal, no matter how wacky TGND acts in group. That leaves walking in the woods, talking, talking, talking with the other patients, or the library. I scoped it out yesterday and it's useless. It's full of copies of the *Big Book of Alcoholics Anonymous* and similar self-help fare. The thought of reading anything like that, in addition to hearing it twice a day during group *and* therapy, makes me want to poke my eye out with a sharp stick.

On the other hand, if someone told me a week ago that I'd be contemplating reading Shakespeare as a way to pass the time, I'd have told them to pass me another drink. But now that I'm here, and drinking's not an option, why the hell not?

I take the book to a comfy corner in the library, curl up, and am immediately, surprisingly, semi-engrossed.

"That's contraband," a woman says to me an hour later as Hamlet's talking to his murdered father's ghost about "*murder most foul.*"

I keep reading. "What?"

"That book. It's contraband."

Hold on a second . . .

I look up. TGND is standing in front of me. Oh my God. TGND is talking to me.

"How can Shakespeare be contraband?"

She flops down next to me, curling her feet under her short jean skirt. "If it's not on the bookshelf, you're not supposed to be reading it."

"Why not?"

"Who the fuck knows?" She plucks the book out of my hand. "So, Shakespeare, huh? Serious stuff."

"It's actually really good."

"Yeah, he knew how to write." She squares her shoulders.

"'What a piece of work is man! How noble in reason! How infinite in faculty! In form and moving how express and admirable! In action how like an angel! In apprehension how like a god! The beauty of the world! The paragon of animals!' Doesn't that give you goose bumps?"

Wow. She doesn't just croak. She quotes the goddamn bard.

"Do you know the whole thing by heart, or is that just a party trick?"

She gives me a coy look. "Wouldn't you like to know?"

Well, yeah. Duh.

"Methinks the lady doth protest too much."

She laughs. "Looks like you have a few party tricks of your own."

"Nah, I just totally pulled that out of my ass."

"Nice image."

"Sorry. I come out a little crass sometimes."

She waves a hand at the room. "We're in rehab. Crass is the vernacular."

If she's trying to impress me, it's working.

"Got it."

She hands the book back to me. "Enjoy. Maybe I'll borrow it when you're done."

"Sure."

"You're Katie, right?"

"Yeah. And you're Amber."

"That's me. What'd you say you did again?"

"I'm a writer."

"Like literature?"

"Like journalism."

Her shoulders tense. Shit.

"I write about music."

She relaxes. "Oh. For *Rolling Stone*?"

"I wish. I write music reviews for a couple of weekly papers."

"Cool."

She glances around the room, and I can tell she's losing interest.

Say something interesting, Katie. Quickly.

"You read a lot?"

OK. That wasn't it.

Her large green eyes track back to mine. "You think I'm too busy partying to read?"

Whoops. Really not it.

"Sorry, I didn't mean it that way."

"It's OK. You've probably seen all that stuff on TV, right?"

I'm not quite sure what the right answer to that question is. "A little."

She smiles. "I'm sure you've seen enough. But it's not really like that living it, you know? Or ... I don't know ... maybe it is. I'm not saying things weren't out of control. They just weren't quite as bad as they looked."

Right. I'm sure that was the first time you ever smoked crack. Your bad luck that it was caught on tape.

I play along. "I know what you mean. Today in my therapy session, Saundra asked me about my childhood, and then she picked it apart until I felt like it was an *After School Special*."

"I was in an *After School Special* once."

"Which one?"

A blush creeps up her cheeks. "That one about incest . . ."

"That was you? There was this line that became this catch-phrase at my school . . ."

She scrunches her shoulders, and I can see the six-year-old girl peeking through. She speaks in a breathy voice. "I don't like it when my daddy touches me."

"That's it. That's totally it!"

"Why do people always remember the worst thing you've ever done?"

"Because negative things are way more interesting."

"Right. I should definitely know that by now." She swings her legs off the chair and stands up. "Anyway, I should let you get back to that."

"OK. Nice talking to you."

"Yeah. You too. You know . . . you might just be the first normal person I've met here."

Shit, shit, shit. I'm not supposed to be normal. I'm supposed to be damaged.

"Thanks."

"See you around."

I watch her walk away, noticing again how very thin she is. When I'm sure she's gone, I grab a pen off the desk and begin scribbling notes into the empty pages at the back of *Hamlet*, trying to get the gist of our conversation down while it's still fresh in my mind.

Bob's going to be *excited!*

Chapter 6
One Step, Two Step, Three Step, Four

"Step One: We admitted we were powerless over alcohol—that our lives had become unmanageable," Saundra says during our second session in her Dogs 'R' Us office. "Do you have any questions about the step?"

I tuck my yoga-panted legs under me, pretending to ponder her question. Do people actually have trouble understanding this step? Why would you be in rehab if your life was manageable? Yeah, yeah, OK. I mean, why would one normally be in rehab?

There is one thing that's bothering me though . . .

"Why are the steps written using the royal 'we'?"

A crease forms across Saundra's forehead. "Pardon?"

"You know, like how the Queen speaks about herself. 'We are not amused.' It's called the royal 'we.'"

"It's the way Bill wrote them."

I should probably know who that is, right?

"Bill . . . ?"

"Bill Wilson, the founder of Alcoholics Anonymous."

"Oh. Well, I think it's weird."

Saundra picks up the dog collar and holds it between her hands. I'm sure it's just an unconscious gesture, but it's freaking me the fuck out.

"I think you might be focusing on the wrong thing, Katie."

You don't say?

"Let's start at the beginning. Are you ready to take the first step?"

"I think so."

"You've admitted your problems, that you're powerless over alcohol? That your life has become unmanageable?"

Oh, I've got a problem all right.

"I thought I had to admit that *we* were powerless over alcohol—that *our* lives had become unmanageable."

She looks disappointed. "Please don't turn this into a joke, Katie."

"I'm sorry." I take a deep breath and look as serious as I can. "I'm powerless. My life has become unmanageable."

Like, why else would I be here?

"That's good, Katie. I know that took a lot of courage." She opens the file folder sitting in the middle of her desk. "I'd like to discuss the results of the psychological assessments we did a few days ago."

"Am I crazy?"

She gives me that disappointed look again.

"I wasn't making a joke. I really want to know."

"You don't seem to have any serious underlying disorders, but the tests indicate that you might be depressed and that you have some issues with honesty and commitment."

Yikes. And I was answering truthfully too. I knew I should've gone with the answer-"C"-to-everything strategy.

"I don't think I'm depressed."

She considers me. "Then why do you drink?"

Well, duh. Because it's *fun*.

"It makes me feel good."

"Are you unhappy when you're not drinking?"

Why do I feel like she's tricking me?

"I have good days and bad days, like everyone."

"But you drink every day?"

That's what I told Dr. Houston, right?

"Yeah."

"So, most days you need something to make you feel happy?"

I knew it was a trick!

"I guess."

"And if you weren't drinking, would you be unhappy most days?"

My eyes wander to the oblong window above Saundra's head. The sky is gray and cloudy.

"I don't know . . . I really don't think of myself as unhappy . . ."

"Katie, when you're using alcohol regularly to alter your mood, it's generally an indication that there's something that needs to be altered."

"So, you think I'm depressed?"

"As I said, you show some signs of it, but it's only through the deeper work we'll do here that we'll figure out if depression is the cause or the effect of your drinking."

This conversation is depressing me.

"And if it's the cause?"

"We'll try to get at the root of it."

"And if it's just an effect?"

"Then if you stop drinking, the symptoms should disappear."

Great. Only . . . what if the thought of never having another drink makes me depressed?

"Are you ready to do the work, Katie?"

"I'm ready."

"And are you prepared to work for as long as it takes?"

"Yes."

For as long as Amber takes, anyway.

She smiles. "That's good, Katie. That's very good."

I leave Saundra's office feeling like I've spent an hour talking to a confessional camera on a reality show. You know how there's always some closet where the players confess their inner thoughts? I've often thought that if I went on one of those shows, I'd pretend to be this sweet, helpful thing, then let out the inner bitch when only the audience at home could see it. But the reality of actually having to be nice to a bunch of crybabies and schemers who talked, talked, talked about themselves all day long always dissuaded me from applying.

Oh, the irony.

When I get back to our room, Amy is lacing up her running shoes to go for a run. She looks fit and healthy in her dark blue shorts and sleeveless T-shirt. Except for the thin, pink scars on her arms and legs, of course. Scars too regular to be anything other than self-inflicted.

"You want to join?" she asks as she springs up and starts running in place.

"The last time I ran for anything other than a cab was in high school."

"It's a really good way to clear your head."

"Maybe tomorrow."

She pulls a mocking face. "Don't put off to tomorrow what you can do today."

"Is that one of the twelve steps?"

"Oh boy, you really are a newbie, aren't you?"

I point to my chest. "'Day Five: The First Step to Sobriety.'"

She mimics me. "'Day Twenty-seven: Advanced Coping Mechanisms.'"

"I'm so jealous. Enjoy your run."

"Thanks . . . and thanks for last night."

"No problem."

She leaves and I lie down on my bed. I place my hands behind my head and try to block out my conversation with Saundra. What I really need is an angle to get closer to TGND.

What does Bob expect me to get out of her, anyway? Should I be rooting through her room to figure out what kind of underwear she wears? Why the hell did I agree to do this in the first place?

At least I know the answer to that question.

When Amy comes back from her run, I tuck *Hamlet* under my arm and we go to the cafeteria for some lunch. The beautiful picture window is streaked with rain, making the view of the lawn and the woods look blurry, like a Monet. Everyone from group but Amber is already here, filling the gap in their lives left by drugs and alcohol.

Amy and I collect sandwiches from a hair-netted lunch lady and sit down at one of the round bistro tables occupied by The Former Child Star and The Novelist.

TFCS (real name, Candice) is thirty-five but still acts like she did when she lisped cute/precocious thoughts that summed up that week's situation comedy. Her white-blond hair is even curled the same way, and she holds her Prussian blue eyes open in an expression of youth and innocence that must take a lot of work. It must've killed her when Amber came through the gates pursued by enough cars to be an inauguration day cortege.

Mary, The Novelist, is a dumpy forty, with frizzy dark hair that's mostly gone gray. She has deep lines on her face that make her look older than she is. Her life spiraled out of control as her first novel climbed the bestseller lists, and she's worried she'll never write anything worth a damn while sober.

Listening to the stories they tell about the things they've done, the depths they've sunk to, makes me amazed/pissed off that anyone could confuse me for someone who needs to be in rehab. I mean, showing up hungover to an interview might be stupid and unfortunate, but it pales in comparison to giving a guy a blow job so he'll share his drugs, right? Even up-talking Elizabeth should be able to see the difference.

As I eat my tuna fish sandwich, Candice begins to complain about the fact that Amber's allowed to miss meals. Her high-pitched half-baby voice grates on my nerves.

"Why do you care?" I ask when I can't take it anymore.

"It's not fair."

"So? Life's not fair. Deal with it."

She gives me a disgusted look, stands up, and storms off without saying another word.

"Thank gawd," Mary says in her coastal twang. "I thought she'd never shut her gob."

"How have you guys been able to stand her?"

"Oh, she's not that bad, really," Amy says. "She's gotten worse since Amber arrived. Besides, it is kind of ridiculous that she doesn't have to follow the rules."

"You can get away with anything when your Q score is high enough," Mary says.

"True enough." Amy stands and picks up her tray. "Katie, do you mind if I take a nap in the room? I'm kind of wiped."

"No problem. I've got my book."

Amy and Mary leave together, and I pick up *Hamlet*. I still feel fidgety from my session with Saundra, though, and I can't concentrate on the complicated language. I put the book down on my orange food tray and watch The Producer, The Judge, and The Lawyer as they gesticulate and guffaw across the room.

"How are you making out with *Hamlet*?" TGND says, plunking herself down next to me. She's wearing a white gauzy dress that makes her look wispy and pale, and her long black hair falls loosely past her shoulders.

Excellent. Now, just remember to ask some questions, but not too many.

Yeah, yeah, I got it.

"It's slow going."

"But better than the alternative, right?"

"My thoughts exactly."

She motions toward my half-finished sandwich. "That any good?"

"Yeah, it's not bad."

"Tasting food has to be the one good thing about living clean."

"You couldn't taste your food?"

What the hell was she on?

"Nope, everything tasted pretty much the same. Like *cheap wine and cigarettes*," she sings a snippet of The Wallflowers' "One Headlight" in a good, pure voice.

"I love that song."

"Me too. You know, I met him once."

"Jakob Dylan?"

"No, the dad."

"You met Bob Dylan?" My voice comes out all high and squeaky.

"I think so. He wrote that 'Everybody Must Get Stoned' song, right?"

How can you be unsure if you've met *Bob Dylan*?

"You mean 'Rainy Day Women Nos. 12 & 35'?"

"I don't think that's what it's called . . ."

"No," I say before I can help myself. "That's what it's called. Lots of people don't know that, but . . ."

"If you say so . . ." Her eyes begin to wander around the room.

Change topics, dum-dum, before she leaves.

"You have a good voice. You should make a record."

Oh, brilliant comment.

She makes a face. "Nah."

"I bet it'd probably be pretty easy for you to get a record deal."

And now you kind of insulted her. Bravo.

Will you stop? This is really not helpful.

"Yeah," she says. "I've been offered one, but I turned it down."

"You turned down a record deal? Why?"

She eyes my sandwich like someone who hasn't eaten in a while. Like maybe a week.

"It's a little embarrassing . . ."

"You don't have to tell me."

Please, please, please tell me.

"Well . . . I have stage fright."

Yes, yes, *yes*. Bob, you are an evil genius.

"But, you're an actress . . ."

"Oh, I'm fine in front of the camera . . . but the one time I tried to do a play, I froze in front of the audience, and the thought of singing to thousands of people . . ." She shudders.

Geez, that's kind of arrogant, thinking you'll be singing in front of thousands of people. Then again, there probably would be thousands of people at a TGND concert.

"Isn't imagining the audience naked supposed to help?"

"Nah, the only thing that helps is large amounts of drugs and alcohol."

I smile. "So, no record deals?"

"No record deals. Besides, I've got enough projects to work on." She picks up my copy of *Hamlet* in a distracted way.

"Like what?"

"Well," she lowers her voice and leans toward me. "I really shouldn't be telling you this, but . . . the reason I knew that quote is because my production company's working on a script of it right now."

"A script based on 'One Headlight'?"

"No, silly. *Hamlet.*" She waves the book at me.

"You're producing a movie of *Hamlet*?"

"Uh-huh. Plus I'm going to star in it."

"You're going to play Ophelia?"

"No, that's a stupid part. I'm going to play Hamlet."

Say what?

"But he's a man."

"So? They're changing that."

"Isn't that kind of a major change?"

She opens the book and starts flipping through the pages. "Not really."

Changing the sex of Hamlet isn't a major change? That Oscar nomination has really gone to her head.

"Are you sure that's a good idea?"

"Why not? Men played all the parts back in the day."

"Yeah, but they were pretending to be women."

"Po-tay-to, po-tah-to."

I take a bite of my sandwich, but my appetite is gone. I don't know why I feel the need to defend Shakespeare against the likes of TGND, but I'm ready to raise my dukes.

Amber starts to laugh. "You should see your face right now!" She laughs harder. "I got you so good!"

"You're not starring in a remake of *Hamlet*?"

"Nah, I don't even have a production company."

And I should totally know that, given what I'm here to do.

I try to smile. "You really had me going."

"Sorry, I couldn't resist." She starts flipping through the book again, looking for something. Maybe that passage about smiling, smiling, and being a villain.

Well, at least she owes me one now, right? I can probably use this. I'm not sure how exactly, but . . .

My heart skips a beat. Shit, shit, shit, my *notes* are in that book. My notes about our conversation in the library are about thirty pages away from her tapered fingers. I am so busted.

Do something, Katie. Quickly.

I pluck the book out of her hand and hold it over my skipping heart. She gives me a quizzical look. I guess my Most Normal Person She's Met in Rehab title is in jeopardy.

"I don't like it when the pages get creased." I try to keep the high note of psychosis out of my voice. I'm not quite sure I manage it.

"That's cool," she replies, looking bored again. She glances at her watch and stands. "I've got a couple of things I've got to take care of before group."

That's right, run away from the psycho. I don't blame you.

"OK. See you then."

She gets a wicked grin on her face. "Yeah, I definitely wouldn't miss group today."

"Why not?"

"You'll see."

I show up to group wondering what Amber's got up her sleeve. And the answer is . . . nothing. She waits until we're all sitting in a circle and walks into the room naked as a jaybird.

Well, not totally naked. When she gets closer, it's clear that she's wearing some kind of body stocking made out of several pair of nylons. She's glued on flowers and leaves to hide certain strategic areas, but still, the overall effect is *totally nekkid*.

Saundra's not impressed. "Amber, this is completely unacceptable."

"What?" she says, all innocent eyes as she sits in the chair next to me and crosses her legs slowly. Every pair of male eyes watches this movement, including The Director, who I thought was gay. Hell, maybe he is gay. She's just that magnetic.

"You know what, Amber. Please go change."

She ignores Saundra. "So, what are we talking about today? Cocaine? I fucking love cocaine."

"Amber."

"Hey, Rodney," she says, addressing The Director. "Tell that story again about the party in the Hills with the bowls of cocaine. You tell it so well, I almost feel like I'm using."

"Which party?" Rodney asks, interest lighting his angular face.

"You know, the one where De Niro was there. Or was it Pacino? Some big fucking guy. You remember."

"Amber!"

"What!?"

"Do you want me to send you to Dr. Houston?"

She spins toward Saundra and puts her hands on her bony hips. "What's he going to do, sedate me? 'No drugs allowed on the premises'? Hah! Not unless they're administered by Nurse Ratched here, that's the real truth!"

"Amber, please calm down."

"Why? Why should I calm down?"

"Because you're disturbing the other patients."

No, I don't think so. By the look on everyone's faces, she's the best entertainment they've seen in a long time. And this is a group that's seen a lot of entertaining things.

"What about me? Doesn't it matter that I'm upset?"

"Of course it does. That's why I want you to see Dr. Houston."

Saundra nods toward the doorway. Two burly male orderlies are standing there dressed in identical white Polo shirts and pressed khakis.

Where did they come from? Saundra must have one of those "I've fallen and I can't get up" panic buttons from the late-night infomercials in her pocket.

"Evan, John. Please escort Amber to Dr. Houston's office."

Amber narrows her eyes. "Saundra, why are you such a complete fucking bitch?"

Saundra doesn't flinch. "Amber, you know that kind of hostility is not acceptable. I'm revoking your outside privileges."

"But you can't do that!"

"Yes, I can," Saundra says softly but firmly.

"Motherfucking-slut-of-a-bitch!"

"That's enough. Evan, John."

"You're so going to pay for this, Saundra!" she screams as Evan and John drag her out of the room. "I know people! I fucking know people!"

We all listen as her cries become more and more distant and then look at Saundra expectantly.

"All right, everyone. Let's get back to work."

Chapter 7
God Knows

Some crazy shit, I write in an email to Bob two days later. *TGND's very thin (but we knew that, right?), and she never eats in front of anyone. She's allowed to violate certain rules (attending all meals) but not others (no acting up in group—she's been in "solitary" for two days for same). She doesn't seem to be taking rehab very seriously (example: "I fucking love cocaine!"). She shows up to group therapy as a different character every day. She has a sense of humor (sometimes mean). She's smart. She likes tuna fish.*

Amber was a no-show in group again today, and I start to worry that she's left. After group I hurry back to my room to check the Internet. TGND leaving rehab again is sure to be headline news, but CNN and Fox are focused on some congressman's sex scandal. However, I do find a website called "Amber Alert" with streaming live video from the front gates, which assures me that she's still somewhere in the building.

You know, whoever decided to call his stalkerazzi website "Amber Alert" is one sick motherfucker.

Of course, people in glass rehab houses really shouldn't throw stones.

I send off my email to Bob and answer a short one from Greer. We've been emailing regularly over the last couple of days. She's been sending me links to hilarious clips on YouTube like the one about a spider on drugs (if you haven't seen it, watch it immediately). She seems to know just when I need a distraction or a laugh.

I haven't heard anything more from Rory. Not even after I wrote a page-long email that simply said *I'm sorry* over and over and over. I've never gone this long without talking to her. I feel like part of me is missing.

I put down the iTouch and turn back to *Hamlet*. "*Whether 'tis nobler in the mind to suffer / The slings and arrows of outrageous fortune, / Or to take arms against a sea of troubles . . .*"

What would Shakespeare make of rehab, I wonder.

"What's up?" Amy asks as she enters the room in her running clothes, her face glowing.

I shove the iTouch under my leg.

Way to call attention to it, dumb-ass.

"Not much."

Amy doesn't seem to have noticed. Phew.

"Are you getting edified, reading that?" she asks, nodding toward my book.

"I do feel kind of smarter."

"I guess that counts for something."

She drops to the floor and starts stretching.

"How do you manage to look so put together after working out?"

"It's not supposed to be about how you look."

"Easy for you to say."

She makes a face. "Don't tell me you're one of those girls."

"What girls?"

"The ones who don't know how pretty they are."

I laugh. "I'm *so* one of those girls."

I sit down on the floor next to her, putting one leg in front of me and one folded behind. It hurts, but in a good way. I think.

"You should go outside once in a while," Amy says.

"You're right."

"Is that Katie-code for fuck off, I'll do what I like?"

"Sometimes. But not today."

"The grounds really are beautiful."

"I know. I grew up around here."

"Is that why you chose this place?"

"I guess."

"So forthcoming with the personal details."

"Sorry. It doesn't come naturally to me."

She looks sympathetic. "It must be rough for you in here, then?"

"I'm managing. Better than Amber seems to be, anyway."

"That's not saying much."

I try to imitate the way Amy leans over her leg and touches her forehead to her kneecap. Is my back supposed to be making that sound?

"Do you think she's trying to get kicked out, you know, acting out like that in group?"

She shrugs. "Maybe, but I heard she's here on a legal hold, so I think she's stuck here."

"What's a legal hold?"

"It's when you're court-ordered into rehab. The facility has the power to hold you for a certain amount of time and makes recommendations to the court about when you can leave."

"Would you have to file legal papers to get that?"

"Of course."

"Is that stuff public?"

She sits up from her stretch and gives me a quizzical look. "Why are you so curious?"

Oopsy daisy.

"Oh . . . I'm not, really."

Amy springs to her feet and I follow suit much more awkwardly.

Jesus. I think I pulled something in my back. And I'm guessing rehab means no painkillers. Perfect.

Amy looks concerned. "Katie, can I give you a word of advice?"

"What?"

"Amber's trouble. I wouldn't get caught up in her little drama if I were you."

"I won't."

She persists. "No offense, OK, but I know girls like her, and you're not going to be friends. She might make you think you are, but you won't be."

I feel a flash of annoyance. Who says I can't be friends with TGND? I was popular in high school, goddamnit.

"If you say so."

"It has nothing to do with you, Katie. It's just what she's used to. It's this whole fucked-up world that you don't want to be involved in. Trust me. I know."

I look into Amy's troubled eyes and can't help thinking of the emotional and physical scars she carries around. Maybe she's right. The only problem is, it's my job to get into TGND's whole fucked-up world.

"All right, I hear you."

I sit gingerly on the bed and pick up *Hamlet* while Amy gets her shower things together.

"Hey, Katie?" Amy says from the doorway.

"Yeah?"

"Still friends?"

I look into her uncertain face and make a decision.

"I haven't been going outside because I don't want to run into my ex-boyfriend," I say.

"Your ex-boyfriend's a patient here?"

I sigh. "No, he's one of the gardeners. I ran into him the other day, and I'm scared I might run into someone else I know and they'll tell my parents they saw me here."

She raises her eyebrows. "Your parents don't know you're here? You really keep it close to the vest, don't you?"

"I told you."

"So why did you come to this treatment facility? You could have gone anywhere."

Anywhere where there's a celebrity who's crash-landed.

"Well, obviously, I didn't think things through. In my defense, though, I wasn't thinking too clearly."

She smiles. "Your secret's safe with me, Katie."

I sure hope so.

"Step Two: Came to believe that a Power greater than ourselves could restore us to sanity," Saundra says during our session on Day Seven: Accepting Our Higher Power. She's wearing a white sweater that has several breeds of dogs scampering over it. They move every time she breathes, and they're kind of freaking me out. "Do you feel ready to do that?"

"No, I don't think so."

"Why not?"

I hesitate. I have a feeling Saundra's not going to like what I have to say.

"Because I don't believe in God."

She regards me impassively. "You don't have to believe in God to take the step, Katie. Your higher power doesn't have to have a religious connotation."

That is such a load of crap.

"Can't I just skip this step, if I do the other ones?"

"No, it doesn't work like that."

"Then I guess AA isn't going to work for me."

She looks concerned. "You have to make it work for you if you're going to stop drinking."

Good thing I don't really need to stop drinking then.

"Are you saying that AA is the only way to stay sober?"

"It's the only thing I know of that works consistently."

"But I thought it only works for like 12 percent of patients."

She speaks carefully. "Yes, that's true. Most treatment programs only have a success rate of between 10 and 20 percent."

I wonder what the success rate is for undercover rehab operations. They probably don't keep stats on that sort of thing, right?

"Including this one?"

"Yes."

"How come you never told me that?"

"Do you think it's helpful to know that you're more likely to fail at this than succeed?"

"Maybe not, but I'm not sure unrealistic expectations work, either."

"Do you think it's unrealistic to say that you have the power to overcome your addiction?"

"I thought I was power*less*."

She shakes her head. The dogs move. I'm so going to have dogmares tonight.

"No, Katie. You're only powerless to change the things you cannot change. You're an alcoholic. That will never change. But you have the ability to make choices about what that means for you."

"But what does that have to do with God?"

"Your higher power is where you get the strength to make the right choices." She gives me a patient smile. "Let's come at this from another angle. Why are you so resistant to the idea of a higher power?"

"Because I don't believe in it. I never have."

"Why do you think that is?"

I think about it. "Have you read that book *Eat, Pray, Love*?"

"I've heard of it."

"It's about this woman who decides to spend a year exploring three aspects of life: pleasure, faith, and finding a balance between the two."

"I don't see the connection."

"Well, I really liked the book, especially the eating and loving parts. Those are things I can believe in. But the middle part, where she's in this ashram in India, meditating all the time, and she has this, I don't know, out-of-body experience or whatever, and she thinks she *sees* God, well, all I could think of when I was reading it was yada yada yada."

"Is that some kind of yogic chant?"

"No, it's the noise my brain was making when she was talking about seeing God."

"Why was your brain making that noise?"

"Because I didn't believe it, and the only time I connected with it was when she was kind of making fun of her experience."

Saundra looks pensive. "So, the only connection you felt to her experience with God was when she expressed her uncertainty that she really had experienced God?"

"Bingo."

"Well, Katie, I haven't read the book, but from what you tell me, I think you might have been missing her point."

No shit.

"Maybe."

Saundra and the creepy moving dogs consider me. "Katie, as I said before, it doesn't have to be God. It merely has to be something outside you. A constant that you can hold on to. So, homework. I want you to spend some time over the next few days trying to find something that's stronger than you. Do you think you can do that?"

Do I have a choice?

Pretty sure you signed your choices away when you took Bob up on his offer.

Maybe that explains the malicious glint in his eye?

"I can try."

After dinner, I follow the crowd to watch yet another romantic comedy. Tonight's offering is *Kate & Leopold*. It's about a rich inventor from the nineteenth century who discovers a way to travel to modern-day New York and Meg Ryan.

Amber sits down next to me about three-quarters of the way through the movie, just as Kate and Leopold are discovering that their relationship might not work out, given, you know, the whole time-space continuum thing. The television's glow makes Amber's face look ashen.

"I can't believe the shit they make us watch here," Amber says, rather loudly.

"Shh!" The maybe-gay Director hisses from behind us.

I shoot him an incredulous look, though, come to think of it, he's been at the movies every night (as, clearly, have I) and seems to enjoy the genre.

We watch the movie. Leopold goes back to his own time and is sad. Kate stays in her time and is sad. Then Kate figures out that being happy is more important than being a successful career woman in the twenty-first century and that she has, like, twenty minutes to get to the Brooklyn Bridge before the hole in the time-space continuum closes forever. She hurries from the party being thrown to announce her huge promotion and . . .

I give a disgusted snort. "Oh. My. God. She's not going to run there is she?"

"Looks like it," Amber says.

"Have you ever noticed how these kinds of movies always end with someone running after their one true love to tell them how they really feel?"

She giggles. "Like in *When Harry Met Sally.*"

"Right."

"Maybe it's just Meg Ryan movies?"

"No, it happens in *The Holiday* too. Cameron Diaz runs through the snow to get to Jude Law."

"You can't blame her for that."

"True."

Amber looks thoughtful. "I guess if it's not worth running toward, it isn't true love."

"Not in the movies, anyway."

"Shh!"

Meg/Kate leaps from the Brooklyn Bridge into the wormhole. After a little more running, she finds Leopold, and casts aside her old life of lonely independence. I guess the fact that she could, you know, vote in the twenty-first century wasn't enough to keep her there. "Suffragette City," eat your heart out.

The credits roll and someone flicks on the lights. I catch The Director's eye as he gets up to leave. The look he gives me could wither a hundred-year-old tree.

"What's his problem?" Amber asks.

"I guess he was in some doubt about whether Kate and Leopold would make it back together."

She snickers. "He must really be starved for entertainment. I know for a *fact* that he won't touch a rom-com script in real life."

"Maybe he'll be more open after this?"

"Maybe. Bet he still won't cast me in his next picture, though, the asshole."

Something clicks into place. "Is that why you've been doing all that stuff during group? So he'll notice you?"

"Partly," she confesses. "But it doesn't seem to be working, and I'm running out of ideas."

"But aren't you worried that everyone will think you're . . ."

"Just another Hollywood brat?"

Nailed it.

"Yeah."

"I don't care what anyone here thinks about me."

"But what if someone told the tabloids?" I say without thinking.

My blood runs cold. Am I a complete idiot?

She shrugs. "I pretty much assume that's going to happen, these days."

Is it possible to hear someone else's heart beating from this distance?

"It doesn't bother you?"

"Sometimes . . . I guess I'm used to it." Amber stands and stretches her hands above her head, giving a big yawn. "I think I'm going to turn in."

For once, I'm happy to see her go. This whole conversation has my blood pressure through the roof. Though, come to think of it, maybe I could score some points here . . .

"Hey, Amber."

"Yeah?"

"Try a dog next time."

She smiles broadly. "Now why didn't I think of that?"

I wake up with my heart pounding, pounding, pounding. My first thought is that Amy's fallen down another K-hole, but the room is eerily quiet. Too quiet, in fact.

I look over at Amy's bed, listening for the sound of her breathing. I hear nothing, and as my eyes adjust to the darkness, I see only the tangle of her sheets.

I snap on the light and look at my watch. It's 1:37 in the morning, a time when everyone should be tucked into their beds, fast asleep. Hell, even the infernal crickets have stopped rubbing their legs together.

Something about her absence doesn't feel right. Maybe I should go looking for her?

Why the hell do you care? She's not the mission.

But she's been really nice to me. And she has those creepy scars on her arms . . . maybe she's in trouble.

Whatever. It's your funeral.

I step out of bed and creep quietly across the cold floor toward the door. They do bed checks periodically throughout the night, and I have a feeling that being caught out of bed is a punishable offense. By extra sessions with Saundra, most likely.

I hold my breath and listen for sounds of life in the corridor. Hearing none, I turn the door handle gently and say a little prayer to the Gods of Night-Time Capers who have kept me out of major trouble until now. If they helped me avoid detection when sneaking out of my parents' house, my altruistic motives should be enough to keep me safe tonight, right?

I look down the hall. The lights in the corridor are dimmed, but there's a bright light escaping from under the bathroom door.

It's probably just my two-in-the-morning brain (which has had all kinds of bright ideas in the past, let me tell you), but something about that light doesn't feel right.

You going to go check it out, or just stand there until you get caught?

I thought you didn't want me to check on her?

Better to be stupid than indecisive.

Can it.

I close the distance to the bathroom with a few quick strides and open the door.

Jesus fucking Christ.

Amy is crouched on the floor in front of one of the shower stalls, holding someone's bright blond head in her lap. The shower is running full blast, beating down on the unconscious woman's pale, twisted legs. And there's blood, *everywhere*.

"Amy, is that . . . ?"

She turns toward me. She looks terrified. "It's Candice. She tried to . . . I need help."

The sight and smell of the blood escaping from the horizontal cuts on Candice's arms freezes me to the spot. I want to move, but I can't. I'm not sure my heart is even beating anymore.

"Katie! Please! Get help!"

My heart starts up again. I turn and wrench open the door. Mary is standing in the doorway of her room across the hall pulling her robe closed. Her gray hair makes a frizzy nimbus around her head.

"What's all the fuss . . . ?" Her mouth falls open as she gets a look at the carnage behind me. "Aw, shit."

We cross each other in the hall, and I rush into her room, looking for the white panic button. I find it above the lamp and push it. Long, long, long. Short, short, short. Long, long, long.

Goddamnit! I did not sign up for this.

I sprint back toward the bathroom. Mary's on the floor next to Candice holding a towel to her left wrist. Candice's face is white and her eyelids are fluttering. Amy is trying to rip another strip of towel with her teeth while holding the wound on Candice's right wrist closed with her fingers.

I look down the empty hall. What's taking them so long? She could die, for Chrissake.

Wasn't I just saying something about a funeral?

You've got to be kidding me!

I think I hear the sounds of clattering footsteps in the distance, and I run toward the end of the hall, my bare feet slapping against the wood floor. As I turn the corner, I almost smack into Dr. Houston and one of the orderlies. They're wheeling a hospital gurney between them.

"This way!"

I lead them to the bathroom. Inside, Dr. Houston quickly takes charge, tying tight tourniquets on Candice's upper arms with rubber tubes that he takes from his medical bag. The blood stops flowing, and the orderly wraps a blanket around Candice's torso and turns off the tap in the shower, soaking his arm up to the elbow.

The bathroom is suddenly incredibly quiet, with only Amy's whimpers echoing off the walls. Mary is standing in the corner with her arms wrapped around her chest and her eyes wide with shock. I realize that my hands are shaking, and I ball them into fists to try to stop them.

"How long ago did you find her?" Dr. Houston asks Amy.

"I d-d-don't know . . ."

"Think. It's important."

"Ten minutes . . ."

He looks grim and turns to Mary. "Do you know when she left your room?"

"Maybe half an hour ago. I was sleeping."

"All right. Go back to your rooms. Someone will come check on you later. Evan, let's lift her."

They lift a limp Candice onto the gurney. She looks like the little girl she used to be.

I hold open the door so they can wheel her out. In the distance, I hear the approaching whine of an ambulance. Mary follows them down the hall, holding tightly to Candice's hand.

I let the door close and turn toward Amy. "Are you all right?"

She wipes her tears away with the back of her hand. She leaves streaks of blood across her face.

"I'm cold."

I walk to one of the other shower stalls and turn on the hot water.

"Get in here. I'll go get you a towel and a change of clothes."

She moves slowly toward the shower, and I head back to our room. I change quickly into a fresh pair of sweatpants and a T-shirt, and gather up clothes and some towels from Amy's dresser.

When I get back to the bathroom, Amy is still standing under the spray, fully dressed. The parts of her toffee skin that aren't covered by her sleeveless nightshirt are red from the heat.

"Amy?" I say loudly.

She doesn't respond. I walk around the pool of blood on the floor and reach into the shower to turn it off. I take her by the hand and lead her out. She walks mechanically, like her consciousness has just been transferred into a T2000.

"Amy, you have to get these clothes off."

She pulls her nightshirt over her head and lets it drop to the floor, then dries herself off with one of the towels I brought. I watch her slowly come back to herself.

"How did you find her?" I ask.

"I went to the bathroom."

"That'll teach you."

The corner of her mouth twitches and her movements become more fluid. She slips into a pair of boxer shorts with hearts across them and a long-sleeved T-shirt.

"Ready to go back to bed?"

"Yeah, I guess."

We collect her clothes and towels and walk back to the room. We climb into our beds and I reach to turn out the light.

"Do you think you could leave that on for a while?"

"Sure."

I turn onto my back and stare at the ceiling. All I can see is the blood pooling around Candice's pale, pale arms. I try to push the image away, but it's stuck, like I burned it into my retinas by staring into an eclipse.

Christ. That was not on the fucking schedule. I am so not equipped to deal with this. I can barely deal with the details of my own life. What I wouldn't do for a drink right now, or twenty.

"Amy, do you think she was really trying to kill herself?"

She sighs. "I doubt it. She was probably just looking for attention."

"Why do you say that?"

"You need to cut vertically if you're really serious," she says matter-of-factly.

Ugh. I guess an expert cutter would know.

Amy slaps her hand against the wall. "I can't wait to get the fuck out of here. Thank God I'm leaving tomorrow."

"And yet she gives no thought at all to the fact that her poor roommate will have no one left to talk to but Saundra."

She gives a small laugh. "You still hating her?"

"She might be growing on me."

"Like mold?"

"Yeah, the infectious kind. Heck, I'll probably start wearing dog-wear soon."

Amy yawns widely. "I bet we could make a fortune marketing a whole line of dog-wear."

"For all the Saundras in the world?"

"People *are* crazy about their pets."

"And yet they function like normal people."

She snuggles down into her covers. "You ready to go to sleep?"

"Sure."

I turn out the light and close my eyes. The images of Candice are waiting for me and there isn't a drink to be found. I open my eyes and listen to Amy's breathing slow and even. I stare at the ceiling, watching the shapes the moon and the clouds make. Sleep has never come easily for me, and I've become well acquainted with the pattern of cracks above me, but at least I'm not waking up screaming for my life every night.

I fall asleep counting moonbeams, and my blessings.

Chapter 8
You Say Goodbye, and I Say Hello

The next morning at breakfast, we get word that Candice is fine and will be rejoining us in a few days. The cafeteria is abuzz with talk of her, and Mary, Amy, and I are very popular when it becomes known that we were somehow involved in the drama.

I'm glad that Candice is going to be OK. As annoying as she is, she deserves a chance to be well. And maybe now I can erase the sight of her nearly lifeless form from my memory.

Not a chance.

After breakfast, Amy asks me again to go for a run with her. And since it's her last day here, I agree to do it.

"Are you nervous about leaving?" I ask as we walk along the path cut into the rim of the property next to the gray stone security wall. I'm wearing a pair of her running shorts that amazingly kind of fit me. According to my weigh-ins, I've lost almost ten pounds since I arrived. Ten pounds in eight days! Who knew rehab would be the best diet I've ever tried?

"Of course."

"Are you worried you'll fall back into your old ways?"

She gives me a sharp look. "Geesh, Katie. Thanks for the vote of confidence."

"Shit, I'm sorry. You'll be fine, Amy. I know you will."

"Thanks. You will too."

Yes, I will. Just as soon as I get the hell out of here.

"Right."

She bounces up and down on her heels. "So, are we doing this thing, or what?"

"Lead the way, Nike."

We start to run at a medium pace. Moments later my lungs are on fire, and I feel like I'm going to collapse. The tall pine trees above us block out the sun, making me feel claustrophobic. I count slowly to a hundred in my head, trying to distract myself, but it's not working.

I stop suddenly and double over with a cramp.

"Are you all right?"

I clutch my aching side. I can't believe anything outside of childbirth hurts this much. Not like I've been through childbirth. I've just heard it's the worst.

"How long have we been running?" I pant.

She looks at her watch. "About five minutes."

Five minutes! How can it only be five minutes? It feels like at least fifteen, maybe twenty.

"How long do you usually go for?"

"Around fifty."

Fifty? Ten times as long. Impossible.

"I think you should go on without me."

"Are you sure?"

I take several deep breaths. It still fucking kills.

"Yeah. I'll walk it off and head back."

"See you back at the room."

She turns and jogs off easily, her thin frame soon disappearing around the corner.

I sit down on a rock, trying to catch my breath, rubbing my side until the pain begins to recede. How did I let myself get so out of shape? Oh, right. One drink at a time.

You know, if I were a better person, I'd make this time in enforced healthfulness really count and start an exercise routine. It wouldn't kill me, right? Even if this pain in my side feels like it is going to kill me, it's just because I haven't exercised in years.

OK. Resolution time. I'm going to run every day, and I'll add a minute a day. So, that means six minutes tomorrow. Six minutes, no excuses.

I can't believe my side still hurts. Maybe five minutes tomorrow will be enough, and the next day I'll bump it up to six. Or five and a half. We'll see how I feel tomorrow. Five minutes for sure.

When the pain recedes I get up and decide to walk for a while. I follow the path until it leaves the woods and crosses a meadow full of new grass and wildflowers that smells like clover. On the other side of the field, TGND is standing in the bright sun staring bleakly at the security wall. She's wearing a pair of worn jeans and a black T-shirt, and looks tired. In fact, it's the first time I've seen her that I haven't been struck by her beauty.

"Thinking about escaping?" I ask when I get closer to her.

She keeps her eyes on the wall. "Do you think I could make it over?"

"You have any superpowers I don't know about?"

"Nope."

"Then I'm thinking no."

She smiles briefly before her face settles back into bleakness.

"Amber, is everything OK?"

"No, but who fucking cares, right?"

"Don't say that. Lots of people care."

In fact, the whole world cares in a way. I wouldn't be here if they didn't.

She shakes herself, and I can see the actress taking over, her expression changing from bleak to bland.

She turns toward me. "Forget it. Whatcha you doing out here, anyway?"

"I'm thinking about taking up running."

She throws her head back and laughs.

"What's so funny?"

"You don't strike me as the type."

"What's the type?"

"Oh, I don't know. More earnest."

"OK . . ."

"I'm just thinking of this guy I know who runs, that's all."

"Is he your boyfriend?"

"Oh no. I'm much too damaged for him. He thinks I'm selfish. And spoiled."

"Sounds like a real charmer."

She smiles thinly. "He has his moments. What about you? You with someone?"

"I'm in-between at the moment."

Amber pulls a pack of cigarettes out of her pocket and shakes one free. "You want?"

"God, yes."

Those who can't run, smoke.

I take the cigarette, and she hands me a bright pink convenience-store lighter. I touch the flame to the end, inhale deeply, and immediately start coughing.

"First time?" she says through the cigarette clenched in her small white teeth.

"Of course not. It's probably just the first cigarette I've had without a drink in my hand since I was fourteen."

Scratch that. I've never had a cigarette sober. Not even at fourteen.

Amber inhales deeply and lets the smoke out in a long stream. "Thank God we can still smoke here. It's the only thing keeping me sane."

"Rehab: the last bastion of cigarettes."

I take another haul and instantly regret it. Who knew smoking without alcohol was this awful? I stub the cigarette out on the bottom of my shoe and put it in my pocket. Maybe it'll taste better later.

Amber looks amused. "That's really very eco of you."

"I haven't completed my deprogramming from my hippie parents."

"Lucky you."

"Yeah, yeah. I was walking, you want to join?"

She shrugs her assent, and we walk in silence for a few minutes. Now that I can breathe properly again, I can appreciate the clean, clean air, even though my mouth tastes like the inside of a bar. When I get back to the city, I need to get out of the city once in a while.

The path ends at the gravel road that passes through the front gates. We stand in front of them, each of us lost in our own thoughts.

"Do you think there's a way to sneak out when a car comes through?" Amber asks.

"That seems awfully risky."

She gives me a reproachful look. "What's life without a little risk?"

"You'll be able to leave soon enough."

"Maybe not. My parents' little court order makes them the boss of me. I can't leave until they say so, and they're listening to Saundra and Dr. Frankenstein."

So, Amy was right. I've got to let Bob know about this tidbit.

"Maybe you can get it lifted?"

"Fuck that. Court stuff always takes too long. You gonna help me bust out of here or not?"

Sure, of course. I can just imagine the conversation with Bob. *You helped her do what?*

"I don't think that's a good idea. There were a bunch of paparazzi waiting outside the gates when I got here. I assume for you."

"Those guys are still there?"

"They were eight days ago."

"Fucking paps. Though . . . did you get a good look at them?"

I try to recall the faces of the smoking men I wasn't good enough for. "I was kind of out of it when I arrived . . . why?"

"I have an arrangement with a couple of them. Sometimes I tell them stuff about me, and they turn the other way when I want them to."

I shudder at the thought of what she wants them to turn away from, given the stuff she seems all too happy to have captured on film.

There's a loud clicking sound and the gates start to open, slowly revealing a familiar green classic pickup truck.

Oh shit. I knew going outside was a bad idea.

I grab Amber's thin arm and drag her off the path behind some spruce hedges.

"What the fuck?"

"Shh!" I push her head down so we're both hidden from view.

I peer around the hedge. Zack and his wife, Meghan, my high school frenemy, are getting out of the truck. He's wearing a pair of khaki gardener's pants and a gray long-sleeved shirt. She looks like she's on her way to shoot a cover for *Martha Stewart Living*—pressed tan pedal-pushers, soft pink cardigan, black headband holding back her honey-blond hair. If I tried hard enough, I'm sure I could smell her honeysuckle scent.

"Why are we hiding?" Amber hisses in my ear.

"That's my ex-boyfriend," I whisper back.

She gives me an incredulous look and then starts to laugh.

"Shh! I don't want him to see me like this." Again.

She slaps her right hand over her mouth. Her shoulders shake with laughter.

I watch Zack give Meghan a loving kiss and a hand into the driver's side of the truck. He closes the door gently behind her.

"Who's the girl?"

"Me in another lifetime."

Meghan turns the key in the ignition, puts the truck in gear, then stops and rolls down the manual window. *We need toilet paper,* I imagine her saying. *I love you more than I've ever loved anyone else,* he obviously replies.

Meghan rolls up the window and backs the truck through the gates.

Amber nudges me in the arm. "Do you think he could get us some blow?"

"No!"

Shit. That was way too loud.

"Who's there?" Zack calls, looking wary as the gates close behind him. This probably isn't the first time he's encountered desperate patients in the woods surrounding the Oasis.

"Well, we're busted now," Amber says.

Fuck, fuck, fuck.

I stand up slowly, tucking the loose hairs that have escaped my ponytail behind my ears.

"Hey, Zack."

His eyes widen. "What are you doing?"

Amber walks out from behind the hedge. "We were thinking about escaping. You want to help?"

I hear a loud rushing sound in my head. I think it's the sound of my career being sucked away.

"She's kidding," I force out. "We were just taking a walk."

Of course, this doesn't explain why I was hiding from him for the second time in a week, but I'm hoping he lets that one slide.

Zack squints at Amber, assessing her. His tanned skin crinkles at the corners of his eyes.

"You're Amber Sheppard."

Zack is cute, but he never was that bright.

"And you are?"

"This is Zack."

He shifts his gaze to me. "You've got a leaf in your hair." He reaches out and removes it gently. "There you go."

I feel a shudder of memory from us in high school, when we were the Golden Couple and the way we were felt like the way it would always be. I ran away from that future, and if it wouldn't mark me as a complete freak, I'd turn and run away from him now. I might not make it very far, but it's the effort that feels important.

I tuck my arm through Amber's. "We should get going."

Thankfully, Amber plays along. "Yeah, I've got a performance to get ready for."

Zack looks confused, but that's OK. We turn and walk

down the road. When we're not quite far enough away, Amber says, "What the hell was that all about?"

I glance behind me. Zack's pushing a wheelbarrow full of dirt toward one of the flower beds that line the road.

"I think it's called bad karma."

Amy and I are finishing up our lunch in the cafeteria when the sound of something scraping across the floor grabs my attention. I turn to look. Carol is climbing onto a chair near the entranceway.

I nudge Amy in the arm. "Check it out."

She looks over her shoulder. "Oh shit."

"What?"

"You'll see."

Carol claps her hands loudly to get our attention. The din in the room dies down to a low murmur.

"Thanks, everyone. So, I'm sure you're all in a bit of shock from last night. Remember, if you need to talk it out, that's what we're here for, OK? You just have to ask."

She sends a sympathetic smile around the room. Nobody looks like they're going to take her up on the offer, even though it's been all anyone's been talking about today. If Candice really was looking for attention, mission accomplished.

"Now, as most of you know, Amy is leaving today. She's done some great work while she's been here. She's proof that the program works if you work it."

"Just get to it already, will you?" Amy mutters under her breath.

"Get to what?" I ask.

She shakes her head. "You've got to hear it to believe it."

"As most of you know, we have a little tradition at the Oasis, a special way we like to say goodbye. Will you join me up here, Amy?"

Amy grits her teeth as she pushes back her chair and rises reluctantly.

I wonder what this is all about.

Amy stands next to Carol and faces the room. She'd probably look happier if she were facing a firing squad.

"Ready?" Carol says.

Several heads nod. Carol grins and begins to . . . sing. A Green Day song. "Good Riddance (Time of Your Life)," to be precise.

Where the hell have they sent me?

I look around the room, expecting this group of cynical alcoholics and drug addicts to reject such a campy gesture. But to my surprise, after a few measures, everyone joins in, even the stuffy Judge who doesn't seem to know any of the words. A few measures later, I even find myself singing.

It feels silly, and yet, it seems to work. It's not long before Amy's smiling, and by the end of the song, she's singing too. Maybe it's like the song says.

Something unpredictable can be right in the end.

When the goodbyes are over, I walk with Amy to the front door to say goodbye. The lobby is empty and smells faintly like wet dog, though there's no sign of Saundra.

"Will you send me anything I forgot?" she says, her voice echoing off the beams in the vaulted ceiling.

"Of course. Hopefully, I'll see you in a few weeks."

"Yeah, I'd like to keep in touch." She looks around nervously. "Where the hell is the van? I'm going to miss my plane."

"I'm sure it'll be here soon. Don't worry."

Her eyes touch mine briefly, then jump away. "I can't help it."

I feel an odd impulse to comfort her. This place must be getting to me.

"This time is going to be different from the others, Amy."

"How can you tell?"

"I just can. I'm a very good judge of character, you know."

The corner of her mouth twitches. "Oh yeah, just like all of us here."

"Seriously. You're going to do great."

"From your lips to God's ears."

There he is again. Maybe Amy can tell me where to find him?

I hear the van pull up outside the front door. Amy picks up her bag.

"I guess this is it," she says. "Candice will be OK, right?"

"That's what they said."

"Will you let me know?"

The van toots its horn.

"Of course. Now quit stalling and get out of here."

We walk outside. The sky's clouded over and it smells like it might rain. I hug my sweatshirt close to keep out the chill. Evan gets out of the van and helps Amy load her suitcase in the back. He closes the doors with a soft thud and walks back toward the driver's seat.

Amy reaches out and hugs me. I hug her back without too much effort. When she lets go her lip is quivering.

"I'm glad I met you," she says.

"Me too." My throat feels tight and there's something wet sliding down my face.

Oh God, I'm actually crying about someone I met a week ago. Sign me up for the next season of *Big Brother*.

I wipe my tears away. "Now get into your pumpkin and get out of here."

"All right, I will."

She climbs into the passenger seat of the van and closes the door behind her. The engine roars to life, and in a moment, she's gone.

What with the crying and all, I arrive at group a few minutes late.

As I search the room for a seat, I see that Amber wasn't joking when she told Zack that she had a performance to prepare for. She's wearing brown cords and a brown shirt, and her hair is in two side ponytails. Her tongue is even protruding slightly from her mouth.

I stifle a giggle as I take a seat next to her. The air in the room is tense. Saundra's shoulders are hunched, though she's trying her best to keep her tone light and professional.

"As I was saying, I think it's important that we discuss what happened to Candice last night, and how you're reacting to it. I know some of you have addressed this already in your individual therapy sessions, but I thought it would be good to discuss it together. Would someone like to start us off?"

"Where were you?" Amber pants out of the side of her mouth.

"Working on your escape plan," I whisper back.

"Really?"

"Amber, Katie. Is there something you want to share with the group?"

Amber narrows her eyes. "Katie just wanted to know where you got that sweater."

The room erupts in laughter. Saundra's wearing a sweater that makes her upper body look like a poodle.

"I'd ask you both to be more respectful, especially considering the topic."

"Sorry, Saundra, it won't happen again," I say.

Amber shoots me a dirty look. "Suck ass."

She slumps down in her seat, staring fixedly out the window. Her posture would be more convincing if she wasn't in a dog costume.

The Screenwriter raises his hand and starts to recount his own suicide attempt, but that's not what's got my attention.

Or Saundra's. "What is it, Amber?"

Amber's sitting there, dumbstruck by something she sees out the window.

"Amber? Are you OK?" I ask.

Amber raises a shaking hand and points her index finger. "What the fuck is he doing here?"

Our eyes follow Amber's finger. A gasp escapes someone's lips. The van is back from dropping Amy off. And climbing out of it is . . .

"Isn't that James Bond?" The Lawyer asks.

"No," says Amber, in a dead-sounding voice. "It's the *Young James Bond*."

Chapter 9
The Monkey on My Back

I'm standing at the edge of the path slowly, slowly lacing up my running shoes, trying to put off running as long as possible.

It's after breakfast, and the air is already hot and cloying.

A heat wave in May! Go, global warming, go.

I'm here to run. I don't want to, but I'm going to do it. I'm going to keep the resolution I made yesterday to run at least five minutes even if it kills me. Or was it six?

I adjust Amy's watch on my wrist. I found it on my bed when I returned to my room after the commotion caused by Connor Parks's arrival. Her simple gesture brought me to tears for the second time that day.

Alcohol-free Katie is getting too bloody soft. I need to get out of here before I lose all my self-control.

When I was done with the crying, I checked the web. Amazingly, no one seemed to know that Connor Parks was in rehab. And here I was in the perfect place to learn all sorts of confidential things about him.

Things were looking up.

I stand up slowly. My movement startles a bird from its nest. The loud *thawp, thawp, thawp* of its wings echoes through the forest.

I wonder what YJB is doing here. Does he really have an alcohol/drug problem, or is this just about Amber? And how the hell does the world not know he's here?

Well, whatever the reason, I took care of that. Or rather, Bob did.

I can't sit on this kind of scoop, he responded to the email I sent him. *Even if it blows your cover, it's worth it.*

The story broke quickly. When I checked Amber Alert a few hours later, it had a red flashing headline that read *CAMBER REUNITED* above a picture of Connor and Amber with their arms around each other at some red-carpet event.

Amber Alert can confirm that Camber are now both patients at the Cloudspin Oasis, a $1,000-a-day rehabilitation center. As we were the first to report, Amber checked into rehab after a much publicized video showing her smoking crack appeared on a rival website (damn you, TMZ!). Insiders report that Connor also suffers from drug and alcohol addiction. All patients staying at the Oasis commit to a minimum 30-day stay. Conditions are said to be rustic but comfortable. The residents take part in both individual and group therapy. One can only assume that Camber's reunion in such circumstances was bittersweet.

Surely this means my future at *The Line* is secure?

I place my earphones in my ears and queue up Matt Nathanson's "Come on Get Higher."

OK, OK. No more putting it off. One, two, three, run!

I take a couple of running steps, and it's not so bad. It's cooler here under the tall, green trees. Step, step, hup, step. Step, step, hup, step. It's pretty, in fact. I should've done this a long time ago. I feel healthier already. Five minutes will be no problem.

Shit. I didn't start the watch.

I stop and press the buttons to get the chronograph to show. Amy's time from her last run is still displayed. Fifty-six minutes! How is that even possible?

OK, focus.

I clear the clock until the zeros appear. *Beep!* Run along, Katie.

Good. I'm in the woods. I'm running. I kept my resolution, big step for me. I just need to think of something to distract myself from the running.

My mind wanders to Zack, and a guilty tingle creeps up my spine.

I push the feeling back down. Our breakup wasn't my finest moment, but that was a really long time ago. Besides, he's married to Meghan. He married *Meghan*? How did that happen?

OK, this is not helpful. Think of something else.

Got it! I have to find something outside myself to appease Saundra and her desire for me to believe in a higher power. That tree's really big. Maybe that'd work? Oh, Big Tree, will you help me stay sober even though I don't really have a drinking problem? Will you help me play along with Saundra so I can stay incognito and learn things about TGND and her exboyfriend? What's that, Big Tree? You don't want to help me with my nefarious deeds? Can't really blame you.

Shit. My lungs hurt. I must've been running for . . . what? At least five minutes. But maybe it's less. Should I look at the watch? No, that'd be a mistake. I should run until I really can't anymore and then look at the watch. Maybe I'll make it up to ten minutes, and I'll be way ahead of myself. Yeah, if I make it to ten, then I can take tomorrow off.

Step, step, hup, step. Step, step, hup, step.

What the hell is that pain in my shoulders? I know this sounds crazy, but it feels like there's some monkey-sized thing sitting on my shoulders bouncing up and down.

Hey, monkey, get the hell off my back! I mean it, monkey! Go away, shoo! Fine, you want to play that way? I'm going to stop and you'll disappear!

I stop running, and the weight eases off my shoulders.

What the hell was that? Running is making me cuckoo.

Well, at least I did it. I ran way more than five minutes, for sure.

I pull the earphones from my ears and look at Amy's watch. It says I've been running for four minutes. Even with forgetting to start the watch there's no way I ran for five.

Goddamnit. I did five minutes yesterday. I was supposed to do six today. Well, at least five and a half. But I can't take another step, I can't. Running clearly doesn't agree with me. I mean, it has me talking to imaginary monkeys!

"Are you all right?" a deep voice asks me.

I turn around in a panic. There's a man with short red hair and a smattering of freckles across his nose standing on the path. He's about six feet tall, in his early thirties, and he's wearing gray running shorts and a matching sleeveless T-shirt.

I've never seen the guy before. My mind spits out possibilities. New patient? Staff member? Escaped convict? Ax murderer?

Fight or flight? Fight or flight? I can't run anymore, so I guess it's going to have to be fight.

Only, I don't know how to fight.

"I got a cramp," I say.

Idiot! Now he knows you're helpless.

He looks sympathetic. "In your side?"

But he doesn't sound like an ax murderer. Is this his MO? Distract me with kindness before going in for the kill?

"Kind of all over . . ."

And yet you keep answering his questions. You are a moron.

"Did you just start running?"

"No."

That was better.

"Well . . . if you're OK, I'll be off."

Shit. Maybe he was being nice, and I'm totally overacting?

I try to make my face seem friendly. "Thanks for stopping."

"No problem. See you around."

He pushes some buttons on his watch, and I watch him as he lopes off through the woods with the easy gait of a long-time runner.

Well done, Katie. A nice man asks if you need help, and you scare him off. No wonder you're single.

Shut up, monkey.

"I think I found my thing," I say to Saundra in therapy later that morning. I'm wearing designer-knock-off black yoga pants topped by a pumpkin-orange hoodie. My hair is tied back and still wet from my shower.

She gives me a puzzled look from across her desk. "Your thing?"

"You know, my replacement-for-God thing. Like you asked me to."

"It's not supposed to be a replacement for God, Katie. It's supposed to be what you place your faith in so you can work the steps."

"Right, I know. I get it. Anyway, I think it's running."

She shakes her head. Her miniature-dog dangle earrings dance. "I don't think a higher power can be a sport, Katie."

"It's not the sport. It's how I feel when I'm doing it."

"You feel good?"

"No, I feel awful."

"That doesn't sound like a promising beginning."

"But that's just it. It's the only thing I can think of that takes me outside myself. It's the only thing that's bigger than me . . . like when I was running today . . . well . . . this is going to sound crazy . . ."

"Don't worry about that, just tell me."

"Well . . . I was running earlier, and all I had to do was five minutes, or maybe six . . . anyway, that's not important . . . so, I'm running, and I'm hating it, and I hurt everywhere, and I'm trying to distract myself by thinking of something that could be my higher power when it happened."

"What happened?"

I hesitate. She is so going to think I'm bonkers.

"The monkey showed up."

She stares at me blankly, her hand poised above her yellow pad.

"It sounds crazy, right?"

"I'm sorry, Katie. I was just surprised. Keep going."

"It wasn't an actual monkey. It just *felt* like there was one."

"What was the monkey doing?"

"It was sitting on my shoulders."

"And?"

"That's it."

"I don't get it."

Neither do I now that I'm saying it out loud.

I try again. "I don't know. It felt like it was something outside myself. Something I can hold on to."

She contemplates me. The dogs wiggle, wiggle, wiggle. "I think what you experienced is a feeling that runners often get when their muscles are oxygen-deprived. What you need to find is something permanent. Something that's always there. It can't be something transient."

"Well, that's what I'm going to use as my higher power," I say petulantly.

"Then we still have a lot of work to do," Saundra replies gently.

After lunch, I wander to the library, hoping desperately that something a little less taxing and depressing than *Hamlet* has magically appeared on the floor-to-ceiling bookshelves.

A mad hope.

Sobriety, Moment of Clarity, Working the Steps, it goes on and on, and there's not a beach read among them. I know we're supposed to be working on ourselves (that's why I'm killing myself through running, right?), but this is taking it way too far. Reading any one of these books would stress me out, not dry me out. No surprise that most of the books look like they've never even had their spines cracked.

"It probably doesn't matter which one you pick up," a man says behind me. "I'm sure they all say the same thing."

I turn around. It's the potential-murderer guy I met on the running path earlier. He's wearing khaki shorts and a blue-gray Oxford that matches his eyes. He has a book tucked under his arm.

"What's that?"

His eyes twinkle. "Don't drink. Don't do drugs."

"Good point. What are you reading?"

He shows me the cover. It's *Running with Scissors,* Augusten Burroughs's really bleak tale about his depraved childhood. It's full of gay sex, drugs, and Oedipal feelings. I bet he's a fun person to party with.

"There's no way you found that here."

"Mr. Drink and Do Drugs? Of course not."

"Didn't he dry out in his next book?"

"Really? How disappointing."

We exchange smiles and move toward the comfy navy armchairs tucked into the corner of the room. As we sit down, I catch a whiff of his aftershave. It smells spicy and expensive.

"So, how did your run end up?" he asks, tapping the fingers of his left hand against his knee.

"End up? Oh no, you saw the end of my run."

He smiles. "It'll get easier if you stick to it."

"That seems to be the theme of this place."

"Right. But I can promise you that it's true for running."

"And for the rest of it?"

A bleak look crosses his face. "Who the fuck knows? I hope so."

Who is this guy? He's definitely not a patient.

"Can I ask you something?"

"Sure."

I gather my courage. "Well . . . I know this is going to sound . . . *odd,* but when I was running, I had this weird feeling in my shoulders . . ."

He nods. "Like something was sitting on you?"

Oh, thank God.

"Yes, exactly. Do you know what that is?"

"Maybe your muscles weren't getting enough oxygen?"

"That's what Saundra said."

"Who's Saundra?"

How can he not know who Saundra is? Now I'm really confused.

"You're not a patient, are you?"

"Nope."

I cock my head to the side. "But if you were on staff, you'd definitely know who Saundra was . . ."

"A leading character, is she?"

I smile. "Kind of. She leads group, and she's my individual therapist."

"That sounds like a lot of therapy. Does it get boring?"

"Sometimes, though it can be entertaining listening to some of the other patients."

Nice. I just said I enjoyed listening to other people talking about the most painful moments in their lives. I'm a bad, bad person.

"I'd hate it," he says.

"Listening to others, or talking about yourself?"

"The latter."

I flex my feet, trying to stretch out my calves. "That's pretty definite."

"When you know yourself, you know yourself."

"What made you so enlightened?"

He gives me a rueful smile. "Well . . . when every girl you go out with says the same thing, you can either accept it or put your head in the sand."

"*Every* girl?"

"Yup."

"But don't women like the strong, silent type?"

He shrugs. "Apparently, not so much."

"Maybe you just need to be with someone who's spent time in here. After listening to twelve narcissists spill their guts day after day, you learn to appreciate someone who can keep the cap on."

"So, you're saying I should focus my dating strategy on women who've spent time in rehab?"

Yo, dum-dum, you're a woman who's spent time in rehab.

"No . . . I guess not," I stammer, a blush spreading across my face.

I stand up stiffly. Less than five minute of running has left me feeling achy in places I didn't know I had.

He rises too, and we stand there inside an awkward silence.

"Well," he says eventually. "It was nice talking to you . . . um . . ."

"Kate. Or Katie. Whichever."

He extends his hand. "OK, Kate, Katie, whichever. Nice to meet you."

I place my hand in his. A shiver crawls up my spine.

"It's nice to meet you too . . ."

"E.," Amber says, coming up behind me.

He drops my hand. "Hello, Amber." He gives me a nod. "See you later, Kate."

He strides past us and leaves the library without looking back.

"What was that all about?" I ask Amber.

"I can't believe he brought *him* to rehab. That little fucker."

"Amber? Can you please tell me what's going on?"

She blinks slowly. "E. is Connor's personal assistant."

"Does he have a drug problem too?"

"E.? Hah! No way. Connor just can't live without him, the big fucking baby."

"But I wasn't even allowed to bring my cell with me, let alone a whole other person."

"Connor always gets what he wants," she says in a resigned tone.

"But isn't dealing with your own shit kind of the whole point of rehab?"

She makes a face. "Welcome to the lives of the rich and famous."

I notice the time on the clock on the wall. Group starts in five minutes.

"Shit, it's almost three. We'd better get to group."

Amber mutters her assent, and we walk to group together. We sit in our usual folding chairs next to Mary and just-returned-from-the-medical-wing Candice. Candice is babbling on about how hot it is to a bored-looking Mary. The tight, white bandages on her wrists give me the creeps.

Amber slumps next to me and gazes out the window. A minute later, Saundra walks to the head of the circle and clears her throat to get our attention. "Today I want to talk about the moment you realized you needed help, when you hit your bottom." She turns toward me. "Katie, I don't believe we've heard from you yet. Would you like to share what it was that brought you here?"

Jesus. Don't I do enough sharing in therapy? Am I going to have to spin this bullshit in front of an audience too?

"I don't feel like sharing today, Saundra."

"Participating in group's an important part of getting well, Katie."

"Ah, why don't you leave her the fuck alone?" Amber says, shifting her focus away from the window.

"Language, Amber, please."

Amber sits up straight and stares intently at Saundra. "You want someone to participate? Fine, I'll fucking participate. All right? That make you happy?"

"What would you like to tell us, Amber?"

"I'll tell you what everyone's dying to know, how about that?" Amber looks around her. She has everyone's full attention. "Don't you all want to know how *I* got here?"

Uh, yeah. I really, really do.

"How did you get here, Amber?"

"Young James Bond, that's how," she replies loudly. "That's right. The big star who's drying out somewhere in this building *can take all the credit.*" She half sings, half yells these last words, maybe hoping that Connor can hear her, wherever he is.

"You can't blame another person for your addictions, Amber."

"*Oh yes, I can!*"

"There's no need to shout."

"You wanted someone to share, right! Well, I'm sharing. I'm putting it out there for everyone to see!" She waves her hands around in big sweeping gestures. "Can you see it? Am I sharing enough for you? Am. I. Sharing. Enough. For. You?" She flings her arms out wide.

"That's enough, Amber."

"But it isn't. It's never enough. I can never have enough."

"I think we've all had enough," Mary says.

The Director and The Judge twitter at Mary's remark. Amber shoots her a dirty look and storms out of the room.

Bloody Mary. What did she have to go and do that for? This was just getting interesting.

I glower at her, but she doesn't notice, high on the laugh she got out of the impossible-to-please boys.

At least someone's getting high in here.

Chapter 10
Sing Along If You Know the Words

When I get back to my room after group, I find Amber sitting on Amy's bed with her knees tucked under her chin, her arms wrapped tightly around her shins. Her cheeks are stained with mascara, and she's rocking back and forth.

My eyes dart nervously around the room. My iTouch is out of sight, but my journal is sitting on the nightstand next to *Hamlet*. I removed the offending pages from the book after my near miss the other day, but TGND's proximity to everything I've gathered about her is *not good*.

I sit down next to her, blocking her access to the nightstand. "What are you doing here?"

"I just couldn't stand being in my room anymore," she sniffles. "Do you mind?"

"No, it's OK. Do you want to talk about it?"

"I'm sick of talking."

"No problem."

I scoop up my journal and walk toward my dresser, grabbing a few loose pieces of clothing along the way. I tuck them into the top drawer and glance at Amber over my shoulder. She's still rocking and staring off into space.

I breathe a sigh of relief and pick *Hamlet* up off the night-stand. I lie down on my own bed and fight off the urge to try to get Amber to talk by reading.

"Must be nice to have something else to focus on," Amber says after I've read a couple of pages.

I lower the book. Amber's wiping away her tears with the back of her sleeve.

"Yeah, but I feel kind of guilty reading it."

"Why?"

"Well . . . I stole it from this lady at the airport."

Despite herself, she laughs. "You stole Shakespeare?"

"Yeah . . ." I fill her in briefly on the details. "Pretty scuzzy, huh?"

"Maybe she just forgot it?"

I shake my head. "No, I don't think so. She was annoying me, and I stole her book. End of story."

"You stole Shakespeare."

"I stole Shakespeare."

Amber hugs her knees harder. "Why is he here?"

"I don't know, Amber."

"He's *always* doing this. He can't let me have one thing to myself, not even rehab."

I sit up and swing my legs over the edge of the bed. "Maybe he's trying to get help too."

"Why does he need to do that here, where I am?"

"Maybe he needs your help to get better."

"He's never needed me for anything."

"I'm sure that's not true. I mean, haven't you guys been together forever? He must care about you."

"It's just this thing we do. Screw up each other's lives. I wouldn't call that caring." She lies down on her side and scrunches up the pillow under her head. "Do you mind if I stay here for a while?"

"Stay as long as you like."

The next day at lunch, I join Amber at one of the bistro tables. The sun streaming through the picture window lights her up like she's on a film set. She's wearing a pair of skin-tight black jeans and a loose black sweater, with her hair in a side ponytail, and she's eating an omelette. Made of real eggs, yolks and all. There might even be a little cheese thrown in.

I place my tray on the table and sit next to her, feeling slightly frumpy in my boy-cut blue jeans and a white striped button-down. She puts a small piece of egg in her mouth and chews it slowly.

"Bad day?" I ask.

"The baddest."

It doesn't seem like she wants to talk, so I pick up my turkey sandwich and start eating.

"Jesus Christ," Amber says a few bites later.

I look up. "What is it?"

Amber nods toward the cafeteria entrance, unable to speak. Connor Parks is shuffling into the room with E. holding his elbow.

He looks like, well . . . a young James Bond. Straight black hair, blue eyes, square jaw, and a build that's meant to be swathed in an Armani tuxedo. His very handsome face is worn out, like he's spent the last few days puking his guts out and spacing out on the same trippy pills Dr. Houston gave me. His three days of stubble makes him looks rugged and dangerous, like he could kill you with his bare hands.

E. is wearing an expensive-looking pair of dark jeans and a light gray pullover. He looks cute and stressed.

The room has gone silent, and everyone (and I mean everyone, from the lunch ladies to Carol and Saundra, who are eating a few tables away from us) is watching YJB. It's like we're all holding our breaths, waiting for something to happen.

"This is fucking ridiculous!" Amber says, pushing her chair back, her face flushed. She stands angrily. "What's everyone looking at, huh? He's just a person, not a god. Stick a needle in his arm and he gets high just like the rest of us!"

The twenty or so pairs of eyes that were watching YJB swivel as one toward Amber, including Saundra's. Saundra says something to Carol, stands, and walks purposively toward us.

I reach up and tug on her arm. "Amber, Saundra's coming."

"Let her come."

Amber climbs onto her chair and from there onto the table. "What's wrong with you? Are you so starstruck you can't speak? Hey, I can't blame you. Look at him. He's so famous he's allowed to bring his own little entourage to rehab. Say hi to E. everyone! Give him a big ol' Oasis welcome!"

Saundra has reached our table. "Please get down from there, Amber."

"OK, so you don't want to say hello to nobodies. I get it. But I know you'll say hello to the one, the only, Cooonnn-nooorrr Paaarrrkkksss!"

"Amber, I mean it. Get down right this minute."

Amber gazes down at Saundra with loathing. "Ooohhh, are you going to count to three like my daddy? Why don't I just save you the trouble?"

Amber stoops to pick up a napkin, wrapping it into a tube. Her hands are shaking.

"One, and two, and three . . ." She starts singing Sara Bareilles's "Love Song" right at YJB. He watches her, his face devoid of expression.

When she gets to the chorus, Amber's voice wavers and peters out, and my heart goes out to this damaged girl. I want to help her. Somehow. Some way.

So, I do the only thing I can. I stand and sing. I climb onto the table and walk toward Amber. Still singing, I take her hand, squeezing it tightly. She gives me a grateful look and joins her voice to mine.

We run right through the song, holding the last note. When we finish, there's a momentary silence before the room erupts in cheers and clapping. We have one exhilarating moment in the spotlight, and then Evan and John haul us down from the table and out of the cafeteria.

Evan leaves me in Dr. Houston's office. As I wait for him to show up, I walk restlessly around the examining room, opening the cupboards that aren't locked, looking for something, I'm not sure what. Inside one of them I find a six-month-old issue of *In Touch* magazine. Better than nothing.

I sit down on the examining table. The sanitary paper crinkles under me. I leaf through the magazine. On page eight, there's a picture of Amber dancing on a table with a drink in her hand at an Absolut Vodka event. She looks like she's having the time of her life. I wish I could Alice-through-the-looking-glass myself into the party so I could be having the time of my life too.

After a moment, I realize that both YJB and E. are also in the photo. (What's E. short for, anyway? Eric? Ethan? Elliott? God, I hope not. Elliott is *so not sexy*.) They're sitting behind her at a table littered with several empty cups and vodka bottles. E. seems to be watching Amber with a scowl on his face, but maybe it's just a trick of the neon light behind him.

"What have you got there?" Dr. Houston asks as he comes through the door buttoning up his white lab coat.

I haven't seen him since the night Candice almost died, and a flash of that gory scene leaps before my eyes.

"Nothing. Just a magazine."

I toss it aside. It falls opens to the page I was looking at.

Dr. Houston picks it up. "You know, we see this a lot."

"See what?"

"Patients who aren't used to being around celebrities getting caught up by their glamour."

I'm not caught up in her glamour. I've been hired to expose her. Big difference, pal.

"That's not what's happening. We're just friends, that's all."

He gives me a concerned look. "Katie, I don't think befriending Amber is the best way to promote your recovery. You should be finding new patterns of behavior so you don't slip back into the ones that led you here."

"But can't we help each other?"

"I don't think so." He holds up his hand to stop me from asking why. "I can't disclose confidences, Katie. Will you trust that I'm looking out for your best interests?"

Right, just like I'm looking out for mine.

"I guess."

"Good. How have you been feeling?" He sits on his stool and wheels himself over to me.

"Pretty good."

"Have you been having any cravings?"

My eyes wander to the magazine. "Some."

"How are you dealing with them?"

"Pretending they don't exist?"

He frowns.

I try again. "Saundra and I have been talking about it."

"Excellent. Have you been having trouble sleeping?"

"Only for as long as I can remember."

"How have you dealt with it in the past?"

I remember Joanne's dwindling supply of investment wine. "I think it's called self-medication."

"You use alcohol to sleep?"

Nope. I *used* alcohol to sleep. Past tense for ten days now. Or eight, I guess, since I used those nice little pills you gave me the first two nights.

"Yes . . . but now I count moonbeams."

He smiles. "I can give you some strategies to help you sleep if you'd like." He flips through the papers on his clipboard. "I see from your weigh-ins that you're losing weight."

Twelve pounds and counting.

"A little."

"Have you had eating issues in the past?"

I don't have an eating issue, buddy. I have a lack-of-access-to-alcohol-and-crappy-food issue. Savvy?

"Maybe it's because I've taken up running."

His face clouds. "Yes, I wanted to talk to you about that. Saundra tells me you've been experiencing hallucinations?"

Jesus Christ.

"No."

"Perhaps I misunderstood. Did you tell Saundra that you're seeing a monkey when you run?"

Somehow it sounds even sillier when cute Dr. Houston says it.

"Well, not exactly . . . it's this feeling I get when I'm running. Like something's sitting on my shoulders . . . I called it a monkey, but it could be anything . . ."

His pen is poised over his clipboard. "I see. And this . . . monkey . . . does it talk to you?"

"Of course it doesn't talk to me. It's not a real monkey . . . I'm not crazy."

"But you want to use this monkey as your higher power?"

"Not the monkey, exactly, but what the monkey represents. It's just . . . I can't explain it . . . I mean, it could be a tree or a leaf, right . . . ?"

Dr. Houston bends his head and writes something. From upside down it looks like: *Repeat step.*

"No . . . I don't need to repeat the step. I understand it, I swear."

He looks up. "I'll discuss this with Saundra. In the meantime, I suggest you try to locate your higher power in the real world."

He kicks the ground with his feet and his chair slides across the room. He spins artfully, opens a drawer, and pulls out a pamphlet. Another kick and he's handing it to me. "This contains some useful tips that should help you with your insomnia."

"Thanks."

"You're doing better than you think, Katie. Keep it up."

I leave Dr. Houston's office and walk back toward the cafeteria. What with the singing with Amber on the table and all, I never finished my lunch, and I'm pretty hungry.

As I stroll through the hall, the song we were singing floats into my mind. I wonder why Amber chose to sing that song to YJB. Does it contain clues to their relationship, or was it simply the first song that popped into her head?

"Haven't we heard enough of that song today?" E. says, standing before me with an amused expression. He's wearing his running clothes, but he must be pre-run because he still looks clean and fresh.

Shit! Was I singing out loud? That's embarrassing.

I place my hands on my hips. "What? You didn't enjoy our little show?"

"I'm going to plead the fifth on that one."

"You would."

"Anyway, you guys were singing the wrong song. Their relationship's much more Britney Spears than Sara Bareilles."

"How so?"

He sings a snippet of "Toxic" in falsetto, doing a surprisingly good imitation of Britney Spears. Surprisingly good.

"That's quite the talent you've got there."

He colors. "Don't go spreading that around, all right? It's not good for my man-cred."

"Man-cred?"

"Being able to sing like a girl is not really the way to get chicks."

"Not the way to *get chicks. Right.* Plus you have that no-talking-about-yourself thing working against you."

He raises his eyebrows. "You've got quite the memory."

"So I've been told."

We smile at each other, and I wonder if I'm the only one feeling nervous and awkward.

"Can I ask you something?" I say, a moment too late for normalcy.

"How many addicts does it take to screw in a lightbulb?"

"Nope."

"Whether I prefer crack or old-fashioned cocaine?"

"Wrong again."

He grins. "I'm out of guesses. Shoot."

"What does E. stand for?"

His smile drops. "It doesn't stand for anything."

"So, your name is E., like the letter, full stop?"

"No . . . that's just something Amber calls me. You know, like Eric on *Entourage*? Because of the red hair and . . ."

"Because you work for Connor?"

"I guess."

"So, what's your real name?"

"It's Henry."

I roll his name around my tongue. "Henry. I like it. It suits you."

"Thanks, Kate, Katie, whichever. Anyway, I should get to my run . . . unless . . . did you want to join me?"

"I already went this morning."

"Maybe some other time?"

"Sure."

He lays his hand on my shoulder and squeezes gently, then leaves through a set of French doors that lead outside.

As I watch him jog easily over the lawn I can still feel the heat of his hand on my shoulder. Is this a good thing, or a sign that I should avoid any further contact?

I think the evidence to date (liking it when he touches me, awkward silences, *grinning* at each other) points toward avoid-any-further-contact, since I'm, you know, in rehab, and spying on his boss's girlfriend.

Yeah. Henry is definitely off limits.

Chapter 11
Apple Peels and Other Fairy Tales

The scraping of a branch against my window wakes me from one of those vivid, realistic dreams that starts to fade as soon as you wake up. Only the taste of it remains, and this dream tastes like alcohol. Tequila shots, I believe.

Why, oh why, did I have to wake up?

I open my eyes. I can tell by the total blackness that it's late, late, late.

I peel back the covers and walk toward the window. I peer at the manicured courtyard. The sky is a bowl of stars that falls right to the horizon. Black clouds whip across the moon.

I feel hot and feverish. I reach through the bars and pry open the window. The cold night air rushes in. The wind feels good against my cheek.

I climb back into bed and search out my nighttime friends, the cracks in the ceiling. I try to reach back into my dream, to rejoin the party, but something about it feels off and wrong.

Oh God. I didn't just have a user-dream, did I? No, no, of course not. Yes, I dreamt I was drinking, getting drunk even, but my dream was nice, right? Fun, even. Nothing like Amy's drugmares.

God, I miss Amy. Without her, the room feels empty and lonely. I hope she's doing well, and that take-three sticks.

I shut my eyes firmly, willing myself to sleep.

It works eventually.

It's Day Eleven: Identifying Patterns of Behavior. I'm standing on the path, trying to psych myself up for my run.

OK. Eight minutes today. No more of this wimpy five or six minutes shit. Just find the longest song you have and run for its entire length. I scroll through the songs on my iTouch. The winner seems to be "Hotel California."

OK, then. Although . . . do I really want to listen to a song about a place you can never leave given where I am right now?

I look for the next-longest song. It's the Pogues's version of "And the Band Played Waltzing Matilda," clocking in at 8:11. No, no that's worse. Shane MacGowan's whiskey-soaked voice is not going to take my mind off the lingering taste of last night's maybe-user-dream.

"Hotel California" it is.

I stretch my last stretch, place the earphones in my ears, and put one foot in front of the other. It's as painful as it is every other day; running just doesn't seem to get any easier. At least not for me.

I remember the last time I danced to this song. It was with Zack at our high school graduation dance. I knew I was leaving for the city right after I threw my mortarboard in the air. My university classes didn't start for several months, but I wanted some time to acclimatize and find a job to help me finance the tuition my parents couldn't afford. I'd told Zack I was leaving but not that I didn't want to try the long-distance thing. He'd been bugging me and bugging me to let him come with me to the city for the summer, and I kept putting him off. He brought it up again as we twirled in the gym. I'm not sure what it was, but I snapped and told him no.

It happened right when the song speeds up. You know, where the drums kick in and you can't slow dance properly? He let his hands drop from my waist and shrugged off my arms. A minute later, the song was over and he wasn't mine anymore.

The drums kick in, and I pick up the pace to match it. Dah, dah, dah, dah, dah, dah. Boom, boom, boom, boom.

The song ends as I come to the gravel road that passes through the front gates. Amber's standing in the middle of the road with her arms crossed over her chest, staring at the gates again. Her hair is pulled back in a ponytail. I pull the earphones from my ears and look at Amy's watch.

Eight minutes. I did it! And not a monkey in sight.

"What's up?" I ask.

She peels her eyes from the gate. "Not much. Thanks for yesterday by the way."

"Don't worry about it."

She looks me up and down. "Your face is awfully red . . ."

"A hazard of healthy living."

"E. gets all red when he goes running too. Red hair, red face, red all over."

"Right. So, where did they take you yesterday?"

"Just to my room. You?"

"I got a lecture from Dr. Houston."

She smirks. "About how you should stay away from bad influences like yours truly?"

"He did say something like that, actually."

"Figures." She kicks at the ground with her foot. "Don't you think Connor looks like shit?"

Yes. The right answer to this question is yes.

"I guess. I've never met him, though, so I don't really have anything to compare to."

She looks unhappy. "I wish I could say the same."

"What was that all about yesterday?"

"Just telling it like it is."

"Well, at least you got over your stage fright."

"With a little help from my friends." She flicks her eyes toward the front gates again.

"You figure a way out of here yet?"

"Not yet."

"I know one way."

Her head snaps towards me. "What?"

"Just do your time. They'll let you out of here eventually."

A trace of a smile crosses her lips. "You're no help at all."

"I'd like to come back to something we touched on the other day, Katie," Saundra says during our session. "About your family."

I lean back in my chair and stretch out my legs so they touch the front of Saundra's desk.

Isn't therapy supposed to involve couches? I could really use a lie-down right about now.

"What about my family?"

"Are you close to them?"

"Not particularly."

She takes a sip of coffee from her white Dog Lover! mug. "Why do you think that is?"

"I don't know. We used to be, but something changed along the way."

"Because of your drinking?"

A wave of tiredness passes through me. "No, it was . . . before that."

"Can you situate it?"

I think back, past the Christmases and birthdays when I stayed away. Before all of the phone calls from my mother I avoided or half-listened to. Pre whatever it was that made my sister go from worshipping me to blaming me for everything that's gone wrong in her life.

"I guess it was when I went away to university, or before that even. I just remember feeling like my parents were something I had to run away from. And whenever I came back, I felt further away from them."

She watches me over the rim of her mug. "But yet you chose a facility that was close to them when you decided to get help."

Right. But that was Amber's mistake, not mine.

"I didn't think about it like that."

"Do you think that maybe, subconsciously, you knew they were part of what you needed to get better?"

"I don't know. It's possible."

"You should consider asking them to come to the family therapy program. I think you would really benefit from it."

My body tenses. "Yeah, maybe."

"Do you want to be close to them again?"

"Everyone wants a happy ending, right? Complete with loving parents, the perfect man, and a white picket fence."

She smiles. "I'll bet that feels a long way away right now."

"Sure. I mean, you can't get a happy ending if you've never been in love."

Oh God, why did I say that? My lack of sleep is making me punch-drunk. And everyone knows that drunks do and say stupid things.

"Do you want to be close to someone?"

"Yes, of course."

"So, what's keeping you from getting there?"

"I don't know. I guess I haven't met anyone I want to spend time with long term."

"Well, where do you usually meet men?"

Somehow I knew it was going to come to this . . . and yet I still brought the subject up. Clever, clever.

I should give this conversation my full attention before I let something worse loose.

I sit up straight. "Well . . . in bars mostly . . ."

"And what kind of men do you meet in bars?"

"The kind you'd expect."

"Meaning?"

I shrug. "They're just immature and looking for a good time, for the most part."

"Have you ever had a serious boyfriend?"

"Yes, two."

"Did the end of these relationships have anything to do with your issues with alcohol, or was this before?"

"Not the first one . . ."

Nope. I was just running away from him and the promise ring I'd heard through the small-town gossip mill that he'd bought me.

"And the other?" she persists.

I wish I could deny it, but . . . shit, alcohol was totally the reason Greg and I broke up. Greg was my boyfriend in university, and he was smart, cute, funny, and into me. We dated for two years, but I got drunk at a party one night and fooled around with this guy who I didn't even like. I thought we could work things out, but Greg couldn't trust me anymore.

"Yes, maybe."

"Maybe how?"

I sink down in my chair. "I cheated on him when I was drunk, and he broke up with me."

"How did that make you feel?"

"I was sad for a while."

"But you weren't in love with him?"

"No, I don't think so."

"Why not?"

For a million reasons that are way too depressing to say out loud.

"Because I never noticed how he peeled an apple," I say instead.

"What does that mean, Katie?"

"It's just how love gets described in the movies. Like in *Sleepless in Seattle* . . ." This is the movie they showed us last night. "Tom Hanks's character is musing about why he fell in love with his dead wife, and he says that it was because she could peel an apple in one long strip, or something like that. And I was reading something similar in a book recently, only that was about peeling an orange . . . anyway . . . I've just never felt like the way someone peels fruit would be a reason to spend the rest of your life with them."

Saundra's eyes grow serious. "I don't think your idea of love should be based on what people say in the movies."

"I know, but don't you think the core of what they're saying is kind of true?"

"What's that?"

"That love should be simple, I guess."

"Love isn't simple, Katie, and neither is life. Things that are worth having are sometimes complicated, and they evoke complicated emotions. You know, one of the reasons people often turn to alcohol or drugs is that they can't deal with complications."

"But everyone here's life *is* complicated. I mean, look at what Candice tried to do."

"Yes, of course. Because alcohol and drugs don't actually make things less complicated. You have to make room in your life for a little messiness, Katie, if you want to fall in love. And also if you want to stay sober."

We finish up our session, and I wander through the fragrant courtyard, thinking about our conversation. Something Saundra said isn't sitting right with me. Is messiness really the answer? Hasn't my life been messy enough up till now? I mean, I've slept with twenty-seven men. Isn't that a little messy?

My first time was with Zack, of course. We did it in his single boyhood bed on a Sunday afternoon while his parents were visiting his grandmother. It was uncomfortable, he was sweet, we used a condom. By the time I ran away, we'd had sex one hundred and forty-two times. Yes, I counted. No, I didn't write it down, I just have a good memory. Zack thought it was weird that I counted too.

It got easier after that to bring sex into a relationship. Sometimes, not a lot of times, but a few times, I went home with someone I met that same night. Once, I didn't even know the guy's name. Of course, alcohol was involved. But it wasn't a big deal to me at the time. In fact, I remember the twenty-two-year-old me being impressed that I did it. And part of me still kind of is.

But with the exception of Zack and Greg, I didn't care about any of those guys. They were just a distraction, something to help me pass the time until my real life began.

So, I know what messy is, and it isn't love. No, love is supposed to be simple. It's supposed to be about brushing raindrops off eyelashes, and looks across a crowded room. It's supposed to be about watching a shooting star, or the way a leaf falls off a tree and floats to the ground.

It's supposed to be about apple peels.

Chapter 12

Messages Sent and Received

"I'm a method writer," Mary says during group a few days later. "I take on the persona of each of my characters so I can write them as real people." She stops, looking uncertain.

We're sitting in our usual folding chairs in a sloppy circle facing Saundra. The coffeepot is bubbling loudly on the sideboard. The sun hasn't been out in a couple of days, and there's a persistent fog seeping down from the mountains. Today it's enveloped the lodge, and the view out the picture window looks like we're in a tree house in a rain forest.

"Go on, Mary," Saundra encourages.

Mary tucks her hands into her oversized fisherman's sweater and takes a deep breath. "The book I was writing is about a runaway who's living on the streets. She keeps her innocence for a while, but then she gives in to the temptations around her. She becomes a heroin addict."

I glance around the room. The other patients look bored, staring into their coffee mugs, slumped in their chairs with their eyes on the ceiling, but The Producer perks up when Mary uses the word "heroin."

"What did you want to tell us, Mary?" Saundra encourages. Her salt-and-pepper hair has gone wild in the humidity. It's barely being contained by a wide, black headband that has a line of dogs chasing one another across it.

Mary looks and sounds miserable. "I was so into getting every detail exactly right that I . . . I started using heroin."

"And you became addicted?"

Mary nods.

"Say it, Mary. Admit it."

Tears start to trickle down her lined face. "I'm addicted to heroin."

Mr. Fortune 500 gives an audible snort of disdain, and The Banker snickers next to him.

Mary wipes her tears away and shoots them a dirty look. "Oh, fuck off, Ted."

"Did you want to say something, Ted?" Saundra says.

He holds up the palm of his right hand and examines his fingernails. "I would've thought her story would be more impressive, that's all."

"What the hell has that got to do with anything?" Mary says, leaning forward angrily. "This isn't story hour. This is group fucking therapy."

"That doesn't mean you can't entertain us at the same time."

Mary wipes away her tears angrily. "What? Like Rodney's stories about bowls of cocaine and big movie stars? Like Amber? Should I sing you a song?"

I look at Amber. She's sitting quietly in her chair next to me watching the exchange between Mary and Ted like it's a tennis match.

Saundra clucks her tongue in disapproval. "Mary, let's not personalize."

"Just because I'm not a big movie star doesn't mean I don't have anything worth talking about."

Speaking of big movie stars . . . YJB is sitting across the room wearing dark distressed jeans and a cornflower-blue crewneck. His color is healthier than it was a couple of days ago, and his face is clean-shaven. Except for his shaking hands, he looks only a few minutes out of character. All that's missing is a tux and a Walther PPK.

He hasn't spoken much in group yet, so I haven't had any news to report to Bob since the singalong in the cafeteria. He loved that shit.

"Ted, Mary, this kind of exchange is hardly helpful."

"It's not fair. No one else gets mocked when they're talking."

"I think we could all learn a lesson from this," Saundra says, looking around the room. "Group is supposed to be a safe haven. A place where everyone can speak their mind and learn from one another's experiences. There are enough people in your lives who'll stand in the way of your recovery once you leave here. You should be listening to one another, helping one another, accepting one another. This is not a place for judgment. It's a circle of truth. A circle of trust. Does everyone understand?"

"Yes, Saundra," we say as one.

By the end of the day, the wind has picked up and swirled the fog away. When I get to the cafeteria at our retirement-home dinnertime, I can see the sun setting behind the mountains for the first time in days. The sky is streaked with orange and purple above the bright green trees. It's breathtaking. Not that anyone here would notice.

I get some baked chicken and vegetables from one of the women behind the counter and join Mary's table. She's sitting, surprisingly, with YJB, Henry, and The Banker.

"Bette Midler and Susan Sarandon," The Banker says. His fingers are laced across his large belly.

"Dude, why'd you pick two old broads?" YJB drawls, his voice a mixture of the Midwest town he comes from and a lingering British upper-crust accent.

"'Cuz I don't want to fuck the old lady from *Titanic.*"

"Not even to get Scarlett Johansson?" Henry says, winking at me as I sit down across from him. The white lettering across his crimson sweatshirt speaks of an impressive/expensive university education.

"Well . . ."

"What are you guys talking about?"

"They're playing Two Equals One Hundred," Mary explains. "You have to pick two famous people to sleep with whose cumulative age is at least one hundred."

"Isn't that a drinking game?"

"So?" The Banker replies.

I catch Henry's eye. He looks amused.

"Forget it."

"What's your pick?" Henry asks me.

I think about it. "Um . . . Sean Connery, and . . ." I catch a look from YJB that seems to me like a challenge. "Can we pick celebrities we know?"

The Banker shakes his head. "No, no, no."

"Why not?"

"Nobody you know. That just causes fights."

"All right . . . Sean Connery and . . . Daniel Craig."

YJB smiles at me seductively. "Too bad you can't pick someone you know. It might've been interesting."

"I thought we could only pick *celebrities.*"

Henry and The Banker hoot with laughter.

YJB taps Henry's shoulder. "She's lively, Henry, watch out."

"Something Mary said yesterday is kind of bothering me," I say to Saundra during our next session. It's Day Fourteen: Rebuilding Your Career. I'm wearing a pair of pink board shorts and a dark blue T-shirt with palm trees on it. My look says: I'd rather be surfing.

"What's that?"

"What she said about how she became a heroin addict."

"You could relate?"

"No . . . not at all."

"So, why did it bother you?"

"It's just . . . think about the level of commitment she has."

"To using heroin?"

"No. For trying it in the first place. I mean, I can't even commit to writing every day, and she cares so much about her work, about its . . . verisimilitude, that she actually tried heroin. Just to get her story right."

Saundra looks up from her notes. "It sounds like you admire her."

"I do."

"Katie, I know you like to tease me . . ."

"No, I *do* admire her. I wish I had what she has."

"A heroin addiction?"

"No, of course not."

"Then what?"

I pull my feet up onto the chair, resting my chin on my knees, searching for the right words. "I don't know . . . something . . . a drive that's strong enough to overcome the easy temptations around me, I guess."

"Have those temptations affected your career, Katie?"

"Yeah."

"Would you like to tell me about it?"

I think back to that day at *The Line*. The way my brain wouldn't work. The way I puked and puked and still didn't feel like myself.

"I had this opportunity to get the job of a lifetime, and I went out the night before . . . it was my birthday, or the day before my birthday . . . anyway, I was just going to have one drink . . ."

Oh my God. I can't believe I'm telling a "just one drink"

story, the staple of every group session. These stories make me want to scream. Like in the movies, when the dumb girl goes into the basement to check out the noise she's heard *after* she's received a dozen creepy phone calls. *Don't do it, dummy! There's a psycho down there!*

But here I am . . .

"And?" Saundra prompts.

"Of course, it didn't stop at one . . ."

It never does in these stories.

"You missed the interview?"

"No, I made the interview. But I was still drunk, and I lasted about five minutes before I puked my guts out in the bathroom. And that was the end of that."

"Is that what made you realize you should come here?"

That'd be one way of putting it.

"Yes."

"Was this the only time that alcohol has affected your career?"

"I guess I've never been good at finishing what I start, and alcohol doesn't help."

"Why do you think that is?"

"I just seem to get distracted."

"By alcohol?"

"By life."

"So it's not a drinking problem, per se, but a Katie problem?"

Oh, I'm definitely the problem all right.

"Yeah, I guess."

Saundra smiles. "Katie, I think you have to give yourself a break."

"What do you mean?"

"You have to accept the things you cannot change."

Ah, the Serenity Prayer. *"God grant me the serenity / To accept the things I cannot change; / Courage to change the things I can . . ."* For some reason, reciting it never leaves me feeling very serene.

"Look, I know we say that every day, but what does it really mean?"

"It means you have to accept yourself. All your flaws, and your good points too. You only have to live with one person, Katie, and that's you. But once you've done that, once you've accepted your limitations, you can't use them as an excuse anymore. If you want to finish something, do it. You control what you do. You decide."

"That sounds too easy."

"It is easy, Katie, in a way. If you take it one day at a time."

I think about the various half-finished drafts of the novels I've started and abandoned, cluttering a bookshelf in my bedroom in the city. It's such a cliché, right, a journalist with half-finished novels lying around. But doesn't everyone have an idea for a novel, some semi-autobiographical tale that's just waiting to be the next *Catcher in the Rye*?

Only, none of my books have anything to do with me, which is probably part of the problem. Like book number two, which was inspired by Sheryl Crow's song "Home." That song kills me. Anyway, my book was going to be about a woman struggling to stay faithful to her longtime love. I wrote thirty pages, realized I knew nothing about faithful love, made myself all kinds of promises about doing some research on the subject, and went to Rory's twenty-eighth birthday party. I ended up sleeping with partner number twenty-four much later that night. His name was Chris. No, Steve. Chris. Steve. Shit.

Anyway . . . Did I decide to never finish what I start? Or was I just letting myself get easily distracted, allowing myself to fail? And has that really been my problem all along? Not making decisions? Letting life act on me instead of acting on it?

My head is spinning out questions, but I don't have any answers. I feel like they're floating in front of me, but they haven't taken shape. And instead of making progress, I'm in suspended animation, waiting, hoping, for something to happen, but unable to make it so.

Given my turmoiling brain, it's no surprise that I have trouble sleeping. Again.

None of the tips in the pamphlet Dr. Houston gave me seem to be working. Go to sleep at the same time every night. Check. Exercise regularly. Check. Try not to fixate on issues in your life that are troubling you. Impossible.

So, as it happens, I'm wide awake sometime after eleven, when there's a soft rapping at my door.

"Who is it?"

"It's Henry," a deep voice says in a loud whisper. "Let me in. I think I hear someone coming."

Damn. I'm wearing a stretched-out shirt and a pair of men's boxers, and my hair is bed-tousled. Oh well, it'll have to do.

I jump out of bed and ease open the door. Henry slips through.

"What's going on?"

"I need you to do me a favor."

"What is it?"

"Can you turn on the light?"

I flick on the small lamp by my bedside and light floods the room. Henry's wearing a broken-in pair of jeans and a white T-shirt. His feet are bare. His red hair curls across his forehead, giving him a boyish look.

"Shit. Someone might see the light." I take the towel I used to dry my hair earlier off my dresser and hand it to him. "Put this along the bottom of the door."

He looks impressed. "What are you, CIA?"

"Nope, I just have years of practice hiding the fact that I was up from my parents."

He bends down and fills in the gap with the towel. "How disappointing."

"You, on the other hand, obviously have experience getting into places where you don't belong."

He stands up and faces me. "I'll take that as a compliment."

We look at each other, and there's an odd current in the air. A whiff of danger I haven't felt in a while. Not like something bad is going to happen, but like I might do something bad.

"So . . . what are you doing in the girls' section?"

"Passing notes."

"Seriously?"

"Unfortunately." He reaches into the front pocket of his jeans and takes out a folded piece of paper. He hands it to me.

"Is this for Amber?"

"Yup."

"You want me to take it to her now?" I check the clock. "At 11:37 at night?"

"Yup."

"Why don't you just deliver it to her yourself. In the day-time?"

He pulls a face. "You don't think I already tried that? She wouldn't take it."

I walk back to my bed and sit on the edge. He sits on Amy's bed, facing me.

"I assume the note's from Connor?"

"Yup."

"He wants her to meet him?"

"Probably."

"They'll get in a lot of trouble if they're caught."

"Then they'll have to do their best not to get caught."

"Why does he want to meet her?"

He gives me an incredulous look. "Why do you think?"

"That's not an answer. He must've told you something."

"Guys don't talk about that kind of stuff, FYI."

"*FYI*, girls don't believe guys when they say that."

We grin at each other, having another one of our moments that is both awkward and not.

"What if she doesn't want to meet him?" I ask eventually.

"Why wouldn't she want to meet him?"

"Well . . . given what happened the other day in the cafeteria . . ."

He looks certain. "She'll go."

"Despite the Britney Spears toxicity of their relationship?"

"Are you trying to get me to sing again?"

"Would you?"

He shakes his head. "No way. That was a one-time-only performance."

"Too bad."

I meet Henry's gaze. It has an intense quality to it that makes me blush.

I look down at my knees. "If they're so bad for one another, why are you acting as his messenger?"

"Life's full of little ironies."

You have no idea, buddy.

There's a sound in the hall. We stand and step toward each other, startled. We're close enough that I can feel the heat of his body and hear the sound of his breathing. It's strangely intimate.

I listen carefully, my breath drawn in. It must be Carol doing bed checks.

"Quick," I whisper to him. "Get under the bed."

He nods and slides under Amy's bed. I make sure that the blue-striped bedspread reaches the floor on the side facing the door and then leap toward my bed, snapping off the light. I hear Carol open the door to Mary and Candice's room two doors down.

"Kate," Henry whispers. "The towel."

Shit. I jump out of bed, grab the towel, and climb back into bed as quietly as I can. I just manage to pull the covers over me as the door opens. I close my eyes and try to keep my face looking like that of a sleeping person's.

A patch of light passes across me. The door closes.

I let out a sigh of relief, the sound of my pounding heart filling my ears.

Christ. I'm thirty years old and clasping a foolscap note to my chest, worried I'll get caught after lights out with a man I barely know hidden under a bed. How the fuck did that happen?

"Is the coast clear?" Henry whispers.

I get out of bed and put the towel back under the door. I turn on the light and lift the bedspread. Henry's on his side surrounded by dustballs. He looks like he's trying not to sneeze.

I stifle my giggle with my fist.

"What's so funny?" he asks.

"You having fun under there?"

He wiggles out and stands up, dusting himself off.

"You know it." He runs his hands through his hair, making it stand on end. "Shit, that was close. What do you think would happen if I got caught in here?"

"I'm guessing we'd get kicked out."

He looks surprised. "You don't sound that concerned."

Right. Shit. I'm in rehab. I'm supposed to need to be here. I'm supposed to want to be here.

"Of course I am. In fact, I'm very mad at you for putting me in this compromising position."

He laughs quietly. "It won't happen again."

"Good. So," I wave the note, "what am I supposed to do with this thing?"

"Sneak into Amber's room and deliver it."

"But what if I can't get it to her?"

"I managed to sneak in here."

"Ah, but you have previous experience."

"Maybe."

"Do you know where her room is?"

He gives me a look. "I thought you were her new BFF."

"Am I?"

"It's the next hall over, second door in. Will you do it?"

"I'll try."

"Thanks. I'd better get out of here before I get caught."

"Good idea."

"Wait five minutes before you go." He squeezes my shoulder, letting his hand linger for a moment. "Good luck, Kate."

He opens my door, peeks out, and leaves.

I sit on the edge of my bed, watching the minutes on the clock tick over, resisting the extremely powerful temptation to read the note. Although . . . aren't I here to get exactly this kind of inside information? I can hear Bob's voice in my head. *Open the goddamn note.*

I unfold it and read the scrawled message.

Babe, renkonti min ĉe la benko de la grande arbo ĉe nokto-mezo.

You've got to be kidding me.

I read it again. It's still garbled garbage.

186

How frustrating. I wonder what he wants to meet her for anyway. Probably for sex, right? Or maybe drugs? Maybe sex and drugs? Amber really is going to get in serious trouble if she gets caught. She might even get thrown out this time, despite the legal hold.

What do you care? Just deliver the note like a good little enabler, and don't get caught.

Right, good point.

I tuck the note into the band of my boxers and leave the room stealthily, sliding my feet along the polished wood floor so they don't make a sound. When I reach the end of the hall, I freeze against the side of the wall and peer around it. The coast is clear. I skitter to the next hall, stopping outside the second door.

I hear a noise. It sounds like it's one hall away, but it might be closer. I raise my hand to knock, then decide to enter and take my chances. I turn the handle gently and slip into the room. Someone with long dark hair is sleeping on her side, the covers tucked around her slim shoulders. Surely, this must be Amber.

"Amber," I whisper.

She doesn't react. I take a step toward her bed and put my hand on her shoulder. Out of nowhere, she reaches up and grips my wrist tightly.

"What the fuck are you doing in my room?" she hisses.

"Amber, it's me. Katie."

Her grip loosens a little. A very little.

"Who?"

"Katie. Katie we sang together in the cafeteria."

Katie I'm here to use your life for my own personal gain.

"Katie?"

"Yes."

She lets my wrist go and sits up. "What are you doing in my room?"

"I have a note for you. From Connor."

She sits there silently. I can't see the expression on her face in the dark, but the set of her shoulders is that of a person in deep concentration.

"Can I turn on the light?" I ask.

"Yeah, all right."

I spy a towel lying folded over the desk chair and use it to block the space between the door and the floor. I turn on the light. Amber's wearing flannel pajamas and her hair falls across her shoulders in soft waves. She looks like she just came out of hair and makeup.

She holds out her hand. "Can I have the note?"

I dig it out of my waistband and hand it to her. I watch nervously as she unfolds it. What if I didn't fold it back up in the right way? Maybe they have some special folding code? That would be bad. Very, very bad.

She stares at the note for a moment and tosses it onto the bed.

Some of the tension eases from my shoulders. "What does he want?"

"For me to meet him in the woods."

"Are you going to go?"

"Not sure yet. Did he bring this to you?"

"No, Henry did."

She snorts. "I should've known. God forbid he should deliver his own notes."

Though every fiber of my being wants to probe her for more information, I think the better move here would be to leave.

"Anyway . . . I should be getting back to my room."

"Will you stay with me for a bit?"

"Sure." I sit down on her twin bed.

"What time is it?"

I check my watch. "Ten to twelve. What do you think he wants?"

"What he always wants."

Sex? Drugs? Rock 'n' roll?

I notice that her hands are shaking. She catches me looking and clenches them shut.

"Yeah, I know. Whenever I think about him I want to use in the worst way."

"Then maybe you shouldn't go."

"That's what my head's saying."

"And your heart?"

She looks bleak. "My heart? My heart's saying . . . Connor Parks is waiting for you . . ."

Connor Parks is waiting for you. *Connor Parks.* Even I'm tempted to go meet him, and I know he's not waiting for me.

"So . . . you're going?"

"Yeah."

She stands up and walks to her dresser. She takes out a pair of black jeans and a dark shirt. She drops them onto the bed and pulls her pajama top over her head, revealing her rather large, naked breasts. I turn away so she can change with some privacy, though she obviously doesn't care.

"Goddamn rehab food," she mutters.

I look at her. She's concentrating on buttoning the front of her pants.

"What was that?"

"Nothing. Thanks for delivering the note."

"No problem . . . I couldn't sleep, anyway. Especially not after being visited by a man in the middle of the night."

She gives me a penetrating look. "You like him, right? E.?"

Shit. What's made her so perceptive all of a sudden?

"I just met him."

"Don't worry, I won't say anything." She applies lip gloss and puckers her lips. "What do you think? Will I do?"

"For an assignation in the woods with your maybe ex-boyfriend?"

"Exactamundo."

"Note perfect."

She flashes me a smile. "Cool. I'll see you later?"

"Sure. Be careful out there."

"Not a chance."

Chapter 13
Trust Me

I'm standing on a platform twenty feet in the air with a harness around my waist, chalk on my hands and a net waiting to catch me. I'm holding an extremely heavy trapeze bar with my right hand. My left is clinging for dear life to a guy wire. Any second now, the muscled man in tights behind me is going to yell "hep!" and I'm supposed to swing into the nothingness in front of me.

As if!

I'm up here because today is Trust Day.

When Saundra told us about it earlier, I'd conjured up images of the kind of trust games I played at camp. You know, where you wear a blindfold and fall backward into the waiting arms of your bunkmates? Well, that's what I thought was waiting for me. I never imagined that a few hours later I'd be up here in the stratosphere, about to jump.

I've been in a bad mood since I woke up this morning.

I'm in a bad mood because, for the first time since I got here, I'm feeling kind of guilty. Guilty about being in rehab.

Guilty about the reason behind my burgeoning friendship with Amber. Maybe even guilty about the truth behind some of the stories I've been telling Saundra.

I'm not sure what's brought this feeling about, but I don't like it.

I don't like the way it woke me up at the crack of dawn, a few hours after I finally managed to drift off after delivering the note to Amber, or the way it accompanied me on my otherwise impressive nine-minute run. I don't like the way it made me chatty in my session with Saundra (look at me, look at me, I'm as fucked up as any of the other patients!), or the way it robs my appetite at lunch as I sit alone mechanically eating a hamburger.

And most of all, I hate the way it keeps reminding me that if I wasn't in this stupid place, I could have a couple vodka tonics, and I'd be feeling too good to feel guilty about anything.

If you weren't in this place, you wouldn't have anything to feel guilty about.

I know that, OK?

I'm just saying.

Will you leave me the hell alone?

"Who're you talking to?" Henry asks as he sits down across from me with his lunch tray. His hair is damp, and he's wearing a pair of taupe Bermuda shorts and a black T-shirt with an alt-rock band logo on it.

Why does this guy always catch me doing embarrassing things?

"No one."

"Seemed like it was a pretty animated conversation to me."

"Right."

"Look, if you'd rather be alone . . ." He starts to leave.

Aw, shit.

"No! Don't go."

Wow. Major overreaction.

"Stay," I say in a more moderate tone. "And sorry. I'm just feeling grumpy today."

He sits back down. "How come?"

"I didn't get much sleep last night . . ."

"Because you followed Amber and Connor into the woods?"

"No!"

"Weren't you tempted to? It must've been such a touching scene," he says sarcastically.

"So, why didn't you follow them?"

He takes a big bite from his burger. "Because I'm not a girl."

"Nice. Mmm . . . you have some ketchup on your chin . . ."

I reach out to wipe it off, then pull my hand back.

He gives me a curious look as he wipes the ketchup off with his napkin. "Thanks. So why didn't you go?"

"Because it wasn't any of my business."

"I see. Tell me . . . you ever read a gossip magazine?"

My hands start to sweat. Where the hell is he going with this?

"Of course."

"Well, none of those 'Celebrities Are Just Like Us' moments are anyone's business either."

"I know, but at least I'm not the one invading their privacy."

At least, not in those particular magazines.

"But you're one step removed. And if no one read those things, then the paparazzi wouldn't be there in the first place."

If no one read those things, I wouldn't be here in the first place.

I try to laugh it off. "So, if a celebrity gets drunk alone in the forest, it doesn't make a sound?"

He smiles. "Exactly."

"But don't some celebrities want the attention?"

"Sure, but does that mean they're not entitled to any privacy?"

"I never said that."

"What *are* you saying?"

That this conversation is hitting way too close to home.

"That I'm as curious as the next person about how extremely well-paid, beautiful young things live their lives, but I still didn't spy on Amber and Connor in the woods last night."

"But you read the note?"

"No . . ."

He leans toward me. "Only because you couldn't understand what it said."

"Why wouldn't I be able to understand what it said?"

"Nice try. Admit it."

"Only if you tell me why I couldn't read the note."

"Because it was in Esperanto."

"Esperanto? That fake language that was supposed to replace English?"

"Yup."

"They communicate in Esperanto?"

"Yup."

"But that's . . ."

He smiles a knowing smile as he pops several french fries into his mouth. "Incredibly geeky?"

"Says the man who can read Esperanto."

He raises his hand to his heart. "You wound me, Kate, Katie, whichever."

"You'll survive."

When I leave Henry to go to group, the guilty feelings return. Maybe it's because group is all about guilty feelings, but as I sit there listening to today's "I was just going to do one line" stories, I feel more alone and down than I have since I blew the interview for my dream job on my thirtieth birthday.

I feel like I need something dramatic to pull me out of this funk. And since I don't have access to what I usually use to cure this kind of ailment, when Saundra tells us about Trust Day, instructs us to put on comfortable clothes, and asks for a volunteer, my hand shoots in the air like it used to do in grade school, when I was sure I knew all the answers.

Sign me up for anything but hanging out with myself in my head.

I feel that way right up until we enter the gym and I see the trapeze apparatus set up in the middle of the basketball court.

"Trust," Saundra says, looking younger and more athletic than usual in a pair of black stretch pants and a shirt emblazoned with the words "Puppies Love Us!" in the same scrawl usually used for slogans like "Porn Star!"

"It's the most difficult thing to give and the easiest to lose. Each of you has lost the trust of those closest to you because of your addictions. You need to learn how to get people to trust you again. But first, you need to learn how to trust others, and trust yourself. And that's what this exercise is about."

"How is acting out an episode of *Sex and the City* going to do that?" The Director asks. The right leg of his sweatpants is pulled up to his knee. He looks like a member of a chorus line.

"That's a good question, Rodney. The exercise works in two ways. First of all, you have to trust the equipment and the people operating it. But also, it's scary up there. It's going to require courage to step off that platform. Finding that in yourself will help you start to build your confidence. You'll need that confidence to inspire trust in others." She looks around. "Any more questions? No? Good, let's get to work."

We spend the next half hour learning how to fly. It's the easiest thing in the world on solid ground, and I begin to relax. Maybe I can do this after all.

When we've learned the basics, one of the instructors (a well-muscled, slightly effeminate man in a dark blue circus leotard) chalks his hands, climbs the rope, and positions himself on the platform.

"Hold the bar like this in your right hand," he bellows down to us, his voice sounding far away. "When I say 'Ready,' let go of the guy wire, grab the bar with your left hand, and steady yourself. You jump on 'Hep!'"

He jumps and swings out over the large net beneath him.

"At the far point of the swing I'll say, 'Legs up.'"

He leans backward, brings his knees to his chest, and tucks his legs over the bar.

"Next comes: 'Release.'"

He lets his hands go and is swinging by his knees.

"When I say, 'Hands up,' bring your hands back up and release your knees."

He follows his own instructions and is swinging by his hands again.

"The second 'Release' means let go."

He falls gracefully onto the net. He walks to the edge and flips to the ground.

Candice applauds, and even the most uptight guys, The Lawyer and The Judge, look impressed. He's made it look easy, but we all know it isn't.

"You ready for your close-up?" Amber asks me. She's dressed like a ballerina, with her hair scraped back into a neat bun, a pink leotard, and matching tights that end mid-calf. One can only wonder what possessed her to bring that outfit to rehab.

I, on the other hand, look more like a bit player from a Jane Fonda workout video from the eighties. All I'm missing is the bright red headband and matching leg warmers.

"Nuh-unh."

"But you volunteered," she mocks me.

"Yeah, I have to remember to keep from doing that."

Amber laughs, and I realize that she's in a good mood. And not in the I-got-one-over-on-Saundra kind of mood she's sometimes in after group. Nope. This is a genuine my-life-is-kind-of-good mood I've never seen before. Things must've gone well in the woods last night.

"You want to take my place in line?" I say.

"Sure, why not?"

"You're not scared?"

"Nah. I've done this before."

She walks to the head of the line, and Carol clips her harness onto the safety rope. She climbs nimbly up the ladder and waits for her signal to fly. When it's given, she hops gracefully off the platform, brings her knees to her chest and over the bar, and hangs from her knees as easily as the instructor did. A few more swings and she's right way round again without any apparent effort and falling through the air toward the net. A hop, skip, and a jump later she's back on the ground beside me.

Her eyes shine brightly. "I forgot how much fun that is!"

"I thought we were supposed to be learning a lesson about trust."

"Fuck that. I've had enough lessons to last me a lifetime."

Amen, sister.

"Katie?" Carol calls. "You're next."

My heart starts to pound. "I don't think I can do this."

"Of course you can."

Since when did Amber become Miss You-Can-Do-It?

I square my shoulders and walk toward Carol. I make it up the ladder by taking one step at time with my eyes closed. The instructor reaches down and hauls me onto the platform by my armpits. When I stand up from my ungraceful landing, the world tilts away from me.

I take several deep breaths as the instructor unclips me from the climbing line and reattaches me to the safety line. He positions me on the edge of the platform facing the bar, then uses a pole with a hook on the end to bring the bar toward me. I reach for it and the weight tips me forward, ready to pull me toward nothingness. My left leg starts jittering up and down uncontrollably.

"Are you all right?" he asks.

"I'm kind of afraid of heights."

"You should've said something before you came up here."

"Yeah, well . . ."

"Do you want to go down?"

Yes, please!

"Give me a minute."

I take several deep breaths and concentrate on my chattering leg. You're harnessed. You're tethered. There's a net. It's perfectly safe. You can do this.

"It's no problem if you want to go down."

"I know. I just need a minute."

I realize that these are the exact same words I used what seems like eons ago when Elizabeth was talking to me through the bathroom door.

Just give me a minute.

The story of my life.

"You can do it, Kate!" someone shouts from below.

I look tentatively over the edge of the platform. Henry is sitting a very long way down on the bleachers next to YJB. He has his hand cupped around his mouth so his encouragement can reach me all the way up here.

Can he see my leg shaking?

Jesus. If you're OK enough to think about that, then you can definitely jump off this platform.

"OK, I'm ready," I say in a small voice.

The instructor pulls the left side of the bar in so that it's parallel with my body.

"Let go of the wire and grab it firmly."

Easier said than done.

"Go for it, Kate!" Henry's far away voice floats up to me.

I loosen my grip on the guy wire and grab the bar, distributing its weight evenly between my hands. It feels like it could sweep me off into oblivion if the instructor wasn't holding onto my harness firmly.

"You feel ready?"

NNOOOO!

"I guess."

"Remember, hop when I say, 'Hep.'"

Can you say hep, hep, hep, hep a hep?

"Right."

"Ready . . . and hep!"

I bend my knees, close my eyes, take a little hop, and . . . I've done it! I'm trapezing!

"Legs up!"

I try to bring my knees up to my chest, but they don't quite make it.

"Legs up!"

I squeeze my stomach muscles tighter than I've ever squeezed them before and hook my ankles over the bar. Another push with my legs and the bar is now firmly behind my knees.

Yes!

"Release!"

I release my hands. My body falls backward, and I can feel my weight being held by my knees, the bar digging in.

"Hands up!"

I swing my hands above my head, groping for the bar, but I can't reach it.

"Wait for my signal!"

The bar swings back to the platform and then away from it. At the furthest point, the instructor screams, "Hands up!"

I reach my hands up and this time I grasp the bar firmly.

"Legs down!"

I pull my knees toward my chest and my legs slide off the bar. Not in a fluid motion like the instructor's or Amber's did, but still, I'm swinging by my arms again and all that's left is . . .

"Release!"

That's what I was afraid of.

"Release!"

Here goes nothing.

I open my hands and fall through the air. I feel the hard jerk of the rope on the harness and my feet are touching the net. I topple over.

Always so graceful.

I flip onto my hands and knees and crawl to the edge. There's no way I'm going to be able to do that cool, over-the-head flip thing. Instead, I sit on my bum, swing my legs over the side, and push off with my hands, landing unsteadily on the ground.

"Well done, Katie," Carol says, beaming at me.

"Thanks."

I brush some of the chalk off my hands and walk toward Amber, Connor, and Henry. My heart is pounding, pounding, pounding, but I feel exhilarated and happier than I've felt in a long time, invincible almost. This must be what being on coke feels like. I'm beginning to see its appeal.

"Yeah, Katie!" Amber says throwing her hands over her head in a parody of a cheerleader. "Wasn't it totally fun?"

"Oh, totally," Connor drawls in his half-British accent.

She swats him playfully. "Shut up, you."

I meet Henry's gaze behind them, and he rolls his eyes. I stifle a laugh.

"So, what'd you think?" Amber asks, her fingers playing with the back of Connor's hair.

"It was a once-in-a-lifetime experience."

"The good kind or the bad kind?" perceptive Henry asks.

"The once-only kind."

"Aw, come on. You *totally* have to do it again!" Amber says.

"Once was enough."

"Well, then *you* have to go, Connor."

"We'll see."

"Con-nor!"

He shrugs her hand away from his neck. "Knock it off, Amb. I'll go if I feel like it."

Amber turns toward me. "You guys haven't really met, right?"

I'm pretty sure telling her about our semi-flirty exchange when we were playing Two Equals One Hundred in the cafeteria is a bad, bad idea.

"Nope."

"Connor, this is Katie, the only normal person here."

"Hi, Connor."

His eyes meet mine briefly. "Hey."

"Katie runs just like E. does! Doesn't she, E.?"

Who *is* this girl?

"Yeah, I guess," Henry grumbles.

"And she writes about music for *Rolling Stone,* right, Katie?"

"Not for anything as prestigious as *Rolling Stone . . .*"

"Oh, don't be so modest."

Seriously, who is this girl?

Wait a minute. Wait just a damn minute. I know who Amber is. She's TGND. Literally. She's acting like the character she played on *The Girl Next Door.* Hyper. Bubbly. A little dumb. What the fuck?

"Connor," Carol calls from across the gym. "Your turn."

Connor gets an I-don't-think-so expression on his face. "Maybe later."

"Come on, Connor."

"Yeah, come on, Connor," Henry mocks.

Amber shoots him a dirty look. "What are you even doing here, E.? You're not a patient."

Connor makes an aggravated sound in his throat. "Amb, we talked about this. You know why Henry's here."

"Well, I'll never understand why he doesn't have to stay in his room all the time, at least."

"Would it be OK if I came out for meals?" Henry asks.

"Connor!" Carol calls again.

Connor emits a sigh and stands. I watch his face as he stares at Carol and the apparatus behind her. He has a strange look in his eyes. It's almost as if . . .

No way. *No way.*

I look again. It's unmistakable. Especially if you've just been through the same thing.

Young James Bond is scared. Scared shitless.

Connor shuffles toward Carol. Amber bounces up and follows him, chatting away about how much fun he's going to have.

I'm not sure what's more surprising. That Amber reverts to a television character when she's around Connor, or that the guy who jumped from a flaming speedboat onto a ladder hanging off a helicopter is afraid of a little trapeze.

"What's up with that?" I ask Henry.

"You mean Amber?"

"Yeah, she's so . . ."

"Annoying? Silly? Stupid?"

"Different."

He grins. "How politic of you."

"Is she always like that around him?"

"Yup."

"You say 'yup' a lot, don't you?"

His mouth twitches. "Yup."

"Want to go watch the show?"

"Sure."

We walk toward the trapeze, where Connor's getting some last-minute tips from Carol. There's a muscle twitching in his jaw.

"I can't believe he's really going through with it," Henry mutters to himself.

"Because he's scared out of his wits?"

He turns to me with surprise. "How'd you guess that?"

"Takes one to know one."

"Can you keep a secret?"

Uh, *yes*. And no.

"Of course."

He lowers his voice. "Connor doesn't do his own stunts."

"But what about his whole too-cool-for-school persona?"

"It's an act."

"He's not that good an actor."

"Yes, he is."

"Shit."

"Yup."

I think about it. "He didn't jump from that boat?"

"Of course not. He's afraid of the water. And of heights."

"He didn't leap from that building onto that other building?"

"You're not listening to me. He's afraid of *everything*."

"You're shitting me."

"Nope."

"But . . . how does he get away with it?"

"How do you think?"

"CGI?"

"No, silly."

"Then how?"

"Drugs and alcohol, baby. Drugs and alcohol."

Chapter 14
Visiting Rights

I wake up on Day Sixteen: Reconnecting with Family and Friends in a much better mood, but with every inch of my body aching. It literally feels like I've been stretched on a rack. No wonder this is how they used to torture people in the Middle Ages.

I sit on the floor and try some of the stretches Amy showed me, but they don't seem to be working. In fact, all they do is remind me of the location of each of the muscles I used to bring my knees up and over the bar yesterday. Obviously, a few halfhearted sit-ups after my pathetic runs aren't enough.

Speaking of which . . .

After the movie last night (*The Lake House,* which wasn't half bad), Henry mentioned something about seeing me out on my run today. Typical guy, he didn't actually ask me to go running with him, or tell me what time he'd be going so I could casually run into him. Of course not. He just said, "See you on your run tomorrow?" gave me his patented shoulder squeeze, and left.

After a few more stretches, I pull on my running stuff and

check that the battery in my iTouch hasn't run down. It's fine, and I don't have any emails from Bob, either. I guess he finally trusts me to let him know when I learn something important. That, or he's too busy managing his other spies.

I slip my earphones in my ears, queue up today's playlist (David Gray's "Slow Motion" and Brett Dennen's "The One Who Loves You the Most" for a ten-minute total), and head out.

Outside, the air still feels crisp and smells sweet. The blue sky is full of big, puffy white clouds that roll lazily toward the horizon.

I jog to the path, willing myself not to look for Henry. If he wanted to run with me, he only had to ask. Besides, I've got my tunes, so I'm all set.

I put my hands against a tree and stretch my legs away from it. Ugh! This is going to be agony.

Someone places a hand on my shoulder and I nearly jump out of my skin. I spin around, clutching the iTouch to my chest like I'm about to be mugged. It's Henry, of course it is, but that doesn't keep my heart from shuddering against my ribs.

He mouths something to me that I can't hear, and I take the earphones out of my ears.

"What?"

"I said, sorry I scared you."

"That's all right. I'm kind of getting used to it."

"Just what every guy likes to hear."

"Doesn't it add to your man-cred?"

"You really do remember everything, don't you?"

"Is that going to be a problem?"

His eyes glint at me. "Not sure yet."

OK, moving on.

"So . . . are you here to run or just to terrorize me?"

"Oh, obviously terrorize. In fact, this is my usual terrorist wardrobe." He waves a hand to indicate his black running shirt and light gray running shorts.

"Smart-ass."

"Sorry, I couldn't resist."

"You want to run with me?"

Why else would he be here, idiot?

"Sure."

"I'm pretty slow."

"I can handle it."

We walk to the path. When we get there, I start running, trying to go a little faster than I normally do. Henry trots along easily next to me.

"How are you feeling today?" Henry asks.

"Everything hurts."

"Yeah, Connor too. I still can't believe he actually made it up that ladder."

I smile, thinking back to Connor's tentative climb up the ladder. His approach was similar to my own (one foot at a time, eyes closed). But while I didn't even attempt to hide my utter terror, Connor tried to act completely blasé. He didn't quite manage to pull it off. It's hard to look as cool as a cucumber while you're shaking like a leaf in sweatpants, even if they are P. Diddy's brand.

"Yeah. That. Was. Funny."

"Do you feel more trustworthy now?"

"Ha. Ha."

"What's on today's menu? Astronaut training? Or just the usual therapy?"

"No. Therapy. Today."

"Why not?"

"Visiting. Day."

"Oh, cool. Are some of your friends coming to visit? Or your family?"

I shake my head, unable to even stutter out words anymore, and stop running. I place my hands on my knees, using them for support as I try to catch my breath.

Henry puts his hand on my back. "You OK?"

"I can't talk . . . when I'm . . . running."

"Sorry, I'm kind of chatty when I run."

"I thought you were . . . the strong . . . silent type."

"I guess running is my kryptonite."

My breathing returns to normal and I straighten up. "Didn't any of your girlfriends figure that out?"

"None of them liked to run."

"Their loss . . ."

And what did you mean by that, Miss Henry-Is-Definitely-Off-Limits?

Not another word.

I look away from him. "Anyway, should we run?"

"Sure."

We continue down the path. I decide to ask a question while I can still talk.

"So, what is your job, exactly?"

He glances sideways at me. "Are you trying to take advantage of me?"

"Never."

"I'm Connor's manager."

"Amber said. You were. Personal assistant."

"She would."

"What does. 'Manager' mean?"

"I manage Connor's career. You know, help him pick the movies he's going to do, endorsements, what talk shows he goes on, that sort of thing . . ."

As we run, Henry babbles on (literally, he is babbling) about how he and Connor grew up together, and how his job is mostly making sure Connor doesn't make stupid business decisions. Except for lately he's also had to keep him away from the paparazzi because of all the drinking and drugs and—"I really shouldn't talk about that, anyway . . . it's kind of hard to explain"—he knows it sounds stupid, like he works for a rapper or something, but really, it's just transitional, while he figures out what he really wants to do—when Connor asked him to come to rehab, that was almost the last straw, and it took a lot of wrangling and a huge donation to an outpatient drug program run by the Oasis before they agreed to let him in. He knows everyone thinks it's weird that he's here, but Connor said he needed him, and he couldn't abandon him when he was finally trying to clean up his act, right?

His talking is strangely comforting and almost makes me

forget I'm running. Almost. Until my entire body feels like it's on fire and the monkey is back with a vengeance.

Please let us have run for at least ten minutes.

I stop and look at my watch. Twelve minutes, two seconds.

I pump my fist in joy. Yes, yes, yes! Ohmygod it hurts.

"You done?" Henry asks, breathing easily, a slight tinge of pink on his cheeks.

"Oh yeah."

"Cramp?"

I nod. "A bad one . . . do you mind if we head back to the lodge?"

He agrees, and we walk slowly while I rub my side.

"So, do you like what you do?"

"Sometimes. It's fun hanging out with Connor, living the life. But . . . sometimes it's weird that my best friend's my boss. And sometimes I feel like I'm living his life."

"So why do it?"

He shrugs. "I'd just finished grad school when he invited me out to LA. I wasn't quite ready to jump into the real world, so I went."

"How long ago was that?"

"Coming up on eight years now."

"That's a long time."

"Yup."

"What'd you go to grad school for?"

"English lit."

"You a writer?"

"Nope, a teacher."

"Really? That's pretty far removed from manager of a huge Hollywood star."

"Imagine the pay cut I'd be taking if I gave it all up."

"Sounds like you're addicted to him."

He shoots me a look. "Excuse me?"

You know, Katie, just because everyone around you is being confronted with brutal truths about themselves 24/7 doesn't mean Henry wants to be.

"Sorry. Forget it."

He stops. "No, tell me. Why did you say that?"

I stare down at my shoes. They're covered with mud. "Well, it's just . . . the way you describe it sounds sort of like an addiction. Being stuck in a pattern you can't get out of because it would mean making sacrifices. Your whole life becoming about it . . ." I look up at him miserably. "That's what it's like to be an addict."

"I know what it's like to be an addict," he says quietly.

Shit.

"Forget I said anything, OK? I've spent too much time lately expelling every thought."

He looks pensive. "No, you might be right. I am kind of addicted to the lifestyle. I have a great car and a big apartment, none of which I'd be able to afford if it wasn't for Connor."

"Sounds nice."

"Yeah, but it's also easy."

"Just because something's easy doesn't mean it's bad for you. And at least being addicted to Connor gets you money and stuff. Most addicts can't say that."

He smiles. "And chicks. Don't forget the chicks."

"Right, how could I forget the *chicks*? You know, if you could invent a pill that got you money, stuff, and chicks, you'd be a gazillionaire."

"I don't think that's a word."

We start walking again. A whippoorwill trills above us, its repeating call the soundtrack of my childhood. My mind wanders briefly to my parents, not far from here as the crow flies. Would they come and visit me if they knew where I was and what I'm up to?

"So, are you really going to leave it all behind and become a teacher?"

He sighs. "I'm thinking about it. But I can't quit until Connor gets better."

"You're a good friend, Henry."

"Thanks. Anyway . . . you never said. Are any of your friends coming to visit today?"

I feel a pang of homesickness for Rory. Is she ever going to speak to me again?

"No, I don't think so."

"How come?"

"Oh, I don't know . . . I've caused my friends enough trouble, I guess."

"I bet your friends are really proud of you for coming here."

"Maybe."

"Trust me."

I make a face. "Trust Day was yesterday."

"So, what are you going to do with all your free time?"

"Hope someone put something readable in the library?"

He smiles. "I wouldn't count on it."

"Miracles can happen."

"Well, if no miracle transpires, we could hang out . . . if you want."

Did he just look nervous when he said that?

"I'd like that."

We turn the last corner of the path and the lawn sprawls out before us. There are more cars in the parking lot than usual. New faces are milling around. A group of four people is walking toward us. Something about them seems vaguely familiar.

"Do you know those people?" Henry says. "They're waving at you."

I follow his gaze. No . . . it can't be.

"Hey, lassie!" Greer bellows from across the lawn, her face a wide grin. "Who's the hottie?"

Twenty minutes later, Rory and I are walking toward my room so I can take a shower.

When our group hug dissolved, Henry graciously offered to show Greer, Scott, and Joanne (!) to the common room while I freshened up. Rory asked to come with me and, of course, I agreed. On the way she explains that she ran into Joanne soon after I left, which is how she learned where I really was. I ask her how they knew where to find me.

"Scott figured it out from the phone number you gave Joanne."

"Who knew he was so smart?"

"Yeah, he's not a bad guy."

I look at her curiously. Rory's never approved of Scott, or Greer, for that matter. I wonder what it means that they're all here together.

I open the door to my room, and Rory sits on Amy's bed while I get my things together for the shower.

"It's nice," she says, glancing round. "Do you have a room-mate?"

"I did. She left."

"Oh. What was she like?"

"She was pretty great."

"I'm glad."

Rory stares nervously down at her sandals, her hands folded in the lap of her tan pencil skirt. It occurs to me that this is the first time I've seen Rory in casual clothes in a long time. It suits her. She even looks like she's gained a few pounds, and her skin is a shade or two darker than the last time I saw her.

"You look good, Rory. Have you put on weight?"

She looks up. "I have."

"That's great."

"Yes, well, your coming here was a bit of a wake-up call for me. In fact, I'm, um, going to see a therapist to discuss my, um, issues with food."

I'm stunned. Besides our fight in her office, this is only the second conversation about her weight we've ever had. Not that I haven't wanted to discuss it with her a thousand times, but since anything near the topic was always greeted with such stony silence, I'd learned it was better to leave it alone.

"I'm really proud of you, Ror."

"Forget that. I'm the one who's proud."

"Please, don't be."

"I mean it, Kate. I'm so impressed that you acknowledged you had a problem and came here before it got totally out of control. And I feel really bad that I didn't respond to your emails as soon as I found out where you were."

"Forget it. I know you went out on a limb to get me that job. I'm really sorry I couldn't take it."

"What you're doing is so much more important than some stupid job."

Great. Just great. I thought I was going to get a lecture, a lecture I deserve, a lecture I can handle. What I can't handle is the fierce, proud look on Rory's face.

"Please don't be impressed with me, Rory. I don't deserve it."

"What are you talking about?"

Crap, crap, crap. I've never been able to lie to Rory.

"Because I haven't done anything to be proud of."

"Don't be silly."

If we talk about this for one more second, I'm going to spill. And it won't be pretty.

I pull her into a hug, finally putting something I've learned here to good use. "I'm sorry, Rory. All we do in here is talk about this kind of stuff, and I'm sick of it. I'd love to just have a normal day with you guys. Is that all right?"

Everything I've just said is true. So why do I feel like such a godawful liar?

Because you are one.

Shut up, shut up, shut up.

"OK, I understand."

"Thanks, Ror. You're the best." I let her go. "Hey, you're never going to believe who I ran into . . ."

After a shower, which erases the sweat from my body but not the guilt from my mind, Rory and I rejoin Greer, Joanne, and Scott in the common room. Henry is still with them, playing host. I thank him for keeping them company and apologize that I won't be able to hang out with him.

"Don't worry about it. Have fun with your friends."

He leaves without giving me his standard shoulder squeeze. I wonder briefly if that means anything until my focus is shifted by Greer's demands for food.

"We-must-be-on-time Joanne insisted we leave at an ungodly hour. I'm ravenous."

"I didn't want to get caught in traffic on the bridge," Joanne says huffily.

"Actually, it was kind of cool," Scott says. "I've never seen the city so quiet."

"Didn't you leave that girl's apartment at six in the morning a few weeks ago?" Greer teases. "It must've been quiet then."

"What girl?" I ask.

"She was no one. And I was still drunk, so I wasn't noticing the peace and quiet."

Rory's eyes dart toward me. "I don't think you should be talking about drunken evenings right now, do you?"

Scott looks chastened. "Shit. Sorry, Katie."

"It's OK. Besides, what do you think people here talk about all day long? I've heard it all."

"I still don't think it's appropriate," Rory says.

"I agree," Joanne chips in.

Rory looks absolutely horrified that she and Joanne agree on something.

I start to laugh.

"What's so funny, lass?"

"Nothing. I'm just happy to see you guys. I'm really touched that you came."

"Geez, are we going to hug again?"

"Shut up, Scott."

"Can we eat now?"

After lunch, we go for a walk around the property, catching up and shooting the shit. The three of them are divided on whether I really need to be in rehab. Joanne, of course, falls into the "it should've happened a long time ago, but better late than never" camp, while Scott seems genuinely surprised.

"Were you just being proactive?" he asks, looking at me intently. "It's cool if you were."

Greer is pragmatic. "It's good to take a break once in a while, give your body a chance to recover, yah?" I agree, but I feel odd around her, like I've got an itch I can't quite reach.

Rory and I are mostly silent, but it's not a bad silence. Each of them tells me in their own way that they're proud of me. I skim over their pride and talk of other, trivial things, and the afternoon passes gently away.

When visiting hours are almost over, we head back toward the parking lot.

"That's never Connor Parks," Greer says.

I look toward the lodge. Connor and Henry are passing a football back and forth on the lawn.

"The one and only."

Scott is excited. "That's awesome! Do you think he'd mind giving me his autograph?"

Joanne rolls her eyes. "Don't be such an idiot, Scott."

"What's the big deal? I'm sure people ask him all the time."

Greer taps him on the shoulder. "Right. But not in rehab, yah?"

"OK, OK."

We watch them make a few more passes.

"That Henry's cute for a ginger," Greer says. "You working on something there?"

"We're just friends."

"If you say so, lass."

Amber comes out of the front door of the lodge and walks toward Henry and YJB. Her hair is in a loose ponytail, and she's wearing a flowy cotton skirt.

Joanne reaches out and grabs my arm, her fingers digging in. "Is that . . . ? Ohmygod, I *love* her."

"You do?"

"I've watched every episode of *The Girl Next Door*."

"You have?"

"The girl next what's it?" Greer asks.

"*The Girl Next Door*. Don't you get television across the pond?"

"Yeah we get telly, you prat. We just don't get shite telly."

Joanne's eyes widen in anger, while the corner of Greer's mouth twitches. She knows who TGND is, of course she does, but she can't help pulling Joanne's leg.

"You're such a bitch."

Rory steps between them. "Let's not ruin Kate's visiting day."

I smile at them all fondly. "Don't worry, you're not."

"Goodness, lassie. Are you going to make us hug *again*?"

Yup.

Chapter 15
This Means War

The next morning, I get a furious email from Bob with a link to the Amber Alert site. They managed to get some photos of Amber and Connor on the lawn passing the football back and forth with Henry. Apparently, one of the visitors took the photos with a cell phone and sold them to the highest bidder.

How come you didn't tell me that they were back together? Bob writes. I can imagine the angry stab of his fingers against the keys. *What am I paying you for?*

Christ. What does this man want from me? Isn't it enough that I have to expose the inner workings of my brain, deal with attempted suicides, and act as a spy?

Bob, sorry for not keeping you up-to-date. They're definitely back together, but if you print what I'm about to tell you, it'll blow my cover. Anyway, here's what's been going on . . .

I type a long description of their midnight reunion and their odd way of communicating in Esperanto. When I'm done, my fingers hurt, and I have a sharp pain between my eyes from staring at the vivid screen for so long. I also feel empty and guilty, but I'm getting used to those feelings.

Bob's reply is almost instantaneous. *Apology accepted. Keep up the good work.*

I stick my tongue out at the screen and turn off the iTouch. Time for my punishment.

"Step Four: Made a searching and fearless moral inventory of ourselves. Do you feel ready to do that?" Saundra asks me on Day Seventeen: Admitting Our Faults and Forgiving Ourselves.

I bite my thumb, not liking the sounds of this. "You really don't think that royal 'we' thing is weird at all?"

"Please stop deflecting, Katie."

"Sorry. I've just been feeling . . . down since my friends left."

I mean, how would you feel if the most interesting thing you'd done in the last eight years is drink enough for half your friends to believe you need to be in rehab?

"Why, do you think?"

I look at Saundra's kind, expectant face, waiting for me to serve up an answer.

"Maybe it's because I'm not sure any of this is working."

"That any of what is working?"

My life. My head. My heart.

"This. Rehab. Therapy. Group. Nobody seems to be getting any better. Not The Producer or The Former Child Star, or anyone."

"Why do you think that?"

"Because they all still talk about drugs and alcohol like they're describing a lover they wish they could get back."

"What patients talk about in group isn't the only measure of whether they're getting better."

"It's the only thing I see."

"Perhaps that's your problem."

"What do you mean?"

"Well, besides Amber, you don't seem to have connected with any of the other patients."

I cross my arms across my chest. "I liked Amy."

"Amy's not here anymore."

"But I don't feel like I have anything in common with them."

"You have your disease in common."

"So, if I had cancer, I'd have to make friends with people on the cancer ward to get better?"

"Maybe."

"That's ridiculous."

"We all have to work together, Katie. You have to learn from your experiences, but also from other addicts. You have to learn to rely on others. And until you do, you're always going to seek refuge in a bottle or a pill or a needle."

"I don't like needles."

"You know what I mean."

"Yeah, I guess. I just don't seem to manage it somehow."

"You could start by learning their real names," she says mildly.

Oh, touché.

"I'll try."

"Good. I think the inventory will help you."

"But how can making a list of all of the worst things I've done make me feel better about myself?"

"I know it sounds counterintuitive, Katie, but writing them down is the first step to letting them go."

Or the first step to a front-page headline.

"I hope so."

After lunch, I get some paper and seek out a peaceful place to take my moral inventory. I decide to do it in the library. I seem to be the only person who spends any time there, and if all else fails, I can stare out the window at the view.

I take a seat on the comfy tan chenille couch that sits in the middle of the room and place my feet on the wood coffee table. I twirl my pen as I think about the pathetic state of me.

Can it really be as simple as Saundra says? Can I really just write the worst of me away? I'll never know unless I try, so . . . these are the top five worst things about me in no particular order:

1. When I left home, I left more than Zack behind. I dropped every single one of my friends from high school except for Rory. And as much as I love her, I probably would've dropped Rory too if she hadn't moved with me. I've always told myself it was because they were my proximity friends and we didn't have much in common. But deep down I know the truth. I liked my high school friends. I had things in common with them, but I didn't want to anymore. I dropped them as deliberately as I

did the accent, big hair, and blue eyeliner that were the hallmarks of me in high school. I felt like they'd drag me down, and so I cut the cord.

2. Four months ago, I wrote something nasty about Greer in the men's bathroom of our favorite bar. She'd pissed me off by swooping in on this guy I was flirting with. He'd seemed interested too, until she showed up with her auburn hair, porcelain skin, and enticing accent. He trailed off in mid-sentence as she sat down at our table, and it was like I didn't exist anymore. She dated him for a week; I went home alone. But not before I used my left hand to write her phone number, email address, and some lewd phrase to imply she gave great blow jobs above the urinals with my lipstick. She got so many calls, texts, and emails, she had to change all her information. She doesn't know who the perpetrator is, but I've heard what she wants to do to that person, and it ain't pretty.

3. Three weeks after Rory and Dave started dating, I ran into him at a bar with his buddies and threw myself at him after downing two pitchers of watery beer. He fended me off, and neither of us ever told Rory. To this day, we're awkward if we're ever left alone together, even though I've apologized a gazillion times.

4. Half of my good friends think I'm a twenty-five-year-old grad student. Enough said.

5. I agreed to go to rehab to write an exposé of Amber Sheppard. Once again, enough said.

Christ, I want a drink. Just one little drink to quiet the noise in my head. And I know it's pathetic, to be thinking about, to be missing, *drinking* when I've just written out a list of the worst things about myself, a list that's supposed to be a step on my road to not drinking. But the more I tell myself that, the more I want a drink.

Just.

One.

Little.

Drink.

And now, instead of counting the days of sobriety, I count the days until I can leave here. Until I can do what I want, when I want. But I don't know when I'm leaving because I don't know when Amber's leaving. Which brings me back to number five on my all-time shame list. Which makes me want to have a drink.

Just.

One.

Little.

Drink.

Fuck, fuck, *fuck*. I'm not sure what feels worse. Admitting the worst things about me, or admitting how badly I want a drink right now. And if I want a drink that badly, what the hell does that say about me? I have a feeling that the answer to that question is more truth than I can handle without One. Little. Drink.

Swish. A paper airplane flies past my ear and lands in my lap. I snap my head around and catch the retreating back of— was that Henry?

I pick up the airplane and unfold it. It reads: *War games begin at 11:15 tonight in the game room. Be there,* followed by a series of directions on how to avoid the staff patrols. From the looks of it, someone, I assume Henry, has spent quite a bit of time mapping out the staff's movements.

Should I go? If we get caught, we'll probably get kicked out, and then what?

Then you can have a drink.

Finally, a good idea.

I flatten the airplane on my knees. *I'll be there,* I write, underlining it until the ink almost bleeds through the paper.

At 11:08 p.m., five minutes after Carol's checked my room to make sure I'm all tucked in, I gingerly open my door as per Henry's instructions. My pillows are under the covers, and I'm dressed in my best pajamas. My hair is brushed and I'm wearing makeup. (Just a little mascara and lip gloss, but still.) I chose the PJs because I figure if I get caught in the hall, I can attempt an "I was sleepwalking" defense. I put on the makeup because . . . well . . . one needs/wants to look one's best before hanging out with one (OK, two) major movie stars, right?

Oh, come off it. You're totally doing it for Henry.

OK, OK, but I shouldn't be.

I scoot quietly to the end of my hall in my bare feet, hugging my flip-flops against my chest, and wait for two minutes before turning the corner to the hall that leads to the library and the game room. I arrive at 11:15 on the dot without having seen or heard anyone.

I *rap, rap, rap* on the door gently. Amber opens it and I scurry inside.

YJB and Henry are sitting at a green baize–covered table, both also in their pajamas (a pair of green hospital scrubs for Connor, gray cotton shorts and a white T-shirt for Henry). There's a game board on the table I don't recognize. The room is dimly lit by a lamp in the corner, and someone's drawn the curtains across the ubiquitous French doors that lead outside.

Amber lays a towel along the bottom of the door. She's wearing black leggings and a gauzy nightshirt. "Glad you could make it."

"Hi, Kate," Henry says, giving me a quick once over.

Makeup was definitely a good idea.

YJB nods in my direction. "Katie. Excellent."

"So, what's all this?" I ask, sitting next to Henry.

"It's *Risk*," Amber says. "Have you ever played?"

"I don't think so."

"These are the rules," Henry says, explaining the game. The board is a map of the world divided into territories. Each player has a number of armies they can use to control a territory. The ultimate goal is to control the world, which is achieved by waging war against the other players.

"More armies doesn't necessarily mean you'll win. But it increases your chances."

"Can you take prisoners of war?"

"Nope. An army is either alive or it's dead."

"Harsh."

"You'll get the hang of it as we go along. I'll help you in the beginning."

Connor pulls a pack of smokes out of his pocket. "You most certainly will not. It's every man for himself."

"I don't think that's a good idea," Amber says as Connor flicks his lighter under the end of his cigarette.

"Cut the mother hen crap, Amber."

"I just don't want to get caught, baby."

He scoffs. "Since when have you cared about getting caught?"

"How about we just open a window, OK?" Henry says, rising to crack open one of the barred windows.

"Well, then, can I have one?" Amber asks.

Connor tosses her the pack. "Let's get this show on the road."

"I want to be pink."

Henry hands me the red army, takes the blue for himself, and gives the black to Connor. We roll for position, and stake our initial claims around the world. Henry gently corrects my early mistakes, much to Connor's disgust, but stops giving me hints when I win a skirmish with him for Quebec.

As our armies slowly cover the map, the room fills with cigarette smoke and I almost feel like I'm at a bar back in the days when you could smoke in bars, except for the obvious lack of drink, of course. I reach for one of Connor's cigarettes to stave off a craving for a nice cold . . . anything, really. I'm not feeling that picky.

"I wonder who's going to rehab next?" Connor says, apropos of nothing. "It always happens in threes."

"That's celebrity deaths, moron," Henry replies, rolling a six and defeating Connor's army for control of Australia.

My turn comes and I decide to make a play for Asia. It goes badly.

"Rookie mistake," Henry says, his eyes twinkling as I go down to him in defeat. "But aggressive. I like it."

Connor hunches over the board gleefully. "'You fool! You fell victim to one of the classic blunders! The most famous is: Never get involved in a land war in Asia . . .'"

"'But only slightly less well known is this: Never go in against a Sicilian when death is on the line!'" I complete the line from *The Princess Bride*.

"I love that movie," Amber says.

Connor cocks his head back and blows smoke rings. "Everyone loves that movie."

"*Con-nor*, why are you always so mean to me?"

"Your turn, Amber," Henry says.

Amber rolls the dice, trying not to look upset. I wonder (not for the first time) what she sees in Connor. He's cute, of course—he's gorgeous. But Amber's right. He *is* mean to her.

I decide to let her win the part of South America I control. She's beyond thrilled when she plunks her pink army down where my red one used to be.

There's a loud noise in the hall and we all look up from the board, startled. Henry stands up quickly and snaps off the lamp in the corner. He pulls open the curtain so we can see by the light of the half moon.

"What should we do?" Amber whispers.

"Shh!"

Henry walks to the door and pulls the towel up off the floor. He presses his ear to the wood. His face contracts with concentration, and he motions to me to come to him. I walk as lightly as I can and stand next to him.

"Someone's talking, but I can't hear what they're saying," he whispers. "Can you?"

I put my ear to the door. I can hear the rumble of voices, a man and a woman by the sound of it. I strain harder.

"Amber . . . not in . . . bed . . ." says the female voice.

"Smoke . . . games . . ." replies the man.

Oh crap.

"They know Amber's not in bed, and they're coming this way."

Connor springs into action. "Amber, try to clear the smoke. OK, let me think. We'll stay here, but you two need to get."

Amber picks up the towel and begins waving it vigorously.

"Connor, I don't think that's a good idea," Henry says.

"We'll be all right. But she'll get kicked out if she's caught." He points at me and gives Henry a meaningful look.

"Henry, he's right," I say. "Amber's been able to get away with all kinds of things that I never would . . ."

There's another noise in the hall, closer this time.

I grab Henry's arm. "Let's go, Henry."

A frustrated noise escapes his throat, and we move together

toward the French doors. I try the door but it's locked. Henry pulls his wallet from his pocket and slides a credit card between the door and the frame. He wiggles it in an experienced way and the lock gives.

"Quickly!"

He pulls me outside and along the building so we're a few feet away from the door. I'm sweating with fear and the cool breeze sends a chill down my spine.

"Shh," Henry says. "Your teeth are chattering."

I clench my jaw shut. Henry wraps his arms around me, pressing my face into his chest. He rests his chin on my head and places his hands loosely on my waist. I can smell his expensive, spicy aftershave and the same soap I've been using.

"Quiet on the set!" Connor hisses loudly.

The door to the game room opens. Someone flicks the light switch, and light falls out the French doors, illuminating the ground next to us.

"Amber, Connor, what are you two doing out of bed?" Carol says.

"Fuck," Henry says so quietly I can barely hear him. "Come on, Amber."

"I'm sorry," Amber says in her best *The Girl Next Door* voice. "I was having some really bad cravings, and I needed a cigarette. I thought it was better to smoke in here than in my room."

"Mmm ... and what about you, Connor?"

"What can I say," he drawls. "Great minds think alike."

I can imagine Connor's charismatic smile spreading across his face.

"We had some things we needed to talk about," Amber says. "I asked him to meet me."

"You know that's not allowed, Amber."

"Please don't tell on us."

"I'm sorry, but I have to report this. And you've both lost your outside privileges for two days."

"*Car-ol . . .*"

"Enough, Amber. Get back to bed immediately."

They shuffle away from the door, and for a moment, I think we might be safe.

"Carol, someone tripped the alarm," a man says.

Uh-oh.

"Amber, Connor, did you go outside?"

"I opened the French door," Amber says faintly. "To let the smoke out."

"John, can you make sure these two get back to their rooms? I'll take care of it."

Henry grinds his teeth together into the top of my head. "We are so fucked," he whispers.

I can hear Carol walk across the room. Henry pulls me deeper into the shadows, closer to his chest.

"However . . . ?" Carol mutters, then shuts the door firmly. We both start at the sound of the lock clicking shut. Her retreating footsteps echo faintly. The light snaps shut and we're left in darkness.

We stand there for what feels like a very long time, breathing in and out, waiting. My breathing falls into a rhythm with Henry's. We breathe well together.

"So, what do we do now?" I say eventually.

"I'm guessing they've put the alarm back on, so it looks like we're stuck out here until morning."

Shit, I was afraid of that.

He loosens his arms and I step away from him. I hug myself to keep out the cold.

A sweater seems like a better idea than makeup at this juncture.

"We can't stay out here that long."

He gives me a reassuring smile. "'Course we can." He shows me the face of his watch. The glow-in-the-dark dial says it's 2:12. "It'll be light in a couple of hours."

"But what if someone sees us?"

"We should probably go to the woods. There'll be less chance of us getting caught there."

"Right, good point."

I follow him away from the building, my flip-flops slapping softly. It's extremely dark under the trees and it's difficult to pick out the path. I've always found woods at night particularly creepy. Every crackle sounds like the pad of a hungry bear. I try to raise my feet high as I step like my dad taught me when I was little, but I trip and stub my toe on a large root.

Henry catches me before I hit the path and sets me right, his strong hands holding my forearms tightly.

"Thanks."

"No problem." He releases me. "Maybe we should stop here. I doubt anyone will find us."

And if they do, at least I'll be able to tell Bob I got kicked out in pursuit of his two favorite targets.

Henry sits on the ground against a large rock. His white legs and arms are the most visible thing about him, and I notice that he's wearing shorts and a T-shirt.

"Are you cold?"

"A little. Will you sit here?"

I can't see where he's indicating, but I know what he means. It seems like a bad idea, but what other options do we have? Hypothermia or huddling together for warmth. The choice seems obvious.

I sit down in front of him and scoot backward. He bends his legs so his feet are flat on the ground, making a little cage around me. We're both shivering.

He slips his arms around my waist. I lean my head against his chest. I can hear his heart thudding.

"So, is tonight making your career-change decision any easier?"

He sighs. "Tonight is just one of the many things in my life that isn't quite right."

"What? Cuddling in the woods with a strange girl you met in rehab while trying to avoid detection isn't what you wanted to do when you grew up?"

"Cuddling in the woods, yes. Hiding from the authorities in rehab, no."

One out of two ain't bad.

Chapter 16
Technical Difficulties

I wake up in Henry's arms at dawn.

Moments before, I was dreaming. Something about escaping from a mental institution with James Bond. Only this Bond has red hair above his black tux. He still likes martinis, though, and I flirt with him outrageously to get one. It's dry and feels like fire as it slides down my throat. When it's gone, I feel warm and bold. I throw my arms around his neck and press my mouth to his.

"You taste like cigarettes," he says.

My eyes flash open. I can see the reddish-blond hairs on Henry's arm. "What?"

"I said, we smell like cigarettes."

"Oh . . . right." I push myself gently away from him and stand stiffly. My mouth tastes like three olives, straight up.

Christ almighty. If I have to have user-dreams, couldn't they at least come with a breath mint?

"What time is it?"

Henry checks at his watch. He looks tired. "Just before six. We should get back."

"How are we going to get into the lodge?"

"They unlock the doors around now."

I brush twigs and dirt from my backside. "How the hell do you know that?"

"I tend to wake up pretty early."

"Come to think of it . . . how did you know how to use your credit card like that? And how come you know when bed checks are?"

He smiles. "I picked up the credit card trick as a teenager, and as for the rest of it, well . . . I have an awful lot of time on my hands in here, so I've been tracking the staff for fun."

"For fun, or so Connor can meet up with Amber?"

His smile drops. "You sure call me on my bullshit, don't you?"

There you go again. Always saying just the right thing to make sure you're alone.

"I'm sorry, Henry, I don't know why I do that."

"It's OK, you're right. I'm the perfect little enabler. Shit, I just slept in the woods to prove it."

"I thought you were out here to keep me from getting kicked out."

"Maybe I am." He brushes his hand across my cheek. I think for a second that he might kiss me, but then the moment passes.

"You go first," he says. "I'll follow you when the coast is clear."

"All right. Thanks."

"For what?"

I don't really know, so I shrug and walk away.

After a nap and a shower, I take out my iTouch to send Bob my daily update. Only this time, when I hit the little icon that's supposed to connect me to the Internet, nothing happens. I notice I'm not connected to the network, so I use the steps I memorized nineteen days ago to locate the Oasis's network. It prompts me for a password. I type in the word "catalyst." *Invalid password* says the screen. I type it in again, more slowly this time, watching each letter turn into an asterisk. *Invalid password.*

I feel a clutch of panic. They must've changed the password. What the fuck am I supposed to do now? There's no way Bob can last twelve more days without his daily fix of The Rehab Lives of Camber. This is an emergency.

Right. It is. Good. Wishes-he-was-a-field-officer-running-CIA-agents Bob has a plan for emergencies.

I check the "Notes" section of my iTouch and there it is, a little note called *In case of emergency.* I open it. It contains a ten-digit phone number. Perfect. Just perfect.

I spend lunch (which I'm happy, for once, to eat alone) trying to figure out how to call the number. The obvious route is to use one of the pay phones on the wall outside the cafeteria. We're allowed to use the phone for ten minutes a week, using tokens that last five minutes each.

But the phones are in the most public part of the lodge. Patients, staff, doctors, Saundra—everyone walks by those phones all the time. It's impossible to have a private conversation, which is probably the point of their location. Like the one phone in the house when I was growing up, which my parents put in the kitchen. No kid would be stupid enough to plan a wild night of drinking within earshot of their mother, right? Hah!

Fuck. I wish I could pull a Matthew Broderick in *War Games* and get myself sent to the principal's office. Then, while he was distracted, I could sneak his desk drawer open and steal the new password. What could go wrong?

"Can I get your attention, everyone?" Carol says from the front of the cafeteria. "Now, as you all know, Gerry and Keith are leaving us today . . ."

She gives her usual spiel about The Lawyer and The Producer's departure, winding her way toward the group singalong . . . Hold on a sec. This is good. In about thirty seconds, everyone in here is going to be singing their lungs out for about three minutes. The perfect diversion.

I stand up and walk briskly from the room, ignoring Saundra's look of disapproval. I'm sure I'll hear about my lack of connection to the other patients in my next session. Again.

I pull my two tokens from my pocket and thrust them into the phone, then punch in Bob's number, my heart in my throat.

The phone rings three times, then, "This better be an emergency."

"It is."

"Has she left?"

"No."

"Are you in a secure location?"

"No."

"Can you give me a hint?"

I cup my hand around the receiver. "Password."

I hear a hand slam into a desk. *Whack!* "Damn it! I was worried about that. How much time have you got?"

"Not long."

"What's that godawful noise?"

"It's singing."

"What the fuck?"

"Don't ask."

There's silence on the other end of the line. I think I can hear his slightly wheezy breathing, but it's hard to tell over the really bad singing.

"You still there, Bob?"

"Don't use my name."

"Sorry."

"OK. We can get the new password. Can I call you there?"

"No."

"Can you call me again?"

"Not for a week."

"Fuck. Any thoughts on how to get it to you?"

Like I'm not doing enough already.

I wrack my brain. "Send me a care package."

"Don't they check those?"

"Sure, but only for the obvious."

He clucks his tongue three times. "Yeah, OK, I don't see a better alternative. Do you have a friend you trust?"

"Why?"

"So she can send it. It can't come from here."

Right. That would be bad. But who the hell can I trust with something like this?

"I'll see if I can get my friend Greer to call you."

"Tell her the minimum."

"Of course."

The phone clicks and my ear is filled with the sound of a dial tone. So pleasant to talk to you, Bob, as always.

The singing in the cafeteria stops as I hang up the phone. What the fuck did I just agree to? Even assuming I can get my hands on some more tokens, there won't be another singing diversion until Mary leaves in three days. There's no way I can explain myself to Greer on these extremely public phones.

"Who's Bob?" Amber asks behind me.

I start in surprise and my already racing heart finds an extra gear. I turn toward her curious face. "Jesus Christ, you scared the life out of me."

She grins. "Sorry, but you looked so secretive, I couldn't help it."

What do you say when the F-word doesn't cover it? Because right now, all my head is making is white noise.

"Nn . . . no secret." I clear my throat. "It was just someone from work."

"Are you in trouble?"

"Sort of."

She scrunches her face. "Tell me about it. I'm supposed to be filming a remake of *Rebecca* right now."

"Sucky. Anyway . . ."

I turn away from her to try to make my escape. I need a couple of hours in a rubber room to calm the fuck down.

She grabs my arm. "Oh no you don't, Missy."

Make that several days.

"What?"

"No way I'm letting you get away before I hear all about," she leans toward me and lowers her voice. "Your night in the woods with E."

Endorphins rush through my body and I work hard to suppress a hysterical laugh. She just wants to gossip. In the good, between-girlfriends way.

I give her what I hope is a coy smile. "Not here. Come by my room after group, OK?"

She winks at me. "Got it. I want full details, though."

Don't we all.

An hour later, I've got a new plan and a new rush of adrenaline coursing through my veins. I feel like I did when I was flying through the air on Trust Day: terrified and exhilarated.

I'm walking through the flower gardens looking for Zack. Really. Actually seeking him out rather than hiding from him. Is that progress? Only time will tell.

I find him where the edge of the lawn meets the woods, shoveling fertilizer onto a big patch of lilies that haven't bloomed yet. His arms are muscular and tanned. His eyes are shaded by a pair of Oakleys.

"Hey, Zack."

He lowers the shovel and rests his arm on it like it's a crutch. "Hey, yourself. Haven't seen you around much lately."

"I've been . . . busy."

"Sure enough."

I lace my hands together. My palms are slick with sweat. "Do you think you could do me a favor?"

"I don't know. Depends."

"Could I borrow your cell phone?"

He pushes his shades up onto his forehead. His eyes look cautious. "What for?"

"I need to make a private phone call, and that's kind of hard on the pay phones inside. It's not for anything bad. I mean, I'm not ordering drugs or anything like that."

"Gee, I don't know, Katie. We're not really supposed to do stuff like that."

"I know. Forget I asked, OK?" I lower my head and kick my foot at the ground in the way I remember doing back when I could get Zack to do whatever I wanted.

I'm actually sad to say, it still works like a charm.

He sighs. "It's really not for anything you shouldn't be doing?"

I keep my head down. Lying is easier this way. "I promise."

"I guess that's all right then."

I look up at him, smiling brightly. "Thank you, Zack, you're a lifesaver."

He doesn't look so sure, but he reaches into his pocket and pulls out his cell phone.

"I'll be back in a sec."

I walk the phone far enough away so he can't overhear my conversation and lean against a tree, hiding myself from the lodge. I dial Greer's number, praying she'll pick up. Instead, I get her voice mail.

"This is Greer. Make it short."

Fuck. Well, here goes nothing.

"Hey, Greer, it's Katie. Thanks again for visiting me the other day, that was awesome. Anyway, I, um, need a favor. I know this is going to sound weird, but it would really help me out if you could call this guy. His name is Bob. He needs to send me something here, but for reasons I can't get into, he can't send it to me directly."

I pause. That totally sounded like I'm asking her to make a drug-connect. Shit.

"OK, that came out kind of wrong. It's something for work, not drug or alcohol related, I swear. And I'll explain it all to you when I get home. For now, I'd just really, really appreciate it if you could call Bob and do what he asks without asking any questions. I totally get it if you don't want to, but if you don't, please just call Bob anyway and let him know, either way. Anyway, sorry for the long message. Bye."

I hang up the phone, shaking my head in disbelief. This was such a stupid fucking plan. No way Greer's going to call Bob, particularly not after that message. Shit, she's probably never going to call me again.

Plus, you didn't even give her Bob's number.

Motherfucker.

I check the time on the phone. It's 2:50. I need to be in group in ten minutes. I look over my shoulder to where Zack is halfheartedly moving the earth around the flower bed while watching me. I signal to him that I'll be a minute.

I hit redial.

"Hey, Greer, me again. Crazy Katie. I forgot to give you Bob's phone number." I recite it. "Anyway, you would really be doing me a huge favor if you called him, so . . . OK, I'm hanging up now."

Oh, well done. Now you've just guaranteed that she's not going to call him.

Will you fuck off, I'm under enough stress here.

I click the phone shut and cup it in my palm as I walk back to Zack. He takes it from me and slips it back into his pocket quickly like I've just passed him some little packages filled with dope.

"Thanks, Zack. I really appreciate it."

He nods. "You doing all right?"

I try to smile. "Some days are better than others."

"No, I meant . . . you look pale and you're sweating. Are you sick?"

I wipe my arm across my forehead. I feel like I'm burning up. "I don't know. Maybe. Anyway, I have to get to group."

"Sure. See you around."

I start to walk away, but something stops me. I turn back.

"Zack?"

"Yeah?"

"Thanks. And . . . I'm sorry."

246

He frowns. "What for?"

"For leaving. For all of it."

"That was a long time ago, Katie."

"I know. I'm sorry for that too."

He gives me a half smile, his hands stuffed in his pockets. Eighteen-year-old Zack isn't far from the surface.

"Goodbye, Zack."

"Bye, Katie. Don't be a stranger."

"I won't."

Two days later, there's a package waiting for me in my room when I return from breakfast. The packing-tape seal has been broken, and there's a "cleared" stamp on it in red ink. Inside, there's an envelope above several items wrapped loosely in newspaper. I pull out the card first. It has a stick figure drawn on the cover with a balloon coming out of its mouth. *So, you're in rehab. What's a girl to do?* I open the card. The stick figure is sitting in a lounge chair, reading a book and smoking a cigarette. Its hand is reaching into a box of candy. The caption above it says: *Smoke, eat, and <u>read</u> trashy novels. Love, Greer.*

I unwrap the newspaper packages, unveiling a carton of cigarettes, a large package of red licorice, and three romance novels with bodice-ripped covers, but no password.

Shit. She must've called Bob, right? Why else would she have sent me this package? So, where the hell is the password? OK, OK, calm down. It can't be in an obvious place; that would defeat the purpose. There must be a code in here somewhere. But where?

Got it! Greer's card must be a clue. I look at it again. She's underlined the word "read."

I pick up the first book and flip through the pages one by one. Nothing. The second book has a woman on the cover who looks vaguely like Greer. Same long auburn hair, same glint of mischief in her eyes. Way less clothing. On page thirty-eight, the word "healing" is circled. I take out the iTouch and get to the password screen. I type in the word "healing" and . . . yes! We have liftoff.

I check my inbox. There's an email from Greer waiting for me.

If you're reading this message, you're smarter than I thought! No need for explanations, lass. The intrigue was worth it.

I laugh out loud. People surprise you every goddamn day, even in rehab.

Chapter 17
It's Going to Be a Bumpy Ride

On Day Twenty-four: Preparing for Your New Life, Carol raps on my door and introduces me to my new roommate, Muriel, the desperate housewife of some Internet CEO. Her three Louis Vuitton suitcases take up twice as much space as she does, her blond hair must come from a bottle, and every inch of her face has been Botoxed so that no wrinkle would even dare attempt to take up residence. She has a jittery, post-detox nervousness about her. My newly trained eye diagnoses her as a prescription-painkiller addict.

She takes one look at me in my patented rehab look (yoga pants, long-sleeved T-shirt, hair in a messy ponytail) and tells Carol she couldn't possibly room with anyone, she needs total silence, she's sure it's crucial to her recovery.

"Muriel, I've already explained that you can't have your own room," Carol replies patiently.

"Not even if I pay double?"

"It's not a question of payment—it's part of the program."

If her forehead was capable of a response, Muriel would be frowning. "We'll see about that."

Carol ignores her. "Katie, would you mind showing Muriel to group?"

"Sure, no problem."

"I'll check on you tomorrow, Muriel."

"Yeah, whatever."

Carol leaves, and I watch my new roommate as she drags her suitcases toward the closet. She opens the door and recoils in horror.

"You've got to be fucking kidding me."

"Not what you're used to, huh?"

She gives me a look that makes me feel unwelcome even though I'm the one who's been living here for weeks. "Excuse me?"

"The closet. I know it's pretty small."

Her eyes become two narrow slits.

Wow. Her skin doesn't move *at all*. How'd they do that?

"Let's get one thing straight right now, Kristie."

"It's Katie."

"Like I give a fuck."

"What the hell's your problem?"

"My problem is I don't want to have a little chitchat about *your* problems, or anything else. I just want to be left alone."

I start to laugh.

Muriel looks pissed off. Or at least she would if her face could make an expression.

"What's so funny?"

"I don't know where you think you are, Garbo, but if you just want to be left alone, you came to the wrong place."

"Do I have to room with her?" I ask Saundra the next day.

Muriel didn't say another word to me the entire day. She spent a loud hour getting ready for bed (I counted three separate face creams, two toners, and several tweezing devices, and I wasn't even paying close attention to what she was doing), then snapped off the light while I was in the middle of a graphic sex scene in one of the romance novels Greer sent me. And then, as I was actually about to drift off to sleep at a decent hour for once, she started to snore. And not some cute, feminine snore. No, sir. It was jackhammer, woodpecker quality.

"Is there a problem?" The corners of Saundra's mouth might be twitching.

"Let me count the ways."

Or maybe not.

"Katie . . ."

"Well, I'm never going to be able to sleep again, for one. She snores like a middle-aged man."

"That's not her fault."

"Well, it's not mine, either."

"We could get you some earplugs."

"She won't even talk to me."

"I'm sure she's feeling very raw right now, Katie. Remember how you felt when you got out of detox?"

Damn straight, I remember. I felt elated.

"I guess."

"And wasn't it helpful having Amy to be able to talk to?"

"But Amy was nice."

"And so are you. Remember, Katie, you're Amy in this scenario."

Right. How the hell did that happen?

"Does that mean I'm working the program well?"

She smiles. "I do think you're making good progress, Katie, don't you?"

"Yeah, things seem to be getting . . . easier, if that makes any sense."

"It does. And that's why I think you're ready to go on today's field trip if you'd like."

"You mean, leave the grounds?"

"That's right."

Oh yes, I'd like.

I leave Saundra's office so excited I skip down the hall to lunch. Henry, Amber, and Connor are already sitting at "our" table next to the picture window. It's a perfect, sunny day, but I wouldn't care if it were snowing.

"My therapist said something about that to me too," Amber says after I tell them I can go on the field trip. "Apparently I'm showing 'newfound respect for the program' and am ready to move on to 'advanced coping mechanisms.'"

I bounce up and down in my seat. "That's great. So, are you going?"

"Calm down there, sister," Henry says teasingly.

"Just wait until you've been here for as long as we have."

"I'm pretty sure I won't be squealing with delight, no matter how long I'm here."

I punch him lightly in the arm. "Don't be so sure." I turn to Amber. "Will you come?"

"Oh, I don't know." She watches Connor plow through a huge plate of pasta. "Can you go, Connor?"

"Doubt it."

"*Con-nor*, don't you want to go?"

"*Am-ber*, you know he's not going to be allowed to," Henry mocks.

She flicks him a look of disgust. "Oh, fuck off, Henry."

I tug on her arm. "Come on, Amber, it'll be fun. Besides, we get to go outside the compound. Haven't you been dreaming about it for weeks?"

"Well . . . when you put it that way."

A smile breaks across my face until I catch Henry laughing at me.

"What?"

"Nothing," he replies, but when he gets up to return his tray, he leans in and whispers, "You're cute when you're excited."

Uh-oh.

Despite my excitement, I almost turn back when I learn where the field trip is going—to the mountain where my father's the assistant manager.

I stand staring at the sign-out sheet, chewing the end of my ponytail in indecision. Amber comes up behind me.

"What's the holdup?" she asks. She's wearing a pair of biking shorts and a zip-up technical shirt covered with logos for French water.

How many suitcases did she bring with her, anyway?

"Oh, nothing, I'm . . . uh . . . just having second thoughts."

She gives a snort of disgust. "You must be kidding. I'm only going because *you* talked me into it."

"I know . . . it's just . . . remember when we ran into my ex-boyfriend, Zack?"

"You mean when we hid in the bushes?"

"Yeah, yeah. Anyway, I'm trying to avoid a repeat, but I'm probably just being silly."

What are the chances I'm going to run into my dad on that big mountain, right? It's not like I'm going to stroll into his office or anything.

"Well, then, let's get this show on the road."

I scribble my name on the sheet with a sense of foreboding, then follow the group outside and clamber into the van. We sit in the backseat, while Candice sits in the front. Carol climbs into the driver's seat and revs the engine.

"Why'd it have to be mountain biking?" Candice whines to us in her little-girl voice. "I'd kill for some good shopping."

I snap. "Deal with it, Candice. You didn't have to come."

"You don't have to be such a bitch . . ."

Amber hangs over the edge of the seat. "What are you even still doing here, Candice? Aren't you ever going home?"

Candice turns her shoulders toward the window. "I'm not talking to you guys anymore!"

Amber and I roll our eyes at one another, and watch the trees and mountains passing by. The sun reflects off the rippling, dark water. I point out the trailhead where I started countless hiking trips with my family.

"Are your parents coming to that family therapy thing?" Amber asks. Day Twenty-seven: Advanced Coping Mechanisms also coincides with Optional Work: Family Therapy.

"No way. Are your parents coming?"

"Sure."

"But I thought you hated them."

"So?"

"So, what am I not getting?"

She glances at Candice, who's still pouting out the window.

She lowers her voice. "I figure if I cooperate, they'll let me out of here earlier."

I probably shouldn't get my hopes up, but ... please, please, please let that be true.

"Got it."

The van turns off the highway onto the road to the mountain, and a flood of memories hit me. Walking from the parking lot to the lodge, my skis a weight across my shoulder, trying to keep up with my dad. Turning through the same gates over and over again, trying to improve my time. Chrissie and I drying our socks by the roaring fire.

Oh my God. I think I miss my parents. I *hate* rehab.

Carol parks the van, takes us to the bike shop, and gives us strict instructions to meet her in three hours. With a final admonishment to "be good," we're free to go biking, hiking, or to walk into the bar on the top floor of the lodge. We could even thumb a ride out of here and never look back.

It's good to have options.

It's been years since I've been here. Thankfully, I don't recognize anyone in the bike shop. Amber and I rent a pair of mountain bikes, grab a map, and decide to take the gondola up to one of the trails that will give us a great downhill ride rather than a huge uphill climb.

Our bikes are attached to a rack on the outside of the gondola, and we take a seat with a group of teenaged boys covered in mud. They start nudging one another and looking at Amber with wide eyes. As we fly up the mountain, I watch them, wondering if they're going to work up the courage to ask if it's really her. Amber seems oblivious, resting her chin on her arms and gazing out the window at the spectacular view of the mountains.

The gondola reaches the top, and the nudging and whispering among the boys increases.

"Do it, dude!" one of them hisses loudly.

As we stand to leave, the boy sitting across from Amber starts to talk to her in a stammering voice. "Um, excuse me, bbbutt, are yyouu . . ."

Amber smiles her dazzling smile. "That actress? God, no."

We're all surprised by her answer, and she takes the moment it gives her to grab my hand and pull me out of the gondola. An attendant hands us our bikes, and we follow the signs to the less scary of the downhill slopes.

"How come you didn't tell them who you were?"

"Who do you take me for, *Candice*?"

I chuckle. "I guess it must be annoying being recognized all the time."

"Sometimes I like it. But today I don't feel like dealing with a bunch of stupid boys following us around all afternoon."

"I hear you."

"Thanks for playing along." She puts her helmet on and snaps the strap closed under her chin. "Ready to die?"

"Oh yeah."

We mount our bikes and pedal toward the trail. It starts off gently enough, but after a few minutes the pitch increases, and I squeeze the brakes to slow myself down.

Not Amber. She lets out a wild "Aiiieeee!" and leans over her handlebars. The mud from her wheels sprays up and hits me in the face, muddying my goggles. I squeeze my brakes harder as I hit the mud patch, and my bike starts to skid.

Ah, shit!

I hit something, a root I think, and my bike leaps in the air. I let go instinctively, hoping to land on soft ground.

I slam into the trail and my bike shudders to the ground a few feet away. I lie spread-eagled on my back, barely breathing. I ache everywhere. I might be dying, and yet, I can hear the birds chirping, and a yelp of joy from somewhere in the distance.

Jesus. I wish I believed in God so I could pray to him, it, she, whatever, to take me away, and make the pain stop. But, I don't. So, all I can wish for is that my brain does me a favor and checks out for a few minutes, at least until the medics arrive with their pain-relieving drugs.

Drugs. Fuck. I'm so screwed.

"Are you OK, ma'am?" a voice that sounds way too familiar asks.

I must be hallucinating. Maybe it's a prelude to passing out?

I raise my hand to wipe the dirt from my eyes. I recognize the fuzzy shape standing above me, and now I'm sure, potential head injury and all, that I'm not hallucinating.

"Dad?"

"Katie?"

He kneels next to me and pulls my goggles gently off my face. And there my dad is, looking at me with concerned and bewildered eyes that are the same shade of blue as mine.

"Hi, Dad."

Shit. Even talking hurts.

"Are you OK?"

"I don't know."

He takes off his helmet and lays it on the ground next to me. His hair is almost entirely gray; he looks older than he did four years ago.

"Can you sit up?"

"I don't think that's a good idea," my sister says, coming into view.

Looking at her is like looking at an upside-down image of myself. Same wavy chestnut hair, same slender build, same narrow nose. Totally different life.

I left. She stayed. I went to university in the city and racked up enormous debts. She went to the local college and put money in the bank. I dreamed about the size of my byline. She became a teacher like my mom and got a job at the elementary school.

Somewhere along the way, she also acquired an enormous chip on her shoulder, a chip I mostly blame on her high school sweetheart, Michael, who left her on their wedding day. Seriously. She was at the back of the church in her wedding dress and everything, waiting for the "Wedding March" to start playing. I had to tell her he wasn't coming, that he'd run off with some girl he'd met at his bachelor party. Chrissie took it surprisingly well at the time, or so we all thought, but she hasn't been the same person since.

"Hey, Chrissie."

She looks away. "Don't move her, Dad. She might've broken her neck."

Does she have to sound happy about that possibility?

She pulls her cell phone out of the shoulder strap of her backpack. "Just stay still, Katie."

She punches in a few numbers, then speaks to whoever answers in a crisp, authoritative tone, stating the nature of her emergency.

As I lie there, with my dad murmuring comforting words, some of the pain starts to recede. I breathe in slowly and fill my lungs. It hurts, but I'm no longer wishing to pass out. Mindful of Chrissie's mention of a broken neck, I turn my head gently from side to side. It feels creaky but in one piece.

I put my hands on the ground and push myself up.

Chrissie snaps her phone shut. "Hey, I said stay still!"

"Don't be so bossy, Chrissie."

My father's face contains that look of disappointment he always gets when we fight. "Girls, girls."

I look down at my legs. They're black with mud, but they both seem to be pointed in natural directions. I move them tentatively.

"Well, if you don't care if you're paralyzed," Chrissie huffs.

"Thanks for your concern, Chris. Dad, can you help me up?"

"Of course, sweetheart."

He helps me get to my shaky feet. I push my hair out of my eyes, and take an inventory. Amazingly, except for a few cuts, a lot of mud, and the lump I can feel forming on the back of my head, I seem to be injury-free.

My sister looks at me like she's inspecting one of her students for evidence of contraband. "So, what are you doing here?"

"Mountain biking."

"You know what I mean."

My mind starts to race. What can I possibly say except for the semi-truth?

I hate my fucking life.

"She's with me," Amber answers for me, pushing her bike up to us. Her body is covered in mud, but she still looks like she's about to shoot a cover for *Outdoor* magazine.

She looks me up and down. "Shit, Katie. You're a total wreck."

"Thanks."

"You OK?"

"Just peachy."

"That's Amber Sheppard," my sister says to no one in particular.

"God, Chrissie! Have a little tact."

"Who's Amber Sheppard?" my dad asks.

Amber smiles charmingly at Chrissie. "You must be Katie's sister."

"So they tell me. How do you know Katie?"

Amber turns toward my father. "And you must be Katie's dad. I'm sorry. It's my fault Katie fell. I was riding too fast."

He smiles at me fondly. "Katie always did like going fast."

Two fit, tanned guys in their mid-twenties in tight shorts and red-and-white shirts bike around the corner, skidding to a stop. One of them has a spinal board strapped to his back.

"Did somebody call for help?"

"She did," Amber and I say together, pointing at my sister.

An hour later, I've been checked head to foot, taken down in the gondola (not something I recommend if you're scared of heights), and had most of the mud cleaned off my face. Along the way, my dad finally clues into who Amber is, and my sister asks her enough personal details to give Saundra a run for her money. The only question Amber hasn't answered is how she knows me, but I know it's just a matter of time before that comes out. Sure enough, a few moments later, Carol walks through the door of the paramedics' examining room.

I watch my dad's eyes wander to the Oasis logo above Carol's pocket and back to me. I take a deep breath, waiting for the inevitable.

"Katie . . . are you . . . working at the Cloudspin Oasis?"

Oh, Dad. Thank you for asking that first.

"No, Dad."

"You're a . . . patient?"

"*What?*" Chrissie sputters. "You're what?"

"Yes, Dad."

"*You're* in rehab?"

I ignore my sister and focus on my dad. He looks incredibly sad, but not, you know, surprised.

"Yes, that's right."

"*No way.*"

I shoot her a dirty look. "Will you knock it off, Chris."

"Sorry," she says, sounding contrite but looking like Christmas has come early.

"For alcohol?" my dad asks.

"For alcohol," I agree.

Chapter 18
In a Family Way

"Why didn't you tell your family you were checking into a rehabilitation facility?" Saundra asks me the next day.

"I didn't want to upset them."

"Why do you think it would upset them?"

Because I didn't want them to think . . . ah, hell.

"Wouldn't it be upsetting to you if your daughter went to rehab?"

Saundra gives me one of her reassuring smiles that never quite manages to reassure me. "I'd be proud of her for recognizing she had a problem, and relieved."

"Relieved?"

"Having an addict in the family can be very stressful."

"I guess."

Saundra considers me. "Katie, you're a self-sufficient woman, and I know you like to think you can solve everything yourself, but you can't."

"I know that."

"Then why are you trying to?"

"I don't think I am. I came here, right?"

"Yes, you did. And that's a great first step."

"I thought I was up to Step Five."

The corners of her lips turn into a smile. Maybe I am making progress.

"Yes, Katie. But you also need to work through your issues with your family."

I fold my arms across my chest. "Things with my family are fine."

"I don't agree, Katie. And thankfully, neither do your parents."

I have a bad feeling about this.

"What do you mean?"

"They've enrolled in the family program. They're arriving tomorrow."

Yup, that was the bad feeling.

I feel like stomping my feet. "But I don't want to do the family program."

"I think you'd get a lot out of it."

"No. I don't want my parents to know about any of this." I gesture to the walls of her office as if the dog pictures and calendar can repeat my secrets, like the talking photos in *Harry Potter*.

"I know you might find it difficult . . ."

A flash of rage flows through me. "It's not going to be difficult. It's going to be excruciating, humiliating."

"Katie, being vulnerable in front of people who love you is how you grow and change."

Then I'll stay as I am, thanks.

"What a load of horseshit."

Saundra looks concerned. "Why are you so angry?"

"I told you. I don't want my parents to come here."

"I think that's a mistake."

"Isn't it my mistake to make?"

"Yes, it is. But you'll have to make it fully."

"What do you mean?"

"If you don't want them to come, you're going to have to call and tell them not to." She gestures toward the black, old-fashioned phone sitting on the corner of her desk.

Goddamnit.

"Why?"

"Because part of the program is taking responsibility for your actions."

"But that's not fair. I never asked them to come."

Ah, Christ. I sound like Candice.

Saundra taps her pencil against her pad of paper. "What will it be, Katie? You decide."

I slump in my chair and stare at the phone. All I can see is the expression on my dad's face yesterday when he put all the pieces together.

"Fine," I mutter into the front of my sweatshirt.

"What was that?"

"I said, *fine.*"

"You'll let them come?"

I nod.

She smiles. "I'm glad, Katie. I think you made the right decision."

That makes one of us.

It's approaching midnight and I'm lying in my bed staring at the ceiling. After two hours of counting moonbeams, cracks, sheep, sheep backward, and a million self-hating thoughts, I know sleep is a hopeless cause.

I think briefly about sneaking to the library and reading one of the sure-to-make-me-sleepy self-help books, but the last thing I want to do is spend more time thinking about drugs/alcohol/self-awareness, self-anything.

I listen to the silence around me. It's empty and deafening at the same time. Even Muriel is sleeping quietly.

I wonder if anyone else is awake. Or are visions of sugar-plums, or sugarplum-flavored brandy, dancing through their heads?

Where the hell are Amber, Connor, and Henry when I need them? I could totally go for a *Girl, Interrupted* moment right now.

Henry, Henry, Henry. What the hell am I going to do about him? Do I need to do anything? Does he like me? Like me like a boy likes a girl? Like a boy likes a girl he has chemistry with even though he met her in rehab? I think he does. I *think* he does, but I'm not sure. Not sure sure. Not sure enough to know if I should be pushing him away.

But if he does like you, why push him away?

I would've thought that was obvious, given what I'm here to do.

Well, maybe you can have a little fun while you work?

Maybe you can let me go to sleep?

I'm just saying . . .

No. I want to go to sleep.

So you can dream about Henry?

Fuck off.

Maybe he's awake too?

Now there's a thought . . .

Working quietly so I don't wake Muriel, I place my pillows under the covers, stop at my dresser to run a brush through my hair, and leave my room. I'm at the end of the hall before I realize something kind of important. A fatal flaw in my plan, really.

I don't know where Henry's room is.

Shit.

Bravo, Katie.

Will you shut the fuck up?

I'm just saying . . .

You're always just saying. I've had just about enough of you this evening.

OK, think. I know the men's rooms are on the floor above mine, and there must be two separate hallways full of bedrooms, just like there are on my floor. I concentrate, thinking back over our conversations, looking for some clue . . . Got it! Wasn't Connor saying something about sending messages through the floor to Amber the other day when we briefly considered having another *Risk* night? So, that must mean . . .

I ease open the door to the stairway. The red exit sign casts a devilish glow over the stairwell. When I get up the stairs, I put my face to the glass panel. The hall seems deserted. I open the door and count doorways until I'm standing in front of the door to Amber's room, one floor up.

So this must be Connor and Henry's room. Which means, of course, that Henry *and* Connor are in there. Which is totally something I should've thought about before. Do I want Connor to know I visited Henry in the middle of the night? And what do I mean by "visiting," anyway? Well, in for a penny, in for a pound.

I reach out and turn the door handle gently. "Henry?"

I hear what seems like an answering sound and push the door open a little wider, letting the light from the hall fall across one of the single beds.

Oh crap. When am I going to learn my lesson about opening doors in the middle of the night?

There are two men in the middle of . . . fraternizing on the bed in front of me. In the light from the hallway, all I can see is that one of them has dark hair and one . . .

"Get the hell out of here!" yells the definitely gay Director.

"Sorry, sorry." I pull the door shut and shove my fist into my mouth to keep my laughter from escaping. The Director and The Banker. Who knew?

So, what now?

Good question.

I have two options. Walk back to my room and resume the endless staring at the ceiling, or hope to find Henry's room by some miracle without being discovered.

And if I'm discovered, I'll probably get tossed out. And tossed out means I've been doing all of this for nothing. That my parents are upset, my sister's feeling superior, my friends are falsely proud of me, for no good reason. And most importantly, that any future at *The Line* is history.

So, I already know what the decision has to be. But still, I hesitate.

Decisions have never my strong suit. Go home at a reasonable hour or have the next drink? Give a guy my number, or invite him to my apartment? Lie to my friends and family, or be frank and honest? I've always chosen drink, invitation, lying.

And tonight? What the hell am I going to do tonight?

Just go to bed.

That's the first sensible thing you've said . . . well, maybe ever.

I creep stealthily back to my room and crawl into bed. Muriel's lying flat on her back, snoring like a drunken sailor. I hug my pillow to my chest and wait for sleep to come.

"Are you staying in the same room as Connor?" I ask Henry in what I hope is a casual tone the next morning after our run (eighteen minutes!). It's a cloudy, cool day, a good match for my sleep-deprived, can't-believe-my-parents-will-be-here-in-an-hour state of mind.

Henry wipes the sweat from his brow with the back of his arm. "Nope."

Crap. I should've asked him while we were running. He'd probably have drawn me a map by now. Can I risk one more question?

"So, where do you sleep then?"

"Why are you so curious?"

I guess not.

"Just making conversation."

His eyes twinkle down at me. "I see."

Changing topics!

"My parents are coming today."

Now why the hell did I tell him that?

"For that family therapy thing?"

"Yeah."

He stares at me intently. "You don't sound psyched."

"Would you be?"

"I don't know if I'm qualified to say," he says gently. So gently that I feel like I might start crying.

Again with the crying! Well, no way, I'm not crying in front of Henry.

I speak quickly through the lump in my throat. "I'd better go take a shower."

"You OK?"

"Sure. I'll see you later."

"Good luck."

"Thanks."

We lock eyes for a moment. He places both his hands on my shoulders and pulls me toward him. His arms feel warm and strong around me. He smells like salt and soap.

"You'll do fine, Kate, Katie, whichever," he says close to my ear.

Crap. I'm so going to cry now.

"I've got to go." I place my hands on his chest and push him away, keeping my head down.

And before he can say anything else nice or sweet, or wipe a tear off my face, I turn and run.

My parents arrive around ten, pulling up in their battered old navy VW station wagon. I'm waiting for them on the rock retaining wall that encloses the parking lot wearing the nicest clothes I brought to rehab—a jean skirt and a light green shirt that needs pressing.

My parents climb out of the car in unison. My mom is wearing a loose khaki skirt and a white blouse, and her long gray hair is swept back in a neat bun. My dad (who wears shorts from April 1 to November 1 no matter what the weather or occasion) is wearing a pair of plaid golf shorts and a dark red polo shirt.

We hug hello, and then the day goes from bad to worse.

"What, no hug for me?" Chrissie smirks as she leans against the car. She looks smart and angry in a light gray shirtdress and more makeup than she usually wears.

What does it say about my family that we all thought Family Therapy Day had a dress code? Rehab casual by the Sandfords. Available at a Tar*get* near you.

"What's she doing here?" I ask my dad.

"This is family therapy, Katie," he answers reproachfully.

"Hah!" Chrissie sputters. "Since when has she given a shit about our family?"

I watch her angry face with regret. When I left town and didn't look back, my parents started off being proud of me, and the brand-name university I got into. But Chrissie just started off being mad. That I left her behind? That she didn't have the grades to follow me two years later? I was never sure, and, to be honest, I never bothered to ask. Then the Michael thing happened, and it was all downhill from there.

"What's your fucking problem, Chrissie?" I say loudly enough to catch the attention of Mr. Fortune 500 and several other patients who are close by.

My mother cringes. "Katie, please."

"I'm sorry, Mom, but this is hard enough without Miss Chip-on-Her-Shoulder blaming me for everything that's gone wrong in her life."

"I don't do that!"

"Yeah, you do. You know, I'm not the reason Michael cheated on you."

She flinches at the sound of his name. "He was staying at your apartment when it happened."

I turn toward my father. "You see what I mean, Dad?"

I give him my don't-you-want-to-please-your-little-lost-girl look, and I can see him softening. He's never been able to discipline me.

"Chrissie, maybe it would be better if it was just me and your mother . . ."

Chrissie's face turns red. "Unfuckingbelievable."

My mother shakes her head firmly. "No, Topher. Don't let her manipulate you."

Since when did my peace-loving mom start calling me on my shit? This is a bad, bad day.

"Mom . . ."

"No, Katie," she says, without quite looking at me. "We're all here, and we're all staying."

I can tell by the tone in my mother's voice that she's not going to cave, and I'm sick of being this minute's entertainment for the other patients. "Fine, whatever. We're late."

My sister raises her chin defiantly. Is it possible to hate someone who looks just like you?

I lead my happy family out of the fishbowl parking lot to the first session of the day: group therapy with parents and sibling in the common room. Yay.

Four of us are participating in the family program: Me, Amber, Candice, and Mr. Fortune 500. We sit around Saundra in a circle made up by the metal folding chairs we use in group.

Amber's parents are old-money WASPs with perfectly tailored clothes and accents. Amber sits between them sullenly as they each hold one of her hands. They seem sad but stoic. Candice's mother is a sixty-something version of Candice with a bad facelift who is clearly waiting for an opportunity to jump in and make it all about her. Mr. Fortune 500's wife is short and pretty in a plain, faded way. She looks miserable, but given who she's married to, I can't blame her.

Saundra welcomes us, gets everyone to introduce themselves ("My name is Topher, and my daughter is an alcoholic," says my dad nervously), and then launches into an explanation of addiction and the role that family can play in enabling it. Then she talks about ways our families can help us break past patterns and become a force in our battle to remain sober.

While Mrs. Fortune 500 and Amber's parents ask questions at regular intervals, my parents don't say anything the entire morning. They just listen to Saundra. Occasionally, my mom writes something down on the small notepad she always keeps in her purse. *Enabling,* she writes at one point. *Support system,* she writes later.

Chrissie spends much of the morning staring out the window at the lake, looking like she wants to make a break for it. I can't help but smile to myself. I'm not Miss Talk-Things-Out, but Chrissie makes Amber's WASPy, contained parents seem like contestants on *The Bachelor.* I can only wonder why she wanted to be here so much.

I don't get a chance to find out. When the session breaks up, my sister announces that she's leaving.

"But you made such a fuss before," my dad says, his eyes troubled. "Why don't you stay out the day?"

"And sit around and listen to more reasons why *we're* responsible for Katie's bullshit? No, thanks."

Amber smiles at me sympathetically as she heads toward the door with her parents.

"So leave," I say. "I never asked you to come here in the first place."

Chrissie glares at me. "No, and you never would, right?"

Sigh. We used to be so close that we liked it when people mistook us for twins. And now, I wouldn't have a clue what to say to keep her here, even if I wanted to.

"No, I wouldn't."

My mother sucks in her breath sharply, and my father makes a clucking, disapproving sound in the base of his throat. Chrissie just picks up her purse and stalks out the French doors. I watch her walk away, her shoulders stiff with anger. I know I should run after her, but I don't have the energy, or know what I could do to fix what's wrong between us.

I turn and face my parents. My father's arm is draped across my mother's shoulders, holding her close.

"Do you want to leave too?" I try to keep the note of hopefulness out of my voice.

"We're staying," my mom replies firmly, finally looking me in the eye.

OK, then.

It's time for lunch, so I take my parents to the cafeteria, where we pick at our chicken Caesar salads and make small talk. I spy Henry sitting with YJB a few tables away. He gives me a friendly wave, and I wave back.

My mom catches me at it. "Who's that?"

"Connor Parks," I answer, though I know that's not who she means.

"No, dear, not him. The one you waved at. The red-headed one."

This is so one of the reasons I didn't want my parents coming here.

"His name is Henry."

"Is he a patient?"

"No."

"Does he work on the staff?"

"No."

My father pats her arm. "Marion, honey, I don't think she wants to tell you who he is."

"Well, why not? It's a simple question."

"Maybe it's private."

"I don't think rehab is really about privacy."

"Marion, we talked about this . . . we should be supporting Katie, not pushing her."

She shakes her head. "No, I don't think that's right."

Serenity now. Serenity now.

I stand up. "We need to go to Saundra's office."

My mother looks like she wants to say something but then gives in. "All right, dear."

At her office, Saundra greets my parents and leads us into a small meeting room next to it that I've never been in before. It has a round oak table with four matching chairs and a high oblong window that lets in the light. There are (of course) framed photographs of dogs on the walls.

"What a lovely room," my mom says stopping in front of a picture of an ordinary-looking dog. "Did you take these photographs?"

Saundra beams. "Yes, I did, thank you. Dogs are a passion of mine, particularly dachshunds."

"Those are the little ones that look like hot dogs, right?"

Saundra flinches slightly at the word "hot dog." "That's right."

"How delightful. Do you breed them?"

"Yes. And I show them in competitions."

"Oh, like in that movie." My mom turns toward my father. "What was it called, Topher? That one with that actress, the funny one."

Best in Show. Catherine O'Hara.

"I don't know, honey."

"Sure you do. We watched it a couple of weeks ago. You know, the one about that dog show with those two funny men doing the commentary?"

"Best in Show," I say.

My mother's face clears. "Ah, yes. That's it. Don't you remember, Topher? *Best in Show.* It was very funny."

"You must have seen it with your other boyfriend," my father grins.

"That's one of our little jokes," my mom explains to Saundra. "Of course, I don't have a boyfriend."

Saundra looks like she doesn't know quite what to say. "Of course."

"Did you see that movie? *Best in Show*?"

"Yes, I did. It was very funny."

Oh. My. God. Aren't we supposed to be talking about me?

"I think that same cast did another one about a movie. They were trying to get an Oscar . . . Oh, now, what's *that* movie called?"

For Your Consideration. Shoot me now.

Saundra clears her throat. "Perhaps we can discuss this a little later."

"Oh yes, of course." My mom sits next to my dad and pulls her notebook and pen out of her purse, looking at Saundra expectantly.

"As we discussed this morning, the purpose of today's session is to discuss the extent of Katie's alcoholism and the way it's been affecting her life, and yours."

"So, she is an alcoholic?" my dad says, suddenly serious.

I look down at the floor and place my hands under my thighs to keep myself from launching across the table and strangling Saundra. Even though I know it's not her fault, I want to blame her anyway.

"Yes," she replies.

"Is it only alcohol?" he persists.

Yes, Daddy. Pot, hash, 'shrooms—I heard you. I did what you said.

"Perhaps Katie can answer your questions."

He turns toward me. I keep my eyes steadily on the carpet pattern. "Yes, Dad. Just alcohol."

"A lot of alcohol?"

"Sometimes."

"What does 'a lot' mean, dear?" my mom asks, her pen hovering above her notepad.

Why the hell is she taking notes, anyway? Is she really going to have trouble remembering today? Or are they going to become one of her many keepsakes, like my bronzed baby shoes and the teeth I left for the tooth fairy?

"What does it matter?"

"Katie, your family is simply trying to understand the magnitude of your problem. Be patient with them."

Impossible request.

I stare back at the floor. "Sorry."

"When did this happen, Katiekins?" my dad asks, using a nickname he hasn't used since I was thirteen, when I forbade it after he called me that in front of a boy I liked.

"I don't know. It happened gradually."

One delicious cocktail at a time, in fact.

I can hear the scratching of my mother's pen. "Is it because you're unhappy in the city? Do you find it overwhelming?"

"No."

"Is it because you don't have a boyfriend?"

"Marion, honey, that's enough."

"Can't I ask my daughter a few questions?"

"Why don't we let her tell us what she wants to tell us?"

"But she doesn't seem to want to tell us anything."

That's right. I don't. I want to scream. I want to stomp my feet. I want this session to be over. Immediately. But I don't want to tell my parents anything.

Maybe there's a way to make that happen. Not a nice way, but being nice doesn't feel like a priority right now.

"Saundra says it's because Dad let me drink when I was a child," I say, raising my eyes to catch Saundra's reaction.

My dad sucks in his breath sharply, and my mom begins to cry, her notes forgotten.

I am a terrible, terrible person.

My parents look at Saundra, waiting for an explanation. And even though I'm miserable, and guilty and sad, I feel a little bit of pleasure as her feet squirm under the table.

"Marion, Topher, what Katie is alluding to is certain discussions we've had regarding her early experiences with alcohol, which I believe occurred in family situations. This does not mean, however, that you are to blame for Katie's alcoholism. In fact, no one is to blame."

Oh, someone's to blame all right.

My dad shifts in his seat. "But it's true, we . . . I . . . let her drink when she was young. Not frequently, but . . ."

"Topher, please believe me when I tell you that there's no way of knowing whether that made a difference one way or another. In all likelihood, Katie would have developed a drinking problem regardless."

You're not getting off that easily, Saundra.

"But you said that the pervading permissiveness in my childhood was one of the reasons I failed to recognize that alcohol was detrimental to me."

Now my dad looks like he's on the verge of tears.

I am a terrible, horrible person.

"Topher, Marion, would you mind giving me a moment with Katie, please?"

My dad takes my mom by the elbow, and they both stand up. "Of course not."

They leave, and Saundra closes the door behind them. I avoid Saundra's gaze, feeling like a caged animal.

"What's going on, Katie?"

"I told you I didn't want them to come here."

She sits down next to me. "Are you trying to get them to leave?"

Well, duh.

"I don't know. Maybe."

"Katie, you're going to be leaving in a couple of days, and you need a support network so you can begin to repair the holes you've created in your life."

"Don't you mean the wide, gaping chasms?"

She almost smiles. "I don't think they're that wide, or gaping. But I am curious about something. I remember you telling me that your parents were great parents."

"Yes, they are."

"So, why are you so angry with them?"

The funny thing is, I didn't even realize I was angry with them until a few seconds ago. But I am. I'm angry with my dad for not looking surprised when he found out I was in rehab. I'm angry with my mom for trying harder to understand my "disease" than she ever did to accept my career. And I'm angry with my sister for not caring enough to stick it out to lunch. But that's just my shit, right? I came here, and now they think they have to deal with an alcoholic in the family. I shouldn't blame them for trying to understand her.

"Bring my parents back in and I'll explain."

Saundra opens the door and beckons them. I stare at the patch of gray sky I can see through the high window, not looking at them as they sit back down.

"Katie has something she'd like to say to you both."

Here goes nothing.

I force myself to look into their sad faces. "Mom, Dad, I'm sorry for what I said before."

"That's all right, dear, we understand."

"No, it's not all right. And it's not your fault. It's mine . . ." I search for the right words. For something that has a core of truth that will reassure them. "It's my fault. I'm here because I made bad choices. And I said those things because I didn't want you to come here, and I guess I was punishing you. But I wasn't being fair, and what I said wasn't true."

My dad places his hand over mine. "Why didn't you want us to come here, Katiekins?"

"Because I didn't want to involve you in this . . ."

This lie, this sham.

"But we're your family, dear. If you need help, we want to help you."

"I know, Mom."

"We love you, Katie."

"I know, Dad. Thank you for coming. Thank you for wanting to help me. It means a lot."

My mom wipes a tear away with the corner of her thumb. "Thank you for saying that, dear."

Saundra is beaming at the three of us. "I think we're making some real progress here. Don't you?"

"Yes," my dad says with a glint in his eye that isn't related to tears. "But there's still something I want to know."

"What's that?"

"Who was that man in the cafeteria?"

Chapter 19
The Last Thing I Have to Do

In group the next day, Candice raises a hand and announces that she wants to tell us why she tried to kill herself. No surprise that everyone is immediately on the edge of their seats, their faces shouting tell-me-tell-me-tell-me. We've reached rock-bottom as far as new stories are concerned. Even Connor's stories of snorting cocaine off starlets' asses are starting to wear thin.

The only one we haven't heard is the one everyone has tried to get out of Candice since she came back from the medical wing with bandages around her wrists.

Saundra looks concerned. "Candice, if you're not ready . . ."

"No, I want to."

Oh, thank God. I thought for a moment Saundra was going to talk her out of it.

"Remember, Candice, this is a safe space." Saundra looks around the room, giving The Director and The Banker a particularly hard stare.

Candice crosses her legs. She's wearing white lacy socks that disappear into a pair of black ankle boots. In fact, her whole look today is kind of Molly Ringwald circa *Pretty in Pink*.

"I'm not stupid, you know. I know most of you don't like me and make fun of me behind my back. The Former Child Star is what you call me, right?"

A shiver runs down my spine. Has she been reading my journal?

She raises her chin. "But that's not why I did what I did, OK? It wasn't because of any of you. It was because of me. Do you know that this is the *fifth* time I've been to rehab? I've spent two hundred thousand dollars on 'taking it one day at a time' and 'Kumbaya' and *It's. Not. Working*. I don't feel any different inside. I still want to use whatever I can get my hands on, and I know, when I leave here, that's exactly what I'm going to do.

"So, that's why I did it. To make the feeling inside go away." She pounds her chest. Hard. "But I couldn't even do that right. I'm still here, and nothing's changed. And I don't know what to do." She hangs her head dramatically.

The room is so quiet you could hear a pin drop. And then The Director starts to applaud in a slow, mechanized way.

"Oh, bravo," he calls. "Well done."

Mr. Fortune 500 starts to clap too. Pretty soon, half the room is clapping and throwing out wolf whistles. I even hear someone, I think it's Connor, shout, "Encore!"

Saundra raps her hand on her chair. She looks upset and angry. "Everyone, please! This is completely unacceptable! How can you violate Candice's trust after everything we've worked for . . ." Her voice trails off as she catches sight of Candice.

Because Candice isn't crying, or upset, or ashamed.

She's taking a bow.

I lean back in my chair in amazement. Despite being exposed to Amber's antics over the last four weeks, I didn't see it coming. I have to give her props, and so I clap along with the rest of them, despite the dirty looks Amber shoots me.

A few moments later, Evan and John appear to break up the disruption. Candice goes quietly. At the door, she blows us a kiss over her shoulder and says, "How do you like me now, bitches?"

"We've almost completed your program," Saundra says near the end of our session on Day Twenty-nine: Letting Go. "Do you feel ready to go home?"

Shit. I've been worried someone would tell me to leave before my work here was done.

"But I'm only up to Step Seven."

"You don't have to finish all the steps while you're here. You'll continue working on them in your AA meetings once you leave."

"Right."

Saundra looks like she hopes I'm joking. "Katie, it's very important that you keep up with meetings once you get home. Thirty in thirty is the minimum we recommend."

"Yeah, I know. So, you really think I'm ready to go home?"

She nods. "We've made some good progress on identifying the roots of your addictive patterns of behavior. We had a real breakthrough with your family, and we've started working on your sobriety plan. So, yes, I think you're ready. But it's important that you feel ready, as well."

"And if I do?"

"Then there's just one more thing you have to do."

"What's that?"

"Confess."

I join Amber for a late lunch, setting down my bowl of clam chowder on the table. She's eating a grilled cheese sandwich, taking small, even bites in a way that reminds me of Rory.

"Where are the boys?"

"Saying goodbye to Ted."

"Shit. I missed the singing?"

She smiles. "You can sing for me tomorrow."

"What do you mean?"

"I finished my program, and since I've been a model patient lately, my therapist said I could leave tomorrow if I wanted."

"Huh." I swallow a spoonful of my creamy soup. "I'm leaving tomorrow too."

"That's great," she says with mild enthusiasm.

"So, we're both leaving tomorrow?"

"Sounds like it."

I put down my spoon. "Then tell me something, why don't we seem happier about it?"

She gives me a bright smile. "'Cuz we're stupid?"

"I think we're in shock." I give myself a shake. "No more therapy, no more group, no more Saundra. This calls for a toast."

I raise my glass toward hers.

She grins and follows suit. "What shall we toast to?"

"Fortitude."

"Fortitude?"

"Yeah. Strength and endurance in painful or difficult situations."

"Sounds about right."

We clink glasses, and I down the rest of my grape juice. Not quite my usual toasting fare, but one can't be picky when celebrating one's last day in rehab.

I slap my glass down on the table upside down, like it's a shot glass. "So, what do you want to do on your last afternoon?"

She wipes away her milk mustache. "Skip group?"

"Excellent idea. I just have one thing to do first."

I wait nervously for Henry near the front door. He and Connor are finishing up their goodbyes with The Banker. Typical guys, there's not a tear in sight.

As I watch Henry throw his head back and laugh I have a moment of doubt about what I'm about to ask. But he's the only person in this place since Amy left who I feel comfortable enough with. And if another message gets sent at the same time, so much the better, right?

When the last palm has been slapped, Henry and Connor walk in my direction. Henry's wearing a rugby shirt over his cargo shorts. He looks about twenty-two.

He flashes me a smile. "Hey."

"Hey. Hi, Connor."

Connor nods hello distractedly. "You seen Amber?"

"I left her in the caf."

"Righto. Catch you later, man?"

"Later. What's up, Kate?"

I nibble on the end of my thumb. "Um . . . well . . . I'm leaving tomorrow."

"Hey, that's great."

"Yeah, it is. Amber's leaving too."

"Really? I never would've thought that she'd leave before Connor could."

"Yeah, that surprised me a little too. But he's got, what, eight, nine days left?"

"Eight days, four hours."

"But who's counting? Can we sit?"

"Sure."

We walk to the library and sit in the armchairs where we had our first real conversation. It seems fitting, since after tonight, this will probably be our last conversation.

Henry looks at me expectantly. I don't know what he's expecting, but I'm sure it's not what I'm about to say.

"Um . . . I wanted to ask you a favor."

"Sure."

"But you don't know what it is yet."

"Is it that bad?"

"Well, you might consider it an imposition, and please feel free to say no . . ."

"Just ask me, Kate."

"OK. Well, you know about the twelve steps, right?"

He waves his hands at the books that surround us. "It would be hard not to."

"Right. So, one of the steps is that you have to admit, like, the 'nature of our wrongs' to another person, and well, usually, it's to a priest or something, but I don't believe in that so . . ."

Oh. My. God. I sound like a Valley girl.

Henry furrows his brow. "You want to confess your wrongs to me?"

"If you wouldn't mind."

"Isn't that kind of personal?"

"Well, that's kind of why I wanted it to be you . . ." I pause. Here comes the hard part. "Because, um, I think it's important to confess to someone you trust but who isn't really a part of your life, so I can confess, and start to move on."

The unsaid words "without you" hang in the air between us.

"I see."

"And I trust you . . ."

His face is expressionless. "And I'm not really a part of your life . . ."

His measured words hit me like individual punches to the chest. Bam, bam, bam, bam. But hey, I asked for this.

"Will you do it?" I force myself to ask.

He looks away. "Yeah, all right."

"Thanks. Are you free after the movie tonight?"

"Won't you be breaking curfew?"

"I don't think that really matters anymore."

He turns back to me and it's like he's looking at a stranger. "OK. This is your show."

I guess it is. But then, how come I don't know how it ends?

After Henry leaves, I spend the rest of the afternoon in the library working on the list of things I'm going to confess to him.

I don't really know why I'm even going through with this step, but I feel like, somewhere along the way, all of this went from being a big joke to being something important. Maybe it was the sessions with my parents, or maybe it's the things Saundra's been saying since I got here. It's not that I think I really, truly, deeply have a drinking problem, but I can see why someone might think I do. And regardless, I need to make some changes in my life. Clearly.

Besides, all this soul-searching is somehow easier than thinking about the blank expression on Henry's face when the reason I was asking him to take my confession sunk in.

Well, he's better off without me. He'll know that once he's heard the worst about me. And since nothing's ever happened between us . . . no harm, no foul, right?

So, I'll confess my sins, and he'll walk away, and then I can just be the girl he went running with while he babysat Connor in rehab, and he can be one more guy I pushed away before things got messy.

When dinnertime comes around, I fold up my notes and take my usual seat next to Amber in the cafeteria. Connor and Henry sit opposite us. We all seem a little out of sorts, like nobody wants to acknowledge that this is our last night together.

Near the end of dinner, Amber says, "So, I've arranged a pickup tomorrow if you want a lift back to the city."

"You're going to drive back?"

"I don't like to fly if I don't have to."

"OK, sure, thanks. What time?"

"Right after breakfast."

"Sounds perfect."

Henry stands abruptly and picks up his tray. "Should we watch the movie?"

Connor eyes Amber across the table. "We'll catch you later."

Amber's gaze is locked on his. "Yeah, later."

Henry and I walk to the common room. Candice and Muriel are sitting together near the screen, whispering conspiratorially. I wave to Muriel. She looks affronted and whispers something emphatically to Candice. A match made in rehab heaven.

The lights dim, and in keeping with the perpetual romantic-comedy theme, tonight's movie is a BBC adaptation of Jane Austen's *Persuasion*. Anne, the smart middle daughter of a foolish baronet, falls in love with a poor, handsome naval officer named Frederick. Her family is very much against the match, and they part. Eight years later, a now rich Frederick moves back to the neighborhood, still angry with Anne for ditching him all those years ago.

As we watch the movie, I'm hyperaware that Henry is sitting next to me, and of what we're going to do afterward.

Maybe it's just the melodrama unfolding on the screen, but it seems like a part of my life is ending, and I'm feeling every second of it.

I shake these thoughts away and try to enjoy the movie, which is quite good and faithful to the book until . . .

"No, no, no," I mutter under my breath.

On screen, Anne is running through the streets of Bath, trying to find Frederick after he confesses his constant love in a letter.

I give a snort of disgust. "This so did not happen in the book."

"What? Women didn't run after men in Austenian England?"

"Of course they didn't."

Anne finally catches up to Frederick and tells him that nothing will keep her from marrying him this time. They kiss (a sweaty, panting kiss in the middle of the street!), and it's the end. As the lights go up, I rant to Henry about the need to modernize a story that was perfectly good just the way it was written.

Henry gives me a teasing smile. "Why do you care so much?"

"Because the original was perfection."

"Oh, really?"

"You've never read it?"

"Do I look like a girl?"

"No, an English grad student."

"Touché."

We lapse into silence as we both remember what comes next.

"You ready?" I ask.

Henry puts his hands in the front pockets of his jeans. His expression is the same inscrutable one from earlier. "Sure. Should we go to the library?"

"No. Follow me."

We walk along the path we've run on so many times, finding our way by the light of the moon. The air is still warm from the day, and it's a clear night. A thousand galaxies are half visible through the canopy of trees above.

I'm looking for a particular place, a tall maple that dwarfs the sky, a tree that always astounds me whenever I run past it. I can see it up ahead, its leaves blowing gently in the breeze. We reach it and I drop to the ground, crossing my legs.

Henry sits down in front of me. "So, what do I do?"

Please, don't hate me.

"Nothing. Just listen."

I take out the paper I wrote on this afternoon. It doesn't contain the whole truth, it can't, but it's mostly there. The worst of me is there.

I take out my iTouch and turn it on so I can see the harsh words on the page. It glows brightly, making a cocoon of light around me. I can almost imagine I'm alone.

I clear my throat. "This is my confession. I am a liar. I keep people at arm's length. I use alcohol as a shield. I have betrayed my friends. I have betrayed people who aren't my friends . . ."

I read slowly until I get to the bottom of the page, giving each sentence its due. Then I turn it over and read everything I wrote on the back too.

Henry listens. I can hear him breathing, but he doesn't say anything.

I get to the end. "I am a liar," I repeat, reading the last thing I've written. The last and the first thing about me are the same.

Do you get it, Henry? Do you get it?

I use my left hand to clear the leaves from the patch of ground between us. I snap off the iTouch and reach into my pocket for the lighter I brought with me. I hold it to the edge of the paper, waiting for it to catch.

"Do you think that's a good idea?" Henry says.

"Shh."

The fire catches hold. I drop the paper onto the patch of cleared ground, watching the flames eat away at the lines I wrote. The charred bits break away and float up toward the trees.

I watch until it's all burned away. Until there's nothing left.

"What now?" Henry asks.

I try to meet his eyes, but it's too dark to see.

"Now, we forget that any of this ever happened."

Chapter 20
Pavlovian Response to Bullshit

The next morning, after Amber and I have been sung to in the cafeteria, I find Saundra in her office, doing paperwork. She looks up when I rap on her door.

"I was just coming to say goodbye."

She smiles and puts down her pen. "I'm glad you did."

"And I wanted to say thank you, you know, for putting up with me, etc."

"It was my pleasure. Good luck, Katie."

"Thanks." I hesitate. "Can I ask you one last thing?"

"Of course."

"I know this is going to sound silly, but it's something I've been wondering about for a while . . ."

"Go ahead."

"Who's that dog collar for?"

Saundra's laughter follows me down the hall to the lobby, where Amber's waiting for me with Carol.

As I sign my discharge papers I wonder whether Henry's going to show up. But then, there he is, talking to Amber. He says something in a low voice that I can't make out, and she shakes her head. He turns away from her looking aggravated but gives me a small smile when he catches me watching them.

"You all set?" he says, walking toward me.

"I think so."

"Maybe I'll see you around the park sometime . . ."

"Sure."

He looks into my eyes, staring at me intently. We're both waiting for the other to say something (Call me? Stay? I'll miss you? Thank you?), but neither of us wants to be the first to speak.

"Take care of yourself, Kate, Katie, whichever," he finally says.

"Thank you, Henry."

"You bet."

He gives me one last shoulder squeeze and walks away. I watch him go, but like with my sister, I don't know what to say to bring him back to me, or even if that's what I want.

I brush my tears away quickly, and follow Amber outside. We climb into a huge black SUV while the driver puts our bags in the back.

We don't talk much on the long drive, both of us lost in our thoughts. When we get to the city, everything looks different from when I left a month ago; it's like the movies, when a fast-motion camera speeds up the seasons. Then the trees were budding; now they're in full bloom. People everywhere are wearing less clothing. Winter is a faint memory.

"Hey, Katie," Amber calls to me through the sunroof as I climb up my front steps.

I turn. Only her head is visible above the roofline. Her long black hair swirls around her. A few pedestrians stop to look, trying to figure out who she is.

"Yeah?"

"Thank you."

"For what?"

"You know . . . for everything."

One of the pedestrians across the street figures it out. He pulls out his phone and begins snapping pictures.

"Forget it. And you're on *Candid Camera*," I nod toward the dude snapping away.

She spins around and gives him her patented smile. "You got your shot, lover?"

The pedestrian looks flustered. "Sorry."

"Don't worry about it. Just get a good price for it, OK? The Girl Next Door Returns from Rehab ought to be worth something."

He looks like he doesn't quite know what to do with this information. "OK."

She turns back to me, laughing. "I'll call you later."

Her head disappears through the roof. The SUV slips into gear and disappears into traffic.

Well, that's that.

I haul my suitcase up the front stairs of my building and into my apartment.

"Joanne?" My voice bounces off the walls, and I can tell there's no one home.

I wheel my suitcase into my room, then head to the kitchen

to see what's in the fridge. It's half empty, and what's there is labeled "Joanne's" in black indelible marker. God forbid she should break with that habit while I was away.

I help myself to some of her leftover beef in Thai basil sauce, eating it cold from the carton. God that tastes good. Thirty days without Thai food—how did I ever survive?

I polish off the container leaning over the sink in our tiny kitchen, looking out the small window at the brick-wall view. Maybe when I get the job at *The Line* I'll finally be able to afford a better apartment sans roommate?

I guess I should call Bob and let him know I'm back. Or maybe I'll just send him an email. I'm sure he has bigger things to worry about than me. Yeah, I'll send an email. That'll be fine.

Why don't you want to call him?

Are you still here?

Where would I go?

I thought I might've left you behind.

No such luck.

Shit.

So, why don't you want to call him?

Because I'm tired, and I don't feel like dealing with that right now.

Dealing with what?

You know.

What?

You *know*. Why I went to rehab. The article.

You don't want to write the article?

Not at this moment, no.

Why not?

Oh, will you just leave me alone.

I toss the empty food container into the garbage, making sure to bury it halfway down so Joanne won't notice it. I head to the living room to sit on the worn couch and watch TV. I hold the remote lovingly in my hand. Ah, TV. I've missed you, my friend.

I channel surf until I come to a rerun of *Lost*. It's the first episode. Jack has just woken up on the beach, the sound of a whirring jet engine blocking out the screams of his fellow passengers. I pull a blanket off the back of the couch and lay it across my knees, snuggling down for a good escape to a desert island. It'd be nice to go there. You know, without the smoke monster, and wild boars, and those pesky Others.

As I watch Jack race around the beach saving lives, I can feel my eyelids getting heavy. Instead of fighting it, I give in, letting myself float away, though the dialogue is still reaching some part of my brain. Kate is sewing Jack up, and she's scared. Give yourself five seconds to be afraid, he says. And then you have to stop.

Just five seconds.

I'm having a dream that's a mixed-up jumble of *Lost* and what I've just left. "You can do it, Kate," Jack says, before dissolving into Dr. Houston. "Count to five and you can go to sleep."

"But I *am* sleeping," I say.

"So, wake up then."

"I don't want to."

"Well, too bad."

The blanket is pulled from my knees, and I feel cold. Why is Jack/Dr. Houston being so mean to me?

"Why did you eat my food?"

I open my eyes. Joanne is standing above me holding the Thai food container I buried in the trash. It's covered with coffee grounds and a few pieces of broken eggshell.

"Is this your way of telling me you missed me?"

Joanne folds her arms across her maroon polo shirt. "Well?"

I guess not.

"Relax, Joanne."

"But that's what I was going to have for dinner."

"So we'll order some more. My treat."

Her eyebrows rise. "You're paying? Fine. I want chicken pad Thai, extra spicy."

"Then that's what you'll have." I stand up and stretch. I have a terrible crick in my neck. "What time is it, anyway?"

"About six thirty. When did you get home?"

"Around one."

"Have you been sleeping this whole time?"

"Pretty much."

"Tough day at the office?"

"Knock it off, Joanne."

She looks contrite. "Sorry. How come you didn't tell me you were coming home?"

"Don't take it personally. I didn't tell anyone."

"I wasn't taking it *personally.*"

"If you say so. I'm going to take a shower."

She picks up her cell phone. "Do you want me to order for you?"

"Nah, that's OK. I'll just eat some of yours."

She frowns. "You didn't change one bit in rehab, did you?"

"Oh, I've changed a few things."

The food arrives just as I've finished drying my hair. I fork over forty bucks to the delivery guy and tell him to keep the change, feeling generous and, finally, a little celebratory.

We unload the pad Thai and mee grob Joanne ordered for me onto plates and munch in companionable (sort of) silence around the tiny circular table tucked into the corner of the living room. I look around our apartment, sensing that something's different, but I can't quite put my finger on it.

"Did you move some of the furniture?" I ask.

She puts a large pile of noodles in her mouth. "No."

I push my seat away from the table and put my hands on my protruding stomach, enjoying the comfortable almost-eaten-enough-to-be-sick-but-not-quite feeling.

"You've lost weight," Joanne says, looking jealous.

Fourteen pounds to be exact. I'm back to where I was when I started university, and feeling pretty good about it.

"True."

"It suits you."

"Thanks, Joanne."

Our doorbell buzzes, the loud *zzzttt* making us both jump.

"Could you get that?" she asks.

"It's probably those Mormon guys again. They'll go away."

Zzzttt!

Joanne gives me a furtive look. "I think you should get it."

"Joanne, what did you do?"

"Nothing."

"Cut the crap, Joanne."

"I may have called a few people."

Zzzttt!

Shit.

"You could've asked me before you invited people over."

She picks up our plates and walks them toward the kitchen. "Well, soorrryyy for trying to do something nice for you. It won't happen again."

I walk to the door and press the intercom button.

"Who is it?"

"IT'S US!"

I press the buzzer and open the door. Greer, Scott, and Rory clomp up the stairs, grinning at me like I've just given birth. Rory's wearing a peach dress that complements her glowing olive skin. She looks like she's put on a few more pounds since she visited me in rehab.

"Are you surprised?" Rory asks as I close the door behind them.

"Very."

"What's with the stealth homecoming?" Scott says. His sandy hair is a little longer than he usually wears it, and it falls across his forehead in a seductive, I'm-probably-no-good-for-you kind of way.

Greer throws her arm across my shoulder. "Yeah, lassie. We wanted to throw you a party."

Rory looks shocked. "Greer! I'm sure Katie doesn't want a P-A-R-T-Y."

"I haven't suddenly turned into a three-year-old, Ror."

"Sorry."

"That's OK. Anyway, you're right. I'm not really up for a party right now, but I would love to hang out with you guys."

Greer plops down on the couch and plunks her worn-in cowboy boots on the coffee table. Her braids hang over her shoulders. "Excellent."

"Hey, no feet on the table," Joanne says as she comes out of the kitchen.

"Ah, Joanne. How lovely to see you again."

I sit down next to Greer. Scott sits on my other side, and we both put our feet on the coffee table next to Greer's, giggling.

"I said . . ."

I sigh. "Oh, will you relax already, Joanne? You found this table on a street corner."

"It's an antique."

"It was in someone's trash."

"Hey, I thought this was supposed to be a party," Scott says. "Where do you keep the mixers?"

My eyes flit to the corner of the room. I finally realize what it is about the apartment that's changed. The liquor cabinet, and the wine stand that sat next to it, are gone.

"Joanne, did you toss all the alcohol?"

Her chin lifts. "Yes."

I feel a flash of anger that's replaced by something closer to . . . gratitude, I guess.

"Wow, that's, um, really sweet of you, actually."

Greer is incredulous. "It's a crime, that is."

"We don't need alcohol to have a good time, do we?" Rory asks, looking at me with apprehension.

"Of course we don't."

Scott looks disappointed, but Greer simply looks philosophical.

"What do you guys want to do?" Scott asks.

"Anyone up for a game of *Risk*?"

I wake up the next morning early, feeling confused. I reach out my hands, expecting to hit air. Instead I come across more mattress, and I realize that I'm in my own bed, in my own apartment, free.

I look at the clock. It's 7:02. Outside of rehab, I haven't been up this early in a good way since I can't remember when. I've seen it plenty of bad ways, of course. Coming home from after-hours places, doing the walk of shame, waking up to puke.

But enough of that. That's the past. I have my future to start. So, action plan. Get up. Go for a run. Call Bob. Write story. Land dream job.

Piece of cake.

I pull out the snazzy shorts and workout top I got when

Rory bought me that gym membership. They're loose on me despite the massive dinner I ate last night. Oh rehab diet, please let your effects be permanent.

I let myself out of the apartment quietly and walk down to the street. I decide to run ten minutes in one direction, and then head back.

I put the iTouch on shuffle, and the first song it kicks up is The Fray's "How to Save a Life." I never really listened to the words before, which is clearly why I never realized this song is about an intervention.

I hit the skip button. Coldplay's "Fix You" starts to play.

This is ridiculous. Has my iTouch achieved sentience?

I hit the skip button again. OK. Matt Nathanson's "All We Are." Much better. A nice little love song. Or, maybe not. In fact, this is so not the song to make me forget about how much easier running was when I had Henry's constant chatter to listen to.

Maybe I don't need to be listening to music right this very minute.

I turn it off and concentrate on the patterns on the sidewalk and the sounds of the city waking up around me. It feels strange running here. The air is different, for starters. And then there's the noise. At the Oasis, I was in, well, an oasis. The only noises were the birds, the bugs, the frogs, or the very occasional car that drove past the road on the other side of the wall. But here, delivery trucks backing up, horns tooting, and the babble of very busy people on their cell phones assaults me. And the smell. Old garbage, car exhaust, millions of bodies.

I don't remember the city smelling this bad. Maybe I'm just used to the sweet smell of dew-covered grass and spring wild-flowers, but I feel raw, like a new baby brought home from the hospital in a little pink cap.

This is probably why people run in the park, right? Isn't that what Henry said? "Maybe I'll see you around the park sometime?" That was a clue. Only Henry's still in rehab, so maybe he was speaking generically? Or maybe he was warning me? Telling me he runs in the park so I could avoid it if I didn't want to see him. And I don't want to see him, right? That's what the whole Confessions of a Thirty-Year-Old Drama Queen was all about, wasn't it?

Argh! So glad I've brought my spinning brain home with me, intact.

I loop around the block and head back to the apartment, finally falling into a good, mindless rhythm. I sprint the last block, feeling exhilarated. I check my watch. Nineteen min-utes, thirty seconds. I shaved half a minute off on my way back. I rock!

I bound up the stairs to the apartment. Back in my room, I find a piece of paper on my bed with Joanne's scrawl across it. *Bob says show up at his office ASAP or else.*

Time to face the music.

"What the fuck is that?" Bob says, shoving a picture of a black SUV in my face an hour later.

"A picture of a black SUV?"

"Don't play cute with me, Kate. Who's in the fucking SUV?"

I take the picture. It's the SUV Amber and I left rehab in yesterday. And just visible through the tinted windows are Amber and . . . me.

"Amber's in the SUV."

Bob folds his arms across his expensive blue business shirt. "That's right. And what's wrong with this picture?"

I notice the white logo in the corner. "It's on TMZ's website?"

"Right again. And what I want to know is why it's not on *my* website?"

I expel a long breath. I was worried about this briefly yesterday when we were attacked by the paparazzi who'd waited patiently for Amber for thirty-five days.

"I didn't want to blow my cover."

He looks down at me in a way that's almost menacing. "*I see.* You didn't want to blow your *cover.*"

Uh-oh.

"There were only a few people who knew Amber was leaving, and they aren't the type who'd alert the paparazzi. She would've known it was me."

"So?"

"So . . . I thought it was a good idea to maintain my cover as long as possible."

"No. You had to maintain your cover as long as you were in rehab. Now that you're out, I don't give a fuck."

"But I'm still gathering stuff for my article . . ."

Bob's eyes narrow in anger. "Kate, I have a Pavlovian

response to bullshit. And let me tell you, my salivary glands are working overtime right now."

"What do you want me to say?"

"I want you to tell me that everything is on track, and that your article is going to be on my desk by next Friday."

"Or what?"

Whoops.

Bob's face gets red. "Or I'm invoking clause seven of your contract, and you owe us $30,000. I may even sue you for damages if I can stomach talking to our lawyers more than I already have to."

Clause seven? $30,000? Shit. I really should've read that thing more closely. Or, you know, not made such a major life decision in the time it takes for words to travel through the space between two people.

"You're not going to have to do that."

"You'll deliver?"

"Yes."

"Everything?"

"Yes."

"Good."

He walks behind his desk, his mind clearly already onto the next thing. I rise to leave, my shoulders slouched, my head down.

Fuck, fuck, fuck! This is by far the stupidest thing I've ever done. Why the hell did I ever agree to this? Oh, right . . . wait a minute . . .

"Um, Bob."

He barely looks up from the papers he's shuffling through. "Yes?"

"What about the job at *The Line*?"

"It's still available."

"Available for me?"

"Maybe. If you deliver."

His eyes meet mine, but I can't read his expression. I wish my salivary glands could tell me whether he's being truthful, or whether he's simply keeping this possibility alive to get what he needs from me.

"I'll deliver."

He smiles that same slightly perverted smile he gave me a month ago in this very office. "You'd better."

Chapter 21
Detritus

Day One: Operation Write Killer Exposé about TGND.

I'm sitting at my computer looking for a way into the story I have nine days to write. And that sounds like a long time, right? It sounds like . . . 216 hours. But I have to sleep, so it's really like . . . 144 hours, if I get a good night's sleep. Which I'm probably not going to, so it's probably more like 171 hours. But then I need to eat at least three times a day (20 hours), and take showers (4.5 hours), and take breaks (10 hours), leaving me 136.5 hours. Shit, I forgot running. Not that that takes much time, but still. OK, minus another five hours for running (let's be optimistic), which makes 131.5 hours.

And now I've just wasted at least ten minutes figuring that out. Great time management.

OK, focus. What am I going to write? What have I learned? What am I trying to say?

I have no frickin' idea.

I can't even pick a title.

All I can think of are silly variations on existing titles like

Amber, Interrupted and *Amber Doesn't Live Here Anymore.* It's all derivative and boring.

Maybe I'm derivative and boring, and I'll only be able to write a derivative and boring article? Maybe if it sucks they won't run it, and I can get myself out of a sticky spot without any collateral damage? Yeah, that might work. But then, of course, no job at *The Line,* either. And really, who cares if it's badly written? Was the piece that made *Gossip Central* famous actually well written? Did anyone read it and think, now there's a nice turn of phrase, or, what a little gem of alliteration? Hell, no. The only important thing was, is, the information, and so long as it makes it from my brain to the page, it won't matter if it's written in the passive voice or full of dangling participles. It won't matter to anyone but me.

So, what do I write? What leaves my brain and what stays behind?

My mental state is not being helped by the fact that I received a text from Amber as I walked home from Bob's office. (Writer's procrastination tip number one: Walk everywhere.) We'd exchanged phone numbers on the ride home, but I didn't really expect her to keep in touch.

But *beep, beep* went my phone, and there it was, a text from TGND.

Where RU?
Walking. U?
Luxuriating.
Big word.

Big soft bed.

Alone?

Course!

What's up?

Hiding from the paps. U?

Trying to get a job.

Good luck.

Thx.

Did I really just solicit Amber's luck to get a job at her expense? What the hell is wrong with me?

Fuck, this is depressing. You'd think that after having sat around doing essentially nothing for the last month I'd be full of get-up-and-go. Full of vim and vigor. Full of . . . shit, I'm all out of aphorisms. Wait, is that the right term? No, I don't think so. Argh. OK, OK, it'll come to me . . . idiom? Right, idioms. Anyway, I'm all out of idioms, or stupid phrases that mean I should be full of energy.

My stomach rumbles as my phone *beep, beeps.* I stretch my arms over my head. My entire body creaks and pops from sitting in one spot for so long. (OK, it was just a couple of hours, but it felt really long.) I dig my phone out of my purse and read Greer's text.

Party 2nite?

Party?

Oops.

It's OK.

How bout dins @ the pub?

? time.

Any.

CU soon.

:)

Perfect. Exactly what I need. (Writer's procrastination tip number two: Have long meals with friends.) I'll distract myself for a few hours having dinner with Greer, get to bed early, and work a solid eight hours tomorrow. I'll be wasting a few hours, but that will still leave me at least a hundred if I start bright and early.

Plenty of time.

Meeting Greer at the pub starts to feel like a bad idea about thirty seconds after I enter the place. That's as long as it takes to shift my attention from the smell of stale beer to the pretty rows of bottles behind Steve's head.

The problem is, I haven't fully decided if I'm really giving up drinking for good, or just until I turn in my article and secure my future. Either way, it means I'm not drinking right now, and that feels harder than I thought it would in this environment.

I slide into the red vinyl booth across from Greer. She's wearing a white peasant blouse and her long curly hair cascades past her shoulders. She looks striking, as always, though I notice that the whites of her eyes are bloodshot.

"Rough night?"

She takes a sip of her Bloody Mary. "You don't even want to know."

She's probably right, but I can't help feeling a little jealous.

"Anyone I know?"

She waves her hand dismissively. The smell of alcohol wafts toward me. "Just another scrounger. Say, did anything ever happen with that guy?"

"What guy?"

"The one passing the football with Connor Parks."

"Oh, him. Henry."

Henry. The guy I've spent absolutely no time thinking about since I left rehab.

"Yeah, him. Give."

"There's nothing to tell."

"Bollocks."

"Really, there isn't."

And there never will be, thanks to me.

A waitress comes to our table and Greer taps the edge of her drink and raises two fingers. After a moment's hesitation, I order a Diet Coke and try to feel virtuous.

Greer smiles. "Still not drinking, I see?"

"I did just get out of rehab."

"When I got out of rehab I celebrated for three days." She looks thoughtful. "I think that's how I ended up in the city, come to think of it."

"Well, I'm not you," I say a little stiffly.

"Whoa, lass, you don't have to go all *Joanne* on me."

I start to laugh. "You really know how to cut a girl to the quick."

"Just trying to make sure my friend's still in there."

Oh, she's still in here. And I'm sure she'll come out soon enough.

"Seriously, though, lass, if my drinking bothers you, just say the word."

"Thanks. But I'm OK for now."

The waitress brings our drinks and Greer pulls out the celery stalk, raises her glass to her lips, and takes a large sip. She leans back against the booth, giving me the once over.

"So, tell me, what was that cloak-and-danger stuff all about?"

I nearly choke on my Diet Coke. Somehow in all the chaos, I forgot about Greer's involvement in the password fiasco.

"Oh, that. Thanks, by the way."

"No problem. You ready to tell me about it, then?"

I suddenly want to. I want to tell someone all about everything I've done and been through. And not in the way Bob wants me to. Or in the way that Saundra would, either. I don't want to go to a meeting. I don't want to confess. I just want someone to squeal and say, "Oh my God!" and hold me if I have to cry (which, given my recent track record, is fairly likely), and forgive me at the end of it all.

And so, I warn Greer that something big is coming, and tell her all about it.

Day Two: Actually Have to Write Something Today.

The day begins with a run along the waterfront (twenty-two minutes), the healthiest breakfast ever (yogurt and fresh fruit), and a text from Amber wondering if I want to go shopping with her later.

Shit. Doesn't this woman have any friends? It's like she has some sixth sense that she should be bugging me about something.

No, Katie, that's just your conscience bugging you.

I wish it wouldn't.

'Tsha, right.

While I try to decide how to answer Amber, I tear the pages out of my journal and spread them out on the floor. My careful notes from the first few weeks gave way to random scrawls and keywords, which I'm now having trouble deciphering.

Like this one: *Fight Club & Fireflies*. What the hell does that mean?

I remember our conversation about fireflies . . . we went for a walk after the movie one night (*27 Dresses*—skip it), and we came upon a swarm of fireflies, all flashing on and off. It was just like that Andrew Ryan song "Lay You Down" except that Amber and I aren't, you know, romantically involved. Anyway, Amber exclaimed in surprise; she'd never seen live fireflies before.

But *Fight Club*? I scan the movie in my head. Tyler Durden? Brad Pitt? Edward Norton? Nope, nope, nope. Making soap from human fat? No. Punching each other in the face? Not that either . . . wait a sec . . . OK, she was saying she wished they showed good movies, and we started talking about rehab movies, and one of us brought up *Fight Club*, and how Edward Norton's character met his girlfriend in a support group. She told me that she did that sometimes when she was bored. She'd put on a disguise and sit in on twelve-step meetings. AA. Overeaters Anonymous (though she was asked to leave that one, and none too politely). Anger management. People obsessed with being obsessed.

Was this note supposed to remind me to write something about her attending twelve-step meetings as an analogy for our celebrity-focused culture? Was I really being that deep? Somehow I doubt it.

I toss the page aside and pick up another, and another, but nothing good comes of it. Around five, I give up in disgust and hunker down under a blanket on the couch. I pop season one of *The Wire* into the DVD player. (Writer's procrastination tip number three: Get engrossed in a serialized television series, preferably one with many seasons available on DVD.) I watch half the season, and write nothing. Better luck tomorrow.

Days Three and Four: Really Need to Write Anything Now or Tight Feeling in Chest Is Going to Require Medical Attention.

More running (twenty and nineteen minutes—backsliding, I know, but I'm distracted, and barely sleeping), more healthy food. More texts from Amber that I dodge. Many hours spent pondering my dilemma, and the advice Greer gave me a few nights ago.

"Don't write the article," she said matter-of-factly when I asked her what I should do.

"But it's the only way I'll get the job at *The Line*."

"So? There'll be other jobs."

"But I'm already thirty. Writing about music is a young person's job."

"You're thirty?"

Ah, shit.

"Right, that's another thing I forgot to tell you. I'm not twenty-five. And, um, I'm not a university student, at least not anymore."

She looked at me like I was a stranger as the pub music pounded around us. "You're not in grad school?"

"No."

"Why did you say you were?"

"It's just the way I get, I mean got, free food and alcohol . . . hanging out on the university wine-and-cheese circuit."

"OK. But why lie to me once we became friends?"

Good question.

"I don't know. It seemed easier, I guess."

She popped a tomato-flavored ice cube into her mouth. "Interesting."

"Are you mad?"

"I'm not sure."

"Would you be mad if you were Amber?"

"Oh yeah."

"So, what do I do?"

"I told you already, don't write it."

"But if I don't, Bob is going to make me pay back the rehab fees, and probably sue me. I don't have that kind of money. I'm totally broke."

"You're in a bit of a pickle, then."

"Gee, thanks for stating the obvious."

"Sorry, lass."

"You wouldn't happen to have a spare thirty thou sitting around, would you?"

She laughs. "What? For the likes of your lying arse?"

"Not a chance, right?"

"Too bloody right."

So, find a way to get $30,000, or write the article. The two choices loom over me until neither seems desirable or even feasible. Quite the pickle, indeed.

Eighty hours and counting.

Day Five: Surprised to Learn That I Don't Actually Function Better Under Pressure.

After another nearly sleepless night (eight potential work hours recovered, but totally wasted), and more staring at the blank page, I break down and tell Rory. (Writer's procrastination tip number four, just discovered: Confessing to friends takes a lot of time.)

I'm not sure why I choose this exact moment to tell Rory. Is it because I want her to absolve me? Do I think she'll write me a check for $30,000? Am I the worst person in the world if the second possibility is equally likely as the first?

Yes.

OK, OK, I know.

So, I bring Rory takeout to her office and tell her the whole story while our lunch gets cold.

After several minutes of silence, she finally speaks in a tightly controlled voice. "Are you only telling me this because you know I'll find out when the article gets published?"

No. The right answer to this question is no.

"I don't know, Rory. I'm telling you for lots of reasons."

"Like what?"

"Well, I haven't liked lying to you all this time. And because I need your help."

Her sarcastic snort bounces around the room. "My help? To do what?"

"To figure out what I'm supposed to do."

She closes the takeout container and tosses it in the trash. She hasn't eaten a bite.

"It's simple. Don't write the article."

"But then Bob's going to sue me."

"I doubt it."

"No, you don't know this guy. He will."

"Well, then tough shit, right?"

"But I could lose everything."

"Haven't you already lost everything?"

"I didn't think so," I say, hoping to soften the hard lines her face has settled into. It doesn't, and so I leave before she says something irretrievable and irreparable.

Sixty-seven hours left.

Day Six: Crunch Time.

I wake early. I finally slept last night out of utter exhaustion, but it was a bad-dream sleep. Amber, Henry, Connor, Rory, Greer, Scott, my parents, Chrissie all took their turns accusing me of things I've never done, a Ring-Around-the-Rosie of "You Suck, Katie, You're an Awful Person."

And every time I tried to tell them that they had it all wrong, no sound would come out. I woke up several times, but I couldn't escape the dream. It was always waiting for me the moment I fell back to sleep. Ah, there you are, Katie, we've been expecting you. Don't think you can get away from us that easily.

I wipe the sleep from my eyes and tie my hair back with an elastic. Still in my pajamas, I sit down in front of my computer. The light streams in the dirty window and lands on my desk, warming my keyboard. Everything is all set for me to write.

I just have to find a way in.

I wish I had a higher power to pray to, that I believed in something, anything bigger than me. In the tree outside my window, or the little patch of grass between the sidewalk and the street. In the small square of sky visible above the buildings. In me.

I wish this choice didn't feel so elemental, like standing on a precipice. Write the story. Don't write the story. Get everything you've always wanted, but lose everything you already have. Lose everything you've always wanted and be left with . . . nothing, it still seems like nothing.

I am nothing, I am nothing, I. Am. Nothing.

If I say it enough times, I can make it come true.

So do it then.

Do what?

Write. Anything. Everything. Just try. Like Rory said, you have nothing to lose.

I have nothing to lose.

Now you're getting it.

But what about ... ?

Forget it. Tabula rasa.

Start over?

No ... start at the beginning.

I can do that.

When the Stars Go Blue
By Kate Sandford

The first time I see Amber Sheppard in the flesh, she's acting like a frog.

She's been in rehab for six days, detoxing from the combination of cocaine, alcohol, and nicotine that's been her rocket fuel for the last six months. She's very thin, and wearing a green velour tracksuit. Her black hair is slicked back into a bun. She sits on her heels on a chair in a circle of fellow addicts.

She croaks. She has our full attention.

I spend the whole day writing. It spills out of me, day after day, thought after thought, conversation after conversation. The little confidences. The strange behavior. Connor. Everything I know, and some things I guess. A little novella of the days of her life that I shared.

I don't know if it's what Bob is looking for. I don't know what it says about Amber, or about me (though I try to keep me out of it). I only know that as I transfer the memories from my brain to the paper, I feel lighter. Not because I'm doing something good, or right, but because of the weight of it all. The last six days of agonizing about how I was going to write the story, if I was going to write it. That's all gone now. I've written it. Maybe I'll turn it in. Maybe I won't. But I have one less decision to make now, and that feels good.

I run a spell check as the sun disappears behind the cityscape, then press print and listen to the clickety-clack of my printer forming words on paper. I'm going to have to read it all again tomorrow to clean it up, but I want a paper copy in case my ancient computer crashes.

I have two days to polish it, and then the next day, deadline day, I'll decide if I'm going to turn it in.

Sounds like a plan.

I stack the pages neatly on the edge of my desk and stick an old rock from my parents' garden on top of it. I save the document one last time and shut down my computer. I inhale and exhale a long, deep breath.

And then I go out and get completely fucking drunk.

Chapter 22
The Boys Are Back in Town

It all starts when I agree to meet Amber and a few of her friends for dinner.

Why, oh why, would I do such a thing given what I've just spent the day doing?

Am I a total masochist? A glutton for punishment? Have I gone totally insane/developed a superhuman ability to withstand guilt?

No.

I am, however, fond of Amber, and in the small corner of my brain that isn't swayed or controlled by rational thought, I'm holding on to a little bit of hope that everything will work out. That Amber will never have to know about the stack of paper on my desk. And if it doesn't work out (OK, *when* it doesn't), I'll have this one last night as a nice memory.

So, when the Show up @ Stolen @ 8:30, UR on the list, bring a friend if u want text arrives, I don't agonize over whether I should go, or why I want to. Instead, I hop in the shower and start inventorying my wardrobe. When I come to the conclusion that nothing I own comes close to being cool enough for a night at Stolen, I call Greer in a panic and convince her to lend me something in exchange for a tagalong.

Greer arrives forty-five minutes later looking fabulous in a dark brown suede skirt and green halter top, her hair in a perfect tangle. If it weren't for the fact that she's carrying a garment bag containing the perfect outfit, I'd call the whole thing off.

When our cab pulls up at eight thirty on the dot, I'm wearing a black linen dress with a tie at the waist that emphasizes all the great things about by my rehab diet and hides the things that'll never disappear. My hair has been straightened, and it feels good to be made up and feeling pretty.

Stolen occupies a building in the old financial district, and the city's young glitterati snake around the block hoping they'll get inside before last call. We walk to the head of the line past group after group of half-starved beautiful people. I feel kind of giddy, almost like I've had a couple of glasses of champagne. We're on the list! How cool is that?

I give my name to the emaciated woman in a backless black cocktail dress who guards the door. As she runs a red-painted talon down the list her whole aspect exudes, *There's no way you're getting in,* until she finds my name with a plus one just below Amber's. She gives a little shrug of defeat before she puts on a welcoming smile.

A waitress leads us down a grand staircase to the heart of the restaurant set on the old trading room floor. The ceilings rise thirty feet above us, the height emphasized by bright uplights set against velvet curtains. The room feels alive, young, and the right place to be.

Amber's sitting at a table with three nearly indistinguish-
able unnaturally blond women all dressed in short, glittery
designer dresses I recognize from *Fashion Television*. She
waves vigorously as we approach and jumps up to greet me.
She's dressed in a white pantsuit and looks tanned and healthy.

"Katie! It's been *ages!* You look fabulous!"

"Thanks. You too. This is my friend, Greer . . ."

"Hi, Greer! I'm Amber."

"Pleased to meet you."

"Are you Scottish? I *love* Scotland!"

What is this girl on?

I look at her closely, trying to discern whether this newfound enthusiasm is chemically based, but she seems only
excited and happy, not high.

"Have you been there?" Greer asks.

"Loads of times. I've been to Glasgow for the festival, but I
especially love Edinburgh."

I smile inwardly as Amber pronounces the word "Edinbor-
ough." Greer will have to love her now.

Sure enough, Greer gives her a welcoming smile.

Amber introduces us to her three friends: Olivia (her publicist), Eva (her makeup artist), and Steph (her personal assistant). They're all in their mid-twenties, and I recognize them
as the hardcore party girls Amber's been hanging out with for
the last couple of years.

The waitress comes to take our drinks order. Greer and
The Party Girls order cocktails, and Amber orders a bottle of
San Pellegrino for the two of us. We peruse the menu. It's a

collection of Asian dishes served like Spanish tapas. By the look of the dishes on the passing trays, each is just big enough for four people to have a mouthful. The prices are shocking. I hope this Last Supper is on Amber.

"Shall we share?" Olivia asks.

"For sure," Amber enthuses. "Does everyone trust me to order?"

We all nod, and Amber orders a few delicious-sounding dishes that I suspect will be enough food for only two people. The waitress makes a polite suggestion to that effect, but Amber shoos her away.

Sigh. I guess I'll fill up on bread. Only there doesn't seem to be any bread. And San Pellegrino doesn't fill you up in quite the same way as, say, a Cosmo.

We spend the next hour listening to The Party Girls cackle as they recount a dozen incidents that Amber missed while she was "away," as they put it. They're all extremely funny, in a bitchy, it's-funny-because-it's-not-about-you kind of way. At least their talk distracts me from the fact that, as suspected, the food comes in Rory-sized portions.

"You should've seen her, Amb," Eva says as she pops the last salt-and-pepper shrimp into her mouth. She didn't even ask if anyone wanted it, though I was clearly eyeing it. "She was totally copying that look you pulled off at the Teen Choice Awards *last year*."

"And she looked like a *cow* in it," Steph chimes in.

"A mad cow, more like," Olivia says. "She really shouldn't show those legs of hers at her *present weight*."

"Who's 'she'?" Greer whispers to me, giving me a whiff of the Tartinis she's been drinking.

"I have no idea."

After a few more stories, I work out that "she" is Kimberley Austen, Amber's rival for It Girl of the moment status, and for Connor's affections. She's the sexy Moneypenny in the *Young James Bond* movies, and she and Connor were photographed frolicking in Cabo in one of his and Amber's off-again moments.

"Whoever are you texting like a mad person, Amb?" Olivia asks.

Amber shoves her phone into her purse. "What? No one. Should we get the check?"

Steph downs the rest of her drink. "Totally. Where to next?"

"How about Round the Corner?" Olivia suggests.

"Perfect."

Amber hands the waitress her black card and waves off my weak protest that she doesn't have to pay for us. The Party Girls don't even try to pay. I wonder what they did when Amber was "away."

On the way out, Amber catches my arm. "They're back!"

Uh-oh.

"Who's back?"

"Connor and Henry, of course."

That's what I was afraid of.

"Oh."

"Aren't you excited?"

I force a smile. "Yeah, that's great. I'm happy for you."

"What about you? Don't you want to see Henry again?"

No, no, no, beats my heart.

"I guess."

"They're meeting us later."

Of course they are. I should've guessed from the texting. And the frenetic enthusiasm. I've only ever seen her like that around Connor.

"Great."

Amber gives me a look. "You two sure are funny."

"How so?"

"Connor said Henry didn't seem that excited about seeing you, either."

I feel queasy. "Well . . . why should he be?"

"You don't have to keep the sexual tension up until the last season, you know."

"What are you talking about?"

"You like him. He likes you. What's with all the indecision? Just *go for it!*"

Olivia calls to us from the doorway. "Yo, girls! What's the holdup?"

"Coming!" Amber yells. "You ready to go, Katie?"

"I need to use the bathroom. I'll meet you guys outside."

She leaves, and I head to the bathroom, Amber's words spinning around in my head. Fuck, fuck, fuck. Why did I go out with her tonight? I should just sever all ties and move on!

I stand in front of the silver-rimmed mirror. The self that looks back at me is pale under my runner's tan. I'd love to splash water on my face, but that would undo all of Greer's good work.

Just get a grip, will you? So you might see Henry again. So what?

I wash my hands and dry them on paper towel from the dispenser. And there it is—a drink, gin and tonic by the looks of it, sitting nearly full and abandoned on the marble countertop, the ice just melting.

I look around for the drink's owner, but there's no one to be seen. In fact, I'm totally alone in here.

After a moment's hesitation, I take the drink in my hand. The glass feels cold and inviting. I can already taste the quinine on my tongue.

What are you doing?

I'm feeling guilty, guilty, guilty for even touching the glass that holds this drink, that's what.

As you should.

Yeah, but you know what? I've had just about enough of guilt, thank you very much.

I bring the glass to my lips and down it in three large gulps.

Guilt, meet guilt-killer.

Oh how I love that first-drink feeling. It's one part I-can-do-nothing-wrong and one part I-should-do-something-wrong. I'm funnier, the world is brighter, and anything troubling me seems to be no trouble at all.

I join Amber, Greer, and The Party Girls outside the restaurant right when the gin kicks in. As we wait for cabs to take us the short ride to Round the Corner, I catch a look from Greer when I belt out a laugh at one of Olivia's catty comments.

Oops. I've become someone whose whole personality changes after a trip to the bathroom.

"Are you OK?" Greer asks me in the cab. Eva's chatting loudly on the phone, trying to persuade someone to join us at the bar.

"Just peachy." I pull a packet of gum out of my purse and pop a square into my mouth. The mint flavor mixes badly with the gin and tonic, like it's Antabuse.

"What were you and Amber talking about?"

"Nothing."

She leans in closer. "You didn't tell her, did you?"

"No."

"Are you going to?"

"I don't know."

"She's nice."

You are so killing my buzz!

"I know."

"Maybe you *should* tell her."

"Mmm . . . so, you think there'll be any cute men there?"

"Here's hoping," Eva says as she gets off the phone.

Eva directs the cab to pull around to the VIP entrance at the back, where Amber and the others are already waiting. A large man with a blond crewcut leads us into a small elevator that clunks its way to the top floor. We disembark onto a rooftop bar with a terrace that has a 360-degree view and a large square of floor space that's part bar, part dance floor.

The bouncer takes us to an alcove created by three white vinyl couches nestled next to the glass railing.

It's a beautiful night, and the city's lights replace the stars. A line about pretty colored lights from Steve Earle's "Ft. Worth Blues" floats through my mind.

A small army of waiters appears with two bottles of Grey Goose in stainless-steel coolers, glasses, mixers, and ice. The Party Girls make themselves drinks (heavy on the Grey Goose, light on the mixers) as Amber distractedly hands over her black card while simultaneously searching the crowd. I make a virgin mix of orange and cranberry juice, with some seltzer for fizz, and Greer, surprisingly, joins me, muttering something about "cutting down."

Olivia takes a pull from her drink and props her long legs up on the glass coffee table. As she looks around, she narrates the cast of characters. "See that table over there? That's the cast of that ambulance show. They just got picked up for another season. That lead guy is cute, but a total asshole." She looks to her left. "And over there's the cast of the new Will Smith movie—they just wrapped this morning."

"I don't see Will," Greer says.

"Nah, he never parties without the wife. He's creepy that way."

Steph interjects. "I heard he has an open marriage. Apparently he just has to tell Jada first, and she's OK with it."

"As if," scoffs Eva.

Greer considers the crowd. "What do you reckon our best shot is?"

"You looking for relationship potential or right-now potential?" Olivia asks.

"If I wanted to be in a relationship I wouldn't be partying on top of a building."

"Gotcha." Olivia scans the room. "I'd say you're cute enough to break into the *Gossip Boy* crowd."

"What's that?"

"A new spinoff full of beautiful twenty-three-year-old boys."

"Sounds perfect."

"You want an intro?"

"Let's hit it."

I watch them walk off and end up making eye contact with a geeky-looking guy in a suit that's one step removed from leisure. He gives me a how-*you*-doing nod, and I quickly look away.

Maybe I should've rolled with Greer and Olivia . . .

I try to strike up a conversation with Amber, but she's too distracted with watching out for Connor to put coherent thoughts together. Eva and Steph are talking to two guys I recognize from a show about a pizza shop in a mall that got canceled after five episodes.

Bored, and coming off my buzz, I half want to leave, or at the very least have another drink.

But how to get a drink without getting caught?

Why do you care about getting caught, dummy? That's the least of your worries.

Shut the fuck up, will you? And I don't want to hear anything more from you tonight. Now, where did Mr. Leisure Suit go?

Ten minutes later, I'm ensconced at the bar like I own the place. I've downed two double vodkas, given out my phone number to a couple of generic men (OK, Joanne's cell phone number. At least a girl will answer), and I'm feeling all right.

I pop some more gum in my mouth and head back to the table. Greer's the only one there, and we've been invaded by a couple of punks wearing their first business suits. They're both portly and shorter than me. The one on the left has bleached-blond hair jelled straight up, and his sidekick has a mop of black curls that's the only cute thing about him.

Greer's eyes scream, "Help me." "Lassie! Have a seat and meet our new friends, Karl and Arty."

I take a seat next to her. "Nice to meet you."

"What's your name, sweetheart?" Arty drawls in an odd half-British accent that reminds me of Connor.

You've got to be fucking kidding me.

"My name's Candie."

"Nice to meet you, baby."

"No, not Baby. Candie."

Karl lets out a guffaw. "What do you know, Arty? We got a feisty one here."

"I do like 'em feisty," Arty replies as he flags down a passing waitress. "Should we get a bottle? On me?"

Greer gives me a desperate look. I can't blame her. If I weren't already half in the bag, these guys would drive me to drink too.

"Sure, why not?" I say.

Karl flicks a shiny new gold card onto the waitress's tray.

"I thought Arty was paying?"

"Nah, Arty's The King. The King don't pay for shit."

"What makes Arty The King?"

"He's just The King, sweetheart. It's not explainable."

Arty takes out a pack of cigarettes and shakes one out. "You ladies like a smoke?"

"Don't mind if I do," Greer says, letting Arty light it for her.

I follow suit, inhaling deeply. I must be drunk, because this cigarette tastes fucking fantastic. The waitress delivers the bottle, and we mix ourselves drinks.

"So what do you boys do for a living?" Greer asks.

"We're corporate raiders," Karl replies.

"What does that mean?"

He tries to blow a smoke ring, but all that comes out is a blob. "Basically, we buy companies that are in trouble, and we rape them."

I nearly choke on my orange juice. "I'm sorry, did you just use the word 'rape'?"

"Yeah, sweetheart. You got a problem with that?"

"A word to the wise, Karl. 'Rape' isn't a word you should use in casual conversation."

Karl puts his hand on my thigh. "A word to *your* wise, baby. I paid for this bottle, so that means I can say what I want."

I stare hard into his unfocused eyes. "Karl, you're really going to want to remove that hand."

"Or what?"

"Or I'm going to fuck you up, asshole."

I look up. Henry is standing behind Karl looking extremely angry. He's wearing a light gray expensive-looking suit and a white dress shirt without a tie. And ohmygod does he look hot.

"Henry, darling." I climb onto the couch and hold out my arms to him. "You come to rescue me?"

After a second's hesitation, he steps toward me and puts his warm hands on my hips. "You want me to stomp these motherfuckers?"

I cock my head like I'm seriously considering it. "Nah. I wouldn't want you to mess up your hands. Again."

"You're the boss."

"And you're the best."

I pull his face toward mine and kiss him. I feel a jolt of surprise as our lips meet. I'm pretty sure he feels it too, because he starts to lean away, then tightens his hands on my hips. We stay like that for more seconds than it takes to be convincing, and my hands start to tingle.

When we break apart, my heart is racing. Henry's got a look in his eyes that makes me blush.

"You sure I can't hurt these assholes?" he murmurs against my lips.

"It wouldn't be a fair fight."

"At least let me ask them to leave."

"Allow me." I turn to Arty and Karl, whose bravado has slipped significantly. "You've got someplace else to be, right, boys?"

They stand hurriedly.

"'Course we do," Karl says, trying to retain some dignity. "The King has other business to attend to."

Arty picks up the bottle and tucks it under his arm.

Greer waves at them as they leave. "See you later."

I plop down on the seat next to Greer, and Henry sits across from me on the couch abandoned by Arty and Karl.

We stare at one another, having one of our awkward silences.

Greer breaks it for us. "Hi, I'm Greer."

He smiles at her, grateful for the distraction. "I remember."

"Are you here with Connor?" I ask.

"Yeah, he's around someplace."

"So is Amber."

His smile drops. "So I gather."

"When did you get out?"

"Today." He gives me an appreciative glance. "You know, I almost didn't recognize you."

"Were you expecting a T-shirt and sweatpants?"

"What I meant is, you look great."

"Thanks. You too."

We lapse back into silence. I can feel Greer watching us, waiting.

Henry leans across the table. "Can we talk for a minute?"

"Um, OK. Here?"

"How about inside?"

"Sure. You don't mind, do you, Greer?"

"Not at all, lass."

I stand as The Party Girls return, full of tales from inside the bar. I'm knocked back into my seat as they jostle around me. Henry watches The Party Girls with a distracted look on his face. Their chatter fills up the air around us, and Greer whispers to me that she's going to call it a night.

"Do you want to come with?"

I look at Henry. "I think I'll stay for a bit."

"All right, lass. Be safe."

"Thanks for coming."

"Happy to do it." She gives me a quick hug. "He's totally into you," she says into my ear.

Before I can ask her what makes her think so, she snakes out of our outdoor living room and disappears into the crowd.

"I can't believe *she* has the nerve to show up here!" Olivia says, grabbing the Grey Goose bottle and shaking it. "Shit, we need another bottle."

"Hello, Livia," Henry says.

Olivia's head snaps around, and her face falls into an ironic expression. "Well, well, well. Henry Slattery, as I live and breathe." She looks around her. "What, no Connor?"

Henry looks nonplussed. "He's around here somewhere."

"Of course he is. Can't have one without the other."

"That's always been your position."

Oh, I get it. Henry and Olivia used to date. Great, just great. I stand up, and step over Olivia.

"Where are you going?" Henry asks.

"I think I'm going to go home."

He holds on to my wrist. "Wait."

I meet his eyes. I wish I knew what that look means.

"Please, Kate?"

"I'll be inside. Come find me if you want."

I pull away and push through the crowd, my hands suddenly shaking. From the shock of seeing Henry again. From the kiss. From the look on his face when he spoke to Olivia. From the look he gave me when he said, "Please, Kate." From the drink, the drink, the drinks.

Speaking of which . . .

I flag down a bartender and order a double, Scotch this time. I lay down some money and ask him to bring me another before the first one hits my stomach. When that one's gone too, my hands and heart have settled, and I'm on my way to being comfortably numb.

I lean against the bar and survey the crowd. What's that line from *Star Wars* about the den of iniquity? Whatever. It's 2 a.m. and the crowd is getting desperate.

I catch sight of Connor sitting at a table in the corner with a tall woman with strawberry-blond hair. She's wearing a pale sundress that's mostly see-through, and when she laughs and turns her head, I realize it's "she"—Kimberley Austen. I search the room for Amber, but I can't see her anywhere.

Connor is such an asshole!

I'm in the middle of forming a plan to crash Connor and Kimberley's little tête-à-tête when Henry finds me.

"There you are," he says, looking happy and relieved.

I put my arms around his neck without thinking. Ah, alcohol. Always so good about eliminating thinking.

"I wasn't hiding."

He smiles. "I'm glad."

"Me too."

We move toward each other like magnets are pulling us. Our lips meet. Then our teeth, our tongues. His mouth tastes like cinnamon gum, and his hands are hot on the small of my back. Mine are playing with his hair where it meets his neck. The noise of the bar falls away, and the *thump, thump, thump* of the music keeps time with my heart.

It's a wonderful kiss. A marvelous kiss. And we're just in the middle of it when Henry pulls away.

His hands cradle my face. "Kate . . . have you been drinking?"

I can't lie to him in this moment. I nod my head gently, and his hands fall away.

"Jesus, Kate. You've only been out of rehab for a week."

"Connor's over there with Kimberley," I non sequitur, trying to distract him.

"Kate."

"It's true, see for yourself."

Henry reluctantly follows my pointing finger to where Kimberley is sitting in Connor's lap.

"Goddamnit! That fucking idiot." Henry's eyes dart around the room.

"What are you looking for?"

"Spies. Kate, stay here. And don't drink anything else."

He pushes his way through the crowd to where Connor and Kimberley are now making out none too discreetly. Henry says something to Connor while gesticulating angrily. Connor looks pissed but dumps Kimberley unceremoniously from his lap. He stands and starts to shout at Henry. Henry takes it for a minute, and then they're both pointing and shouting. I can't hear a word of it until Henry shouts, extra loudly as the music dips, "Aw, fuck off already!" and storms back across the room to me.

"What happened?"

"Nothing. Let's go."

"Where are we going?"

"I'm taking you home."

I like the sound of that.

"OK."

I jump off the stool and my legs give out. Henry catches me right before I reach the floor.

"My legs aren't working."

He looks grim. "I see that."

"Why aren't my legs working?"

"I'm guessing it has something to do with alcohol."

"I like alcohol."

Oops.

"I know."

Henry leads me toward the elevator, one hand on my waist and the other around my shoulder so I don't fall over.

"How do you know so much about me?"

"You confessed to me, remember?"

I cock my head back and look up at him. He's watching the numbers on the panel above the elevator.

"Why did I do something silly like that?"

"Beats me."

Chapter 23
Fade to Black

I wake up from a total blackout. I don't know where I am. I don't know how I got here. I'm not even entirely sure of my own name.

OK. Let's establish some basics.

My head fucking hurts. My stomach feels like I drank battery acid. My tongue has that scalded feeling it gets when I've been smoking. The room seems to be spinning.

Perfect. I'm both drunk and hungover. Well, I've been here before. I'll survive.

What else?

I seem to be lying in a very big, soft bed. I stretch out my hand, feeling the sheets. They have a really nice hotel feeling. I take a deep breath. The air smells clean, almost antiseptic. Oh shit . . . am I?

My eyes fly open. Relief. There's no way this is a hospital room, not even in the nicest, Angelina-Jolie-gave-birth-here kind of hospital. So, it must be a hotel room, right?

I look around. My eyes grate against their sockets like someone threw sand in them. The room is dark, but there's a crack of light seeping under a door, maybe to the bathroom, that makes it bright enough to see. There's heavy wallpaper on the wall above wood wainscoting, a dark wood desk in the corner, and a nice chest of drawers. Hotel room for sure.

OK, but whose hotel room?

Hearing seems to be the last sense that returns, but after a few moments, I can hear the sound of water running. A lot of water. Someone's taking a shower.

So, I'm not alone. I didn't book myself into an expensive hotel room in a drink-fueled display of wealth I don't have. Good. Only, that means . . .

Did I . . . ?

I do a quick body check. I'm wearing a T-shirt, bra, and underwear. I still feel relatively clean, you know, *down there,* so we clearly didn't have sex last night, or this morning, or whenever the hell we rolled in here.

And who the hell is "we"?

Um, me and . . . me and . . . Nope, no idea.

OK, start at the beginning. What was I doing last night?

I search back. OK. Amber and The Party Girls. We had dinner. Not much dinner, but some. Then we went to that bar. And I had those drinks. And those other ones. Right. This is starting to make sense. The bathroom gin and tonic, and all those doubles makes . . . two, four, *nine* drinks. So, nine belts of liquor + almost no dinner + no drinks for thirty-six days = blackout. Good to know.

But that still doesn't answer how I got here, or who's in the shower. Surely it can't be Amber, or one of The Party Girls.

Even nine drinks + nearly empty stomach + no drinks for thirty-six days ≠ suddenly gay. There weren't any men at dinner. Or at the bar that I remember. I roll through the images like I'm fast-forwarding a movie. Hey, Greer was there! Shit. I hope Greer got home OK. No, wait. I remember her telling me she was leaving. Right around when . . .

Uh-oh.

The water in the bathroom turns off, and I hold my breath. I'm pretty sure I know who's splashing around in there, but what if I'm wrong? More importantly, what if I'm right?

What the hell is he doing in there, anyway? Drying himself off? Getting dressed? Applying self-tanner?

Come out, come out whoever you are.

The door handle turns, and in a panic, I close my eyes. I breathe in and out evenly, feigning sleep. I can hear the soft pad of feet on the carpet, and I wait for the feeling I get when someone's standing over me, watching me, but it doesn't come.

Maybe I should open my eyes? Maybe I should say something? But what is there to say?

More feet-padding across carpet, only they sound heavier this time. He's put on shoes. The noise is getting fainter. A latch turns. Shit. Don't.

"Wait . . ."

But I'm too late. My voice is barely audible, and by the time I've propped myself up and my eyes have focused on the door, it's been closed gently and I'm all alone.

I sit up. Oh boy. Maybe that wasn't such a good idea. The room tilts and whirls and does a loop-the-loop. I hope my legs are working because I need to get to the bathroom right quick.

I fling off the covers and sprint toward the bathroom. I assume the position over the toilet bowl, waiting for the inevitable. It comes before too long, and when I'm done I feel slightly better, though still extremely dizzy. I sit on the cold tile floor, waiting, wondering how I've come full circle back to here.

I'm not sure how long it is before the I-may-ralph-again feeling passes, but it does, and I get unsteadily back to my feet. I strip off my clothes and climb into the enormous tiled shower, swinging the heavy glass door shut behind me. I turn on the spray and let the cold water rain down on me. All I want to do is escape, but I force myself to stand steady and take it. I'm not sure why exactly, but I feel like I need to be punished, and this is the closest thing to hand.

When my skin is gooseflesh and I start shivering uncontrollably, I switch the water so it's as hot as I can stand it. My shoulders turn red, and the glass door is opaque with steam. I open the expensive shampoo in its little two-time-use bottle and slather it onto my hair. It smells like eucalyptus, and leaves my hair squeaky clean. I rinse, turn off the water, and envelope myself in a large white robe I find hanging on the back of the door.

God, I could use some aspirin and a good teeth brushing. There's a toothbrush sitting on the counter near the sink. It looks new, like it's only been used a couple of times, maybe only this morning. What the hell? I slept in the same bed as its owner, didn't I?

When I'm done brushing my teeth, I root through my purse until I find what I was hoping for: a little foil package containing two extra-strength Tylenols. I run the water in the sink until it's cold and swallow down the pills and two glasses of extra-cold water. Not wanting to get back into the clothes I slept in, I search through the dresser until I find a clean T-shirt and some crisp white boxers. They smell like Henry, or at least I hope they do.

Feeling more like a human, I crawl back into the bed and flick on the TV. I do my usual slow march through the channels until I come across a rerun of *Men in Trees*. Perfect. I snuggle down into the bed to watch Jack flirt with Marin in a fisherman's sweater.

This really is the most comfortable bed I've ever been in. I wonder if its owner, or renter, or whatever a hotel guest is in relation to their room, will be coming back soon. Or at all. What if it's not him? What if it is? Ack. These questions are making me dizzy again. Maybe I should close my eyes. That's better. All better. No need to stress. I'll find out soon enough. What will be, will be.

What will be, will be.

"Kate," Henry says sternly, a hand on my shoulder. "Wake up."

I open my eyes. Henry's standing above me. He's wearing a navy sweatshirt and a faded pair of jeans. There's a trace of stubble on his chin. He looks more like rehab Henry than he did last night.

"What time is it?"

"It's coming up on noon. Time to get up."

"I was up earlier," I reply lamely. "I took a shower . . ."

He looks away. "I left a toothbrush for you by the sink."

Of course you did. Because you're perfect, and I'm a nightmare who doesn't deserve you.

"Thanks."

"Forget it."

Henry opens the blinds, letting in the daylight, and I push back the covers and put my feet on the thick carpet. I still feel a little dizzy, but I think that has more to do with the cold look on Henry's face than the lingering alcohol.

I stand up, and Henry looks me up and down with a bemused expression I don't understand until I remember. I'm wearing his clothes.

"Sorry, I borrowed these."

"It's fine."

"Give me a few minutes and I'll be out of here."

"Yeah, that's probably best," he mutters.

The rational part of my brain kind of knows why he's acting this way, but the feeling part of my brain is pissed off. Does he have to be this cold and distant?

"What's the matter, Henry?"

"Nothing."

"That's bullshit."

His eyes flash. "Yeah, well maybe it is, but that's my business."

"Look, I get that you're disappointed in me, or whatever, but I'm not perfect, all right? You don't know the week I've had . . ."

He holds up his hand. "I don't want to hear it. Whatever

excuse you have. I've heard them all, and I've got bigger problems right now."

"God, Henry, I'm not *Connor*, all right. . . . What did you mean by you have bigger problems right now?"

He hesitates. "Amber's missing."

"What?"

"No one's seen her since last night. She stormed off when Kimberley arrived, and she's not answering her cell phone."

"Is Connor looking for her?"

He looks angry. "No."

"How did you find out?"

"Olivia called."

Something pops out of the blackout. I think Henry and Olivia used to date. Why, oh why, is that the first thing I remember?

I wait for something more, but nothing comes.

"Has Amber done this before?"

"A few times. The last time she ended up on YouTube . . ."

"Crap."

"Yeah. *Crap*."

"We should go look for her."

"I know."

"Well, come on then, let's go."

He bites his lip in concentration, looking like he's struggling with something. After a few moments, he sighs. "OK, you can come." He walks toward the door and picks up a shopping bag. "I got you these."

I take it from him and look inside. There's a T-shirt, jeans, a bra, underwear, and a pair of sneakers. A quick check reveals they're all in my size.

"How did you do this?"

He shrugs. "I've had some experience."

All righty then.

I keep my tone light. "From bringing home so many drunken girls?"

I get no answering smile. "Nope. It's part of the job. It's kind of Connor's MO."

"Having an outfit ready for a one-night stand?"

Shit. Why did I just call myself a one-night stand?

"Yup."

"But I thought he and Amber have been together forever."

"Come on, Kate . . ."

"Right. Sorry. I shouldn't be so naive."

His face softens. "No, you really shouldn't."

I carry the bag into the bathroom and take off Henry's clothes. As the shirt passes my face, I can smell him—part fabric softener, part spice. I hold the shirt to my nose and breathe in deeply. If only being with Henry could be as simple as this. Soft, and warm, and smelling good.

"Everything fit OK?" Henry asks through the door.

I hurriedly put the shirt down and pull the clothes out of the bag.

"Yeah. How did you figure out my size?"

Because this bra and underwear (simple white cotton, exactly like the ones I was wearing last night) fit perfectly, and that's kind of freaking me out.

"Practice."

I slip into the clothes and open the door. "How many girls are we talking about, exactly?"

"You don't want to know."

"You're probably right. So, what's the plan?"

"I have a few ideas of places she might've gone."

"Bad places?"

"Yup."

"Lead the way."

We go downstairs, and Henry directs a cab to an area of the city I've never been to but have heard about frequently on the nightly news. The Middle Eastern cabdriver shoots us a look that says, "Why the hell would you want to go there?" and Henry repeats the directions firmly. The driver shrugs and puts the car in gear.

Henry watches his cell phone the whole way, waiting for it to ring. I watch the gray sky, wondering if Henry's ever going to forgive me for being another person in his life that he enables.

The cab pulls up in front of a rundown red-brick building. Henry asks the driver to wait, hands him some bills, and tells me to stay in the cab. On the sidewalk, he hunches his shoulders and pulls the hood of his sweatshirt over his head. He walks up to the heavy wooden door and knocks, says something, and is admitted.

I wait nervously for him to come out. As I watch the door, a guy in his forties wearing grimy clothes casts a nervous glance down the street before knocking on the door. Like Henry, he says something and is admitted into the building. After he enters, an extremely large man with a tattooed face sticks his head out and gives our cab a hard stare. As he pulls the door shut, I catch a glimpse of something black and hard sitting on his hip.

Jesus Christ. How the hell did I end up in "Gangsta's Paradise"?

The cabdriver turns around. He looks afraid. "If your boyfriend doesn't come out in five minutes, lady, I'm leaving."

"No, you can't leave him here."

"Watch me."

"We're not buying drugs, you know. We're looking for a friend who's in trouble."

"Lady, I don't care what you're doing. He's got five minutes."

I peer back out the window. Hurry up, Henry. Why didn't I take his cell phone number down before he left the cab? Stupid, stupid, stupid.

With a minute left, the front door opens and Henry comes out. I move over to let him sit next to me.

"Was she there?"

"No."

"Had they seen her?"

"No." Henry leans forward. "Take a left at the corner."

The driver shakes his head.

"He doesn't want to take us to any more places in this neighborhood."

"Why not?"

I lower my voice. "I think he's scared."

Like me. I'm scared.

Henry makes a face. "It's broad daylight."

"That tattooed guy was wearing a gun."

"There's always a guy with a gun in places like that." He pulls his wallet from his hip. "Look, buddy, we're looking for a friend, a famous friend, who's in trouble. I need you to drive us to a few more places. I'll make it worth your while." He throws several hundred-dollar bills onto the passenger seat.

The driver glances at them, wavering. "Who is it?"

"Amber Sheppard."

His eyes widen. "The Girl Next Door?"

"Yes."

"That girl is messed up."

"Will you help us?"

"Yeah, all right."

"Thanks. Now take a left at the corner."

Henry leans back into the seat. He punches a number into his phone and puts it to his ear. "Hey, it's me. No, she wasn't there. I'm trying that place on Parker next. No, I haven't spoken to him. Can you call him? I'll text you the number. Yeah. OK. I'll call you later."

He ends his call, writes a short text, and resumes his stare out the window.

"How many more places are we going to?" I ask.

"Till we run out of places."

"Shouldn't Connor be doing this?"

"I don't think it's a good idea for Connor to be going into crack houses right this minute." He turns to me. "Shit. I wasn't thinking. Are you OK?"

"God, Henry, I've never been to a crack house."

"Good." He turns back to the window.

I stare at the back of his angry head. "Henry, what happened between us last night?"

"You don't remember?"

"Not much." I take a deep breath. "And not anything that would explain how I ended up in your bed."

He turns and looks at me blankly. "Nothing happened."

"Then how come you didn't take me home?"

The cab jerks to a stop in front of another run-down building.

"You were too drunk to give me your address."

Shame floods through me. "Oh."

"You going in there or what, man?" the driver asks.

"In a sec."

"Give me your cell number so I can call you in case something happens," I say.

I pull out my phone. Henry takes it and types in the number. When he hands the phone back to me, I hit the dial button just to be sure. His phone buzzes in his hand.

He ends the call. "I'll be out in a few minutes."

"Be careful."

He nods and opens the door. I watch him walk to the front step.

"You really think Amber Sheppard's in there?" the driver asks.

"I hope so."

Six hours and eleven crack houses later, the cab pulls up in front of my apartment building. Henry and I are exhausted and defeated, and no one's heard anything from Amber. We've decided to take a dinner break and brainstorm, so we pay off my new best friend, Ahkmed, and climb the stairs to my apartment.

"Joanne?" I call when we get inside. There's no answer. "I guess she must be out. Why don't you take a seat and I'll get the takeout menus."

He sits down on the couch in an exhausted slump. He lets out a sigh, then checks his phone for the millionth time. He places a call. Probably calling Olivia. Again.

"What do you want to eat?"

He lowers the phone, covering the mouthpiece. "I don't care. Order whatever you want."

I walk into the kitchen, pick up the pile of menus from the counter, and shuffle through them, hoping one of them will magically stand out. The phone in the wall rings loudly next to me.

"Hello?"

"Lassie."

"Hey, Greer. What's up?"

"What's up? That's all you have to say to me?"

"What are you talking about?"

"Don't play coy with me, minxy. Joanne told me you didn't come home last night."

I close the swinging door between the kitchen and the living room.

"She what?"

"Calm down. She was worried about you."

"Yeah, right."

"She thought you'd fallen off the wagon, but I assured her you were simply indulging in another vice."

If you only knew.

"Joanne was really worried about me?"

"She was."

"So, is she, like, your new best friend?"

She laughs. "Don't be daft. Now spill."

"Um, well nothing really happened, and he's kind of here right now, so . . ."

"Nothing happened? Even after that kiss?"

"What . . ." I stop myself. Telling Greer that I don't remember the kiss (The kiss? We kissed? Damn you, alcohol!) is going to raise way too many questions. "It wasn't that good, was it?"

"Looked that way from where I was sitting."

Then why did Henry say that nothing happened?

Why do you think, idiot?

"So, you spent the day together?"

"Yeah."

"Sounds serious."

"No, it wasn't like that."

"He's cute."

"Uh-huh. Anyway, I'm supposed to be ordering food right now."

"OK, lass. Run along. But call me tomorrow. I insist on receiving more details."

Right. Just as soon as I remember them.

I hang up and look down at the menus. The one on top is from an Indian place that's pretty good.

"Hey, Henry," I say as I walk into the living room. "You like Indian?"

"Sure."

"Would you mind ordering?" I hand him the menu. "I need to use the bathroom."

He agrees, and I walk down the hall and close the door to the bathroom. I examine myself in the mirror. I look like hell. Hangover city. No wonder Henry didn't want to admit he kissed me.

And kissed me real good, according to Greer. Why, oh why, can't I remember it?

I run a brush through my hair. The phone rings.

"Let the machine pick it up," I yell.

The phone rings once more, then stops, but I don't hear the loud clicks our old answering machine usually makes. I guess whoever it was hung up.

I finish up in the bathroom and head back to the living room. Henry is standing with the phone receiver in his hand. He looks stunned.

"Henry? What is it?"

He replaces the receiver slowly but doesn't say anything.

"Henry, you're freaking me out. Who was on the phone? Was it something to do with Amber?"

"Yeah, it was something to do with Amber."

"Is she OK? Who called?"

He meets my eyes with a blank expression. "It was Bob calling to remind you that your article is due on Friday at five, no excuses. And he'd also heard that Amber was MIA, and wanted you to follow up."

I suck in my breath, frozen in place.

"You answered my phone?"

His face hardens. "Is that all you have to say? Jesus, Kate. Give me a fucking break."

"Henry, it's not what you think."

"Oh, really? So, you're not writing an article about Amber's time in rehab for a fucking gossip magazine, and you're not working me for material?"

"No. I'm not working you for material."

"Kate, will you stop lying to me? Will you please just stop?"

He's angry and disappointed and disgusted. And that's exactly how I feel. I'm angry and disappointed and disgusted with myself. At least we can agree on something.

All the tiredness I've been holding at bay descends. I don't have the energy to lie anymore.

"I'm not sure I know how to stop."

"What am I supposed to do with that, Kate?"

"I don't know. What do you want me to say? What do you want me to do?"

He stares at me. I wait for him to yell, or scream, or walk out. But instead, after a moment, all he says is, "Start at the beginning."

Chapter 24
Hold On Until You Can Let Go

So I tell him everything. Without embellishment. Without leaving anything out. From the day before my birthday until today. I tell the truth and nothing but. I even let him read the article, hoping the fact that it's honest about Amber, but not harsh, will be the beginning of forgiveness.

As I tell him these things, I get some perspective. I finally realize a few fundamental things about myself. Things I already knew, that I'd already *confessed* to but never completely accepted. I am a liar. I have a problem with alcohol. My life has become unmanageable.

And, oh yeah, I think I'm in love with Henry.

These are the only things I keep back, but they're so real to me that I'm sure he can see them too. Like skywriting. Little tufts of clouds that spell liar, alcoholic, and love.

When I finish, Henry sits silently on the couch with his eyes closed, moving his lips in and out.

I wait for the explosion. And come to think of it, why isn't he yelling at me? Why isn't he storming around the room freaking out? Why is he still here?

I watch him, waiting, hoping, nervous. "Henry? What's going on?"

"Nothing. I'm thinking."

"About what?"

"Shush, Kate."

I shush, but my brain keeps spinning. I wish I could see inside his mind, like I've let him into mine. But then again, maybe not. Maybe he's adding up liar + alcohol, and that definitely ≠ wanting me to be his girlfriend.

I stand up and walk toward the hall.

He opens his eyes. "Where are you going?"

"To get changed."

"Stay."

He wants me to stay! But why? Why does he want me to stay?

I sit next to him on the couch. He leans back and closes his eyes. This silence is killing me. I want to ask him a million questions: Why is he looking for Amber? Why isn't Connor? Why isn't he talking to Connor? What's going on with Olivia? Does he like Indian food?

And how did he know how to find that many crack houses?

"Will you tell me what you're thinking about?" I say instead.

"I'm trying to remember something."

"About where Amber might be?"

"Yup."

"Maybe you should go for a run."

His eyes fly open. "What did you say?"

"I said, maybe you should go for a run. It helps me think

things through, and you know how your brain gets all flowy when you run, so . . ."

Henry grabs my face and kisses me hard on the mouth, then pulls away. He looks confused and embarrassed.

"What was that for?"

He turns his face so I can't see his expression. "Nothing. You solved it, that's all."

"I did? How?"

"I'll show you."

"She likes to hang out here sometimes when's she's upset," Henry explains as we walk through the east part of the park along a path I've never been on. It's dark and spooky, even with Joanne's emergency-preparedness flashlights clutched in our hands. They crisscross on the path, searching, but all they reveal are leaves and branches.

"How do you know that?"

"I've seen her here on my runs, usually after she's had a fight with Connor."

We walk silently for several more minutes.

"Henry, I think we should talk."

"About what?"

About the kiss we had last night that I can't remember. About how I ended up in your bed. About how angry you clearly are, and why you haven't left.

"About what I told you before. The article, all of it."

"I don't really think this is the right time for that."

Fair enough.

"Will you at least tell me why you're not talking to Connor?"

He moves the flashlight onto a dark shape on the side of the path. It's a rock.

"Why do you think?"

"Because of Kimberley?"

"I don't give a shit about Kimberly."

"Then why?"

He smacks the flashlight against the palm of his hand. "Because I'm thirty-two years old, and I'm walking through the park at night trying to find his ex-girlfriend. Because I'm supposed to be teaching English to high school students." He expels a deep breath. "Because the only person I can tell these things to is you."

Take your pick. Any one will do.

I put my hand on his forearm. "I'm sorry, Henry." I can barely make him out in the darkness. What I can see of him looks sad and serious. "I wish you were happy about telling me things, that you could trust me."

He pulls away. "Kate, you're the one who told me I couldn't."

I feel weary, and hungry, and defeated. "We should look for Amber."

"We should."

He walks ahead of me. As I watch the stiff set of his shoulders, I feel like he's walking away from me forever.

"I think I see something up ahead," he calls back to me.

I catch up to him. The path turns to the right to follow the arc of a man-made lake. The half moon is reflected in the water.

"I don't see anything."

He points across the water. "Look there."

I squint. There does seem to be a round shape on the ground, which may or may not be human.

"Are you sure it's her?"

"No, but I'm going to find out."

"What if it's some homeless guy who's dangerous?"

"Kate, where do you think I've been all day?"

"Right, good point."

We walk around the edge of the lake. As we get closer, it's clear that it's a person, a small one, sitting on the ground with their knees held to their chest.

"Amber," Henry says gently.

She doesn't look up, she just rocks back and forth.

"It's Henry and Kate, Amber, don't be afraid."

A cry escapes her lips, and now I'm sure it's Amber. We've found her.

We walk toward her cautiously, sidling up to her so we don't scare her off. Her hair is a jumbled mess and the pantsuit she was wearing last night is dirty and torn.

I kneel down next to her. The grass is wet and smells like the bottom of a peat bog. I put my hand on her shoulder. Her skin feels cold through the thin fabric. "Amber, are you OK?"

Amber rocks back and forth on her heels. She's gripping something in her hand. It looks like it's made of glass.

"Give me the pipe, Amber," Henry says.

Amber shakes her head vigorously.

"Come on, Amber. Give it to me."

She shakes and rocks and grips her fist harder.

Henry crouches on her other side and takes her hand in his. He gently pries her fingers open. Lying in the palm of her hand is a glass pipe and a chunk of something off-white that must be crack.

"Amber, did you use today?" Henry asks sternly.

"No," she says in a small voice.

Henry puts his finger under her chin. "Amber, be honest. Did you use today?"

"No. Not yet."

"How long have you been here?" I ask.

She turns toward me. Her eyes look black. "Since Connor fucking Parks shoved his tongue down that bitch's throat."

"Will you give that to me?" Henry says.

She closes her fingers and hugs her hand to her chest. "Why?"

"So I can throw it away."

"No, I may need it later."

"You won't," I say.

"You don't know. I might."

"No, Amber, you don't need drugs anymore."

"That's right," Henry says. "You've made it through the hardest part. You can do this by yourself."

A tear slides down her dirty face. "But it hurts."

I search for the right words. Words Saundra might say. "I know it does. And it's going to keep on hurting, maybe for a long time. But this is going to hurt you more. This could kill you. And I know you don't want to die."

"Maybe I do."

"No, you don't."

"How do you know?"

"Because I've watched you this last month. And sometimes you're unhappy, and you seem to think you need to punish yourself, but you don't want to die, Amber. You have too many things left to do."

"Like what?" she sniffs.

I search for something. "Like convincing Rodney to cast you in one of his films."

I think I see a hint of a smile, but she doesn't loosen her grip.

I catch Henry's eye, and mouth, "Say something."

He nods to me across her head. "Amber, if you give in now, you're letting Connor win."

"So?"

"You don't want to give him that satisfaction, do you?"

She looks at him warily. "What do you care, Henry? When have you ever cared about anyone other than Connor?"

"Amber, that's not fair. Henry's been looking for you all day."

She brushes away her tears. "Doing Connor's dirty work, as usual."

Henry's mouth sets in a hard line. "No, Amber, not this time. I don't work for him anymore."

"You don't?" Amber and I both say together.

"No. I quit last night."

"Really?"

"Really."

Amber stares at him fixedly and he stares right back. Eventually, she extends her hand over his and tips the rock and the pipe into it. Henry dumps the rock on the ground and grinds it with the heel of his shoe until it disappears into the dirt.

"Thank you, Amber. Now, let's get you home."

When we get to Amber's apartment, Olivia and Steph are waiting for us. They lead an exhausted Amber toward her bedroom.

Her top-floor apartment is an enormous ultra-modern loft. There's a wall of arched floor-to-ceiling windows and a kitchen full of gleaming stainless-steel appliances. The furniture is all white: white angular couches, white Formica dining chairs, white shag rugs on the floor. The only color comes from a series of framed playbills that hang on the wall that separates the bedroom from the rest of the apartment.

Olivia and Steph shut the bedroom door firmly behind them, and Henry heads to the kitchen. He washes his hands thoroughly in the sink and pulls several containers and some Cokes from the fridge.

"You want something to eat?" he asks.

"God, yes."

I take a seat on one of the bar stools and ladle some bean and couscous salad onto the plate Henry hands me.

"Sorry. All she seems to have is this macrobiotic shit."

"Forget it. I'd eat just about anything right now."

I tuck in. I've never tasted anything so delicious in my life, and I don't even like beans or couscous. Of course, it's been twenty-five hours since the quarter-dinner I ate yesterday. Coupled with the hangover and the puking, I can't believe I'm still standing.

I grab a container of tofu spread that looks disgusting, but I'm still so hungry I don't care. Henry's also vacuuming up everything in sight.

He catches me watching him and smiles. "Feeling better?"

"More human, anyway."

"Good."

"Look, Henry, about before . . ."

Olivia's heels click across the light wood floor toward us. She looks fabulous and formidable in a pair of skin-tight jeans and an ice blue halter top. Her skin is a perfect, even tan that has to be fake. "Henry, were those paparazzi assholes still downstairs?"

His eyes flit to mine. "Yup."

"How the fuck do they always know when something's going on?"

"Beats me. Any idea, Kate?"

Oh fuck.

I meet Henry's gaze. Please let him believe me.

"No, Henry. I don't have any idea."

Olivia takes a plate out of the cupboard and serves herself some couscous. "I swear someone's tapped her phone. I keep telling Amb to have it checked out, but she never listens to me."

"Is she sleeping?" I ask.

"She's taking a bath. I can't believe she spent the night in the park. Fucking Connor."

"Did you talk to him?" Henry says.

"Briefly. He didn't seem particularly concerned."

A flash of anger crosses Henry's face. "No, he wouldn't be."

I don't think I can stand another minute of this idle chit-chat. I desperately need to talk to Henry. To tell him what, exactly, I'm not sure. But this may be my last chance.

"Henry, can we talk for a second?"

Henry hesitates before he answers, and something about my tone draws Olivia's attention. She gives me a look like she's just noticed I'm here. That I came with Henry. That I've been with him all day.

"It's Katie, right?"

Jesus, we only spent six hours together *yesterday*.

"Yes."

She furrows her brow. "And what are you doing here, exactly?"

"She was helping me look for Amber," Henry says.

Olivia looks from Henry to me. "I see. You guys met in rehab, right?"

"Yes, that's right," I say.

"So, you're an addict?"

"Olivia!"

Thank you, thank you, darling Henry, for defending me. Even though you're still mad at me, even though you may never forgive me.

"It's OK, Henry." I take a deep breath and return Olivia's steady gaze. "Yes, I am."

"So, are you like a Cocaine Girl or a Heroin Girl?"

Henry makes an angry noise in his throat. "I mean it, Livia. Knock it off."

She pouts in his direction and some unspoken communication passes between them. I turn away from their obvious history. I've seen enough.

I stand up and walk my plate to the sink.

"Just leave it there, Kate. I'll take care of it," Henry says.

Olivia stands next to Henry, creating a visual unit. "Yes. We can take it from here."

The "we" kind of breaks my heart, but that's just me being silly and weak. I'll be stronger tomorrow. I have to be.

"Will you say goodbye to Amber for me?" I say to Henry.

"Of course. Thanks for your help today."

"Happy to do it."

Our eyes meet one last time, and I force myself to turn and leave the apartment. It's only when I get to the sidewalk that I realize I never told Henry goodbye.

Chapter 25
The Prisoner's Dilemma

I wake early the next morning feeling both relieved and apprehensive. I'm in my own bed, and I can remember every second of the last twenty-four hours (even though there are parts I'd like to forget). On the dark side, Bob is expecting my article tomorrow at five, and I still haven't decided if I'm going to turn it in.

I don't know why I'm still hesitating. I've told Rory, Greer, and Henry the truth, and at least Greer is still talking to me. And it can't really be about Amber. Yes, I like her. And yes, she'll be pissed and will probably never talk to me again, but I didn't ever expect to be friends with her in the first place.

Zzzttt! Zzzttt! Someone is ringing my doorbell insistently. I glance at the clock by my bedside. It's 7:20. I'm guessing that whatever/whoever's on the end of that godawful sound is something I've been avoiding.

I pull the covers over my head and listen to Joanne's muttered oaths as she stomps toward the front door. I may have to get that new solo apartment earlier than I thought.

The apprehension in the pit of my stomach grows when

I hear Joanne's muffled squeal, followed by the sound of the three locks on our front door being turned hastily. Joanne scurries down the hall and knocks excitedly on my door.

"Katie, get up! You'll never guess who's here!"

Somehow I highly doubt that.

"Coming."

I get out of bed and run a brush through my hair. Despite my good night's sleep, I have dark circles under my eyes and my eyes are bloodshot. It seems like I should look better than this when I face my accuser, but there isn't any time.

I open my bedroom door tentatively and walk toward the living room. Amber's standing under the window staring down at the street. Her hair is pulled back into a ponytail, and she's wearing an oversized pair of dark sunglasses. In her black leggings and ballet flats, she looks tiny and birdlike.

"Hey."

Amber pushes her sunglasses up to the crown of her head and gives me a look reminiscent of those she used to shoot Saundra in group. "Let's cut to the chase."

"Amber, look, I'm really . . ."

The words catch in my throat as Joanne comes through the kitchen door holding a steaming mug.

"Here's your coffee, Amber!" she trills.

"Joanne, get out of here."

She looks crestfallen. "But . . ."

"I mean it, Joanne. Please."

She looks back and forth between me and Amber. Amber's

angry expression is enough to persuade her. She puts the mug down on the coffee table and walks toward her bedroom.

"You *owe* me," she hisses as she passes by.

When Joanne's door clicks shut, Amber walks toward me, pulling a sheaf of papers out of her purse. I don't have to look at them to know what they are: the copy of my article I gave Henry to read. I hadn't even noticed it was gone, but in my defense, I was kind of distracted.

"I'm so sorry, Amber. Will you let me explain?"

She throws the papers toward me. They hit my chest and fall to the floor, fanning out in a haphazard pattern. "Don't bother. I don't want to hear any more of your lies."

"Then why did you come here?"

"I came here to tell you that if you publish that, I'm going to ruin you." Her voice is quavering slightly, but this only convinces me she's telling the truth, even if her words sound like they come from a script.

But you know what, I've had just about enough of people threatening me.

"Take a number," I say.

"Excuse me?"

"Look, I'm sorry I agreed to go to rehab and write a story about you, OK, but I was only trying to get a job. And you were just someone who seemed perfectly happy to have her life splashed all over the tabloids. So, that probably makes me a bad person, but now I don't have any choices left. I either hand in the article or I don't. Either way my life is shit."

"And what makes that my problem?"

"It doesn't. I'm just telling you, if this doesn't turn out the way you want it to, don't be surprised."

Her eyes narrow to slits. "Get the fuck out of my way."

I step to the side, and she breezes past me toward the door.

"I'm sorry, Amber."

She lowers her sunglasses with a flick of the hand. "Fuck you, Katie."

I decide to go for a run to see if my feet pounding on the pavement can help me figure out what I should do, and to get away from Joanne's accusatory looks. I'm feeling a gamut of emotions, but mostly I'm just guilty and scared.

Guilty about what?

Guilty about getting something I've always wanted through a series of fuck-ups, I guess.

Because you're only going to get the job at The Line *because you got drunk, and lied your way through rehab?*

Pretty much.

So, stop doing that.

Doing what?

Drinking. Lying.

I'm not sure if I can.

'Course you can. Just decide to do it, and it's done.

Full of platitudes as always, I see.

Hey, this advice is gold, baby, gold.

Well, if you're so smart, tell me what I'm afraid of.

That's easy. You're afraid of getting what you've always wanted.

When did you get to be so smart?

We've always been smart.

Haven't been acting so smart lately.

Don't look at me. That's all on you.

Yes, yes. So, you're saying . . . publish the article, take the job?

Un-huh.

And stop drinking. Stop lying.

You got it.

And then?

Simple. You live happily ever after.

Now I know you're fucking with me.

Twenty-five minutes of such thoughts brings me full circle to my front stoop. I stretch my legs on the steps, enjoying the limber feeling in my body and my mind. If I could bottle this clarity and sell it, I'd make a fortune.

It's then that it hits me. Maybe there's a way I can get everything I've always wanted, and save a few friendships too. I mull it over. Yeah, that might just work. But first, I'm going to have to convince Amber to speak to me again.

And I have twenty-nine hours to do it.

One hour later I've showered and made my way across town to Amber's apartment. I'm standing in front of the glass doors to her building. There's a large group of men lurking across the street, fast cars and wide angles at the ready. I take out my phone and text her.

I have a way to get back at Connor.

I wait nervously, wondering if she'll respond. But surely, if I've learned anything in the last month, it's how to get Amber's attention.

Beep! Beep!

I'm listening.
It's complicated. Can I come up?
Where RU?
Outside.

I look up at her apartment's large bank of windows. The white curtains twitch, and I catch sight of her pale face looking down at me. One of the photographers behind me yells and points, and a dozen lenses tilt toward the sky. She jerks the curtains shut.

Beep! Beep!

Hanging with your peeps?
U know I'm not.
I can't trust u.
I know.

There's a pause. I can sense that Amber's fighting her own internal demons. I'm banking on them wanting to hurt Connor more than they hate me. But as the minutes tick by, my confidence starts to fail. I'm about to leave when a large man in a business suit and sunglasses walks out of the building and up to me.

"Amber wants to speak to you," he says in a bass voice.

I follow him nervously into the large, bright lobby of her building. Amber's sitting on the edge of a ceramic wall that encloses a Zen waterfall. Her arms are folded tightly across her chest.

"So, what's your big plan?" she asks in a brusque tone.

"I was thinking that there might be a way for us to both get what we want."

"How's that?"

"Well, what if I turn in my article, only we put a different spin on it?"

She looks curious. "What kind of spin?"

"I was thinking a little more Connor, a little less Amber."

"You mean, instead of it being a tell-all about me, it will become a tell-all about him?"

"That's the idea."

"Is that going to work?"

"I don't see why not."

She gets a faraway look in her eyes. I hope she's seeing Connor and Kimberley entwined on the rooftop.

"Where do we start?" she asks.

I know the answer to this question.

"At the beginning."

"Joanne, would you mind giving us a minute?" I say when we get back to my apartment after taking the paparazzi on a mad, heart-stopping chase through the city. Joanne's anger melts away the minute she catches sight of Amber trailing through the door behind me.

She bounces up from the couch. "Oh sure, no problem. I'll just go find my DVDs for you to sign if that's all right?"

"Sure, no problem," Amber replies.

Joanne skips out of the room, and I'm pretty sure she's singing under her breath. Possibly the theme song to *The Girl Next Door.*

"Sorry about that."

"She's harmless."

"Shall we get to it?"

We go to my room, and Amber spends the next several hours telling me detail after detail about Connor. She holds nothing back. The ins and outs of their relationship. His cheating. His drug use. How he introduced her to drugs. His insecurities. The amount of money he spends on a haircut. It flows out of her while I type furiously, barely fast enough to keep up with her constant, "Oh, and here's another thing . . ."

Joanne brings us snacks at regular intervals, and we work through the afternoon and late into the night. When she's finally exhausted her list of grievances, I print up two copies and we read it through.

"No one's going to print this," she says unhappily when she gets to the last page. She's wrapped a blanket from my bed around her shoulders and let her hair down.

"Not unless they want to get sued," I agree from my desk chair. "They're not going to be able to second-source most of this."

"Shit!"

"Don't worry. All is not lost."

"Why? What are you thinking?"

"Well, I think if we go back to what I started with and slip some of this in, we can achieve the same effect in a more subtle way."

She chews on the end of her pen. "But Connor will still know that I'm the source?"

"Definitely."

"And if I want to take something in particular out, you'll let me?"

"Of course."

"OK, deal."

I spin my desk chair around to face my computer and pull up the original article. I print up a copy for Amber.

"Why don't you tell me what you want me to take out, while I work on integrating the stuff about Connor."

She agrees, and we're silent as we each reread the original article.

"I like the way you describe Connor the first time you see him," she says.

"Thanks."

"Maybe you can slip in the haircut stuff there?"

"I was thinking the same thing."

Later, she asks me to take out the scene of her singing to Connor in the cafeteria.

"How come?"

"Because I seem like a complete idiot."

"Nope, just human."

"I don't want to be that human."

"It's your call." I delete the passage she's referring to.

"You know, the article's pretty good."

"Thanks."

"You're still a dirty rotten scoundrel for agreeing to do it in the first place, though. And for pretending to be my friend."

I turn to face her. Her face is angled toward the pages in her lap, but I can tell she's just trying to keep herself from crying.

"I wasn't pretending, Amber. I wasn't being a good friend, but I could've spied on you without liking you."

"Whatever, it's not a big deal."

"I mean it. I'm your friend if you want me to be."

She smiles. "Thanks."

I work on the passage about the day we went trapezing, adding in some text about Connor's inability to do his own stunts, which Amber confirms.

"Does Henry know you're here?" I ask as casually as I can manage.

"No."

"Are you going to tell him about it?"

"No way. He might tell Connor."

"But he quit. And I don't think they're speaking."

"We'll see how long that lasts."

I type a few more sentences.

"Did he and Olivia used to date?"

"What do you mean 'used to'?"

Oh God. I think I might be sick.

I start to type again, but all that's coming out is nonsense. I'm not sure I can stand it, but I have to know more.

"They're together?"

OK, high, squeaky voice is not casual.

"Well . . . they didn't seem very broken up last night."

It takes every ounce of willpower I have not to ask what she means by that. It doesn't leave much for basic necessities like breathing.

"Did anything ever happen between you two?" she asks.

Well, apparently, we shared a hot kiss, but I can't remember it. Oh, and we slept in the same bed. And he kissed me briefly yesterday in the living room. And I might be in love with him. Anything else? Nope, that about covers it.

"No."

"Yeah, that's what he said."

Breathe, Kate. Breathe.

"It must be true then. Henry never lies."

She laughs. "You're right. He doesn't. Isn't that freaky?"

"Freaky." I stand up. My legs are shaking. "I'm going to go outside for some fresh air. You want to come?"

"Nah. I'm not sure we shook off all those guys. I'd better stay up here."

"How about I call you when I get outside to let you know if I see anyone."

"Cool. You mind if I take a look at the new draft?"

I wave toward the computer. "Be my guest."

I walk outside and sit on my front stoop. It's nearly six in the morning, and the sky is lightening. It rained a couple of hours ago, so the air has that cleaned-out feeling, as if the rain scrubbed out all the pollutants as it fell. I breathe it in deeply, trying to shake the fatigue that's descending, and the sadness.

I look around, but there don't seem to be any paparazzi waiting to take Amber's photograph. I open my phone to call Amber to give her the all-clear. I scan my list of recent calls, searching for her number. At the top, there's a number I don't recognize. Oh, right, of course. It's Henry's number. Henry, who seems so far from me, so unreachable, is really just a button-push away.

Before I can talk myself out of it, I highlight his number, punch the dial button, and hold the phone to my ear. It rings once, then clicks to voice mail.

"This is Henry. Leave a message."

I should've known he wouldn't answer at this hour.

"Hey, Henry, it's Kate. Sorry if I woke you. I'm not sure why I'm calling really, but your number was in my phone, and I wanted to hear your voice. Is that stupid? I'm mostly stupid these days, so I can't tell anymore. Anyway, I guess what I really wanted to say was, I'm sorry. And I'd love to tell you that in person if you can stand it. So, you have my number. Call me. Or I'll see you in the park . . ." The line goes dead.

Blast! I talked too long. Maybe I should call back? No, that would be really stupid. And desperate. Not to mention pathetic. He has my number. If he wants to talk to me, he'll call. And if he doesn't, well, then I'm not going to be surprised, right? And I'll live. I may end up in a crying heap on the floor for a while, but I'll pick myself up eventually.

Knowing me, it'll probably be sooner rather than later.

I go back inside. Joanne's making breakfast for Amber in the kitchen—eggs and sausage. It smells great, but there's really no point, since Amber will only eat a few bites. I start to tell Joanne this, but then I see her happy, purposive face, and I don't have the heart to shatter her illusions.

After breakfast (Amber eats three tiny bites and spends the rest of the meal pushing the food around on her plate while Joanne anxiously asks her if she likes it), we spend a few hours polishing the article. It's finally finished around noon, five hours to spare before my deadline.

I print up the final copy as Amber stretches across my bed.

"I can't believe you're still awake," I say.

"Eighteen-hour days are pretty normal on set." She yawns. "So, what's next?"

"I thought I'd take a shower and then go hand this in to charming Bob. What about you?"

"Ditto on the shower, plus a nap. Then I thought I'd go to a meeting."

"An AA meeting?"

"Of course. 'Thirty meetings in thirty days will keep relapses at bay.'"

This was Saundra's constant refrain during group. Thirty meetings in thirty days to reinforce the lessons learned in rehab and to avoid a relapse. Thirty in thirty. It has a nice, slogan-y ring to it.

I, of course, haven't been to a meeting since I left rehab, but I have been from zero to blackout in my first week home. I should learn something from that, right?

"That's what they say," I reply.

"You want to come with? From what Henry told me, it sounds like you could use one."

What I could really use is a few days without any more thoughts of Henry.

"Maybe. Where is it?"

"At the Y on Pearson."

"Fancy."

"It's not about where you are . . ."

"But who you're with," I finish. "What time's the meeting?"

"At three."

"OK, I'll try to make it."

"You really should come, Katie."

I give her a puzzled look. "Why are you being so nice to me?"

"Because the enemy of my enemy is my friend, grasshopper."

"Did you learn that in a movie?"

"An episode of *Roseanne*, actually."

I start to laugh, and it feels so good I give in to it. Amber joins in, and we laugh and laugh until we have tears running down our faces.

Joanne pokes her head in the door. "What's so funny? Come on, guys. Let me in on the joke. Guys . . ."

Chapter 26
Apologies

I'm sitting in Bob's office, watching him read through the article, a red pencil in his hand. As he reads, he makes small tick marks and occasionally draws a line through a few words. Mostly, he taps the pencil against the side of his desk while muttering to himself.

After what feels like a long time, he reaches the end and gives me a smile tinged with his trademark evil glint.

"Well done, Kate."

"You sound surprised."

"I am, a little, given our previous conversation."

"We had a deal."

He laces his hands on his desk over the article. "Yes, we did. Welcome to the team."

My heart starts to race. "I've got the job?"

"Yes, *The Line* will be lucky to have you. Though, are you sure you wouldn't prefer to work at *Gossip Central*? You seem to be a natural."

Remain calm, Katie. Taking him by the throat will erase everything you've worked for.

"No, thanks."

He smirks. "That's not I'm-too-good-to-work-here that I hear in your tone, is it?"

I try my hardest to copy an expression I've seen on Amber's face when she's trying to be charming. "Of course not, Bob." My eyes meet his. I focus on all I've been through to get to this moment.

"All right, then," he says slowly. "Report to Elizabeth on Monday."

I stand to leave before he changes his mind. "Thank you. You won't regret this."

I wait until I've left the building to let myself celebrate. Surrounded by strangers on the busy sidewalk, I let out a whoop of joy and pump my fist in the air.

This is happening, it's really happening.

So why doesn't it feel better than this?

I should be calling everyone I know, happier than I've ever been, but instead, all I feel is that there's something else I'm supposed to be doing, some place I ought to be.

Thirty in thirty. Can that really be the answer?

Will it kill me to find out?

I make it to the Y right before the meeting is supposed to start, and follow the signs and the smell of cheap coffee to a meeting room in the basement. Behind a door with a paper sign that reads ALCOHOLICS ANONYMOUS MEETING, I find twenty men and women of all ages sitting on folding chairs facing a lectern. A man in his mid-forties is leading the meeting. He has a rumpled, absent-minded-professor look about him, complete with a corduroy jacket with leather patches on the elbows and a scraggly beard.

I search the room for Amber. She's wearing jeans and a black sweatshirt, with the hood up over her head. I take a seat next to her.

"How did it go?" she whispers.

"It'll be out on Monday," I whisper back.

A girl in her late teens in the row in front of us is staring at Amber over her shoulder, trying to place her. She has jet-black hair and three rings through her left eyebrow.

Amber fiddles with the rim of her coffee cup. "Oh good."

"Having second thoughts?"

"Every other minute, but it's out of my hands now."

The Professor finishes the preliminaries and calls on the first speaker. A beautiful woman in a tailored business suit takes the podium and introduces herself. I'm surprised to see it's Amy, looking healthy and anxious.

She coughs nervously. "Hi, everyone, my name is Amy, and I'm an alcoholic and an addict."

"Hi, Amy!"

I give her a little wave, which she returns with a smile. Her eyes slip toward Amber and her smile falters.

Amy raises her hand. A round disk on a chain hangs from her finger. "Um, I'm here because I'm sixty days sober today."

Several people clap enthusiastically.

"Thanks, but until I reach ninety, I'm still just counting

days, like all of you. I was talking to Jim before the meeting started . . . Jim, I hope you don't mind . . ." She nods toward an older man who looks like he might live on the street. He nods his bald head in encouragement. "Thanks, Jim. Anyway, he doesn't have much, a lot less than most of us, but he found the courage to show up today instead of taking a drink. And if he can do that, than I can too, and so can you. That's all I wanted to say."

She walks off the podium and we all clap. Amy flushes with pleasure as she sits in her chair in the front row.

The Professor thanks her and calls on the next speaker, a good-looking guy in his mid-thirties who's had a relapse and has been sober for five hours. He wants to make it till tomorrow. The next speaker is there for her fifth anniversary. She holds her five-year chip tightly in her manicured hand, like it might get stolen if she's careless with it.

As I listen, I wonder what it is about talking to strangers that makes it easier to go through a day without drinking. Because sitting here, knowing I might be expected to share something personal, makes me long for a drink, just like it did in rehab. So, if coming here day after day, doing my thirty in thirty, is going to make me want to drink, what am I supposed to do? How am I supposed to move past any of this?

At the end of the hour, we stand, clasp hands, and say the Serenity Prayer. And for the first time, I feel some comfort in the familiar words, from the rote repetition of a hope we all share. "*Living one day at a time; / Enjoying one moment at a time; / Accepting hardships as the pathway to peace.*"

When the meeting breaks up, I say goodbye to Amber and cross the room to greet Amy. We hug hello.

"Well, I see you made it out in one piece," she says, holding me away from her.

"I guess."

"You look better, Katie. Healthier."

"I ran for twenty-five minutes yesterday."

"Hey, hey, hey. I told you you could do it."

We walk up the stairs and out into the late afternoon. The honking cars and exhaust fumes shatter some of the peace I found in the basement.

"So . . . you came to the meeting with Amber?"

"That's at least a two-coffee story."

She looks curious, but undecided. "Well . . . I should get back to work . . ."

"Some other time then. I don't want you to get in trouble."

"You know what? The bigwigs are all out at some corporate golf event, so let's coffee up."

We walk to the nearest coffee shop and settle in with some expensive coffees. Two cups later, I've spilled my guts with the requisite number of gasps and wide eyes from Amy.

She stirs the dregs in her cup. "Sounds like you've had a pretty wild couple of days."

"That about sums it up."

"Why are you telling me all of this, anyway?"

"I guess I'm . . . making amends."

She squeezes my hand. "You don't have to apologize to me, Katie."

"Yes, I do. You were a real friend to me in rehab, and I wasn't honest with you."

"Well, don't beat yourself up about it."

"I'm trying not to."

We walk toward the door of the coffee shop.

"So, what are you going to do now?" she asks.

"Go home and sleep for as long as I can before I start my dream job." I put my hand on the door to open it, but something stops me. "Everything's going to be all right, isn't it?"

"I hope so, Katie."

Sunday night to Monday morning I wake on the hour, every hour. The red numbers on my clock radio angrily announce the time. 1:00! 2:00! 3:00! Nah, nah, nah, nah, nah. Try to sleep if you can.

At 6:00 (!) I give up and stumble out of bed. Mindful (for once) of Joanne, I walk quietly to the kitchen and start the coffee brewing. A double whammy day—I'm definitely going to need extra caffeine.

After a run, two mega mugs of coffee, a healthy breakfast, a shower, and a long struggle with my closet to find the perfect first-day-of-the-rest-of-my-life outfit (I am so putting way too much pressure on this day), I leave the apartment with enough time to walk to *The Line*'s offices, so I don't have to suffer through the stress of being stuck in traffic or underground if the subway breaks down. Nothing, *nothing*, will make me late today.

OK, nothing except . . .

Four blocks from my destination I pass a magazine stand, and there it is, half visible through the heavy-duty plastic wrapping: a stack of this week's edition of *Gossip Central* containing an article by none other than me. I shuffle the stack around so I can get a better look. There's a party, party, party shot of Amber on the cover, and the headline reads: "INSIDE REHAB WITH CAMBER!"

So much for five days of struggling over the perfect title.

I look at the magazine stand. It's tightly shuttered, and the owner's nowhere in sight. Goddamnit! What time does it open? I peer at the sign. Nine. Of course. Nine is when I need to be five blocks down and twenty-nine floors up. Damn you, universe!

But maybe I could just take one? I bet I could use my keys to rip that plastic . . .

No, no, no! I will not start the first day of the rest of my life stealing. Again.

Though . . . I could leave some money, and then it wouldn't be stealing, right? But what if other people take copies and don't leave any money? Then maybe I didn't steal, but I created a situation that invites other people to steal, and that's almost as bad, isn't it?

Hello, idiot! You've got twenty minutes to get to TFDO-TROYL. Forget the magazine. You'll have plenty of time to read it later. In fact, you've already lived it. Get a move on!

I walk away from the magazine stand with a pang of regret but with purpose. I reach *The Line*'s modern waiting room with eight minutes to spare and stroll confidently up to the purple-haired, nose-ringed receptionist.

"Kate Sandford, reporting for duty."

"Huh?"

That line didn't work for John Kerry either. Let's try this again.

"My name's Kate. It's my first day."

"It is?"

Oh my God! Was it all a joke? Was Bob just fucking with me this whole time?

I give it one last try before I run from the building in a total panic.

"I'm supposed to be meeting Elizabeth at nine."

Her face clears. "Oh, right. She mentioned something. I'll call her."

"Thanks."

"You can take a seat over there."

I sit nervously on the couch, eyeing the magazines on the coffee table. There's a copy of last week's *Gossip Central,* but what good is that?

"Kate? Good to see you again?" Elizabeth says a few minutes later. She's wearing a skin-tight pair of dark jeans that taper to the ankle and a pink tank top.

Classy and up-talking as always.

I rise and shake her hand. "Thanks, Elizabeth. You too."

"Great? Follow me?"

She takes me to a wing of the office where there's a long row of cubicles that reminds me of the gossip call center below us. She stops in front of an empty cubicle across from a large, glassed-in office.

"So, this will be your office?"

I look at the nondescript fabric dividers. There are a few stray pushpins stuck into the fabric, a fancy phone, and a desk chair.

"Perfect."

"Are you ready to get started?"

Sure, only . . . once again I'm here for a job, and I don't even know what it is. I guess that's still me. Leap before I look.

"Um, so what will I be doing, exactly?"

"You'll be covering small local bands for now? Reporting to me? But we'll get into more at the story meeting? At eleven?"

"OK, great."

"It'll be in the Nashville Skyline room? You remember?"

Will I ever be allowed to forget?

"Yes. And I'm really sorry about that."

She shows me her teeth. "No problem? I believe in bygones, you know?"

"Thanks."

"Why don't you settle in? Oh, and I have something for you?" She walks into her office, picks something up off her desk, and walks it back to me. "I thought you'd like to read this?"

I take this week's *Gossip Central* from her almost reverently. So much of my life seems bound up in these glossy, gossipy pages.

She goes into her office, and I sit down at my desk to read my article. It's a twelve-page spread, full of lurid pictures of

Amber and Connor. At the front of it all is my name. Reporting and story by Kate Sandford. That's me, that's me.

My phone beeps. It's a text from Amber.

Read it. It's perfect. ☺
Thx.
Phone is ringing off the hook.
RU going 2 answer?
Thinking about it.
Good luck.
CU @ the meeting later?
Thinking about it.
30 in 30.
Yes, Saundra.
#*#!!

Two more texts come in, one from Greer and one from
Scott, both congratulating me. I text them back a thank-you as
my desk phone rings. I stare at it. Can that be for me? I haven't
given anyone this number. I don't even know the number.

"Hello?"

It's the receptionist. "I have John Macintosh for you."

"OK." The phone clicks. "Hello?"

"This is John Macintosh from *FYI* magazine," says a
medium deep voice with a slight Southern twang.

"Yes?"

"Connor Parks is saying that everything you wrote about
him in your article is untrue. Do you have any comment?"

"He's saying what?"

"That you've fabricated the entire story. At least as it relates to him. He *did* confirm what you wrote about Amber, and a lot more besides."

I'll bet he did, the fucking asshole.

"So, do you have any comment?"

I look down at the picture of Amber passed out at Connor's feet. "I stand by everything I wrote."

"And do you have anything to say to Connor's accusations?"

"No, I have nothing to say to him at all."

"Any regrets about going undercover to get the story in the first place?"

Oh, I have regrets, but I'm not going to talk about them with you.

"No comment."

"Have you spoken to Amber since the article came out?"

"No comment."

"Do you know anything about her going missing last week?"

"No comment."

He makes a disappointed sound in his throat. "All right. Thank you, Ms. Sandford."

I hang up, and my phone rings again. This time it's someone from *OK.* Then *People, Us,* and a few British tabloids I've never even heard of. I say the same thing over and over. No, I don't have any comment. No, I won't be giving any interviews. No, I can't reveal my sources.

In between the tabloid calls, I get a call from my mother. She read the article online, and she has a few questions.

Yesterday, I plucked up my courage and called my parents to tell them the whole story. They took it pretty well, considering.

"Does that mean you didn't need to be in rehab?" my dad asked, talking to me on the staticky cordless phone I've been trying to get them to replace for years.

"I'm not sure, Dad. I think maybe I did, but I'm still trying to work that out."

"I think it was a good thing, dear," my mom said from the phone that hangs on the wall in the kitchen where I used to talk to Rory for hours.

"I thought I'd come home next weekend, if you'd like," I say to my mom after I explain what "K" is, and how you use meth. The Rehab Education of Kate Sandford.

"We'd like that very much."

I twine the cord around my fingers. "You could invite Chrissie for dinner too, maybe?"

"Of course, dear. I'll make your favorite lasagna."

"That's Chrissie's favorite dish, Mom, not mine."

"Is it, now?"

When the phone finally stops ringing, I have half an hour until my first story meeting. At *The Line!* Oh. My. God. And all I had to do was sell half my soul to get it.

No sweat.

I start making a list of ideas that will hopefully impress my new colleagues but end up with a list of the people I need to apologize to: Mom, Dad, Chrissie, Rory, Greer, Scott, Amber, Amy, Zack, Joanne, Saundra, Henry, myself.

Myself.

Myself.

Myself.

"Are you ready for the meeting?" Elizabeth asks, coming out of her office a few minutes before eleven.

"Absolutely."

I follow her to the Nashville Skyline room, feeling nervous. Going back to the scene of the crime doesn't really appeal to me.

Laetitia, Cora, and Kevin (all of who I vaguely remember from my interview) are there, and we reintroduce ourselves. Kevin calls me "Undercover Brother," which I actually take as a good sign. If people are going to hate you, they use your name to your face and a nickname behind your back.

"So? What do we have this week?" Elizabeth asks.

"The Jonas Brothers have a new album coming out," Cora says.

Kevin shudders. "Ugh. Please tell me we're not covering that."

"Agreed? That is totally not our demographic?"

"Arcade Fire's new album might be more appropriate," Laetitia says.

"Perfect? Kevin, see if you can get an interview? Maybe we'll put them on the cover? Anything else?"

I raise my hand. "Has anyone heard of a band called The Spread?"

"Nope," Kevin says.

"Well . . . I've been following them for about a year now, and I'm convinced they're going to be massive. They've just been signed, and I thought they'd be perfect for one of those 'Who you'll be listening to this time next year' segments."

I wait nervously while Elizabeth ponders the suggestion.

"Sounds good? Do a thousand words and show it to me? By Friday? Now what else?"

At lunchtime, I swallow my pride and walk two sandwiches up five blocks to Rory's building. I stand in the doorway of her cluttered office watching the best friend I've ever had reading something with such concentration it takes my breath away. It scares me that I've done all the things I have in the last couple of months without her to rely on. She's the only person I've managed to hold on to in my life, and, like Saundra said, self-sufficiency is not something I need to work on.

"Hey, stranger," I say.

Her head snaps up. She looks pale, and some of the hollows have returned to her cheeks.

Did I do this? Did I sabotage her recovery when I sabotaged my own?

"Hey, yourself."

"Can I come in?"

She nods. I remove the large stack of paper from the chair in front of her desk.

"Careful."

I smile. "Don't worry, I won't mess with the system."

"What do you want, Kate?"

I sit down and hand her the sandwich bag. "I thought we could have lunch together."

She drops the bag on her desk like it's contaminated. "And what? Just forget everything that's happened?"

"No. I want to tell you everything that's happened."

Her eyes widen in surprise, and only get wider as I fill her in on the missing details. I take her straight through from the dinner with Amber to waking up with Henry to our tour through hell. By the time I get to turning the tables on Connor, I can tell that Rory has forgiven me. All I have to do is ask.

"So, do you forgive me?"

Rory picks up her forgotten sandwich and takes an absent-minded bite. "For what?"

"For everything. For lying to you. For thinking I could do any of this without you."

"But you have done it without me."

"But I don't want to anymore, Ror. I need you."

Rory reaches her hand across the desk, and I grab on and hold it tightly. Since neither of us wants to cry at her work, we leave it at that.

Ravenous, I unwrap my sandwich and put half of it in my mouth. Those rehab pounds are going to come back with a vengeance if I don't impose some self-control.

"So, enough about me, what's up with you?"

Her face lights up. "Well, they made me a director."

"About fucking time."

I spend the afternoon working on my article on The Spread, and fielding a few more calls from journalists. When I check the Internet, it seems to be all anyone's writing about. What's true? What's false? Will Camber ever get back together? Someone claims they were together Sunday, or was it Saturday?

Connor issues a formal denial, Amber stays mum. This seems like the right strategy, because the coverage is leaning in her favor. Everyone's disgusted with Connor's behavior and his desperate attempts to slur her. Amazingly, no one seems to clue into the fact that Amber must be the source of all the gory details. Except for Connor and Henry, of course. There's no way they don't know.

I leave the office at five, feeling more tired than I have in a long time. An honest day's work, tomorrow will be another. TSDOTROML. One day at a time.

When I get back to the apartment, Scott's there, hanging out with Joanne.

"I thought I'd take you out to celebrate your first day of stardom," he says.

"That's sweet."

Scott gives me a knowing smile. "But . . ."

"But, I have somewhere I have to be."

"An AA meeting?" Joanne guesses.

"That's right."

"I could come with, if you like."

"Scott, that's an incredibly nice gesture, but it's kind of something you have to do alone."

"I don't have any plans, Scott," Joanne says, smiling at him in a way I've never seen her smile before.

Interesting. Joanne's into Scott. And come to think of it, Joanne's looking particularly nice today. Her hair is less Annie than usual, and she's wearing a black shirt over her jeans that makes her skin look milky. Is this just a coincidence or did she know he was coming?

Scott seems disconcerted. "Oh, sure, right. What are you in the mood for?"

"How about that Thai place near campus?"

"OK." Scott turns to me. "You sure you don't want to join?"

"I'm good, thanks."

Scott gives me a what-the-hell-are-you-doing-to-me? look before following Joanne out of the apartment.

Sorry, Scott.

I head to my room and close the door behind me. I lie down on my bed and slap my earphones into my ears, pressing play. My semi-sentient machine matches my mood by tossing out Grace Potter and the Nocturnals' "Apologies," a song about love ending, and what can this make me think about but Henry? Henry, Henry, Henry.

Did I mention that he never called me back?

And I'm pretty sure it's not because he didn't get the message. Or, to be honest, the six messages I left him between Friday and Sunday when *I* finally got the message, and stopped dialing his number.

I've got to get a grip. I've gone further down the road of being "that girl" (that stalking, can't-make-it-without-a-particular-man girl) than I ever wanted to. He doesn't want to be with me. Maybe he did. But he doesn't now, and I have to find a way to move on.

And this music isn't helping. I click it off and stare at the ceiling. How does one move on, exactly?

Beep! Beep!

Maybe another piece of technology will be more helpful?

It's a text from Amber.

U coming or what?

Then again, maybe not.

I stare at my phone, watching the electronic numbers march toward zero hour. If I don't leave in three minutes, there'll be no meeting for me tonight.

And what would that mean? Would I start drinking again? Would I be putting TFDOTROML in jeopardy?

Am I willing to take that chance?

I swing my legs off the bed and stand up.

I don't have any chances left.

Chapter 27
Running to Stand Still

A month later, I'm packing up my meager belongings as Joanne reads a magazine on the couch while pretending not to care that I'm moving out.

"Did you buy this colander, or did I?" I ask her, holding up a lime-green pasta strainer.

"I can't remember."

"I'll just leave it then."

Joanne flips a page of her magazine aggressively.

"We can still hang out, you know."

"Hah."

I stop myself from saying anything more. When have I ever been able to alleviate any of Joanne's moods? And it's not like I'm going to be seeking her out once I leave here, right?

I close the box I've been packing with kitchen stuff and start filling another.

"Holy crap," Joanne says.

"What?"

She flashes the magazine at me. "It says here that you're Amber's lesbian lover."

"Excuse me?"

"Listen . . . 'Amber Sheppard has been seen entering the home of an unidentified woman on at least three occasions in the last month, often late at night.' There's even a picture. It's only the back of your head, but it's definitely you. And look, that's our front door!"

"Let me see that."

I take the magazine. Sure enough, there are several shots of Amber entering my building with the time and date stamped below them. The first is the day we wrote the article together, and the latest was last week. The article goes on to speculate that Amber's so heartbroken over Connor's final betrayal (he's been seen apartment hunting with Kimberley) that she's now playing for the other team.

"God, they're getting really desperate if they've started with that kind of speculation."

Joanne eyes me suspiciously. "It isn't true, is it?"

"Joanne!"

"What? It's not like you ever go on dates."

"You're one to talk."

She looks sheepish. "Actually, I've been meaning to tell you . . . I've got a date on Friday."

"That's great. With who?"

"Well, actually, it's with Scott."

You could knock me over with a feather.

"Scott? My Scott?"

She frowns. "That's right."

"Sorry, I didn't mean it like that. When did this happen?"

"Remember when we went to dinner that time, after your first day of work?"

I don't really.

"Sure."

"Well, we had a really great time, and . . . one thing sort of led to another, it's not a big deal . . ."

"That's great, Joanne."

"Yeah, well, it probably won't work out . . . I mean, he's way younger than me."

"He's an old soul."

Her eyes brighten. "I think so too."

"See, it's a good thing I'm moving out. You can have the place to yourself."

"It's not like he's moving in or anything."

"Stranger things have happened . . ."

"You don't mind, do you?"

"Of course not. I'm dating Amber, remember?"

I look down at the magazine, scanning the rest of the photographs on the page. It's the usual assortment of stars at parties with their arms around one another. But one of them makes my heart stop.

It's of Henry. He's squinting at the camera, looking annoyed. And beside him, beaming, is Olivia.

"They look like a couple, don't they?" I ask, staring at the photograph for the hundredth time.

Amy, Rory, Greer, and I are sitting at the coffee shop near

where Amy and I go to meetings. I asked Rory and Greer to join us after the meeting given the whole Henry-seems-to-be-dating-Olivia fiasco.

Amy looks at the picture I've spent hours dissecting. "They look like they're standing next to each other."

"But what about the caption?"

Because it's the caption that's been torturing me. *Henry Slattery (Connor Parks's manager) and Olivia Canfield (Amber Sheppard's publicist) looked like they were plotting more than a reunion between their employers at Sunrise the other night!*

"That's just gossip magazine drivel," Rory says.

"But they often get things right. I mean, think about my article."

Greer takes a large swig of her triple espresso. "That's the last thing you should be thinking about, lass."

"I know, but I can't help it. Why didn't he ever call me back?"

"He's probably angry," Amy says. "You did lie to him for weeks and write an exposé about his best friend."

Right. Good point.

"He must hate me."

Rory shakes her head. "Don't be so melodramatic. From everything you've told us, he certainly doesn't hate you."

"But he doesn't want to be with me."

"But lass, didn't you do everything you could to push him away?"

"I know, but that was before I realized . . ."

"That you were in love with him?" Rory finishes for me.

I nod.

"Have you ever told him that?"

"No, of course not."

"Well, why don't you?"

"You mean, call him *again* and leave him *another* message, telling him I'm in love with him?"

Rory nods her logical head. "Why not?"

"Impossible."

"Nothing's impossible," Amy says quietly.

"But if it feels like it is, isn't that the only thing that counts?"

She gives me a sad look. "I think the only thing that counts is that love is rare. And when you find it, you need to grab on and not let go."

"Sorry, but that's a little too Hallmark for me." I tuck the magazine away, sick of the sight of Henry and Olivia together. "Let's talk about something else."

"Good idea."

"You guys still doing that 10K race on Sunday?" Greer asks Amy.

Amy smiles confidently. "Of course. You sure you're ready, Katie?"

"For the entire 10K? Probably not."

"Then why do it, lass?"

"Nothing ventured, nothing gained."

Greer raises her coffee cup. "I'll drink to that."

"Greer!"

"Ah, relax, Ror." I raise my coffee cup and clink it to hers. "What are we drinking to again?"

"The possible."

"To the possible."

OK, confession time again. I signed up for the 10K race when Amber mentioned in passing that Henry was going to be running in it. Even though I assumed (but couldn't bring myself to ask) that she'd gotten this information from Olivia, I mentioned it to Amy at AA, and the next thing I knew, we were signed up.

I've been regretting my moment of weakness ever since then. However, I made a promise to Amy, and I'm all about keeping my promises these days.

So, here I am, lining up with thousands of other crazy people at the edge of the park early Sunday morning. I've got a tracking chip attached to my shoe and the number 764 pinned to my chest. My one-month-of-sobriety chip is strung around my neck. Maybe it'll bring me luck.

Amy's standing beside me, looking calm and collected. She's been coaching me on race strategy and sports psychology. I'm pretty sure I've retained exactly none of her wisdom. I search the crowd for Henry, my heart lurching at every glimpse of red hair.

As it gets close to race time, the crowd surges forward, jockeying for position nearer to the start. Everyone's all elbows and knees, and I begin to feel claustrophobic. When one elbow too many gets me in the ribs, I spin on the culprit in anger.

"Watch it, buddy, will you!"

The man I've yelled at recoils, but not because I screamed at him for no reason. It's because it's Henry.

Our eyes lock, and it takes a moment for me to realize that I'm standing there with my mouth hanging open.

Par for the embarrassing course.

I click my mouth shut. "Sorry, I didn't know it was you."

"That's OK."

I search his face. He looks the same as always, only a little white under his tan.

"I'm running in the race," I say, stupidly.

His mouth looks amused, but it doesn't travel to his eyes. "I can see that."

A million thoughts, questions, emotions are running through my brain. And the one that pops out is, "Did you get my messages?"

He looks away. "Yes. I got them."

I search his face again. "Look, Henry, I get why you didn't want to call me back . . ."

Before he can answer, another runner stumbles into me, pushing me toward Henry. He steadies me against his chest, and we stay like that, surrounded and prodded by the eager crowd. My heart beats loudly in my ears, and I swear I can hear his heart too.

"Kate, I . . ."

A horn blares and the starter calls us to our marks. The crush of people becomes twice what it was before. We're separated before Henry can complete his thought, whatever it was.

I search the crowd, but I can't see him or Amy.

"Amy!"

"Katie!"

"Where are you?"

"Over here!"

I see a hand waving above the crowd and push my way toward her.

"Ten seconds," yells the starter through his bullhorn.

"What happened?" Amy asks.

"I ran into Henry."

"Are you OK?"

"I guess."

"Did you say anything?"

"I tried to, but we got pushed apart."

"On your marks! Get set! Go!"

The horn blares, and we move forward as one. It's a faster pace than I'm used to, but the adrenaline of the race, of seeing Henry, pushes me along past the huge digital clock hanging over the starting line.

"Stick with me, Katie," Amy says. "Let people pass you so we can stay on pace."

I slow down, and we run at a comfortable clip for a few minutes while my beating heart returns to almost normal. We round a corner to a straighter section of the path. I can see Henry up ahead, and my heart starts pounding again, taking my legs along with it. I'm running too fast, but I can't seem to help myself.

As I stare at the back of his head, something falls out of the blackout. My hands in his hair. His on my waist. Our tongues meeting in between our mouths. The way the world fell away until he tasted alcohol.

"Katie, we should slow down, you're not going to make it to the end."

"I feel like I can do it."

I focus on Henry's back, his easy gait.

He must like me to kiss me like that.

But that was before he knew you were a liar.

No, I'd already told him that.

Right, but then you showed him.

But I've stopped drinking.

He doesn't know that.

I tried to tell him.

Not very hard.

I'm running after him, aren't I?

I almost laugh out loud as this realization thunks through my brain.

Oh. My. God. It's true. I'm running, for Chrissakes, I'm *running* after a man to tell him how I feel about him. How did I end up at the end of a romantic comedy?

And if I catch him, if I tell him, what then? Why am I so sure he wants to hear what I have to say? Why am I so convinced that his reluctance is a mask for love?

How stupid can you be, Katie?

My energy drains away. My legs aren't working very well anymore, and neither are my lungs. I stop running, doubled over, gasping for breath.

Amy stops and puts her hand on my back. "Katie, are you all right?"

I shake my head, unable to speak. I hear Amy call for help, and she and one of the volunteers supports me to the sidelines. I sink to the grass, wheezing. When I can speak, I tell Amy to go on without me, and she reluctantly agrees.

The kind volunteer woman wraps me in a metallic space blanket and hands me a glass of Gatorade. I drink it slowly as she gives me a ride on a golf cart to the medical tents. When we get there, I'm led to a cot, and a young nurse takes my blood pressure. After the air releases from the blood pressure cuff, the nurse tells me my pressure is low and that I should rest until I feel better. I don't have the heart to tell her that feeling better is not an option.

I lie down on the cot and pull the space blanket up to my chin. I feel utterly exhausted, like every molecule of energy I've ever had has been drained away to nothing. Who knew that running flat out for thirty minutes could induce the same feeling as halfway between shit-faced and sobering up?

Runner's high, I guess. Same damn thing as any other high.

Time passes. After a while, I begin to feel better, and silly. What the hell is wrong with me, anyway? Am I so thin-skinned that one encounter with Henry has me chasing my tail (OK, Henry's tail) until I hit the wall? All this because of a boy? I've got to pull myself together. Like U2 says. I'm stuck in a moment I can't get out of.

You said it, Bono. And nice guitar riff, The Edge. You work that shit.

I sit up, and the world stays steady. I kick off the blanket, and the cool air doesn't kill me. I unpin the number from my chest and unclip the tracker from my shoe, leaving them both on the cot. I tell the nurse I'm leaving, and she reminds me to take it easy.

I find Amy waiting for me outside the tent with Rory. Amy's face is glowing, and she has a medal hanging around her neck.

I give them a small wave. "Hey, guys."

Rory looks concerned. "What happened to you?"

"Turns out I'm not Supergirl." I notice the camera in Rory's hand. "Thanks for coming, Ror. Sorry you didn't get your shot."

"I had a place in my scrapbook all picked out and everything."

"You're such a liar."

"Takes one to know one."

Amy laughs. "You two always have such intellectual conversations?"

"We've known each other since we were five," Rory says by way of explanation. "It stuck."

"How did you do?" I ask Amy.

She looks proud of herself. "Fifty-two minutes."

"That's great! Sorry I slowed you down."

"Are you kidding? I beat my goal by three minutes, even with the medical diversion."

Apparently chasing after Henry makes me a good pace bunny.

"Should we go?"

Amy and Rory exchange a guilty glance.

"What is it?"

"Someone wants to talk to you first," Rory says, pointing over her shoulder.

I look, but I don't really have to. I know it's going to be Henry, and sure enough, there he is, sitting on a park bench with a green-and-orange Gatorade cup in his hand, looking nervous.

"You going to go over there?" Amy asks.

"Thinking about it."

"You know you have to actually walk to get there, right?"

"Fuck off, Ror."

"You want us to wait?"

"Nah. I'll be all right."

I walk toward Henry with as much dignity as I can muster with my worn-out legs, sweaty body, and disheveled hair straggling out of my baseball cap. Henry's face is red above his blue running shirt. His finisher's medal is poking out of his pocket.

"I hear you wanted to talk to me."

"I do."

"What about?"

He pats the bench next to him. "Will you sit for a minute?"

I sit. He plays with the edge of the empty cup.

"So . . ."

"So . . . I wanted to tell you why I never called you back."

My mouth goes dry. "Why didn't you?"

"It's kind of complicated . . . but . . . you see . . . shit, this would be so much easier if we could go for a run."

The thought of running right now is so absurd I almost laugh out loud. "I'm afraid that's out of the question."

He looks at me with concern in his eyes. "Rory said you were in the medical tent. Are you OK?"

"I just ran too fast, that's all."

"That happened to me in my first race too."

"Yeah?"

"Yeah."

We lapse into our standard silence.

Suddenly, I can't stand it anymore.

"Henry, one of us is going to have to do something, or say something."

"I know, Kate."

"*You* wanted to talk . . ."

He smiles. "Which puts me on deck."

"Yup."

"You talking like me now?"

"Seems like."

He reaches over and takes my hands in his. Surprised, I look into his blue-gray eyes.

"Remember when we first met, what I told you?"

I think back to the memories that are still crisp and clear. "You told me that women don't like the strong, silent type."

"Right, and that's what I bring to the table. And I know that's not easy to deal with, but . . ."

"You met me in rehab."

"It wasn't just that, Kate. I could deal with that . . . but then, when you were drinking again, and the rest of it came out . . . everything just seemed way too complicated."

"And the beginning's supposed to be simple."

"It is."

"It's funny, because I thought it felt simple most of the time."

"So did I."

"So it wasn't just me?"

"No. It wasn't just you."

We smile at each other. My hands feel warm in his.

"Do you think we could make it simple again?" I ask.

"I'd like to try."

"Really?"

"Really."

We smile again, and I begin to feel a little silly. I pull my hands away gently.

"So, what happens now?"

"I don't know . . . do you want to maybe get dinner with me?"

"You mean, go on a date?"

"Yeah."

"What's going to happen on this date?"

He brushes a lock of hair out of my eyes. "Oh, you know. You'll wear something sexy, I'll press my chinos, and we'll talk."

"You're going to talk?"

"I promise."

"What about?"

His thumb skims the bridge of my nose. "Maybe I'll tell you about my new job teaching rich prep school kids *King Lear.*"

"So, you're not dating Olivia?"

He drops his hand. "No. God no."

"Good."

"Why did you ask me that?"

"Oh, I saw this photo . . ."

"In *People*?"

"Yeah."

"You of all people should know better than to believe anything you read in there."

"Why? Everything I wrote was true."

His face clouds. "I guess it was."

"Shit, Henry, I'm sorry."

"No, don't do that. Don't apologize."

"But I want to . . ."

"No, Kate."

Henry leans toward me, and our lips touch gently. His feel soft, firm, warm, welcoming, and I give in to the kiss.

Someone lets out a whoop near us and we pull apart.

"I'm afraid that might've been my friends."

He smiles. "Let's give them something to really whoop about, then."

He slips his hand to the back of my neck and pulls me toward him. This time the kiss is hotter, wetter, firmer, full of promise. And, oh yes, I remember this. I remember, I remember.

I pull back, and when I look into his eyes I see the same promise I felt in his kiss.

"So you think we should forget the past?"

"I think that's best. Don't you?"

Kiss me one more time, and I'll agree to anything.

I concentrate. "I think that . . . 'I am but mad north-northwest; but when the wind is southerly, I know a hawk from a handsaw.'"

"You're quoting Shakespeare to me?"

"It feels like that kind of day."

"We're not crazy, Kate."

"Aren't we?"

He tips my chin toward his, and this kiss is one for the record books. Like the last kiss in *The Princess Bride,* it leaves all the others behind. They're dust.

"OK, maybe a little crazy," Henry says when we pull apart, breathless.

"I told you."

"Still, I'm willing to risk it if you are."

Henry waits for me to answer.

Here it is, Kate. Here's the moment. Here's where you have to choose. Are you ready?

"I was running after you. That's why I was in the medical tent."

He laughs. "If I knew you were running after me, I would've slowed down."

"Henry, that might just be the most romantic thing I've ever heard."

"Well, it's a start."

It's our start, anyway.

Katie's Playlist

Acknowledgments

Since the birth of her son, my sister has been taking all the credit. Hey, she says, I grew him inside me, and then I breast-fed him until his six-month size. That kid is mine.

I understand the sentiment, but . . . just like my sister knows others played a part in his existence and growth, I also had a lot of help bringing this book into the world.

So, in no particular order (I have to say that, right?), I'd like to thank:

My best friend, Tasha, for too many things to name here, but especially for being a lifelong friend, for reading the first draft of everything I write, and for having the courage to let me speak at her wedding. I've said it before, and I'll say it again, I have two sisters, and you are one.

All those who read early drafts, especially my mom, Katie, and David.

Amy, for keeping me writing once I got started, and for on-the-money, pull-no-punches insights. Also for great dinners and laughter.

Phyllis, for her long friendship, and for collaborating with me on my first writing project, too embarrassing to reveal. OK, it was a script for *Remington Steele*. Seriously. In our defense, we were thirteen.

The Bromont Gang (in alphabetical order this time): Amy, Annie, Candice, Chad, Christie, Dan, Eric, Katie, Kevin, Lindsay, Marty, Olivier, Patrick, Phil, Presseau, Sara, Stephanie, Tanya, and Thierry. For laughter, good times, and (most of all) encouragement.

My mom, for being a constant reader; my dad, the other writer in the family; my sister, who wants to be called Cam now, but will always be Cammy to me; and my brother, Mike. I love you guys. Also my grandparents, Roy and Dorothy McKenzie, for their love, support, and longevity, and my in-laws, Michael and Jennifer, for always being welcoming.

Janet, for long runs and complaints. Peter, for conversations about music. And the rest of my law partners, for indulging me in this decidedly nonlegal pursuit.

Tish Cohen, Julie Buxbaum, Cathy Marie Buchanan, Leah McLaren, Holly Kennedy, David Sprague, and Diane Saarinen for their early support of my work. And Shawn Klomparens, who always said this day would happen.

My agent, Abigail Koons, for her faith, hard work, and friendship, as well as the whole team at Park Literary. My editor at HarperCollins Canada, Jennifer Lambert, for falling in love with my book and making it better, and my editors at HarperCollins US, Emily Krump and Stephanie Meyers, for believing that more than a few Canadians might enjoy the read.

And David. Thank you for your support, for putting up with me typing next to you while we watch TV, and for letting me talk (a lot).

This is starting to feel like my grad note, so: *Carpe diem.*

Read on for an excerpt from

ARRANGED
Catherine McKenzie

Available in May 2012 from

wm

WILLIAM MORROW
An Imprint of HarperCollins*Publishers*

Chapter 1
Enough is Enough

"I read your emails," I tell Stuart.

His head snaps up from his copy of Maxim. His sock-covered feet are resting on the glass coffee table that sits in front of the leather couch we bought six months ago. An innocent pose, though he's guilty as hell.

"You what?"

"You heard me."

The planes of his angular face harden. "I'd better not be hearing you."

I feel a moment of guilt. Then I remember what I read. "I read your emails. All of them." He opens his mouth to speak, but I cut him off. "How could I violate your privacy? Is that what you were going to say? Don't you talk to me about violations, Stuart. Don't you even dare."

He shuts his mouth so quickly his teeth click. His wheels are spinning. I can almost see the movement behind his eyes, which can be so warm, so sexy, so everything, but at this moment are so cold, so hard, and so damn blue.

"What do you think you read, Anne?" he says eventually, his voice tightly controlled, a blank slate.

"Are you really going to make me say it out loud?"

He stays silent. The light from the reading lamp glints off of his straight black hair. A clock ticks on the mantel above the fireplace, measuring out the seconds I have left here.

I take a deep breath. "I know you slept with Christy. I know you've been sleeping with her for a while."

There. I said it. And even though I knew it, even though I read it, actually saying it brings it to life in a way I hadn't anticipated. It's so much larger now that it's in the room. So much worse. Like Christy is here with us. Like she's repeating the words she wrote to him, in the soft, sultry voice I heard once on the answering machine. Words I can't erase.

The clock keeps ticking. I feel caught, waiting for him to do or say something.

Say something, goddamn it. Say something!

He stands up like he heard me. The magazine slaps to the polished wood floor.

"Well, bravo, Anne, you caught me! What're you going to do about it?"

Jesus Christ. Wouldn't it be great if you could videotape people during a breakup? Wouldn't it be great if you could have access to that videotape at the beginning of a relationship?

Look how this guy's going to be treating you in six, eight, ten months. Look how he treated the girl he spent three years with! Run away, run away!

My breath rattles in my throat, but I get the words out. "I'm leaving."

"You're leaving," he repeats, maybe a statement, maybe a question. Like something he can't quite bring himself to believe.

"Do you really expect me to stay? After what you've done? Is that what you even want?"

His eyes shift away from mine, the first sign of weakness. "I don't know."

"Oh, Stuart, please. This is exactly what you want. You just don't want to be the bad guy. So instead, you've made sure I'll be the one who ends it. And I've been too stupid to figure that out until now."

"You think you're so smart, don't you?"

"I've just finished telling you I've been stupid. But, yes, today I think I'm being smart."

"Well, I'm not leaving the apartment, if that's what you think is going to happen."

"God, you really don't know me at all, do you? After all this time."

He scoffs. "Oh, I know you, Anne. Don't you worry about that."

I consider him: his beauty, his anger, this man I thought I'd marry.

"So, I guess this is it," I say, because this is what people always seem to say in these kinds of situations. At least, that's what they say in the movies, and right now, my life feels like an invented life.

He doesn't answer me. Instead, he watches me walk to the hall closet and reach for the duffel bag I stashed there earlier with everything I need for the immediate future packed inside.

I turn to face him. I look into his eyes, searching for something, I don't know what.

"Goodbye, Stuart."

"Goodbye, Anne."

I hesitate, waiting for him to say something more, to beg me to stay, to tell me, I love you, it's all a mistake, I'm a complete asshole, I can't live without you, please, darling, please.

But he isn't going to give me that. Not now that I'm finally letting him have what he wants. Because he is an asshole, and I'm an idiot for wanting anything from him, no matter how small. So before he can call me on it, or ask me why I'm still here, I hoist the bag over my shoulder and walk out.

Outside, I get into the waiting cab and direct it to my new apartment.

I don't notice the twenty minutes it takes to travel from my old life to the new. The city streets are blurred streaks of light against the black night sky.

The driver raps on the grimy glass between us to get my attention. I exit the cab and stare up at my new building. Four stories, red brick, high ceilings, wood floors, shops nearby. The listing seemed too good to be true when I saw it online yesterday. The rent is more than I can afford, but I needed a new place to live, pronto. And while, in the past, I might have stayed at a friend's or, God forbid, my parents', thirty-three seems too old for that. Too old for a lot of things.

I walk up the thick concrete stairs to the front door. The panel next to my buzzer is blank, ready for me to fill it in.

My apartment's blank too. There's nothing on the pale cream walls but the dusty outline of the posters that used to hang there. The air smells different, alien. My eyes rest on the nook beneath the curved bay window. It's the perfect place for the writing desk I left across town. I have that itchy feeling I get when I need to write. Only, I don't know if I can write about today. Not yet, anyway.

Through the walls (upstairs? downstairs? I haven't figured out the sounds here yet), I hear a woman's voice calling her man to dinner in a loving voice, and it cuts the legs out from under me. In an instant, I'm on my knees, strangled cries in my throat.

Oh my God, how did this happen to me? How did it take so long for me to see through him? How did I put myself, my heart, in the hands of a man who would betray me? Again?

My cell rings next to me. A glance at the screen tells me it's Stuart. He's too late. There's nothing he can say that will erase what I read, what he did.

I throw the phone as hard as I can. It hits the door frame, a loud sound in this quiet, empty place. A chip of paint flies off the wood and the ringing stops. I hug my knees to my chest and stare at the silenced instrument.

Time passes. Eventually, I start to breathe. The hard wood floor makes its presence known.

My cell phone rings again. The force of my anger wasn't enough to silence it permanently. This time, the caller is a life-line. My best friend, Sarah.

"Hey, it's me," she says, concerned, apprehensive. "We still on for that drink?"

My voice is stronger than I thought it would be. "Are we ever. I'll be there in ten."

I wash my face and grab a thin trench coat from my duffel bag. My new neighborhood waits outside. The brick buildings end where the sidewalks begin—seamless—and the only trees stand in the small parks that dot every other block. Their changing leaves rustle in the fall breeze. The air is thick with car exhaust and the mix of smells issuing from the restaurants. The streets feel alive and claustrophobic at the same time.

I liked the silence of my old neighborhood, where the noise of the city was just a whisper in the background. But I like the energy I'm getting from the noise around me now, the people, and the sensation that something could happen at any moment.

A block from the bar, something on the ground catches my eye. Is that my last name? I bend to pick it up, and sure enough, it's a business card that reads:

Blythe & Company
Arrangements Made
♀♂
4300 Cunningham Street
20th floor
(555) 458-4239

Something about seeing my name on the card gives me a thrill. Without really thinking about it, I put it in the front pocket of my jeans and keep walking.

I enter the bar and scan the dark room for Sarah. The White Lion is halfway toward trendy, with red leather stools tucked under a worn mahogany bar. Tiny white lights frame the wall of mirrors behind it. A Taylor Swift song is audible above the murmur of the Tuesday-night crowd.

Sarah's sitting in one of the dark upholstered booths, typing furiously on her BlackBerry. She's wearing a navy business suit, and her curly blond hair is bunched at the base of her neck. Her pale skin seems almost translucent under the muted lighting.

She smiles at me as I sit across from her. Her teeth are small and even. "So?"

"I did it," I say, waving over the waitress.

"Thank God."

"Do you really hate him that much?"

"I really do."

I order a gin and tonic. "And the reason you never said anything is?"

Her cobalt eyes are full of disbelief. "What are you talking about? First of all, I did say something. And second, I figured it would be better for me to hang around and make sure you were okay, rather than have us get into a big fight and never see you again."

Sarah's a lawyer, and she's always making lists. It's the way she thinks—organized. She's been this way as long as I've known her, i.e., since nursery school.

"Thanks for that."

"No worries. I just wish I hadn't dragged you to that party."

I met Stuart at a party three years ago. I was about to turn thirty and was still getting over being dumped by the then love of my life, John. Sarah convinced me it would be good to "get back out there." I wasn't so sure, but Sarah isn't someone you say no to.

I spotted Stuart shortly after we arrived. Straight black hair, clear blue eyes, over six feet tall, slim—he was exactly the kind of man I always fall for, ever since my first crush on a boy. He had a circle of girls around him, vying for his attention. But the girls didn't daunt me. I was used to the girls. You had to be when your weakness was very-good-looking men.

I was working on how to get him to notice me when Sarah did it for me by accidentally spilling her red wine down the front of my white sweater. I seized the moment and overreacted, making a dramatic fuss. It had the desired effect, as all eyes, including Stuart's, traveled toward us. I made eye contact with him, held his gaze briefly, and looked away.

When Sarah and I got back from cleaning me up in the bathroom, we found a spot on a couch. I positioned myself so I couldn't look in Stuart's direction. I could tell, though, that he was watching me.

Later, when the boys gathered to do triple shots of Jack Daniel's, I saw my opportunity and muscled my way into the group. A few of them protested that I wasn't strong enough to handle it. I tied my long red hair into a ponytail and told them I could take care of myself, just pour it. We clinked glasses and opened our throats. Only a few of them managed to get it down in one shot, but I turned my glass over with a flourish and brought it down hard on the tray Stuart was holding. I looked up at him, flushed, seeing the interest in his eyes.

"What finally made you leave?" Sarah asks.

"Have you ever noticed how no story that begins, 'I read his emails' ever finishes with, 'I was completely wrong; he wasn't cheating on me'?"

She wrinkles her small nose. "So he was cheating on you?"

"Of course he was. Just like you said."

"Yes, well. It didn't give me any pleasure to tell you that." She fiddles with the lime on the rim of her glass.

"I know, Sarah."

"Good. I have to say, you're taking this awfully well."

Of course, she didn't see me sobbing on the floor. "Am I fooling you, too?"

"Almost."

"It's amazing what extreme anger gives you the strength to do."

She smiles. "If someone figured out a way to bottle woman-been-wronged, they'd make a fortune."

"What I really need is a product that can cure a broken heart."

"I think it's called alcohol."

I try to smile but end up crying instead. Quiet, salty tears.

Sarah slips her hand over mine. "It'll get easier, Anne. In time."

"I know. It always does." I wipe my tears away with the back of my hand and force myself to smile. "Enough. We're supposed to be celebrating my new life."

I raise my glass. Sarah clicks hers to mine.

"To Anne Blythe's new life!"

"That reminds me. Look what I found on the street." I dig the card out of my pocket and hand it to her.

"Why did you pick this up?"

"Because my name was on it, I guess. I wonder what they do?"

"'Arrangements Made,' and the symbols for male and female . . . it must be some kind of dating service."

"Good point. Maybe, if I get really desperate, I'll call and find out."

Sarah blushes. "You don't have to be desperate to use a dating service."

"Have you . . . used one?"

"No, but I was thinking about it before I met Mike." Sarah smiles the way she always does whenever she speaks about him. He's a stockbroker who works in her building. They met six months ago at a cocktail party. So far, he's disproving my theory that men who are still single at thirty-five are single for a reason.

As for me: newly single at thirty-three? I've got all kinds of theories.

"You're lucky to have him," I tell her.

"I am. And you'll be lucky too, Anne."

"Yeah, maybe. But for now, I think I'm going be alone for a while, and see how that feels."

I try to sound like I mean it, even though being alone has never been my strong suit. Not the old Anne's, anyway. But the Anne who was strong enough to walk away from Stuart today is going to be on her own for a while. At least, she's going to try to be.

We finish our drinks, pay up, and head out into the night. Fall's settling in and it's cooler than it was a few hours ago. I stick my suddenly cold hands in my pockets, hugging my coat around me. Sarah hails a cab and climbs in.

She rolls down the window. "You'll be fine, Anne. Just believe it and it'll come true."

As her cab disappears into traffic, I wonder if she's right. Can I really make myself better if I wish it hard enough?

I close my eyes and click my heels together slowly three times. I will be okay. I will be okay. I will be okay. I open my eyes and look up to the North Star shining brightly above me, the only star visible in this city sky. Feeling silly, I seal my wish on it and head home.

Back in my new apartment, I walk around the empty, echoey rooms, trying to decide where I should sleep. The guy whose lease I took over left his couch and his bed. I'm not sure which would be less creepy to sleep on. I pick the couch and go to the bathroom to brush my teeth. I clean the loose change out of my pockets, along with the Blythe & Company card. I brush my fingers over the raised lettering and feel a prick of curiosity. "Arrangements Made." It seems so formal, old-fashioned.

Should I call and find out what they do? If it's a dating service, should I use it? No, that's silly. Didn't I just decide I needed to be alone? That's right, I did. So, I'll be alone. And then I'll find a new man, the right man, on my own.

I throw the card in the direction of the wastebasket in my old bathroom. It hits the tile with a sharp click. I pick it up and read it again. I feel the same thrill I did earlier. Something about the card feels lucky, like the fortune cookie I once got that said, "You were born to write," which is now hanging, framed, in my cubicle at *Twist* magazine.

I need something lucky right now.

I tuck the card into the black rim of the mirror above the white pedestal sink.

It couldn't hurt to keep it for a while.